Critical acclai

...a tautly plotted thriller . . .
Virtually Maria will not fail you . . .
(Irish News-Belfast)

. . a very slick fish in the growing pool of
cyberthrillers . . .
irrepressible and surprisingly irresistible.
(RTE Guide)

. . . a ground-breaking love story . . .
(The Examiner)

brilliantly conceived, exquisitely executed
and eminently readable . . .
(Commuting Times)

. . published to great critical acclaim . . .
(Ireland on Sunday)

Vi *Maria* – A gripping, action-packed, tautly
plotted thriller . . .
(Publishing News)

Virtually Maria - EASONS Book of the Month

FIRE

&

ICE

A NOVEL

Also by John Joyce

The Virtual Trilogy

Virtually Maria
A Matter of Time
Yesterday, Today & Tomorrow

www.virtualtrilogy.com

Captain Cockle

Captain Cockle and the Cormorant
Captain Cockle and the Loch Ness Monster
Captain Cockle and the Pond

www.captaincockle.com

FIRE

&

ICE

JOHN

JOYCE

This edition published by Spindrift Press 2012

 **SPINDRIFT PRESS**

www.spindriftpress.com

ISBN 978-0-9557637-3-1

The moral right of the author has been asserted

ABOUT THE AUTHOR

Award-winning science writer Dr John Joyce is the author of the *Virtual Trilogy* of technothrillers featuring Theo Gilkrensky – *Virtually Maria, A Matter of Time* and *Yesterday, Today and Tomorrow* – as well as the *Captain Cockle* series of books for children.

He was presented with the Glaxo EU Fellowship for Science Writers by the Prime Minister of Ireland in 1978 and has contributed a great many articles to scientific and technical publications. His first published novel *Virtually Maria* was selected as 'Book of the Month' by the Easons book retailing chain.

John Joyce is currently working on his next thriller *Masterpiece,* describing modern day nuclear smuggling and the theft of the Mona Lisa from the Louvre in Paris.

For information and updates on *The Virtual Trilogy* and other John Joyce books, log on to:

www.virtualtrilogy.com

ACKNOWLEDGEMENTS

I would like to acknowledge the help I have received from all those I met during my research on *Fire & Ice* at the various locations mentioned in this novel.

In the USA, I would like to thank: the staff of the National Parks Service and the Phantom Ranch at the Grand Canyon; our guides around the submarine *USS Pampanito* (SS-383) at Fisherman's Warf, San Francisco and the staff of the Flamingo Casino in Las Vegas; as well as the pilots and staff of Papillon Grand Canyon Helicopters for an unforgettable flight.

On this side of the Atlantic: David Meredith for his expert advice on white water canoeing; Barry Pullen for his advice on the various signals intelligence systems used in this book; the Arts Council of Ireland and the staff of the Tyrone Guthrie Centre at Annaghmakerrig for the peace and quiet to finish this book.

Inspiration for this novel was given by Dr. Konstantin Korotov during our meeting in Dublin in 1998. A personally signed copy of his book *Aura and Consciousness: New Age of Scientific Understanding* has pride of place in my bookshelves.

Finally, as always, I would like to thank my wife Jane for her support with this novel and, in particular, for her strength and patience while accompanying me on an unforgettable research expedition from the rim of the Grand Canyon to its base at the Colorado River and back again.

This book, like those before, is lovingly dedicated to you.

Thank you.

FOR JANE

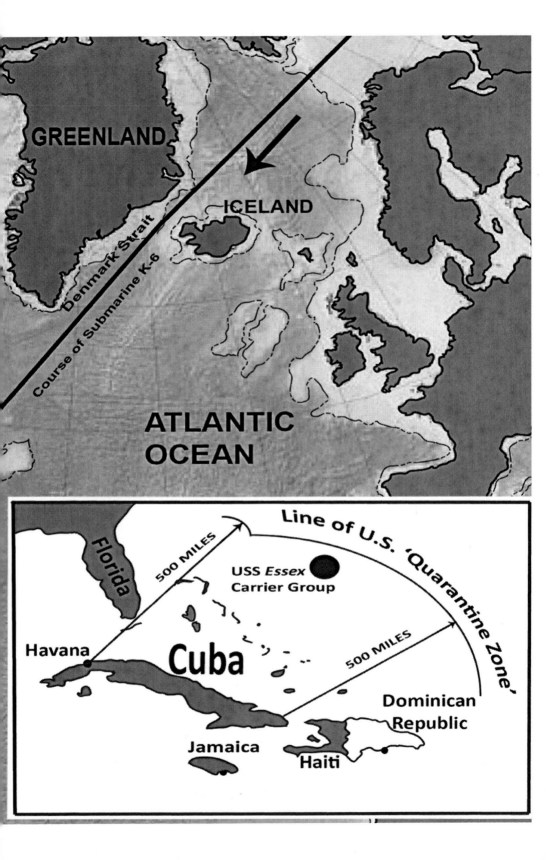

Russian November Class
Nuclear Attack Submarine K-6

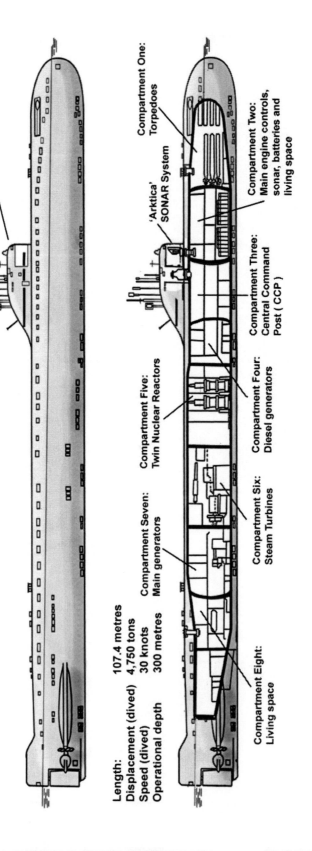

Length: 107.4 metres
Displacement (dived)   4,750 tons
Speed (dived)   30 knots
Operational depth   300 metres

Conning
Tower and cockpit

Periscopes, Radar Masts
and Radio Antenna

Compartment One:
Torpedoes

Compartment Two:
Main engine controls,
sonar, batteries and
living space

'Arktica'
SONAR System

Compartment Three:
Central Command
Post (CCP)

Compartment Four:
Diesel generators

Compartment Five:
Twin Nuclear Reactors

Compartment Six:
Steam Turbines

Compartment Seven:
Main generators

Compartment Eight:
Living space

AUTHOR'S INTRODUCTION: THE PSYCHIC SPY

The use of extra-sensory perception (ESP) as a communications system in war, or as a weapon of war in its own right, is nothing new. In Roman times soothsayers and fortune-tellers were paid to assist generals with the deployment of their forces and to gauge the strengths and weaknesses of enemies.

Native American Indians speak of medicine men who could predict an enemy's advance, as well as the number of warriors and weapons held, by simply going into a trance.

It is known that Hitler placed great store in the power of psychic ability with some initial, although thankfully short-lived success during World War II, and that even Churchill was not above employing some of the more reliable mediums on projects that required their unique talents.

What *is* new however, is the wealth of information now coming forward to demonstrate how seriously the power of ESP was taken by the Soviet Uniton and the United States of America during the years of the Cold War. Highly classified and 'Top Secret' files, now available since the collapse of communism in Eastern Europe and following the fifty-year Freedom of Information Bill in the West, show clearly how far research went in both countries and how, for five nerve-wracking days during the 1962 Cuban Missile Crisis, the fate of the world lay not in the hands of Kennedy or Khrushchev, but in the minds of two hunted women . . . Fire and Ice.

1

THE NIGHTMARE

Ruth looked down on the tight cluster of huts, guard towers and electric fences. Beyond the compound, the dark forest stretched out on all sides like a frozen sea, broken only by the steel ribbons of the railway track, glistening in the moonlight.

"Something terrible happened here," she said.

"Then you're on target," Carpenter said. "What can you see?"

Ruth described the scene in detail, as she had been trained to do.

"Can you see people?"

"Only on the guard towers. There are also men with dogs, patrolling the perimeter."

"And in the camp itself?"

She focused on the parade ground outside the largest hut, and then floated lower. A silver chord connected her to the sky. None of the guards saw her. No searchlights burst into life and swung her way. The world lay silent and still, as if she was swimming underwater.

"I'm going to the largest hut. It looks like a barracks."

Ruth slid towards the closed door and felt the gentlest resistance, as if she had stepped through a spider's web. Then she was inside.

"I see men asleep in bunks."

"How many?"

"Thirty. Maybe thirty-five."

"The sense of evil you felt earlier. Is it there, in that room?"

"No."

"Then search the other huts and tell me what you see."

Ruth moved between the rows of sleeping men, through the far wall and out into the compound. She floated from building to building, passing through stores, a canteen and a meeting room, to an armoury and a garage, reporting all she saw. She heard no noise in this strange, formless world - only Carpenter's voice inside her head, urging her on.

Finally, she came to a low concrete bunker surrounded by its own electric fence and guarded by two men with dogs.

"I'm at the last building. It looks like the focus of the compound, but it's so small."

"What do you feel?"

"I feel hopelessness. I feel forgotten and abandoned. Everything is poisoned, dark and dead. I want to come back now."

"Just a little while longer. Can you look inside the building?"

"There are steel doors."

"That never stopped you before, Ruth. We must know what this place is."

Ruth moved forward. The guard dogs stirred on either side of her. The men holding them looked around but saw nothing. Nobody could see her; nobody could hear her. She was a ghost, a phantom, a disembodied soul.

The doors were at least six inches thick, but she felt only the gentle touch of gossamer as she passed through them into a deep dark space hung with steel cables. She floated downwards into the blackness until she arrived at a tiny room, deep in the earth.

"Where are you now?"

"I'm at the bottom of an elevator shaft, moving through the doors into a corridor. It's brightly lit, like a hospital. There are gurneys and doors with glass windows, windows with bars."

"How does it feel?"

"Worse. I sense terror and pain. Horrible things have been done here."

"Keep going. Nobody can hurt you. Just tell me what you see."

"There are rubber suits inside, helmets, masks and . . . surgical instruments on trays. I see a metal door at the end of the corridor. It looks like an airlock."

"Go on, Ruth. We've come this far. Go inside."

"I...I don't want to. There was evil here, great suffering. It hurts."

"Please, Ruth. Go inside."

She passed through the airlock chamber into a brilliantly lit space. The walls, floor and ceiling were tiled in white, as if for easy cleaning. In the centre of the space stood three heavy metal chairs, bolted to the floor, each with leather straps on the arms and legs. Where the head of each occupant would rest, a thick rubber restraint reached out like a broken claw. Ruth saw teeth-marks.

"People were tortured here. I feel their pain. I must come back now."

"In a moment. We need to know what went on. Can you see notes, instruments, anything?"

"I saw rubber suits beyond the airlock. They had their own air supply. Yet there are teeth-marks on the chair restraints."

"So the people in the chairs had no protection?"

"No. But the watchers did."

"What were they watching?"

Ruth focused on the chairs. She saw gouge marks on the armrests, the brown stains of old blood and a broken fingernail embedded in the leather. A ghostly face appeared, the face of a woman with grey eyes wide in pain and fear. Her arms and legs were strapped down. She sat staring towards the door. Ruth tried to reach her, to feel what she was feeling. She reached out to touch . . . .

Suddenly she *was* the woman in the chair; watching men in white rubber suits stepping out through the airlock and closing the door behind them, hearing the taps turn and the hiss of poison gas. Her eyes burned in their sockets. Her throat turned to fire and her skin shrivelled. Her fingers tore at the padded armrest. A nail caught and ripped out.

Ruth pulled away from the chair. She was back in the white-tiled room.

"They were watching death," she said.

"When was this?" asked Carpenter. "Yesterday? A year ago?"

"I must come back, John. Please! It hurts too much!"

"All right. Just follow my voice. I'll guide you to — "

"Wait! There's somebody here!"

"The guards? A worker?"

The air turned to ice, as if the door of a giant blast freezer had opened.

"No. It's somebody like me. A viewer!"

The presence in the room overwhelmed her. Ruth was pierced by the most intense feeling of dread. She was a helpless child in the grip of a malevolent adult, someone with the power to crush her into nothingness, to break the silver chord that linked her to her living body and trap her in this space forever, cut off from the light and warmth of the world . . . for all eternity.

"Come back Ruth. Come back now!"

She tried to escape, following the silver chord connecting her with reality; back up through the earth to the sky and freedom. But the presence reached out and took her, dragging her back into the white space and the pain. The silver chord broke. The darkness closed in. Ruth lay drowning in a sea of black, limitless hatred.

"Help me! Help me, *pleeeease!*"

Opening Moves

TIME TO EVENT

03:06:55

DAYS : HRS : MINS

TUESDAY, 23 OCTOBER 1962
TUCSAYON TRAILER PARK, ARIZONA, USA
8.55 A.M. MOUNTAIN STANDARD TIME
1555 GMT

"Ruth! Ruth!"

The dark presence fell away. The white room dissolved as light stabbed through her eyelids. She was back in the living world of touch, noise and smell—the coarse sheets and the damp pillow below her head, the clatter of a pan and the aroma of fried bacon.

"Ruth, you'll be late for work. Remember what Bob Herschel said. This is your last chance."

Ruth Weylon opened her eyes. Outside, in the kitchenette, Granny Moon was fixing breakfast. The big Bush radio Old Billy the park janitor had scrounged for them from the dump was playing *Monster Mash* by Bobby Boris Picket and the Kryptkickers in the run-up to Halloween. Its lyrics about monsters, ghouls and zombies brought back the vision of the tortured woman with the grey eyes. Ruth threw off the sheets and the coarse blanket, feeling the cool air from the fan against her damp skin.

"Nightmares?" asked the old woman, setting a cup of coffee and a glass of water on the shelf by her bed.

"You know how it is," said Ruth, reaching for the glass and draining it.

The old woman lifted an empty bottle of Jack Daniel's from the bedroom floor with her thumb and forefinger, as if it had been a dead rat, and dropped it into the trash.

"I do. But is drink the only way you can deal with it? You'll kill yourself if you go on like this."

"What other way is there? I ran out of pills."

"The government trained you to do those things. They must know how to make the nightmares stop."

Ruth's fingers went to the metal dog tags around her neck, rubbed them for a moment and let them fall.

"They don't," she said. "Believe me. All they do is give me pills."

"Then why don't you throw those tags away?" said Granny Moon. "They just remind you of what they did to you."

"I can't let myself forget what it was like. The government men will return for me one day. I won't go back."

"So what *will* you do? You can't go on like this."

Ruth looked past her, through the window of the trailer, to the sky. She heard doors opening and closing, dogs barking, the cough and rattle of engines and the chatter of people leaving for work, the sounds of the real world.

"I'll get Joan to cover for me at the store after lunch, go into Flagstaff and get more pills," she said. "And if that doesn't work I'll get another bottle of Jack Daniel's and hope the liquor doesn't wear off before I wake up tomorrow."

"You'll kill yourself."

Ruth hauled herself out of bed and pulled on the Fred Harvey Company uniform Granny Moon had laid out for her. Then she steadied herself against the rickety dressing table and ran her fingers through her hair. The face staring back at her from the mirror had once been beautiful, a stunning mixture of Havasupai Indian and Texas Park Ranger. But now she looked puffy and tired. Her dark green eyes were red-rimmed, her raven black hair matted and flat. Ruth was only twenty-nine, but she felt fifty. If only she could sleep without the pills! But she had already tried that. The last time her screams had almost got them thrown off the lot.

Ruth staggered to the kitchenette. Granny Moon had borrowed Old Billy's newspaper. The headline glared out at Ruth: PRESIDENT TELLS NATION THAT REDS HAVE ESTABLISHED MISSILE BASE.

On the radio, the eight o'clock breakfast news cut in with a report of the President's address to the nation the night before.

"Maybe I won't have to kill myself," said Ruth, scanning the story on page one. "Maybe the Russians will do it for me."

John F. Kennedy's voice filled the little trailer, just as it had when she had killed the bottle of Jack Daniel's.

"Good evening, my fellow citizens. This government, as promised, has maintained the closest surveillance of the Soviet military build-up on the island of Cuba. To halt this offensive build-up, a strict quarantine on all offensive military equipment under shipment to Cuba is being initiated. All ships of any kind bound for Cuba, from whatever nation or port, will, if found to contain cargoes of offensive weapons, be turned back."

Granny Moon looked up from her coffee. "Billy's building an atomic shelter. He's cut a hole in top of the old septic tank at the back of his shack and cleaned it out with a power hose. They're giving away leaflets at the supermarket on how to survive a nuclear attack. You should read them."

"I don't have to. I know what'll happen if they drop the bomb. We'll all die."

Granny Moon thought about this for a moment. "Are you sure the government men will come for you?"

"There's going to be a war," said Ruth. "You've seen the way people are panicking, building shelters, cramming themselves into churches down in Flagstaff like it's the end of the world. The government men will come for me. They need me to go back to work for them and spy on the Russians. The trick is for me not to be here when they come."

"How will you do that? They must know where we live."

"I've made plans. I've got an escape kit up at the store. If they come, then I'm gone. You run too, back to Havasu Canyon and our people. That's the only place either of us will be safe."

The old woman looked down into her coffee cup.

"Are you sure there'll be a war?"

"I am," Ruth said. "All it'll take will be one person to push the wrong button."

2

The screech of tortured metal tore through the Central Command Post.

Every man in the cramped space froze at his station.

"All stop!" Captain (First Rank) Sergei Nikolai Petrachkov jumped to his feet from the command chair. The order was repeated. The engine noise dropped an octave and faded to a low hum.

He knew what had happened. They had dived with their radio mast extended and ripped it off on the ice. Now they would have to go back, surface and assess the damage, to make sure the outer hull of the submarine was still airtight. That meant finding the hole in the ice they had just left.

"Engines back slow!"

All eyes in the CCP were on him. Each of the one hundred and ten men aboard was only too aware that they were sealed inside a hundred-metre steel pressure hull, held afloat by nothing more than pockets of air between it and a thin outer skin. If that skin was ruptured on the ice and the air let out, then the ship would sink, with no hope of escape for anyone on board. No wonder everybody had frozen on the spot. No wonder eyes turned towards him when he ordered them to go back and risk the ice again. They had done enough damage already.

Petrachkov was a short, strong terrier of a man with dark watchful eyes and broad shoulders bulked out from years of weight-lifting. As a child in an overcrowded State school on the Baltic coast outside Leningrad, his small body had made him a target for bullying. Now, in the cramped conditions of the submarine, it was a positive asset, allowing him to move with ease between the narrow bulkheads, projecting levers and tight corridors that made up the ship. The crowded CCP was no bigger than a small household lounge, yet it contained at least a dozen men. In front of Petrachkov sat the helmsman. On either side of him were the two planesmen, who controlled the small fin-like diving planes at each end of the submarine.

Then there was the diving officer, who controlled the ship's buoyancy when it was submerged, the engineering officer who directed the ship's propulsion, the fire control officer and various enlisted men, all crammed into that confined space, along with a bewildering array of pipes, dials, levers and control wheels. *Kashtan* microphones for the *Nerpa* announcing system hung from the ceiling every few feet like black party streamers, connecting the CCP to every other part in the ship. The compartment resembled a steam room, thick with the smoke of cheap cigarettes, the smell of machine oil, hot electronics, stale air and sweat.

Directly to Petrachkov's right stood Captain (Third Rank) Valentin Rykov, his *Starpom*, or second in command, a tall gangly officer with blond hair and the earnest expression of an academic. In Petrachkov's eyes, Rykov was a dreamer who cared more for abstract theories, party politics and the opinion of his men than he did for the success of the mission. Rykov had been the last man to leave the open cockpit on top of the conning tower above their heads before they had dived.

"Sonar," snapped Petrachkov, "tell me when we reach the gap!"

Rykov still watched him nervously, dreading the moment when the submarine would surface and the results of his mistake would be fully revealed. And there was Igor Muhkin, the thin-faced *zampolit* or political officer appointed by the Party, watching both of them. The Party was everywhere. It was something you lived with, like the weather, the sea and the KGB, a natural hazard you got used to. Petrachkov had seen very able officers have their careers stopped dead in the water by the smallest of transgressions, while he had managed to survive and prosper. The trick was to be good enough to stand out for promotion, but not so good as to attract the attention of the wrong people.

"The ice is thinning, Comrade Captain. We're almost there."

"All stop! Blow trim tanks and surface. Up slow."

Petrachkov shot a glance at the periscope indicator, just to make sure it was safely retracted into the conning tower. Years before, when he had been a junior officer on K-3, Russia's first nuclear submarine, his captain had disgraced himself by diving under the ice with the periscope still raised, and had blinded his ship. Now, at this crucial time in the struggle with the West, Rykov had deafened the K-6 by smashing the radio aerial in much the same way.

Petrachkov's last radio contact with Northern Fleet headquarters at Severmorsk, within the Arctic Circle on Russia's frozen north-west Kola Peninsular, had told him of the worsening situation in Cuba. If he and his submarine were called south into action now, but could not respond because of the communications failure, how would that look on Rykov's record, or on his? It would certainly get the attention of the Party. Muhkin was observing everything.

What would Rykov's fate be once the political officer's report reached Moscow? What black mark would go on his own *zapista*, the personal file the State kept on every man, woman and child from the cradle to the grave?

All eyes in the CCP turned upwards as the submarine started to rise. Petrachkov heard the first scraping of ice as the conning tower broke through the surface and the thud as the hull came to rest against the ice pack.

"Secure ballast tanks," he said, stepping clear of the ladder in the middle of the compartment. "Check the tower is clear, then raise the anti-aircraft radar and stand by the main trunk hatch. Comrade Rykov, get suited up and come with me topside."

Two seamen darted up the ladder, put their hands on the wheel to undo the hatch and turned it. A brief flood of water cascaded into the CCP and drained through the grill covering the floor. Even though he was expecting it, Petrachkov still found the sight of water pouring into his ship unnerving.

As the cascade subsided to a drip and the seamen darted up the trunk to undo the next hatch to the cockpit, Petrachkov weaved his way forward through the men in the CCP to his cabin. It was a modest affair, no bigger than a small bathroom, with a cramped curved ceiling of cheap laminated wood following the line of the hull. But, for Petrachkov, it was a luxury apartment compared to his experiences in diesel submarines. It boasted a narrow desk and chair, a bunk and a big brass clock. Three cheaply framed photographs hung on the wall: a scene of a fishing village, a group of men on the deck of an old diesel submarine and a family portrait of a mother, father and two young sons. Petrachkov glanced at them briefly, as he always did when he entered that space, and then reached down to pull on layer after layer of wool and oilskin over his blue boilersuit.

He had been born forty-two years before in a small village on the Baltic coast, west of Leningrad, his mother a factory worker and his father a Party activist. His early service in the Great Patriotic War against fascist Germany was spent as a young ensign with the Northern Fleet in the bleakness of the Kola Gulf, where he served on the diesel-electric submarine D-2. In an effort to extend the range of these small craft, the Russian navy had used liquid oxygen to allow the diesel engines to be run while submerged, a design that proved to be a serious fire hazard, earning these tiny ships the nickname "cigarette lighters".

Yet, like most children, he had outlived his parents, who were slaughtered as the Nazi war machine crushed his village in its relentless march towards Leningrad. Their deaths fired his ambition for survival still further and he was rewarded with his first command when he was still only twenty-six – a diesel submarine of his own – which he commanded as part of the Black Sea Fleet.

Then, in 1956, he had been selected as part of the top-secret project K-3, the first Soviet nuclear submarine, and had found himself in the middle of a highly guarded operation in which one half of the team did not know what the other half was doing. He and his entire family, his wife Natalya and their two young sons Nikolai and Giorgi, were examined by a medical commission to see if he was fit to serve in a nuclear submarine and they were fit to live in the north. They had been handed long questionnaires and life histories, told how to fill them out and what was expected. Their records had been examined, friends and colleagues questioned. Selection as an officer on a nuclear submarine in the Soviet fleet was carefully controlled by the senior ranks of the fleet's operational and political directorates and the Central Committee of the Communist Party.

After all, how many people in Russia would be as free as the captain of a nuclear submarine? Who else would live and work so far from the eyes and ears of the State, and yet wield so much destructive power? Was that why each vessel carried not only a political officer appointed by the Party, but also a security officer answerable only to the KGB, so that the eyes and ears of the State could follow them wherever they went?

Yet Petrachkov considered it just another challenge in his rise up the ladder of command. On taking up his first post as watch-keeping officer of the K-3, he and his family had been given a government-issued apartment all to themselves. Petrachkov had embarked on an adventure in a new breed of submarines with practically infinite range and endurance limited only by the physical limits of the crew and the supply of food, ships that never needed to snorkel for air and could slide through the water at up to thirty knots, making them ideal weapons for use under the frozen ice cap of the North Pole.

Petrachkov put on his fur cap and walked back to the command post, where Rykov was already dressed and waiting.

He reached up and took one of the hanging microphones.

"Radar, is the horizon clear?"

"Yes, Comrade Captain. Nothing within fifty miles."

"Comrade Rykov. Come with me. Comrade Muhkin, sound the alarm if that changes."

"Yes, Comrade Captain," said the political officer, stiffening with pride. It was a good idea, Petrachkov realised, to give the watchful Muhkin something to keep him occupied, until the damage could be assessed. If the radio aerial could be repaired, then there was no harm done. If it could not, then having Muhkin see the extent of the damage before a contingency plan had been worked out could be dangerous.

Petrachkov felt the temperature plummet as he climbed the slippery steel ladder inside the hollow conning tower. The biting cold struck him like a blow as he emerged into the open air of the tiny cockpit.

He blinked, squinting into the blinding light as his eyes adjusted to the dazzling glare of the sun on the ice. All around him lay a featureless frozen desert, an alien world where the temperature was thirty degrees below freezing and the nearest human habitation was a thousand miles to the south.

But human life did not interest Petrachkov just then. All his attention was on the question of whether or not his ship could still communicate with its base in the northern Soviet Union. He peered back, past the lookouts on either side of the cockpit, the conical radar mast above his head and the stumpy cylinders of the retracted search and attack periscopes, to the shaft housing the *Iva* long-range radio aerial.

He cursed under his breath.

The aerial, a ten-metre folding shaft of steel and ceramics capable of sending a signal around the world, had been torn from its mount. Now it hung like a broken fishing rod over the starboard side of the conning tower, barely attached to the submarine by a frayed cable.

Rykov squeezed his way out of the hatch into the cockpit. He was tall for a submariner, at just under six feet. He too peered aft at the shattered aerial.

"How bad is it?" Petrachkov asked.

Rykov squirmed past him, lifted himself out of the cockpit onto the frozen rim of the conning tower. Petrachkov watched anxiously, as his *Starpom* poked with a gloved finger at the broken seal around the aerial mount.

"The gasket is ruptured. That means there'll be seawater in the core of the mast housing. Even if we could get a replacement, or bring a helium balloon up here and fly an aerial wire out above the ship, we couldn't run it from this connection without shorting the radio."

"Can it be repaired?"

"Not without pulling out the aerial well, and that's a dockyard job."

"And how about the other systems?" he asked, referring to the Low Frequency, Very Low Frequency and Extremely Low Frequency radio sets that could be used to transmit simple code words and messages from the land to the submarine while it was still submerged.

"They haven't worked since we left port, Comrade Captain. Problems with the watertight seals — or so the communications officer tells me."

Petrachkov slammed down his fist on the cockpit rim. Here he was in the middle of a frozen waste on the brink of a nuclear war, let down by faulty rubber seals that had probably been installed as a botched job so that some bureaucrat could meet his quotas.

"There *is* another option," Rykov suggested. "We could run an aerial wire from the communications room out through the CCP and up to the cockpit. From here we could attach it to a helium balloon and raise it over the ice. That should give us a good enough aerial to contact base."

Petrachkov felt his anger towards Rykov subside. He turned to one of the young lookouts scanning the horizon with binoculars.

"Go below and have Comrade Mostock send up one of his engineers to cut the cable and throw the aerial overboard. We can't have it clanking on the hull or breaking free and hitting the propellers when we get underway."

Rykov edged his way down from the rim into the cockpit. When he was safely inside, Petrachkov said, "How did it happen, Valentin? It's not like you to make that kind of mistake."

"I don't know, Captain. I had been up here making sure we were properly rigged to dive. I was doing my final checks. The boy was here too, the one from Doctor Chiker's team. He had never seen the ice before and it fascinated him. The periscopes were stowed and the radar mast lowered in readiness to dive. I was going to lower the radio aerial when he asked me something. It must have distracted me."

"What did he ask you?"

Rykov looked embarrassed.

"If I believed in life after death."

"A strange thing to ask."

"I thought so too. And I was thinking about this question as I watched him climb below. I was looking forward, away from the aerial. I must have forgotten to order that it be lowered before I climbed down myself and closed the hatch."

"I see. It's very regrettable."

"What will happen to me, Comrade Captain?"

"You will resume your duties. I will be obliged to file a report. Comrade Muhkin will file one too. But neither of those documents can be considered, or placed on your *zapista* until we reach port. In the meantime, you must be vigilant, avoid further errors and continue with our mission. Is that understood?"

"Yes, Comrade Captain."

"Then go below, and take that last lookout with you. I'll stand watch here until we make contact with Severmorsk."

For a moment, Rykov looked as if he was about to say something. Then he saluted, turned and made his way down into the warmer world of the submarine.

Petrachkov looked back to the ice. That was the problem with allowing civilian scientists on board an operational submarine. They asked stupid questions and distracted the crew from their duties. Rykov was a good officer and treated his men with respect, but he simply wasn't tough enough when it came to difficult decisions. Far better for him to have been a scientist himself than a serving officer, who had to focus on the job in hand. Once his report and Muhkin's reached Severmorsk and were placed on Rykov's *zapista*, Rykov's career at sea would be over.

"So Sergei Nikolai, we have a problem?"

The lean, wiry man pulling himself out of the hatch was equal in rank to Petrachkov and his senior by three years. But Captain (First Rank) Viktor Mostock had long ago been assigned to a specialisation in engineering and nuclear power, which forever barred him from command of his own ship. His skin, which hardly ever saw the light of day, had at least a hint of colour, in contrast to the ice beyond the cockpit, and his mischievous brown eyes shone at the chance of a challenge worthy of his skills.

"I didn't mean you to come yourself, Viktor. Anyone with a wire cutter would have done as well."

"Ah, why have the monkey when you can have the organ-grinder? Besides, we haven't had much chance to talk lately and I thought you could use a friendly ear."

Mostock had sailed with Petrachkov on his first command in the Great Patriotic War and was the closest friend he had. They had survived the dangers of fascist depth charges, diesel fuel explosions and bad food together in the D-2 "cigarette lighter". And, when Mostock's young fiancée Galina had been taken by the Nazis, never to return, Petrachkov's own wife had practically adopted him into their family, unsuccessfully trying to mend his broken heart by arranging introductions with all the eligible women she knew.

As propulsion engineer in charge of the submarine's two nuclear reactors, Mostock was usually to be found at the main engine controls in compartment two, forward of Petrachkov's CCP and the reactors themselves, which were the heaviest plant on the ship and located amidships to balance the boat. It was a standing joke amongst the crew that it was a measure of how unsafe those reactors were that the man responsible for their operation worked so far away from them.

"I could use an opinion, certainly," Petrachkov said, "but not until you have that aerial cut away."

Mostock climbed gingerly out onto the rim of the conning tower and examined the shattered aerial housing. Then he pulled a pair of heavy-duty cutters from his belt and went to work. Petrachkov heard a loud snap followed by the clatter of the broken aerial falling onto the ice.

"There," said Mostock, lowering himself back into the cockpit. "Rykov will be back with the balloon in a moment. What was that opinion you wanted of me, while we are still alone?"

"Four diesel submarines of the Northern Fleet have been ordered to the Atlantic to protect our comrades who are fighting to save the revolution in Cuba, Victor. Yet here we are, in a *nuclear* boat with twice the speed and unlimited endurance, baby-sitting a gaggle of scientists while they undertake crazy experiments and map the bottom of the sea. Why is that, Viktor? I'm a submariner, not a taxi-driver."

Mostock reached beneath his fur-lined jacket to an inside pocket and pulled out a packet of cheap *papirosi* cigarettes. In a moment the bitter tang of strong tobacco tainted the pristine air.

"It is not our job to question, Sergei Nikolai," said Mostock, grinning broadly. "Who are we to doubt the wisdom of Moscow? After all, the State has faith in science. Science has given us our victories in space and built this wonderful vessel. The Arctic is where wars of the future will be fought, and the future belongs to scientists.

If the State needs a few taxi-drivers to take their beloved eggheads where they need to go, then it is our patriotic duty to oblige them, don't you agree?"

Petrachkov smiled. "Of course, and speaking of science, there is always the test of the nuclear torpedo."

"Ah yes. I heard. Comrade Dudko's little toy. I saw it brought aboard in Sayda Bay before we sailed. He has it under twenty-four-hour guard, by a KGB security officer like himself who sleeps with it as if it was a woman. The man even carries a pistol, so they tell me. Not that any of our boys would steal a torpedo, you understand — even one as powerful as this."

Petrachkov was well aware of the 'special torpedo' that had been loaded into his ship by MINATOM, the ministry that developed such nuclear weapons. Unlike conventional 553 millimetre torpedoes, which had their noses painted grey, this one was painted bright purple. Petrachkov was also aware that such weapons had been tested only once before, by Captain First Rank Nikolai Shumkov of the submarine B-130, below the Arctic waters off northern Russia, near the island of Novaya Zemla. Shumkov had been awarded the Order of Lenin for that test. Now Petrachkov had been ordered to do the same thing. Perhaps there was some glory to be had on this mission after all.

"What have *you* heard about the scientists?" Petrachkov asked.

"Not much. Only that they are working on a new way of communicating with submarines under the ice. I don't know how they are supposed to do it. What can you tell *me*, Comrade Captain?"

"Very little. Rykov is the one dealing with them. They meet every twelve hours, at eight o'clock in the evening and eight in the morning Moscow time, and try to contact the Admiralty in Leningrad. I don't know if they've succeeded."

Rykov's head popped above the hatch rim.

"Excuse me, Comrade Captains, but I have the balloon ready with the connection to the radio room. Would you like to begin?"

Mostock smiled at Petrachkov and flicked his half-finished cigarette out onto the ice.

"Why not?" he said. "And if that doesn't work, we can always join hands around the table with the boys from Leningrad and have a séance."

TUESDAY, 23 OCTOBER 1962
TUCSAYON TRAILER PARK, ARIZONA
1.38 P.M. MOUNTAIN STANDARD TIME
2038 GMT

"Granny Moon, Miss Ruth! Come quick!"

Ruth was back in the trailer, rummaging through the drawers next to her bed for a few dollars and the prescription for her pills, when the knock came on the flimsy metal door. An old Indian in a faded blue baseball cap, oil-stained overalls and scuffed sneakers stood outside. He took off his cap when Granny Moon opened the door, revealing the mane of silvery hair tied in a ponytail that hung halfway down his back..

"What is it, Billy?" asked Granny Moon. "Did they drop the bomb?"

"Not yet, Granny. But they're going to. The Governor of Arizona himself was on the radio just now telling everyone to stock up on enough food and water for the next two weeks. I'm driving into Flagstaff right away and I was wondering if either of you wanted to come with me and get supplies?"

"I'll find the cash," said Ruth. "You make a list, Granny. Did you see my prescription?" She went back to the bedside locker, turned the drawers out on the bed and scrabbled at the papers inside. Coming down from the pills was hard. It made her edgy and nervous.

If there had been any Jack Daniel's left she'd have take a couple of shots to steady herself. She had to get the pills in Flagstaff or she'd go insane.

A crumpled ten dollar bill fluttered to the floor. Ruth grabbed it and turned to where Granny Moon and Old Billy were huddled like an old married couple over the shopping list on the dining counter.

"And get some more bacon," Granny Moon said. "It's only thirty-nine cents a pound in the supermarket. And plenty of beans, if they're not more than twenty cents a can. How much bottled water did the Governor say we'd need?"

"I've only got ten dollars and change," said Ruth.

"I got some back pay yesterday," Old Billy said. "I'll help you out."

"You don't have to."

Old Billy looked up at her from the table.

"There's going to be a war, Miss Ruth, and you and Granny Moon are the closest thing to family I've got. Money won't be no good in a war. What we need is food and water. I'll go start the car."

"How long have you known Billy?" Ruth asked.

"Since I was a child back in Havasu Canyon. We used to play by the river."

"And you never thought of getting together, after Grandpa died?"

The old woman looked up from her list.

"When I was fourteen, he came to my family's *wikiup* to claim me for his wife. But he was from a different tribe. He was Walapai. I was Havasupai. In those days, to marry outside the tribe was taboo."

"My mother did. And so did I."

The old woman looked up from the table.

"I know," she said. "And look what happened."

Old Billy's car was a 1955 Mercury station wagon with peeling wooden trim, a hole in the muffler and the rear doors missing, which made it handy for carrying ladders, but suffocating to ride in unless all the windows were open. Old Billy had the radio on, listening for news of the crisis. NBC's Chet Huntley had called Kennedy's address the toughest and most grim speech by a president since President Roosevelt had spoken to the Congress in December 1941 after Pearl Harbor. The news anchorman said there were twenty-six Russian ships heading for the blockade line. He didn't seem to think they would stop. Ruth didn't either. She was edgy from not having her pills, and every news broadcast made her jumpier.

The radio played *Don't They Know It's the End of the World?* as they neared the crossroads on the long straight road into Flagstaff, turned left into the town and right into the parking lot outside the supermarket.

"Holy shit!" said Old Billy.

Cars, trucks and station wagons covered the lot, parked at odd angles and jammed into tight corners. Horns honked angrily. Crowds of people pushed trolleys piled high with supplies, or struggled under armfuls of bulging paper bags.

Old Billy pulled the old station wagon up on the nearest sidewalk and flung open his door.

"We'd better get in there!"

"You go," Ruth said. "Take the list. I have to get my pills."

She ran across the street from the supermarket to the drugstore. Even that was full of anxious people, stocking up on medical supplies. A couple of women glared up at her from their shopping and then went back to piling bandages and antiseptic creams into their wire baskets. She knew that look. It told her that she did not belong.

She pushed her way to the desk and slapped down her prescription.

A nervous young man in a white coat with a Stars and Stripes lapel pin stared down at her. It was Jerry Jones, the druggist's son. He had that look too.

"I can't fill this," he said.

"Why not? It's all made out. I always get it filled here."

"We've had a run on tranquillisers ever since the Governor's broadcast. People are filling prescriptions in advance. We're fresh out."

"But I have to have them! Where's your father? He always fills it for me."

"He's on Civil Defence Duty up in Phoenix, answering phone calls, telling folks how to dig shelters. He won't be back for days."

"When will you get another shipment?"

"Not until tomorrow. If you want to drive into Phoenix, there are plenty of drugstores there."

"Look, Jerry," pleaded Ruth, leaning over the counter and lowering her voice. "I have to have those pills. I can't sleep without them. I'm going nuts! What do I have to do to get them?" Her hand went to the top button of her shirt.

The young man looked at her again. This time Ruth saw a flash of desire in his eyes, but then he glanced up at the other customers behind her in the crowded shop.

"I keep telling you, we're fresh out. Either drive into Phoenix or come back tomorrow. Next!"

"So you have the pills, but you just aren't going to given them to me!"

Jerry blushed. "I . . . I'm fresh out," he stammered. "Like I said, if you want them, you come back tomorrow or you go to Phoenix."

"Come on! You heard the man. There's people waiting in line here!" a woman shouted behind her.

Ruth turned and ran out of the shop, across the road and into the supermarket parking lot, fighting her way through the jostling crowds to the door. Halloween masks covered the windows, along with orange and black bunting and painted signs for holiday special offers. She pushed her way inside, past the checkouts and into the aisles. She saw row after row of empty shelves, the floor littered with Hallmark greeting cards from an upended Halloween display stand and people fighting over the last box of cereal. Her feet crunched on spilled corn flakes.

"Billy!"

"Over here, Miss Ruth."

He lay across a shopping trolley with his arms spread over the contents. His baseball cap was gone and blood oozed from a gash on his forehead.

"What happened?"

"I told them, Miss Ruth. I said it don't matter if your skin is black, white or red, that atom bomb is going to fry you just the same. The only thing that's going to save you is if you have a shelter. And you and Granny Moon are the only people I'm going to let into mine."

"What did you get?"

Old Billy painfully bent himself upright. In the trolley were four Halloween pumpkins, five tins of beans, some bacon and six bottles of water.

"That was all they had, Miss Ruth. All they had."

"You did well just to get that, Billy."

"But is it what we need?"

Ruth looked around. The crowds were thinning, now that all the produce was gone. She was standing in the farthest corner of the supermarket, over by the liquor counter. She reached out, took two quarts of Jack Daniel's and slipped them into the cart.

"I've got what I need," she said. "Now let's get out of here."

3

TUESDAY, 23 OCTOBER 1962
RUSSIAN NUCLEAR SUBMARINE K-6 IN THE ARCTIC CIRCLE
4.05 A.M. MOSCOW TIME
2205 GMT

"Retract the masts!" Petrachkov ordered, and watched as the big cone of the radar system slid down to fit flush with the top of the conning tower. Above it, the crystal Arctic night was a sea of twinkling stars above the luminous icescape.

"Depth under the keel?"

"Seventy metres, Comrade Captain" came the disembodied voice of Rykov below him in the CCP.

"Clear the bridge! Lookouts below. Prepare to dive."

The blue and white flag of the Soviet Navy, with its big red star, came down. The lookouts stowed the spray screen in the front of the cockpit while Petrachkov checked that the ice around them was clear. Then he went to the trunk hatch, stepped down the ladder after the lookouts, and pulled on a chain to heave the heavy hatch shut. After inspecting the seal to make sure it was tight and that the automatic locking mechanism was engaged, he climbed down the ladder and through a second hatch, into the darkness of the command post.

"Ready to dive, Comrade Captain."

"Status?"

"All hull openings green. All systems aligned," Rykov said.

"Very well. Set depth for forty metres, to take us clear of the ice. Flood the main ballast tanks. Ten degrees down on the planes. Dive!"

Rykov pulled the dive alarm. The outer hull vented with a long, sad sigh as the ballast tanks flooded with seawater from the bottom and air rushed out at the top. Petrachkov heard the crunch and scrape of ice as the submarine slid clear and down into the depths.

The deck tilted and the whoosh of air subsided to a whisper as the submarine took on tons of water. The CCP, already sweltering with heat, seemed to grow even hotter. The deck levelled out. The hull started to pop and creak under the pressure. Petrachkov remembered when he had first heard it as a raw recruit and the fear it had raised it him. But that had been a long time ago.

"Right standard rudder, come right to course one two zero, turns for twenty knots."

"Aye, Comrade Captain, rudder is right standard, coming to new course one two zero. Engine room answers turns for twenty knots."

Petrachkov had his orders now, and a new confidence. Kapitulsky, the young and energetic Communications Officer, had raised his balloon aerial and managed to send off a squirt transmission to Severmorsk, informing the Northern Fleet of their situation. The response, complete with the day's authentication codes, included fresh instructions and news of the worsening situation in the Caribbean. Imperialist American forces had been put on 'Defence Condition Two', the final state of readiness before nuclear war. A 500-mile 'quarantine zone' had been declared around Cuba, supported by a blockade of American warships, to come into effect at 10.00 am local time. Petrachkov's instructions therefore were to abandon the torpedo test, head for open water and return to fleet headquarters, so that his communications systems could be repaired. Petrachkov duly relayed this information to the officers and crew.

"How long until we clear the ice, Comrade Rykov?"

"Approximately twelve hours, Captain."

Unlike the other officers, the *Starpom* looked uneasy at the prospect of rejoining his family at Severmorsk. Petrachkov imagined Rykov thinking about his future, and the reports Muhkin and Petrachkov would have to make as to why the aerial was smashed. He decided to try and ease his *Starpom's* mind.

"How have your Leningrad scientists been doing with their communications experiments?"

"They have had some success. Doctor Chiker says the results are extremely encouraging."

"And how long is it before their next contact session?"

Rykov glanced up at the master clock, set to Moscow time. "Just under four hours, at eight a.m., Comrade Captain. Leningrad and Moscow are in the same time zone."

Petrachkov smiled. "Call me just before then, if you will. I'm interested to see these experiments for myself. After all, it would be useful if we had a working back-up system for communicating with headquarters."

The officers' wardroom, located forward of the CCP in compartment two, was soundproofed and had a lock on the door to keep discussions from the ears of enlisted men. It also contained the ship's safe, where secret instructions, codes and the key to the nuclear torpedo were kept. The six digits of the combination lock were in two groups of three, one known only by Petrachkov and the other only by Dudko, the KGB security officer, so that it could not by opened by either man acting alone.

At first glance, Max Rospin resembled any of the young recruits on the ship. The twenty-one-year-old was tall and thin, with an open innocent face, blond hair and the young puppy awkwardness of looking about to fall over his own feet at any moment. But his eyes gave him away. They were dark brown, almost black, with a strange intensity that made Petrachkov uncomfortable. It was as if the young man could look into his soul. No wonder Rykov had been distracted up in the cockpit, he thought. There is something unnatural about this boy.

Next to Max sat Doctor Alexandr Chiker, from the Department of Psychology at the University of Leningrad, a man in his mid-forties, with thinning black hair, cheap clothes and a neatly trimmed beard. To Petrachkov, Chiker would have looked a lot like Lenin had it not been for his glasses, which were as thick as the bottoms of vodka bottles.

"It is a pleasure to have you witness our work, Comrade Captain," Chiker said, rising.

"It's something I should have done long ago, but the business of running the ship is my chief responsibility. You know Comrade Rykov, our first officer, and our political officer Comrade Muhkin? You understand the difficult challenge we face now, with our radio communications systems compromised and the worsening tactical situation in the Atlantic?"

Chiker smiled excitedly. "I understand perfectly, Comrade Captain. I understand we now have a unique opportunity to demonstrate our technique to you, under as close an approximation to battle conditions as it is possible to get. The University of Leningrad won't let you down, Comrade, or betray the faith our State has placed in us through funding this project."

"Then perhaps you would explain to us what the State has bought for its money?"

"Certainly. It is interesting that your other scientific studies, such as the mapping of the seabed under the Arctic Ocean to find a navigation route from the Atlantic to the Pacific, is an exercise pioneered four years ago by the American nuclear submarine *Nautilus*. On that voyage, the Americans also experimented with a new way of communicating with submarines under the ice where no radio contact was possible, a method they claimed had worked. It is that system we've been working to perfect at the University of Leningrad, and which we shall demonstrate to you in a few moments. It uses mental telepathy to receive and transmit messages from anywhere in the world."

"Are you seriously telling me that this boy can send messages with his brain?" Petrachkov asked.

"I am."

"I should also inform you, Comrade Captain," said Muhkin, "that this research is very highly regarded by number of key members of the Praesidium and has already been used to communicate with our cosmonauts in space."

"I see," replied Petrachkov, taking Muhkin's hint. If powerful officials in Moscow had faith in this new science, then lowly naval officers such as himself would be very wise to show it the proper respect. "Perhaps you could give us a report on the experiments to date, Comrade Doctor?"

Chiker laid a brown cardboard folder on the wardroom table and opened it, displaying a series of cards bearing squares, circles and letters, along with a typed list of words.

"I am a research fellow at the University of Leningrad," he said, "working under Professor Boris Kharkov, the State's foremost authority on psychic research. Comrade Max Rospin here has a natural gift which he shares with his twin sister Tatyana, who is presently located in the Admiralty Building in Leningrad. They are both telepathic, and are able to read each other's minds. Professor Kharkov and I have studied them, trained them, and can now use them as living radio transmitters to exchange messages at any agreed time of the day or night."

Petrachkov glanced over at Rykov and winked.

"It looks as if we may not need our radio after all," he said. But if Rykov had any comments, he did not make them then, not after the political officer had warned of the dangers of debunking the brainchild of the Praesidium.

"The experiments started as soon as we left Severmorsk," Chiker continued. "Every twelve hours, at eight in the morning and eight at night, by Leningrad time, I sit here with Max and calm his mind, to make him receptive to thoughts transmitted by his sister. At the same moment, Comrade Kharkov is doing the same with Tatyana in Leningrad. The first messages we sent were simple geometric shapes, followed in a few days by single words and then by more complex phrases. You can see the score sheets, Comrades. At the last session we achieved a success rate of a hundred percent."

Chiker pushed the folder across the wooden table.

Petrachkov examined the neat columns of figures and passed the file to Rykov and Muhkin. Chiker watched each reader for his reaction. Petrachkov saw the scientist's gaze pass from man to man and noted the ambition in the scientist's eyes. He made a mental note to look out for any trick that Chiker might be playing to advance his career back in Leningrad.

"Can these results be independently verified," he asked. "I mean no disrespect, Comrade Doctor, but in a tactical situation the Navy could be committing even nuclear weapons on the strength of orders transmitted by your technique. It is only right that we prove it beyond doubt."

Doctor Chiker was about to speak when Muhkin reached into his jacket, drew out a sealed envelope and placed it on the table in front of them.

"Before we sailed," he said, "a list of code words was drawn up, much like the codes you would use to authenticate a battle order from headquarters, or to act as shorthand for various tactical situations. Leningrad has a copy of the code words for each transmission and so do I, here in this sealed envelope, but neither Doctor Chiker nor Max are told what these words are until *after* each transmission. There is no chance of trickery, Comrade Captain. The system works, just as Comrade Doctor Chiker has described."

"Hmmm," said Petrachkov, glancing up at the clock on the wardroom wall. The big red second hand slid around the bottom of the face. It was almost eight o'clock in Leningrad. "Let us proceed, Comrade Doctor."

Chiker smiled. "Very well, Comrade Captain. I must ask that only you, as the senior officer present, speak during this session, and then only when I indicate you may do so. I say this with the greatest respect, but I must ensure that Comrade Rospin is not distracted. This technique will work if my voice is the *only* one he hears as I guide him through the process. You understand? There are very real risks if he cannot follow my voice, and mine alone, once his consciousness leaves his body."

Petrachkov nodded grudgingly. He resented being given orders on his own ship, particularly by ambitious academics from Leningrad.

"Very well, Max," Chiker continued. "I want you to place your feet flat on the floor, with your hands in your lap, your fingers and thumbs touching and your back supported by your seat. Then I want you to calm your breathing and gently close your eyes."

The young man settled himself as he was told. Petrachkov noticed a deep serenity come over him that seemed to spread out into the room.

"Max. I want you to be aware of the sounds all around you: the hum of machinery, the whirr of the air extractor, the breathing of all the men in this room, your own breathing . . . in and out . . . in and out . . . in and out. Hear them, feel them, and release them . . . . Now I want you to focus your attention on the soles of your feet. Feel the floor through them. Put your whole being right there on the floor with them . . . and let them go. Now move to your ankles . . . ."

Without wishing to, Petrachkov found himself following Chiker's instructions, from his feet to his ankles and on up his legs to his chest. A deep sense of relaxation flowed over him, a feeling of inner peace. Perhaps this would be good for getting to sleep? He made a mental note to ask Chiker for the technique later, as the scientist's voice droned on.

"Now, Max, I want you to focus your being in the space behind your eyes. This is *where* you are. It is *who* you are. Nothing else exists for you in the world. You have no body, no form, nothing to hold you back. You can reach out through this room, through the waters of the sea and up through the ice. You can reach all the way to Tatyana in Leningrad. Think of her, Max. Think of her reaching out to you. She is speaking. She is telling you the words you need to know. What is she saying?"

The expression of utter relaxation on Max Rospin's face did not change.

"Archangel," he said softly.

"Now Comrade Muhkin," said Chiker to the political officer. "Could you open that sealed envelope containing the KGB codes for this session? Show it only to your Captain please."

Petrachkov watched as Muhkin slit the envelope, pulled out the single sheet of paper inside and opened it for him to see. It was a list of names. The first one was "Archangel.

"Are you sure he's never seen that list before?"

"Please, Comrade Captain, not interrupt," said Chiker softly. "If Max loses his state of relaxation, it will break contact with his sister in Leningrad."

Petrachkov was about to apologise, but Chiker motioned with his finger over his own lips. Then he nodded to Petrachkov and continued.

"Now, Max, what is the next name on Tatyana's list?"

"Mother."

Petrachkov checked. The boy was right.

"And the next?"

"Sunrise."

Right again. It was uncanny. If that list really was genuine and Max had not seen it before, then the possibilities for a serving submariner like himself were endless. A submarine would be able to communicate with its base from anywhere in the world without surfacing to deploy its VHF aerial or relying on the slow and limited ultra-low frequency systems underwater. It could communicate instantly from the deepest reaches of the ocean, from the farthest distances, and from under the ice. The technique could even be developed for use from submarine to submarine. It could not be intercepted or decoded by anyone else. Neither could it reveal the submarine's position.

It was a breakthrough.

Petrachkov nodded his approval as the end of the list was reached. The boy had scored every one of the twenty words correctly.

Chiker watched him intently. "Now, Captain, do you approve?"

"Unbelievable," said Petrachkov softly. "Does it work the other way? Could I transmit a message back to Leningrad?"

"Indeed. What do you wish to say?"

"Confirm that our main VHF aerial is damaged. Ask Severmorsk to repeat the instructions they gave us when we used the balloon."

"And you have code words for those situations?" asked Chiker, turning to Rykov.

The first officer scribbled two words on the reverse of Chiker's list and passed it to the scientist.

"Max," said Chiker. "Reach out with your mind to Tatyana and tell her these two words – 'Volcano' and 'Serpent'."

"She understands," said Max. "She will tell her guide, Comrade Professor Kharkov. He will pass the message on to those in authority and return with a reply in a moment."

Petrachkov nodded and glanced at Rykov and Muhkin. They appeared to be as impressed as he was. Perhaps he could still keep his command and even earn a commendation, rather than a black mark in his *zapista,* in spite of Rykov's disabling of the VHF aerial.

"And the confirmation of orders?" asked Petrachkov, as softly as he could.

Max's face darkened. A deep furrow appeared on his brow.

"Tatyana is troubled," said Max. "The international situation has worsened. Your orders have been changed."

"What . . .?" began Petrachkov, but Chiker motioned to him to be silent.

"Speak to me, Max," the scientist said. "Calm yourself. Listen only to Tatyana. What is her message?"

Petrachkov saw tiny beads of sweat break out on Max's forehead. The young man's eyelids fluttered.

"A mixture of words and numbers."

"What are they, Max?" asked Chiker. "Stay with Tatyana, Max. Listen to her. What is she saying?"

Max was breathing quickly. The message stuttered from his lips.

"The code words are 'Apex', 'Earthquake', 'Volcano', 'Swordfish', and 'Anadyr'. The rest of the message is 'alpha, alpha, six, eight, one, zero, three, delta'."

Petrachkov's heart tightened in his chest. Pictures of Natalya and his boys flashed across his mind. This had to be a mistake. Muhkin and Rykov stared at Max in disbelief.

"Ask . . . ask him to repeat those," stammered Petrachkov, trying to keep his voice under control. Rykov was already scribbling furiously on a piece of paper.

"What is it?" asked Chiker, picking up the concern in the captain's voice.

"Where exactly is Max's sister right now?"

"The experiments are being conducted from the Admiralty Building in Leningrad. Why? Is something wrong?"

"Would it be possible for my superior officers in the Northern Fleet to relay an emergency message to me through Tatyana Rospin and her brother in the event that communications from Severmorsk were knocked out?"

"Theoretically, yes. Admiral Shumanin authorised the experiment. He knows the potential of this technique. Why? What do those words and numbers mean?"

Petrachkov fought to keep his voice steady.

"Doctor Chiker, I have to confer with my officers in private. This is not because I have any doubts about Comrade Rospin's abilities. Quite the reverse. It is simply an issue of vital importance to my mission and to the security of the State. If Max relays any more messages between now and your next contact time, please alert me immediately. Muhkin, Rykov, you stay here with me."

After Chiker and Rospin had left the officers' wardroom, Petrachkov ordered that the door be locked.

"You know what that message means?"

Rykov nodded his head. "If it's genuine, then yes."

"If it is, we have a very serious situation," said Petrachkov, turning to the political officer. "Comrade Muhkin, I need your help."

He pulled back the wooden panel covering the ship's safe and, together with Muhkin, opened it, withdrawing a thick codebook bound in red, along with a series of sealed plastic packets, one date-stamped for each day of the mission.

"What's the matter?" asked Muhkin. "What does it mean?"

"Those words the boy was using," said Petrachkov, "are specific coded instructions for elements of Operation Anadyr—the liberation of our comrades on the beleaguered island of Cuba. The numbers are the authenticator key for the message, known only to naval command and changed each day. Please open today's code packet and check them."

The political officer sorted through the packets until he found the one matching that day's date. Then he broke the seal, glanced at the contents and passed it to Petrachkov. It read "alpha, alpha, six, eight, one, zero, three, delta."

"The message must be authentic," said Muhkin. "They know we are under the ice and cannot communicate by radio. The young lad said that the situation in Cuba has deteriorated. They are sending us new coded instructions. What do they want us to do, Comrade Captain?"

But Petrachkov's thoughts were far away, with his wife and two boys at Severmorsk as they had stood on the jetty and waved goodbye to the submarine as it sailed. Natalya had on her fur coat, the one she had bought in Moscow when he had been told they would be moving north to Severmorsk. She had been so proud of that coat.

"Comrade Captain?"

Petrachkov spoke slowly, as if in a trance. "'Apex' is the code for immediate action in time of war," he said, reciting the information from memory in a monotone. "Any Apex message must be acted on immediately, ahead of all other priorities, including the safety of the ship and crew. 'Earthquake' indicates an attack on Severmorsk, while

4

"You have to be sure the message is genuine?" said Mostock. "Each one of us has families at Severmorsk. We have to know if they are live or dead. And you *have* to be certain, Comrade Captain, if you are to release a nuclear weapon and take us to war."

Petrachkov and his eight senior officers sat in conference around the wardroom table with the door locked. Each of them was present according to their place in the chain of command, and as the senior officers of their own specific compartments of the submarine, which, in the emergency of flooding or fire, could each be sealed off from the rest of the ship by a watertight bulkhead designed to withstand the full pressure of the sea. In the event that those bulkheads were ever closed, and a break in communications with the CCP occurred, each officer was expected to command his compartment as a separate unit.

Dudko, the KGB security officer, was in charge of the torpedo room in compartment one nearest the bow. He exchanged suspicious glances with *zampolit* Igor Muhkin, who ran compartment two, which contained the officers' quarters, sonar room and forward batteries. On Petrachkov's right sat Rykov, who was responsible for the CCP in Petrachkov's absence, and Kapitulsky, the Communications Officer, who commanded compartment four containing the diesel generators, refrigerators, compressors and evaporators. Beside him was Mostock, whose precious reactors occupied compartment five at the centre of the ship. At the far end of the table sat Mostock's assistant, in charge of compartment six, housing the turbines, flanked by officers commanding compartments seven, eight and nine,

'Volcano' tells us that radio communications are down. 'Sv
the code for a strike with nuclear torpedoes."

"Then 'Anadyr' means . . ." Rykov's voice trailed off.

"Exactly," said Petrachkov, turning to face him. "If thi
is as genuine as it appears, then Severmorsk has been dest
we have been ordered to proceed to Cuba and attack the
blockade with our nuclear torpedo."

containing the electric motors, crews' quarters and sick bay, steering gear and provision stores.

The only outsider at the table was Doctor Chiker, who sat to Petrachkov's left, cleaning his spectacles nervously while the military debate went on around him.

"We knew the global situation was deteriorating from our last radio communication with Severmorsk," Petrachkov said slowly as he came to grips with the impossible. "We knew the Americans had put their armed forces on what they call 'Defence Condition Two', the highest possible level of readiness. It is entirely possible that diplomatic relations broke down after we submerged and that we are now at war with the United States. Apart from arranging another communication with Leningrad through the services of Doctor Chiker's team, we have no means of getting more information until we clear the ice pack and launch the balloon aerial again."

"If I may speak, Comrade Captain," said Chiker. "Max will not be able to establish contact with Leningrad until his sister is ready to communicate with him, which is not for another eleven hours. As to the accuracy and authenticity of the message, you yourself witnessed complete success in the final test before the transmission came through ordering you to war."

"Nevertheless," said Petrachkov, "I must be absolutely sure before I commit this ship to the release of nuclear weapons. I have ordered a change of course towards the closest edge of the ice, which we shall reach in just over two hours. We will then surface and launch the balloon aerial, allowing another high speed radio message by VHF to authenticate our orders."

"And what if they *are* authenticated?" Muhkin asked.

"Then we shall proceed as ordered. Comrade Rykov, how long will it take us to reach the war zone around Cuba from our present position?"

Rykov spread a chart of the North Atlantic on the table. A pencil line, stretching from north of Bear Island, through the Denmark Strait, then south-westwards to the United States and the Caribbean, had been drawn on it. Rykov placed his finger on the cross marking their present position and dragged it south-westwards as he spoke. As Petrachkov had, he spoke like a man in a dream.

"If the propulsion system holds up, and we are able to make our best submerged speed of thirty knots over a sustained period, then we should be at the blockade around Cuba in approximately two and a half days," he said. "But if we have to evade any anti-submarine patrols at the choke points between Iceland and Greenland, along the Mid-Atlantic Ridge or during our approach to the American coast, we could be delayed. I recommend we follow a course as close to the edge of the American continental shelf as we safely can. This will not only confuse our sonar signal with those of merchant vessels in the shipping lanes near the coast, but also give us the option of escaping detection in the upwelling currents and saltwater gradients in that area."

Petrachkov listened to these details as if he were an actor in a play waiting for his cue. Natalya and his boys were dead. Nothing else mattered. Not this ship, these men, this mission. Nothing.

"Comrade Captain?" asked Rykov.

Petrachkov pulled himself together. He had once been a husband and a father, but he was still commander of this submarine, and a defender of the State.

"Very good, Comrade Rykov," he said trying to lift the mood in the room. "Comrade Mostock, can those beloved reactors keep us going that long? Or will we have to surface and row to Cuba."

Mostock shrugged. "They can run forever, Comrade Captain. Likewise the oxygen generator and the freshwater still are working well. Mechanically, we can do it. But how will the rest of the crew take the news that their families have died at Severmorsk? How will they react when they know we are at war?"

"Comrade Muhkin, how will the men take it?"

"The morale of the men has always been high, Comrade Captain. Even in this terrible time, I expect they will do their duty to the Party and the State."

"Comrade Kapitulsky, is the balloon fit for a second flight?"

"It is, Comrade Captain."

Petrachkov nodded. "Launching the balloon will be risky Comrades. The weather is bad in the Arctic at this time of year and the sea beyond the ice will be extremely rough, so we'll need life jackets and full immersion suits. We shall also be transmitting well within range of the American air base on Greenland, so I do not want to spend a second longer on the surface than we have to. This part of the mission has to go like clockwork. Is that understood?"

Heads nodded around the table.

"Very well," said Petrachkov. "Let's try and get some rest until we reach the edge of the ice."

He walked back to his cabin, looked at the three photographs on the wall and shut the door behind him. Then slowly, gently, he took the family portrait of a father, mother and two young sons down from the wall and traced their faces with his fingers. His heart burst and suddenly he was kneeling next to his bunk, sobbing uncontrollably into the coarse blanket. It was not supposed to be this way! It was husbands and fathers who fought and died, not wives and children! The pain drowned him. He felt lost in it, small and weak and helpless.

Then a hand touched his shoulder.

"Sergei Nikolai," said Mostock softly. "I know your pain. Natalya was a wonderful wife and your sons were something to be truly proud of. You have been dealt a blow that nobody can recover from, just as I was when Galina was taken. But we need you, Comrade. We need you as our commander to lead us through this thing. Be strong for us, Sergei Nikolai, stronger than even you know how to be, for all of us."

Petrachkov reached back, clasped Mostock's calloused hand and held it tight. Then he got to his feet, still facing the cabin wall and wiped the tears from his eyes.

"Thank you, Comrade," he said. "I'll return to the CCP in a moment."

"Yes, Comrade Captain."

Mostock closed the door behind him. Petrachkov lifted the family portrait and looked at it one last time. Then he opened the drawer of his desk, placed the picture inside and shut it, before turning from the cabin and heading aft towards the control room.

TUESDAY, 23 OCTOBER 1962
GRAND CANYON SOUTH RIM AIRPORT
7.15 P.M. MOUNTAIN STANDARD TIME
WEDNESDAY, 24 OCTOBER
0215 GMT

Ruth sat with her face pressed up against the chain fence at the outer perimeter of the airport watching the flashing lights of the last tour helicopters as they flitted in across the trees.

The sun was setting fast now, throwing long shadows across the airport. In a few minutes the sky would turn to fire in the east, burn for a moment and then fall into darkness. That was the way of things on the rim – a beautiful day, a flaming sunset and then night. She took another swig from the bottle of Jack Daniel's and stared at the slowly turning rotors of the last helicopter to land.

Was it him? What would she do if it was? What would he say if he saw her drunk?

And yet she had to be here. She had to be near him one last time before the bombs fell and everything was blasted into nothingness.

"Miss Ruth?" said Old Billy from the station wagon behind her. "You have to come back now. Granny Moon will be worried for you. You know how she worries when you get like this."

"She knows where I am. She knows you're with me. What's there to worry about?"

From the supermarket in Flagstaff they had come back to the trailer park, where Granny Moon had fixed the wound on Old Billy's forehead and told him it was a shame that decent folks would act like animals that way. Seeing them together, caring for each other, had brought Ruth close to tears.

Then they all went back to Old Billy's shack to watch the early evening news on the old black and white TV he had scrounged from a trash can behind an electrical store a few of months back and fixed with a couple of new valves and his big soldering iron. Walter Cronkite had been talking about "the collision course towards global annihilation", which had been more than Ruth could stand. She had demanded that Old Billy bring her up to the airport but, when they had got there, all she could do was to collapse against the perimeter fence and cry.

She took another large pull at the bottle and fell back against the fence in tears.

Old Billy watched her for a while longer. Then he got out of the car, took the bottle from her hand and capped it, before lifting her gently in his arms and taking her home.

WEDNESDAY, 24 OCTOBER 1962
SUBMARINE K-6 IN THE GREENLAND BASIN
1500 MOSCOW TIME
12 NOON GMT

"Up periscope! Raise signal detectors!"

Petrachkov leant forward as the great steel cylinder slid from its well beneath the command post. He pressed his eyes to the rubber sockets over the lenses and rotated the scope quickly, covering the entire horizon. He was already dressed in a one-piece immersion suit and a lifejacket, as were Rykov and Kapitulsky.

In the cross hairs of the periscope, to the stern of the ship, he saw the white mass of ice they had just left. In front of them, and on either side, towered the rolling grey mountains of the sea.

"It's broad daylight up there, Comrades. We had better do this quickly. Raise the radar mast and complete a sweep for aircraft before we blow ballast."

The submarine rolled sickeningly. While they had been cruising at depth, they had been out of reach of the waves. But close to the surface, the motion of the moving water made itself felt.

"Both radar and sonar report no contacts, Captain," said Rykov. "No ships or aircraft within range. No electronic emissions of any kind."

Petrachkov pressed his eyes to the periscope. A jet aircraft travelling at low altitude could easily sneak up on them before they had time to dive. The ship rolled, catching Rykov off balance. He grabbed the rail around the periscope base and held on.

"Pretty bad sea running too," noted Petrachkov. "We'll all be glad of these immersion suits when we go aloft to launch the balloon. Is everyone ready?"

"Yes, Comrade Captain."

"Very well then. Blow all secondary ballast. Stand by the main trunk hatch. Surface!"

Petrachkov followed the lookouts up into the cockpit. All around him, the rolling waters of the North Atlantic heaved and churned in foam-crested peaks. The submarine, designed for peak performance underwater, had none of the stability of a surface ship when out of its natural element. It rolled alarmingly. Petrachkov gripped the sides of the cockpit as the ship swayed, trying to hold his binoculars steady as he scanned the horizon.

Rykov emerged from the hatch, holding the deflated balloon and a cylinder of helium. Behind him, Kapitulsky threw a coil of aerial wire out of the hatch and disappeared back down to man the radio gear.

Petrachkov reached forward and plugged his intercom headset into the socket so that he could talk to those below in the CCP.

"Anything on radar?"

"Sonar and radar both clear, Comrade Captain. No emissions."

"Good. Report anything you see immediately."

He signalled to Rykov to inflate the balloon and heard the loud hiss of gas. The ship was running with the waves at her stern, heading south-west. White water broke over the hull, slid forward and crashed into the base of the conning tower, drenching the cockpit. Petrachkov wiped his eyes and scanned the horizon, just as another wave broke.

"Come left ten degrees. We're getting drowned up here!"

Rykov had the balloon inflated. It tugged at its aerial like a live bird seeking the sky. Then it soared upwards, jerking to a stop as the wire paid out to its full length, fifty metres above the rolling submarine.

"The balloon is up!" shouted Petrachkov into his microphone. "Do you have radio contact?"

"We have the carrier wave," Kapitulsky replied from below. "We're about to start transmission. It should only take a few seconds if the signal compression works. It—"

"Aircraft contact astern!" shouted another voice over the intercom. "Bearing zero five degrees. It looks like three planes coming at us over the ice."

"How long before they reach us?"

"Less than two minutes!"

"Lookouts below," shouted Petrachkov above the wind and the waves. "Kapitulsky, do we have a reply to that transmission?"

"Not yet, Captain. It would take them a while to decode it and compose a response."

"Diving officer, prepare to crash dive as soon as I give the word."

He trained the binoculars over the stern.

It was all a gamble on whose planes they were, whether or not they were armed with anti-submarine weapons, and how fast Severmorsk could respond to his message.

"Where are the planes now?"

"About a minute astern."

"Can you tell whose they are?"

"No, Captain. But we are a small radar contact running low in the water. Perhaps they won't see us."

Petrachkov glanced up at the bright orange balloon jerking against the sky above his head.

"They'll see us," he shouted. "They probably have the balloon on radar already."

"Forty seconds to contact, Captain."

"Any sign of a reply to our message?"

"None."

Petrachkov saw the planes, three tiny pinpricks above the ice, each trailing a smudge of exhaust gas and heading straight for the submarine.

"Rykov, bring in the balloon! Control room, retract the masts and prepare to dive."

Rykov had his gloved hands around the aerial and was pulling hard, but the balloon was caught in the wind, throwing him against the cockpit casing. Above them, the Albatross anti-aircraft radar mast slid towards its socket behind the cockpit. The wind whipped at the balloon, spun it about and looped the wire around the conical head.

The three dots had taken the shapes of three American Phantom jet fighters. Would they fire on the first pass? Petrachkov was betting the lives of everyone on the ship that they would not.

"The balloon's caught," Rykov screamed above the wind.

"Get it free. We can't afford to lose it!"

Petrachkov watched the jets racing at them silently across the waves. They're travelling at the speed of sound, he thought. That's why I can't hear them.

He leant forward to help Rykov with the aerial wire, but Rykov was already climbing up onto the cockpit lip and reaching for it as the cone of the radar mast slid down.

"No! Don't be a fool!"

A wave smashed onto the rear casing of the submarine, broke against the conning tower and sent a wall of green water over the cockpit. Petrachkov ducked, just as the three aircraft shot overhead with a boom and a roar, less than a hundred metres above. The explosion of their jet engines slammed Petrachkov's eardrums. He glimpsed the red, white and blue markings on the wings as they banked and turned, getting ready for their second run. They'll open fire for sure, he thought, now they know who we are.

"Leave the balloon, Rykov!" he shouted. "Cut the aerial and get below. Crash dive! Dive! Dive! Dive!"

But he was alone in the cockpit.

"Rykov!" he screamed out at the waves. "Rykov!" But there was nothing but the rolling grey ocean, the three jets circling in the distance and the hiss of air escaping from the ballast tanks, shooting spray into the sky.

"Captain, Captain, you have to get below!"

"Man overboard! Abort the dive!"

"Captain, the ballast tanks are already flooding. We are losing buoyancy. You must get below."

A mountainous wave broke over the cockpit, crushing Petrachkov to his knees under the weight of water. Blinded and shaking, he crawled to the hatch and climbed inside.

The last thing he saw before pulling the lid closed over his head and strapping it shut was the orange ball of the balloon, liberated from the submarine and making its bid for freedom on the wind.

5

WEDNESDAY, 24 OCTOBER 1962
THE ADMIRALTY BUILDING, LENINGRAD
3.34 P.M. LOCAL TIME
1234 GMT

Admiral Aleksandr Shumanin of the Red Banner Northern Fleet looked out from the window of his corner office in the Admiralteystvo building in Leningrad and sipped his mid-afternoon cup of black tea from his favourite glass in its silver holder. From this window, he could look inland, right across the Admiralty Gardens to the wide boulevard of the Nevsky Prospeckt.

He would have preferred an office on the seaward side of the building, one that looked out across the river Neva to the Baltic and the glorious memories of his youth. Ideally, he would have liked to be back with the fleet at Severmorsk, rather than managing "special projects" in Leningrad. But on reflection, now that he was nearing his sixtieth birthday, it was better that his life turned towards home, to views of children playing in the park, of lovers strolling among the autumn leaves and of the bustle of life on Nevsky Prospeckt. Leningrad was a beautiful city and it troubled him deeply that everything he saw from his window could be destroyed in one atomic fireball, if things went out of control in the Caribbean.

The Northern Fleet was already on a high state of alert, standing by for war. As of that morning, the Americans had thrown a blockade of warships in a circle around Cuba, threatening to board any Soviet ship and inspect it for weapons of war. Operation Anadyr, which included the deployment of four diesel-powered submarines to protect the Russian merchantmen supplying Cuba with weapons, had been put into effect. Staff worked around the clock to maintain communications, service and feed the radios, switchboards and coding rooms that processed and directed information traffic.

Admiral Shumanin took another sip of tea, looked at his watch and wondered if he would ever get home again to see his wife. He was a short, jolly man who, since leaving active sea duty some ten years before, had become so overweight that he had to have his uniforms specially tailored. To those who met him for the first time, he looked like a favourite uncle who had decided to dress up as an Admiral for a fancy dress party, rather than the shrewd tactician he was, a man who had risen to high rank by combining intelligence and political cunning with a genuine feel for the needs of those under his command.

He returned to his desk, where a pile of messages awaited his attention, and called for his secretary to come and take dictation. He was halfway through a memorandum concerning the deployment of vessels in the eastern Mediterranean, when a knock sounded on the oak door and a nervous captain from the communications centre entered.

Shumanin smiled at the young man and beckoned him into his presence.

"What has you so worried on such a fine afternoon, Anatoly? Have the Americans landed in Moscow?"

The officer glanced at Shumanin's secretary.

"It is a matter of State security, Comrade Admiral. I need to speak to you alone."

Shumanin stiffened slightly. "Very well. Olga, we'll finish this later."

The woman nodded, folded her dictation pad and left.

"What is it, Anatoly?"

"Severmorsk has received another radio signal from submarine K-6, Comrade Admiral. Captain Petrachkov had experienced problems with his VHF radio aerial in the ice and communications had been shut down. He sent a squirt transmission from a balloon aerial yesterday evening, advising Severmorsk of the situation."

"I know. He was ordered to return for repairs."

"Yes, Comrade Admiral. But a few minutes ago Severmorsk received another high speed transmission requesting confirmation of a second set of instructions Captain Petrachkov claims he was given, while under the ice, as part of the Leningrad University experiments."

"Ah, that mumbo-jumbo! We have a whole floor of modern radio equipment here and an antenna array that can send a signal to Mars, yet the Praesidium still has this obsession for fortune-tellers and séances. What instructions does he claim to have received?"

The young Captain hesitated. In the Soviet military there was no more dangerous duty than to report bad news to a superior officer.

"It was a properly coded Apex attack signal, Comrade Admiral."

"An Apex attack signal! Those scientists are not cleared to meddle with Apex signals. What is this? Some kind of a joke?"

"It is no joke, Comrade Admiral. The two signals, Petrachkov's request for confirmation to us and the message he claims was sent through the experimental programme, all appear genuine."

"I want everyone involved in those experiments rounded up for questioning. Do you understand? Everyone! This is a security breach of the highest order."

"That is being done, Comrade Admiral."

"Let me see that confirmation request."

The Captain handed over the flimsy transcript. Shumanin read it twice. Every code word was correct. Every authenticator was in place. It was just as a properly formatted Apex order should be. His hands shook as he laid the paper on the desk.

"What is this? Severmorsk destroyed! An order to carry out a nuclear torpedo attack on the American blockade around Cuba!"

"We have checked with the Kremlin, Comrade Admiral. Severmorsk has not been attacked and the Crisis Room has issued no such order for reprisals. But, as you can see, the authentication codes are correct. Such a message could only have come from someone at the highest level of command."

"And what action is Petrachkov taking on these orders? He's not going to carry them out surely?"

"Severmorsk has lost radio contact with his submarine, Comrade Admiral. By the time they had formulated a response, the carrier wave from his balloon aerial had collapsed. He may have experienced more trouble with his radio, or had to make an emergency dive."

"Or been sunk?"

"Yes, Comrade Admiral, there is that possibility. To send a transmission with a balloon aerial he would have had to surface completely, and there are regular American patrols in the area."

"Are we still trying to reach him?"

"Severmorsk has issued coded instructions for Petrachkov to disregard the signal but, given the absolute priority he would attach to any properly coded Apex order, it is likely that the submarine has submerged again and is on its way to Cuba. Apex protocols would require Petrachkov to do that in the event that Severmorsk or the secondary command centre in Leningrad had been destroyed. But he will surely surface and call again, or at least be in a position to receive countermanding instructions on his balloon aerial."

"And if he doesn't?"

"It is unlikely, Admiral. A commander of Captain Petrachkov's experience would never go through with a nuclear attack on the strength of a single signal from an experimental source."

Admiral Shumanin sat down at his desk, picked up the order and read it though again. "Do not be so sure, Anatoly. Comrade Petrachkov may be an able and experienced officer, but if he believes that Severmorsk has been destroyed and his family are dead, then he may let his desire for revenge cloud his judgement."

Shumanin heard a commotion in the corridor outside his office. There was a loud knock and his secretary looked in.

"I'm sorry, Comrade Admiral but — "

"Comrade Admiral, we have news." Two young men, wearing the dark khaki uniforms of the internal security directorate of the KGB, strode into the room.

"Yes?"

"We have Professor Kharkov of the University of Leningrad in the cells below this building, Comrade Admiral. But the girl, Tatyana Rospin, is missing. Professor Kharkov claims that she left the Admiralty Building after her last session and never came back."

"And what about the naval officer who was supposed to be supervising these . . . these experiments? Where is he?"

"Gone too, Admiral. Apparently he and the Rospin woman were . . ."

Admiral Shumanin swore violently, smashing his fist on the desk and sending his unfinished glass of tea crashing down onto the polished floor.

"I want a full meeting of all Section Heads here in ten minutes. I don't care what they are doing or how important they think it is. Just get them!"

As the officers left, Admiral Shumanin looked at the shattered glass and wondered if he would have a career, or even his own life, in ten minutes. It was a nightmare.

His secretary opened the door and entered with a dustpan and brush. "Never mind that, Olga. Get back to your desk and find me the name of the officer commanding the KGB in the city. I need to see him right away."

His secretary looked frightened. "I already know his name, Comrade Admiral. It is Cherlenko. Comrade Colonel Vladimir Cherlenko."

Yes, Olga, of course, thought Admiral Shumanin. You have every reason to be afraid.

Black Bishop

TIME TO EVENT

02:10:09

DAYS : HRS : MINS

6

Admiral Shumanin already knew of Cherlenko's reputation. He had met him briefly at informal functions around the military circuit in Leningrad. At first, he had taken the young blond officer with the refined features and genteel manners to be one of the diplomatic corps. But at the Mariinskiy Theatre one evening, he had seen Cherlenko wearing the dark khaki uniform and sword and shield emblem of the KGB, a row of medal ribbons from the Great Patriotic War, and had noticed the way that even senior officers deferred to him. When introduced by a mutual acquaintance, both Shumanin and his wife were charmed by Cherlenko's wit and good manners, his knowledge of the arts and his kind offer to help Shumanin's sons, who were interested in careers within the security system.

It was only later, as they were leaving the ballet, that this mutual acquaintance took Madame Shumanin aside and whispered in her ear, so softly that nobody standing more than a few centimetres away would have heard a sound.

"You be careful now, Masha. You know who that was, don't you? That's the 'Butcher of Novocherkassk'."

The incident had happened earlier that year, at the beginning of June, and had only been whispered about in the corridors of power. It had started with a peaceful protest over wage cuts and rising food prices in the steel store of NEVZ, the largest electromotive plant in Novocherkassk. The city was considered to be a centre for students at the time, so very little meat and butter was delivered to the government stores and what there was quickly became too expensive to buy. The protest got out of hand and soon mushroomed into a mass demonstration in the streets. The local militia could not cope.

Placards bearing the slogans 'Give us meat and butter', and 'Make meat from Khrushchev!' appeared. But even then, nobody was hurt or injured, apart from a woman who had been hit through a window by a soldier's gun butt.

Armoured troop carriers arrived but were forced to withdraw as the workers started rocking the vehicles in an attempt to overturn them. The unarmed, disorganised workers were winning out against the might of the State's military machine with surprising ease. They took down Khrushchev's picture from the front of the plant management office, then went through every room, gathered all the portraits and burned them on a large, smoky bonfire.

Tanks were brought in, along with reinforcements of soldiers, but the protest grew and grew as the workers became more and more excited, full of belief in their power and the fairness of their demands. The revolutionary songs grew louder, more harmonious and more powerful. The workers had risen from their knees and were challenging the authority of the State.

Then a worker managed to wrest a submachine gun from a soldier and brandished it above his head. It was unloaded and harmless. The soldier who owned it still had the magazine clip safely in his pocket, but the KGB officer commanding the militia, one Colonel Vladimir Cherlenko, ordered his men to open fire again and again with live ammunition on the densely packed crowds. At least two hundred people were killed.

Afterwards, the corpses of the victims were thrown into trucks and buses and driven away. Not a single body was given to its family to be buried, wounded people disappeared and the blood was washed from the streets by fire engines. Leaders of the protest were rounded up, arrested, and vanished. The city was quarantined for six weeks, so that nobody could leave or enter without a KGB pass. Not a word appeared in the press, but the story was whispered throughout the country and taken as a warning to those in government of how fragile their hold on power really was.

Admiral Shumanin was well aware of Lenin's 'scientific definition of a dictatorship' as 'unlimited power resting directly on force' and that in Soviet Russia control of the masses was achieved through the three legs of force provided by the Communist Party, the Army and the KGB. He also knew that while each one of these forces possessed enormous power, it was always exceeded by the combined strength of the other two.

The KGB was the craftiest of the trio. It could recruit any party leader or military officer as its agent, or destroy them in a compromising situation. The Party remembered how the KGB's predecessor, the MVD, had destroyed the entire Central Committee during the course of a single year, while the Army remembered how the KGB had managed to annihilate all its generals in the space of only two months following the death of Stalin in 1953.

The KGB was an enormous organization with a broad network of special departments in all major government institutions, enterprises and factories, which recruited informers to assist them with their tasks. It controlled domestic security, censorship, propaganda and the protection of military and State secrets. It encouraged neighbourhood vigilantes and informers. It patrolled borders, uncovered and investigated political crimes. It confined dissidents in psychiatric hospitals or deported them to prison camps. It was the dark nightmare behind the Soviet dream.

Shumanin had every reason to fear Cherlenko, and the prospect of telling him the bad news.

An hour later, after his meeting with the Admiralty Section Heads, a discreet knock sounded on Shumanin's office door. He rose and said, "Enter."

The door opened. Shumanin's secretary showed Colonel Vladimir Cherlenko into the room. He smiled at her politely, handed over his cap, coat and gloves and graciously accepted the offer of tea and a cigarette. Then he snapped a crisp salute to Shumanin and, the formalities over, reached out his right hand.

"My dear Comrade Admiral, good evening. How is your charming wife?"

Shumanin took the offered hand and shook it. Cherlenko's grip was cold. His bright eyes made Shumanin think of a coiled snake, ready to strike.

"She is well, thank you."

"And your sons? Advancing in their careers I trust?"

"Indeed."

"Very good. Then how can I be of service?"

"Comrade Colonel, thank you for taking the trouble to come here this evening. Normally I would not have disturbed such a senior official as yourself, had it not been for the supreme urgency of this matter. As you may be aware, we have been conducting experiments in communications with a submarine under the Arctic ice cap. This has involved — "

"Comrade Professor Boris Kharkov," said Cherlenko. "I know the man. He has a laboratory at the university. I'm sorry for interrupting. Please go on."

The tea arrived. Shumanin waited until his secretary was out of the room before continuing his briefing. Shumanin was impressed by how much Cherlenko already knew of the experiments and those involved. If he knows that much about Kharkov, Shumanin thought, then how much does he know about me? Finally, he came to the events of the afternoon, the discovery of the message on which Captain Petrachkov had requested confirmation, and the terrible implications for the State if the submarine could not be recalled.

To Shumanin, Cherlenko seemed almost excited by the prospect of the chase, in spite of the terrible consequences of failure.

"You realize the gravity of the situation, Comrade Colonel?" he said without thinking.

Cherlenko's bright eyes turned to polished steel. The smile dropped from his face.

"And do *you* realize, Comrade Admiral, that this Professor Kharkov of yours was once a dissident who spent time in a Siberian labour camp?"

"No .... No. I didn't. What crimes did he commit?"

Cherlenko reached into the leather briefcase he had placed on the floor beside him and pulled out a thick brown *zapista* with a red line scrawled across the front cover. As Cherlenko opened it, Shumanin noticed the red stamp of the KGB on each of the onionskin pages.

"I *fully* realise what is at stake here, Comrade Admiral. But all this trouble could have been avoided if you had only been courteous enough to consult me before recruiting dissidents and granting them access to secret research programmes."

The threat was obvious. Shumanin saw his career, his family, even his very life, flash before his eyes.

"The Soviet Union has become a powerful empire composed of many peoples and many lands, banded together in a common cause under one flag to fight capitalism," Cherlenko said. "Yet Comrade Kharkov was one of those poor deluded chauvinists who wanted to break all that apart and return us to our peasant roots."

"Like Solzhenitsyn?"

"Indeed. These 'Russianists', as we call them, believe in the Russian Orthodox Church and that the rightful place of every man is on his own land. They are against the collective farms and modern life. They want us all to leave the cities, throw away everything we have achieved in building this great modern empire of ours, and return to grubbing around for potatoes in the dirt. You see now, Admiral, why it is so important that you consult with me before allowing such people to become involved in sensitive work for the State?"

"I do, Comrade Colonel. I will, of course, make sure this is done in future."

"If there is a future."

"I'm sure the submarine can be stopped, Comrade Colonel. I will do everything in my power to make sure it is."

Cherlenko smiled. "I'm glad to hear it, Comrade Admiral. I would not want you and your wife to exchange all the privileges you enjoy here in Leningrad for a forced labour camp in Siberia, or your sons to find themselves assigned to a coal mine."

"No." Shumanin felt himself walking on ice. From now on, his entire future, and that of his family, rested on his every response.

"To business then," said Cherlenko, snapping shut Kharkov's *zapista*. "I understand that my main task is to locate this girl whom Kharkov trained as a telepathic link to her brother in the submarine. Is that correct?"

"It is, Comrade Colonel."

"Very good. In the meantime I suggest you contact your superiors in Moscow personally and inform them of how this situation might develop if we are unable to stop Captain Petrachkov from releasing his nuclear weapon."

Shumanin knew this was coming. At some point, as senior officer in charge of the experiment, he would have to take responsibility for what had gone wrong. He was doomed. All that remained was for him to fall on his sword with as little suffering to his family as possible.

"I will make the call once this meeting is over."

"Then all I need do is put the investigation under way and hunt down these dissidents."

"I will give you every assistance," offered Shumanin, still contemplating the ruins of his shattered career.

"I know," said Cherlenko, sliding Kharkov's *zapista* back into his briefcase. "And the first thing you can give me is an interview with the infamous Professor Kharkov. I understand he is in custody in this building."

7

The old elevator, with its dirty brass doors, screeching pulleys and confined space, made Cherlenko uneasy. It reminded him of being trapped in the filthy maze of ruined machinery which had been Stalingrad's greatest tractor factory. German snipers struck without warning if anyone broke cover for food. The burst bodies of their victims lay stripped of clothes and equipment, abandoned to rot in the slime.

The elevator reached the basement, jerking Cherlenko back to the present.

"This way, Comrade Colonel," said Shumanin, sliding back the door to let him past. "The cell is down here on the left."

But Cherlenko could already tell which cell Kharkov was in from the two naval sentries posted at its door. They both snapped to attention.

"My own guards will be here shortly," he said. "I'm sure your men have better things to do than baby-sit aging academics."

He smiled amiably at each of the three men as he insulted them, knowing they dared not protest. No matter, he thought; the navy had made a complete mess of this whole situation.

"Quite so, Comrade Colonel," said Shumanin, avoiding his gaze. "In the meantime, it would probably be wise for one of them to accompany us into the cell, while we interview the prisoner."

"Is Kharkov restrained?"

"He is handcuffed to the chair, Comrade Colonel," said one of the guards, with his eyes fixed on the wall straight ahead.

"Then I will not detain you any longer, Comrade Admiral," Cherlenko said, still smiling. "Thank you for bringing this whole affair to my attention."

"But — "

"Thank you, Comrade Admiral. And please give my regards to your wife."

Shumanin was an overweight idiot who deserved to be shot, Cherlenko thought. His wife would soon slim down a few dress sizes on the diet she would face on a civilian's pay.

"Yes, Comrade Colonel."

"And don't forget that phone call to Moscow."

Shumanin straightened his back and saluted. Then he walked back to the elevator like a condemned man trying to show courage in front of a firing squad.

Cherlenko turned to the rusty cell door with its eye-level spy-hole and metal *kormushka* food flap.

"Open the cell!"

One of the men took a heavy brass key from a ring on his leather belt, threaded it into the lock and hauled it round. Cherlenko heard the solid 'clack' as the bolt slid back. A stench of stale urine, cheap disinfectant and naked fear wafted out into the corridor.

"Leave it unlocked," Cherlenko ordered. The walls had been painted like a child's bedroom, in pale robin egg blue up to shoulder level, with the rest of the walls dirty beige. The cement floor, badly scuffed at the entrance, had been painted dark brown, as had the inside of the door. A stinking, sodden rag lay at the threshold like a mat. The only light came from a single bulb in a protective metal frame bolted to the ceiling. It shone down on a narrow cot, a table and two metal chairs, all bolted to the floor. One of the chairs was occupied. The man sitting there stared straight into Cherlenko's eyes.

Professor Boris Kharkov looked to be in his mid-fifties. He was small and slightly built, with a full head of thick black hair, turning silver, and a neat tapered beard. Cherlenko fancied that Kharkov's head was so large as to appear out of proportion to his body. He reminded himself that was sometimes the way with people whose limbs had wasted away from starvation, as Kharkov's would surely have during his time in the Gulag.

But it was the eyes that struck Cherlenko most. In his time with the KGB, he had seen the eyes of many men and women trapped in prison cells or interrogation rooms—eyes that wept or blazed with fury, eyes that begged for mercy or the hollow eyes of broken prisoners for whom all hope had died.

Kharkov's eyes were different. They sparkled with the detached amusement of someone who knew nothing could ever touch them, someone with the arrogance of true faith in a higher power, someone to whom life was nothing more than a joke.

I'll enjoy breaking you, thought Cherlenko. Then we'll see who is laughing.

"Good evening, Comrade Professor. I hope you're being treated well."

"I've been treated no better or worse than I expected, Comrade Colonel."

Kharkov smiled at Cherlenko, revealing the bloody socket of a missing tooth. Whoever had administered his last beating had been wearing a ring and had either forgotten to remove it, or had deliberately decided to keep it on. Cherlenko noted the bruises on Kharkov's gaunt face and the gash across the right temple. Amateurs! There were plenty of ways to torture a man without leaving a mark.

He dusted the second chair with his gloves and sat down. Then he opened his briefcase and laid Kharkov's *zapista* on the table between them.

"I want to talk to you about your experiments, Professor."

"Which ones? I have undertaken so many during my quest for scientific truth in support of the State."

"The investigations with the Rospin twins you were performing for Admiral Shumanin and his submarine fleet. The ones concerning telepathy."

"You seem well informed, Comrade. What more can I possibly add that you do not already know?"

"You can start from the very beginning by telling me who conceived these experiments, who ordered them to be carried out and how this was done. You can also tell me how the minds of the Rospin twins are linked, how the girl came to have access to restricted naval codes and then be allowed to transmit them to the submarine. Finally, you can tell me where I can find her so that this madness can be stopped."

"That is an extremely long list, Comrade. An old man like me might have difficulty remembering it all."

"I doubt that very much, Comrade Professor."

Kharkov smiled and glanced down at the thick *zapista*.

"Of course. The KGB knows everything about everyone. Isn't that right?"

The bright brown eyes twinkled at Cherlenko across the table, but he had done too many interrogations on too many people to be concerned. It was just a matter of finding a person's weak spot and probing it until he or she broke.

"That is correct, Comrade Professor. I am aware that you and your wife adopted the Rospin twins, Tatyana and Max, after their parents were killed at the siege of Leningrad during the Great Patriotic War. You raised them as your own children until you were both sent to Siberia."

"You *are* well informed," said Kharkov softly.

"Like you said, the KGB knows everything. You should also be aware that I have the power to have every one of your friends and colleagues at the university arrested, tortured and shot."

"I know that already."

"Do you play chess, Comrade Professor?"

For the first time, Kharkov looked worried. His right hand went to his left and began twiddling the gold wedding band on the third finger.

"I . . . I have done . . . in my time, yes."

"Are you any good?"

Kharkov shrugged.

"If you know the rules of chess, you will surely recognise that I hold you in check on every side. I hold all the pieces. I have absolute power over you and all those you care about. You, on the other hand, are a powerless pawn, a worthless dissident and former mental patient who is alive only because of a talent that is useful to the State. Please consider your next move carefully before trying my patience further."

Kharkov nodded, like a chess player gracefully accepting defeat. Cherlenko pictured him reaching out and toppling his king on the board.

"You assume I am guilty of a crime, Comrade Colonel. But my only transgressions were to believe that mankind can transcend this frail body of his, and to prove it by harnessing the power of science in the service of the State. I have nothing to hide. Where would you like me to begin?"

"At the beginning of my list, Comrade. With the experiments."

"Very well. The research programme at the university was conceived after Moscow learned that the Americans were already experimenting with thought projection as a way of talking to nuclear submarines under the ice. The Praesidium decided we might soon be competing with the Americans in a 'mind race' to develop telepathic communication, just as we have been engaged in an arms race and a space race for many years. Comrade Stalin was a great believer in psychic research. He even ordered the famous psychic Wolf Messing to be taken from the stage during a packed performance in Belarus to appear before him personally in 1940. Did you know that?"

"It is *more recent* history that concerns me."

"Quite so. When I returned from my period of correction in Siberia, I began working here in Leningrad at the Parapsychology Laboratory headed by Dr Vasilev. He took a very methodical approach, measuring brainwaves with an encephalograph, photographing human auras using Kirlian photography, looking for the cold, scientific reason as to why such phenomena occurred. 'We must widen the consciousness of humanity,' he used to say. 'It is vital that the paranormal powers hidden in the human mind be used for good.' Ironic, isn't it, that his work should be perverted to allow us control of nuclear weapons?"

"I appreciate the irony. Please tell me who contacted you to begin the experiments with the navy."

"Why, the KGB of course, Comrade Colonel. It was a Major Leonid Galrikov of your Science and Technology Division, as I recall. Do you know him?"

"Our organization has over a quarter of a million personnel in the uniformed branches alone, Professor. I do not know them all personally."

"A pity. He was a keen chess player and a connoisseur of the ballet. Much like yourself, Comrade Colonel. The two of you would have got on famously."

A cold wind blew across Cherlenko's warm sense of victory. While his fondness for the ballet was no State secret, it disturbed him that Kharkov would mention it. What else did the man know about him?

"And what did the KGB ask you to do?"

"To reproduce and improve on the American work, to develop a reliable working system of transmitting messages over long distances by using the mind. Imagine the applications to our space programme. If our glorious cosmonauts experienced a breakdown on one of their missions, a code number, indicating that particular problem, could be sent back to earth by telepathy. Messages that would take hours to transmit by radio across the vastness of space on a mission to Mars could be sent instantly. And then, of course, there was the application to submarines, which was much closer to home."

"How did you begin?"

"You have to understand that telepathy isn't a science, as Comrade Vasilev believed, but an art. And true artistic talent is something you are either born with, or you are not. If you had musical talent, Comrade Colonel, I could teach you to sing in an opera or play a piano sonata. If you were tone deaf, I could not even teach you to whistle. It is the same with psychic ability. Some people have no gift whatever; they go through life without the slightest intuition about anything, like cattle in a field, ignorant and serene. Others of us have some very basic gift in that direction. We have flashes of inspiration, premonitions and bursts of *déjà vu*. We know *something* is happening inside our heads and we're grateful when it comes to our aid, but we do not know what that 'something' is, nor can we control it or summon it at will."

"Indeed," said Cherlenko, "I've had similar experiences myself."

Kharkov nodded.

"Then," he continued, "there are a very, very few people who are *particularly* gifted in this way. In many instances they do not know what their gifts mean or how to use them. They may have vivid dreams they do not understand or visions they cannot control. Such phenomena may frighten them. They may think they are going mad. If they tell people around them what is going on inside their heads, they may be branded as witches, thrown into mental asylums or even executed by the State. But, if these people are recognised for the power they truly possess, if their talents are nurtured, guided and trained, then there is nothing they cannot do."

A thought occurred to Cherlenko. He gave it voice.

"Are you gifted in this way, Professor?"

Kharkov snorted. "If I was gifted in this way, Comrade Colonel, if I could project my thoughts, read minds and perform any one of a hundred miracles the way such gifted people can, do you think I'd be sitting here as a prisoner before you? No, I'm just a simple scientist who was ordered to undertake a project for the State. But I *was* fortunate enough to find two such gifted people to assist me."

"The Rospin twins."

"Indeed. Max and Tatyana. Two of the most gifted telepaths I have ever met. They were the children of friends of mine here in Leningrad during the siege. Their parents had been killed in 1943 by the German bombing, just as my own children were. It was natural that my wife and I should take them in and care for them. I did not know of their talent until later, of course, when I returned from Siberia, after my wife . . . ."

"Yes. I have read your file."

Kharkov's face darkened. "Of course, Comrade Colonel. You have looked into the black heart of humanity, just as I have. You have seen how —"

"The Rospin twins," said Cherlenko, "what abilities do they possess?"

"Their minds are linked . . . each of them can feel what the other is feeling. If they make a conscious decision to sit down and calm themselves at a particular time of day, they can even exchange thoughts, no matter how far they are apart. I knew they were emotionally close, far closer than a brother and sister normally are and, when I was given this assignment by your organization, I started to investigate this further. They are unique, Comrade Colonel, but, like all prima donnas with unique gifts, they are also highly strung and temperamental. This is where our problem lies. This is why Tatyana ran away."

"Why did she abscond? Why would a woman with her privileges rebel against the State?"

"You have never had children, Comrade?"

"No." Cherlenko's life had been his work. His personal needs had been pushed aside and he had never married. Friendships with others had always been strained, because of his position in the KGB. His mind wandered back to Stalingrad again, and suddenly felt Kharkov's attention deeply focused on him. "Why do you ask me that?"

"Because, if you had been a father, as I was by proxy to this highly strung and gifted pair, you would know how their minds work. Young people . . . *all* young people . . . question everything and rebel against what they do not like. Do you remember how it was to be young, Comrade? Do you remember how it was to feel you had all the power in the world? Do you remember wanting to change the world?"

Cherlenko thought back to when his mother and father had been taken away in a German truck, to his own dark years fighting in the streets of Stalingrad, dodging snipers, carrying food, stripping bodies, and worse. He recalled the years of desperate ambition after the war, to never, *ever* have to face those nightmares again; the relentless quest for the power to shut out the rest of the world and rise above everything that was dirty and obscene. "No, Professor, I don't."

"I understand," said Kharkov sympathetically. "You and I are of a generation whose youth was taken from us by the Great Patriotic War. But Tatyana and Max still question. They strain against their bonds. And now I'm afraid that Tatyana at least may have broken free."

"How so?"

"Have you looked at the picture in her *zapista*, Colonel, or seen her in the flesh? She is very beautiful and very headstrong. I fear that she may have become involved with certain other young people at the university who question the way the State is run, as I foolishly did in my youth. Knowing what she knows about the State and, given her powers to find out more, I fear she may have taken matters into her own hands by ordering that submarine to attack the Americans."

"But why? What good would that do her?"

"A war with the Americans will destabilise the State, Colonel. I know that, and so do you. Be honest: the Russian people are kept in check only by the force of the army, by the Party and by your colleagues in the KGB. You yourself witnessed how powerful the people can be at Novocherkassk, didn't you? It is no secret. Imagine what the population would do if the State were to collapse. The way would be open for a complete shift in regime. That is what Tatyana, Baybarin and a small band of like-minded friends are hoping for. That is why she ran away with them."

"These friends of Tatyana Rospin's, how many are there?"

"A handful, six or seven at most. But then again, how many does it take to start a revolution?"

"You will give me their names."

"Of course."

Cherlenko knew how such dissident idealists operated. Instead of accepting that the greater good, the victory of Communism, sometimes had to be paid for by the suffering of the individual, they chose to pull down the whole structure around their heads. Kharkov was right. Cherlenko had seen it at Novocherkassk. He had heard it in the insults of the workers and the taunts of the women and children. He had seen it too often, in the countless interrogations he had performed so efficiently, to deny that such idealism existed.

"Yes," he said at last. "I understand why she did what she did, but I still do not understand *how*. How did she obtain the secret authentication codes to send Petrachkov off on this spurious mission? How did she actually transmit them to her brother on the submarine while you were guiding her, without your knowledge? Explain that to me please!"

Kharkov sighed. "There was a handsome young officer from Admiral Shumanin's staff working as naval liaison on the project with us. He was close to Tatyana and very attracted to her. He could have been the trigger for all this, Colonel. You asked me where she might have obtained the codes that ordered Petrachkov towards Cuba. I think he is the source."

"His name?"

"Gregor Baybarin. He was a Captain with high security clearance. I am told he went missing at the same time Tatyana disappeared."

"I see. And the opportunity to transmit the codes without your knowledge? How did she accomplish that?"

"It would have been after the last session. We had finished transmitting the list of key words to Max. I thought Tatyana had broken contact with her brother. I left for a moment to relieve myself. She must have kept the link open and transmitted the message while I was gone."

"When was the last time you saw this woman and Baybarin together?"

"He took her to rest in the next room after the experiment. Telepathy is very wearing. It uses a great deal of energy and causes fatigue. That must have been when they left the building. I haven't seen or heard from them since."

Cherlenko considered this.

"Correct me if I'm wrong, Professor but, as I understand it, Tatyana Rospin has the ability to communicate with her brother from any location. She does not need you to be present to do this. Am I correct?"

"I'm afraid you are. While projecting one's consciousness outside the body with nobody to guide you back is dangerous, Baybarin has probably seen enough from previous experiments to act as her guide. Or she may be experienced enough to calm herself and direct her thoughts on her own by now. That is the beauty of the system, Comrade Colonel. It can be operated from anywhere, to anywhere else, all over the world."

"And now this system is working against us?"

"Indeed."

"And the next transmission will take place in just under an hour's time, at eight o'clock. Does Baybarin have access to the new authentication codes for each day to validate the messages?"

"It is possible. But I do not know for certain."

"So the Rospin woman could transmit her signal to the submarine through Max, and Petrachkov would have no idea that anything had changed in Leningrad?"

"All this is possible. Yes."

Cherlenko thought this over carefully.

"If she and her friends are successful, then Petrachkov will release his weapon, the Americans will retaliate, and the conflict will spiral out of control. It will mean nuclear war with America. You know this is true?"

Kharkov nodded silently.

"Are you willing to help me stop it from happening?"

"Do I have a choice, Comrade Colonel?"

"Only in the manner of your approach to this problem, Professor. I can force you to assist me. I can break your body, but I cannot enslave your mind. You know what is at stake here: the lives of millions of people and the future of the very State itself. Will you help me willingly?"

"There is one condition," said Kharkov. "Meet that, and I will do what you ask."

"Name it."

"That Tatyana be captured alive and unharmed. Without her, you have no chance of stopping that submarine anyway. She is useless to you dead."

"You have my word."

Kharkov smiled. "I suppose that will have to do."

"Then I will have you released into my custody, get you a clean set of clothes, and together we will find Tatyana Rospin and this dissident group of hers. Once we find her—alive of course—she will communicate with the submarine, countermand the spurious orders and end this madness."

Cherlenko turned to the door. "Guard, release this man at once."

They climbed the stairs from the cells to the main entrance hall. Kharkov wore a set of blue overalls and a naval coat, several sizes too big for him. His shoelaces had been returned and an orderly had placed an adhesive bandage over the cut on his temple.

They were crossing towards the doors and Cherlenko's car when Admiral Shumanin called out to them from the stairs above.

"Comrade Colonel! I have an urgent message from Moscow." Shumanin seemed to have regained some of his self-confidence. "We have been summoned to the Kremlin. At once."

"This will have to wait. My business is far more urgent than a report to some petty official in Moscow."

The ghost of a smile crossed Shumanin's lips.

"This is no petty official, Comrade. The order is for us to brief the High Naval Command in person. It is signed by the Commander in Chief of the Navy, Fleet Admiral Gorshkov himself."

TUESDAY, 24 OCTOBER 1962
TUCSAYON TRAILER PARK, ARIZONA
9.18 A.M. MOUNTAIN STANDARD TIME
1618 GMT

"You're torturing yourself," said Granny Moon. "Take the day off work and come down to Havasu Canyon with me." She slid fried bacon and a runny egg onto Ruth's plate and pushed it across the dining counter to her. Ruth looked at the grease congealing on the cold plate and pushed it back.

The sun was already high in the sky. The old fan had broken and the trailer felt like an oven. Ruth's head throbbed from the bottle of Jack Daniel's she had killed the night before. Her neck ached from lying up against the fence at the airport. Why had she done that? It had seemed the only thing to do at the time. She glanced back at the photographs stuck to the wall around her unmade bed. She would get rid of those tomorrow . . . or the next day.

"What good would going back to Havasu do?" she said. "If the pills and the whiskey don't work, then what can there be down there that would help me?"

The old woman took a knife and fork and started to eat. The scrape of steel on cheap crockery pierced Ruth's brain like a red hot needle.

"The old ways," said Granny Moon. "The men from the government perverted your gift of entering the Other World to make war there. The pain you feel is a result of that. The Other World is a place of peace. Let me guide you back there and make peace again."

Ruth took a tumbler of lukewarm water and drained it.

"It didn't help my mother," she said.

"She gave up. She gave up and she turned her back on the old ways. You're a fighter. At least your father gave you that. Let me take you back to the waterfall where we set your mother's spirit free, and make peace with the Other World so that these nightmares of yours will stop."

Ruth went to the faucet and refilled the tumbler. The water was even warmer than before.

"What's the point?" she said. "The Russians could drop the bomb at any time. You'd be better off with Old Billy in his septic tank than trudging around Havasu Canyon with me. Besides, I'm late for work."

The old woman smiled mischievously.

"Then what's the point of even going in? Like you said, the Russians could drop the bomb at any time."

8

"I have contact."

"Very good, Max," said Doctor Chiker softly. "Please ask Tatyana to confirm the orders she transmitted to you twelve hours ago."

Max settled into a deeper trance. Petrachkov fancied he could see the young man's eyes moving behind his closed eyelids.

"Tatyana says the orders come directly from the Crisis Room in the Kremlin. They are authentic 'Apex' instructions, to be carried out without delay. Admiral Shumanin confirms the American attack on Severmorsk and sends his condolences to Captain Petrachkov on the loss of his wife Natalya and two sons, Nikolai and Giorgi. He says he remembers the happy times when you all went fishing together and is sure you will do your duty."

Petrachkov was now certain that the orders relayed through Max were genuine. The only person on board who knew anything about his personal life was his old friend Mostock, and Mostock never betrayed a confidence. Admiral Shumanin had met Natalya and the boys. They had talked about fishing. This message had to be genuine. Severmorsk was destroyed. His beloved family was dead. They were at war.

"Very well," he said softly to Chiker. "Please tell Leningrad we are proceeding as ordered and will make contact every twelve hours, through Max, to report progress and check on the naval situation."

He turned to Muhkin and Kapitulsky. "Please come to the CCP with me, Comrades. It is time I addressed the crew."

The loss of Rykov had been a great blow, coming as it had in the midst of his own uncertainty over his orders and the fate of his family. Ever since his *Starpom* had vanished over the side of the cockpit, Petrachkov had been tortured by the possibility that his death had been the result of a young boy's delusions, an experiment gone wrong, or a stupid foul-up in Leningrad. Now he knew there was no mistake. His orders had been confirmed. From here on, the mission was simply a matter of doing what he had been trained for all his life: to strike at the enemy.

Conversation in the CCP stopped as he entered. There was silence as he walked to his captain's chair, reached up for one of the hanging microphones and pressed its switch.

"Comrades, men of the K-6. Since we emerged from under the ice, rumours have been circulating on this ship. Rumours that things are bad in Cuba, that war has broken out, and that Severmorsk has been destroyed."

He paused, searching for the right words.

"I can now confirm that these reports are true, that Severmorsk has been attacked and destroyed, and that we are at war with the United States of America."

A stunned silence filled the ship, followed by shouts of outrage and despair. Petrachkov felt his own grief rising in his chest once more and fought it back. He had to rise above his own pain and be a leader to the men. He waited until the shouting had died down and called his crew to order.

"Comrades, I know that many of you have felt that this ship had been relegated to the sideline, making maps under the ice and playing with our scientific toys while our comrades on the high seas and our loved ones at home needed our help. That time of waiting is over. Today, thanks to a great breakthrough by Soviet science, we have our orders confirmed. This was done, without the use of radio, and without bringing the ship to the surface. It is yet another sign that our work in promoting the use of science has not been in vain and that, with this science and the stout hearts aboard this ship, we shall be avenged."

He glanced to his left, where Muhkin and Dudko, the eyes and ears of the Party and the KGB, stood watching and listening. They were with him. He could see it in their faces. His hand slid to the pocket of his overalls and pulled out a fistful of index cards, listing the names of all the crew on the ship.

"Men of compartment one," he called out, picking out a few of the men for special mention. "Sergei, Alexei, Pyotr. They say the heart of a wasp is in its sting and our sting lies in our new torpedo, the most powerful ever made. Every man on the K-6 is depending on you to deliver the special weapon Comrade Dudko has brought aboard. Men of compartment two — Leonid, Valentin, Victor and Ilya. Your sonar will be our ears on this long voyage. Our enemies will be waiting for us, Comrades. They will be ready to pounce on us if we give them the smallest chance, but with your skills and the equipment at your disposal, we will hear them farting a thousand miles away and know they are there.

"Men of compartments four, five, six and seven. Your machinery, your generators, turbines and reactors are the heart of this ship. Without them, we are dead in the water. Nikolai Zateyev, Ilya Kharchenko and Boris Antokin, this is your first cruise as engineer seamen. Pay close attention to my old friend Comrade Mostock. Never pass up an opportunity to learn. He will keep those atoms in the reactors where they belong and all of us safe from harm. I have known him for many years and can tell you that, while he likes to smoke after sex, he never glows.

"And you men here with me in compartment three. We have all lost a brave and capable comrade in Valentin Rykov. He gave his life trying to save the radio system of this ship while under attack from the air. His life will not be in vain. We shall succeed in our mission thanks to his sacrifice, and I will recommend that he be awarded the Order of Lenin for his courage after we are avenged.

"Because we *shall* be avenged, comrades. But to do that, men of the K-6, everyone aboard, from the commanding officer to the young comrades new to the sea, must work together as a team.

"The Americans think they own the sea, but they do not. We are sailing in support of our brave merchant seamen who are transporting much-needed arms to our beleaguered comrades in Cuba. Fat American battle fleets stand in their way and at the centre of those battle fleets lie the giant aircraft carriers Uncle Sam prizes so dearly. Well, Comrades, we are to take this ship, the finest to ever come out of the shipyards of Leningrad, and sail to Cuba, where we shall engage the enemy. Our time of waiting is over. This ship is going to war."

WEDNESDAY, 24 OCTOBER
MOSCOW
10.30 P.M. LOCAL TIME
1930 GMT

The VIP-configured Tupolev TU-42 circled Moscow from the north, lining itself up for a landing at Vnukovo, an airport reserved for special personnel and closed to the general public. In daylight, Cherlenko would have been able to pick out the golden domes of the old Church of Fili in the north-western suburbs. In the darkness, all he could see were the scattered lights of the city and the concentric rings of traffic.

He had hoped to continue his mental chess game with the dissident Kharkov during the flight, to learn more of what was in the older man's head. There was something about the academic's defiance that fascinated Cherlenko. But then Kharkov had complained of airsickness, huddled himself at the back of the plane and fallen into a deep and troubled sleep. Nightmares of the Gulag, thought

Cherlenko, nightmares of the Great Patriotic War. Even I still get those.

By contrast, Admiral Shumanin seemed a great deal more confident, in spite of his impending disgrace. Cherlenko wondered whom Shumanin knew in Moscow who could have generated that confidence. He was only too aware of the constant war between the KGB, the military and the Party, and ever watchful for the knife in the back or the unseen conspiracy that could destroy a man's career in an instant, even when success seemed certain.

The plane touched down with a jolt and taxied to a halt. Shumanin was right behind him as he climbed out of the aircraft into the freezing night, followed by Kharkov. In a few moments a black Zil limousine was sweeping them into the city along the empty centre lane reserved for official cars. Cherlenko watched the distant silhouette of the Kremlin walls grow closer as the car drove without slowing through Arbat Square, turned sharply on Yanesheva ulitsa, past the military guards outside the Ministry of Defence building and came to a stop in the annex parking lot.

Cherlenko told the driver to wait. Then he buttoned his coat against the wind and led Shumanin and Kharkov across the street to the arched tunnel framing the defence ministry building. Military police with high leather boots and white guard belts stood to attention. Cherlenko saluted them smartly and was about to mount the steps to the main entrance, when Shumanin redirected them to a side door reserved for senior members of the operations and intelligence staff.

"This way to the 'Sardine Can' Comrades," he said, with a trace of a smile. "This is where the *real* decisions are made."

They entered an elevator and descended three floors to the secure sub-basement. Shumanin took the lead and in a few moments Cherlenko found himself standing outside the door of the ministry's "Emergency Action Centre", commonly known as "The Sardine Can". A red light shone above the door.

"High security meeting in session," said Shumanin and knocked. The door opened and they were ushered into a huge, low-ceilinged room. Large-scale charts of the Atlantic, the Mediterranean and the Pacific covered the pea-green concrete walls. A highly polished circular table strewn with nametags, telephones, overflowing ashtrays, half-eaten sandwiches and abandoned glasses of tea dominated the space between them. Cigarette smoke filled the air.

A short, stumpy figure in shirtsleeves, his tie hanging loose, stood at the head of the table directing operations. He looked up as they entered and fixed his eyes on Shumanin. His face broke into a smile.

"Aleksandr Konstantin, my old friend!" he called across the room as heads turned. "What kind of a mess have you got us into this time?"

Ah, thought Cherlenko, who recognised the man coming around the table to put his arms around Shumanin. So that is why we are here: to meet your protector.

Fleet Admiral Sergei Gorshkov, Commander in Chief of the Navy, was the father of the modern Soviet fleet. Khrushchev had put him in place to reverse Stalin's post-war plans for expansion of the naval service and since then had presided longer and through more significant changes than any other Soviet naval leader.

If Shumanin has support from a friend like that, then my job just became a lot more difficult, thought Cherlenko. I will have Gorshkov and the military looking over my shoulder every second from now on.

"Come this way, Aleksandr Konstantin," said Gorshkov, "and let us exchange intelligence." He led them to the other side of the table and a large wall map of the Caribbean. A red arc had been drawn from Florida to Puerto Rico around the north-eastern approach to Cuba. "Right now, we are in a very tense situation. The Americans have declared a five-hundred-mile quarantine area. It is patrolled by warships, including the anti-submarine group centred on the aircraft carrier *Essex*, with two other carriers, the *Independence* and *Enterprise* . . . here and here. We have two merchant vessels, the *Gagarin* and the *Komiles*, within a few miles of the blockade line. We also have a squadron of four submarines in the area to protect them.

The situation is very tense. Comrade Khrushchev has let it be known that the submarines have orders to fire on any American warship that stops a Soviet ship. I am awaiting orders from the Defence Council of the Praesidium as to how to proceed. You can see what a knife-edge we rest on, Aleksandr Konstantin. What is this loose cannon you have unleashed on me? How long will it be before this rogue submarine of yours reaches its target?"

Admiral Shumanin briefed Gorshkov on his side of the situation, from the beginning of the Kharkov experiments to the strange message telling him that Petrachkov and K-6 had gone to war. Cherlenko noted how Shumanin carefully glossed over his own failure to have Kharkov security-cleared with the KGB before the experiments began and how the failure of Petrachkov's radios was explained as poor workmanship by the dockyards and the intervention of fate, rather than any mistakes the Navy might have made.

"I am fortunate to have the full co-operation of the KGB and their top man in Leningrad to assist me in recapturing the woman," Shumanin concluded.

"He refers to you, I take it, Comrade Colonel," said Gorshkov, turning to Cherlenko for the first time.

"It is an honour to be working with our comrades in the navy on such an important task, Comrade Admiral," Cherlenko said, snapping to attention.

Gorshkov smiled. "And they tell me that the two services never work well together! How long do you think it will take to find this woman? Can it be done in time to stop the submarine?"

"Leningrad is a big city, Comrade Admiral. It is a maze of bridges and islands. I understand we have less than seventy-two hours if the submarine proceeds at full speed from its last known position in the Arctic. I will put every resource at the disposal of Admiral Shumanin. The KGB will not let you down."

"Very well," said Gorshkov. "Personally, I think it is time that someone took the American navy down a peg. Their arrogance in putting up a blockade in international waters is beyond belief.

Ah! here comes my summons to the Defence Council. We will know what our orders are in a few moments. Please excuse me."

A Red Army colonel was making his way across the Action Centre. Admiral Gorshkov straightened his tie and took his jacket from the back of his chair.

"Comrade Admiral," said the officer, saluting smartly. "You are called at once to the Defence Council."

"Yes indeed. Please excuse me, Aleksandr Konstantin. You and your colleagues should please help yourself to tea and food while I am gone."

"Excuse me, Comrade Admiral," said the Army officer, "but I have explicit orders to also bring a Colonel Cherlenko of the KGB and his prisoner, as well as Comrade Admiral Shumanin. Is that you, Comrades?"

Cherlenko nodded. He felt Shumanin's anger and Gorshkov's surprise. Kharkov smiled.

Cherlenko had once been told that, if he ever wanted to know who were the most powerful men in the Soviet Union, all he had to do was to look at the positions of the Soviet leaders on Lenin's Mausoleum each year on the 7th of November at the annual military parade in Moscow. He was to take the General Secretary of the Communist Party and the four members of the Praesidium standing next to him. Those would be the members of the Defence Council, the very embodiment of Lenin's 'scientific definition' of the Soviet dictatorship—power resting on force—where the most powerful representatives of the Party, the KGB and the Army met in committee, with unrestricted powers to decide the fate of the entire Soviet Union.

The doors swung open and those very men sat before Cherlenko. On either side of a polished wooden table littered with papers and the inevitable overflowing ashtrays sat five men, wreathed in cigarette smoke. There was Defence Minister Marshal Rodion Yakoulevich Malinovsky, Marshal Zhukov of the Army, Leonid Ilyvich Brezhnev, whom Cherlenko knew to be a close associate of the General Secretary and, to Cherlenko's immense satisfaction, Vladimir Semichastniy, the powerful and much-feared head of the KGB. Sitting at the top of the table, small, squat and powerful, sat Nikita Sereyevich Khrushchev, General Secretary of the Communist Party and the most powerful man in the Soviet Union.

"Come in!" he snapped. "We have matters of the greatest importance to discuss!"

Cherlenko remembered seeing Khrushchev at Stalingrad, in his capacity as Chief Political Commissar of the South-western Front, rallying the people amongst the wreckage of the burned-out city. He knew him as a man who had clawed his way up from a peasant background in the tough mining town of Yuzovka, through the purges of the political system and the court of Stalin, all the way to the very top. It is a great honour to be here now, so close to him, thought Cherlenko.

"Comrade First Secretary and members of the Defence Council," said Admiral Gorshkov. "Allow me to introduce Admiral—"

"We know who they are!" barked Khrushchev. "This is an emergency. We have no time for pleasantries. You will simply answer questions. Is that understood?"

"Yes, Comrade General Secretary."

"Shumanin, you say this submarine of yours has no radio contact with the outside world?"

"I do, Comrade General Secretary. Its main VHF aerial was damaged on the ice and its makeshift balloon aerial seems to have failed."

"Seems to? Don't your submarines carry spares?"

"They do, but this was an unforeseen emergency. They happen. It is impossible to predict them all."

"Indeed. Perhaps the person who fills your shoes tomorrow will have a better means of predicting the future. In the meantime, you can tell us what we must do to stop this Captain . . . Petrachkov, from starting a nuclear war."

"It is possible," said Gorshkov, coming to Shumanin's aid, "that the submarine has sunk. Radio contact was lost abruptly and we have not heard from it since."

"And what if it did *not* sink!" shouted Khrushchev, banging his fist on the table. "I am balancing on the edge of a knife. I have ships up against the blockade. I have the Americans on their highest state of alert. I am on the brink of a nuclear war. One tiny incident, just one, could trigger disaster. Do you hear me? Even now, I have the KGB in Washington trying to open a back door for negotiations with the Americans before all this blows up in our faces, and here *you* are, Gorshkov, calmly telling me that one of your submarines may or may not wander into the middle of this situation and release a nuclear weapon! I want *certainties*. You can all speculate when you are dead!"

This tirade unnerved Cherlenko. Until now, he had always believed that the Defence Council in general, and Comrade Khrushchev in particular, had complete control of every situation. Could it be that the General Secretary had allowed his pride to overrule his head and had blundered into the Cuban situation without thought for contingency plans and strategies? Comrade Khrushchev had always been impulsive in battle. Those in the know were aware that his well-publicised victories at Stalingrad and Kursk in 1943 during the Great Patriotic War were balanced by such disasters as Kiev in 1941, where four entire Soviet armies had been wiped out and hundreds of thousands of Soviet soldiers had died needlessly. Could it be that Khrushchev had gambled against the Americans and was faced with defeat? If so, then the General Secretary would be looking for someone to blame. Cherlenko wondered if that was why he and the others had been summoned – to face a firing squad for Comrade Khrushchev's mistakes.

He glanced at Admiral Shumanin. As the person ultimately responsible for sending Petrachkov the spurious orders, and with his protector Gorshkov out of favour with Khrushchev, Shumanin would be the focus of blame for the Defence Council.

He would be lucky to get out of Moscow with his life.

But, to Cherlenko's surprise, Shumanin seemed suddenly resolute.

"Comrade General Secretary," he said. "I realise I have made a grievous error which could upset the delicate balance of your negotiations with the Americans. I am willing to pay for that error, with my life if necessary, in order to protect the State."

"Your life if worth nothing to me," said Khrushchev. "I need a plan. I need action. I have to know if that submarine can be stopped."

"I have a suggestion, Comrade General Secretary," continued Shumanin fearlessly. "It follows the lines of your own back door discussions with the Americans. When I served in the Great Patriotic War against the fascists, when relations with the capitalist west were better than they are today, I met an American naval officer who was escorting supply convoys for our great struggle from Britain to Murmansk. I got on well with him and we corresponded until relations broke down between our two countries. I understand he is now a high functionary in Naval Intelligence in Washington."

"How can that help us? We already have our lines of communication to the Americans."

"I know an unforeseen emergency such as this must not be allowed to upset your delicate discussions on this crisis," said Shumanin. "There is a very real danger that, when the Americans learn of the potential threat posed by Petrachkov's submarine, they will see it as an act of war and your negotiations might break down. So, with your permission, Comrade General Secretary, and under the supervision of whomever you wish to accompany me from the KGB, I would like to make informal contact with my friend and brief him on the situation. In that way, perhaps we can explain the unfortunate mistake that has occurred and demonstrate it was an accident rather than an act of war."

Cherlenko watched as Khrushchev conferred with his colleagues around the table.

"Go on, Comrade Admiral," he said. "Convince me this could work."

"It *will* work, Comrade General Secretary, because I am certain I can convince my friend that the error was mine alone in allowing dissidents to hijack the experiment. I can convince the American military that you had no part in this, and tell them that if I cannot stop Petrachkov myself, then their navy should feel free to sink his submarine without fear of retaliation by our forces. To use the example of a chess game, Comrade General Secretary, we would be removing a rogue knight from the board and allowing you and President Kennedy to move the other pieces as you see fit."

Cherlenko felt a sudden surge of respect for Shumanin. It would be a pity to lose a man with such an elastic imagination.

"Wait outside. All of you," said Khrushchev. "We will give you our decision when we are ready. You may leave your papers and charts with us."

For thirty minutes, Cherlenko, Shumanin, Gorshkov and Professor Kharkov sat and awaited their fate in the outer hall, beneath overpowering murals depicting the Soviet victory over fascism during the Great Patriotic War. Heroes of that war—Zhukov, Rokossovskii, Bogdanov and Gorshkov himself—looked down like cherubs from the walls.

Nobody spoke or even dared to light a cigarette.

Then the doors of the Defence Council chamber swung open and they were ushered back inside. The air was even thicker than before. Admiral Shumanin's charts and papers were laid out across the polished table. A thin-faced young woman in the uniform of a captain of the Red Army had joined the group. Her hard eyes met Cherlenko's as he entered the room and he had the feeling of being back under the telescopic sights of hidden snipers in Stalingrad.

"You, Comrade Professor," said Khrushchev, acknowledging the academic for the first time. "Are you sure this protégé of yours is the only person who can communicate with the submarine?"

"Yes, Comrade General Secretary, I am."

"Very well. Comrade Colonel Cherlenko, the KGB has made me aware of your record and I know you to be a loyal and zealous member of the Party. There is a great and urgent task for you to accomplish in finding this woman over the next three days and you will need every resource we can put at your disposal. Therefore, to ensure your success, I hereby promote you to the rank of General in the KGB and put the entire city of Leningrad under your command. You are to establish martial law and to spare no effort, no expense and not even civilian safety in your efforts to capture this woman alive and on time. Is that clear?"

Cherlenko felt the enormous power he had been invested with course through his veins like a drug.

"Yes, Comrade General Secretary," he said, coming stiffly to attention with a click of his heels. "You can count on me."

"I hope so. The consequence of failure will be as great as the reward for success. For that reason and, at the insistence of General Zhukov and the Army, I am assigning you an adjutant to assist you. Comrade Captain Slavin will report directly to the Defence Council on progress in this operation."

The young woman's heels clicked as smartly as Cherlenko's had.

Khrushchev continued. "Shumanin, you have made an error of judgement so profound that it has put at risk everything we have toiled for over the years in our struggle against the capitalists. You are to be stripped of all rank. Do you understand?"

"I do, Comrade General Secretary."

"But, before you take off that uniform of yours, you are to accompany Comrade General Cherlenko to the KGB headquarters here in Moscow and make arrangements to contact your friend in Washington. The Defence Council has agreed to your plan. You got us into this mess. Now you can get us out of it. Give the Americans all the intelligence they ask for regarding Petrachkov and his mission. Put your submarine fleet at their disposal if you think they can help stop him because if you fail, and there is still anyone alive to pull the trigger, I will have you and your entire family shot."

9

Carpenter always had a problem with doors.

"It opens outwards," said the young woman with a Jackie Kennedy hairdo behind him, pulling on the big glass door and swinging it open effortlessly. "Fire regulations." She smiled at him.

"Thanks," said Carpenter, feeling the way he always felt when pretty girls smiled at him - awkward and shy. He had no need to be. Carpenter was a tall, handsome man who had just turned thirty, thin and fair-skinned with bright blue eyes and a soft, drawling voice that many women found attractive. The problem was that Carpenter lived most of his life in his head. He felt in control there. Real situations and real people made him nervous.

Carpenter felt nervous now.

The lobby looked like the newly built headquarters of any large multinational. The marble walls, the glass doors, and the corporate logo writ large could have belonged to Texaco, Standard Oil or Pan American Airways. What made this building special were the armed military police on guard, the shrine "to those who died in action", and the words "Central Intelligence Agency" inscribed below the vast eagle's head above a shield and compass rose which formed the centrepiece of the floor.

As a member of the CIA's biggest corporate rival, the National Security Agency, Carpenter had no idea why he had been called to

Langley so late at night. It could be anything from the Cuban crisis to some petty squabble that had erupted on Capitol Hill. His director had called him at home and told him to get over to Langley in "double quick time", but had hung up before he could tell Carpenter what it was about.

He did at least recognise the man walking towards him from the security barrier. It was Sam Hiscock, who held the equivalent of Carpenter's NSA position at Langley. Seeing him, Carpenter guessed that the meeting might even be about the competition between the two agencies for control of the Consolidated Cryptologic Program, a gargantuan budget submission covering America's entire Signals Intelligence (SIGINT) and Communications Security (COMSEC) budgets and running to the tune of ten billion US dollars a year.

"Hi, Sam. What's all this about?" Carpenter asked. Hiscock took Carpenter's security pass, showed it to the guard, who put a tick against Carpenter's name on a list and let him through.

"Not for me to say, John," Hiscock said. "We'll have to wait until we get upstairs."

The word 'upstairs' made Carpenter even more nervous, particularly when Hiscock pressed the top button of the elevator. As in any corporation, the higher up the building, the more important the person and the issues they discuss, and the only offices on the top floor of the CIA complex at Langley belonged to the director, senior management and their staff.

This was big shit. Carpenter only hoped there wasn't a fan around for it to hit.

"Do you know that the President's got a shelter up at Mount Weather big enough to hold himself and the whole cabinet?" asked Hiscock. "It'll hold up to two hundred people for thirty days under six hundred feet of stone. And there's my wife Janice and the kids on a vacation in Florida to see her mother. I've heard it's like an armed camp down there. Troops and airplanes being shipped in all the time in case the President decides to invade Cuba. Do you think I should have her come back? What would you do?"

"So this meeting's not about the budget then?"

"Seriously, John. What would you do?"

"I don't know, Sam. I'm not married."

"Yeah. But if you were . . ?"

The elevator opened. Hiscock ushered him down a long carpeted corridor to a heavy panelled door. Two more MPs in white helmets stood there, both armed. Even in the paranoid world of the CIA, so much security, so far inside an already heavily guarded building, was unusual.

Carpenter hauled his NSA identification out of this wallet and handed it over. Hiscock showed a guard the laminated badge on his shirt pocket. The man checked both their names off another list.

"Thank you, Dr. Hiscock. They're all inside now. You both go right in."

Seen in the context of the big meeting room, with its darkened windows and vast mahogany board table, the group already present seemed small. There were just five men, sitting in silence, along with a stenographer who sat in the warm halo of a desk lamp behind the chairman and to the right. Carpenter sensed the tension in the room. Nobody was smoking. Was it a committee of enquiry, a job interview? Carpenter saw no notes on the table, except for a slim file in front of the chairman, who rose to his feet. He was a sleek, well-built man in his early forties who looked as if he took care of himself. His hair was slightly long but well groomed and his suit was expensive and freshly pressed. Carpenter noticed his tanned face and the glint of gold as the stenographer's lamp caught his cufflinks and the clip on his Ivy League tie.

"Good evening, Mr. Carpenter. I'm Don Birkett, the Deputy Director. This is Admiral Church, our liaison with Naval Intelligence, Admiral Cursey of the Atlantic Fleet, and Walter Sharpe of the FBI. You already know Sam Hiscock of our Technical Division." The accent was educated Boston. Carpenter remembered the jealous rumours within the NSA, which had Birkett connected with the Kennedys and explained his rapid rise within the CIA.

Birkett motioned Carpenter to sit. "Right then, let's get underway. Firstly, I must apologise for dragging you all to this meeting at this late hour but I assure you it would not have been called had it not been to discuss a matter of the utmost importance to national security. Secondly," he said, glancing at Hiscock, "in case some of you are wondering if there might have been a catastrophic deterioration in the Cuban situation and are thinking of calling your wives and sweethearts to tell them to head for the shelters, don't. There has been no increase in hostility, at least none that I am aware of, and you are under the strictest orders not to disclose the existence or the content of this meeting to anyone. You are about to become the founding members of the most exclusive club in the world, gentlemen, even more exclusive than that 'Executive Committee' the President has holed up in the White House to sort out this whole Cuban mess. There will be no notes of this meeting, other than those taken by my stenographer, no whispers and no rumours. You have all sworn allegiance to the flag, either as serving officers or through non-disclosure agreements as part of your duties. If any of that trust is breached, it will be treated as 'treason in time of war' and the ultimate penalty will apply. Do I make myself clear?"

Heads nodded around the table. Carpenter wondered what on earth he was getting himself into and whether or not he had the authority, if asked, to commit the NSA to action at this kind of level.

"As you will be aware," continued Birkett. "The naval blockade around Cuba came into force at ten this morning. At that time, there were twenty-six ships from Soviet and Eastern-bloc countries reported on their way to Cuba, sixteen of which have turned back. Since then, we have had a number of minor incidents around the picket line, some involving sightings of Russian submarines, sent to protect Soviet blockade-runners. We already know the Russians have at least four diesel-powered subs in the Caribbean, which may, or may not, be carrying torpedoes armed with nuclear warheads. You will also be aware that American forces around the world are at 'DEFCON 2', one step away from the release of atomic weapons.

The situation is already explosive. Now a new factor has emerged, one that threatens to push us into a full scale nuclear holocaust."

The men around the table exchanged glances.

Birkett straightened his cuffs. "I would now like to introduce you to Commodore James Amery, currently working in Naval Intelligence, but more importantly a former commander of a destroyer escort flotilla to Murmansk in the Soviet Union during the war. Admiral, if you'd be so kind?"

Admiral Church, a tall proud officer with a steel-grey crew cut, got up from his seat and went to a door at the far end of the meeting room. He came back, accompanied by a short, wiry man in civilian clothes. Commodore Amery had just the kind of tanned leathery face that Carpenter could imagine peering out from the bridge of a pitching destroyer in Arctic waters.

"Thank you, Commodore," said Birkett once the two men had taken their seats. "Now we have representatives from all the relevant agencies present, I'd be grateful if you could brief them as to why they were all pulled away from their wives and families to be here tonight."

Commodore Amery cleared his throat. "It's like this. I met this Russian called Aleksandr Shumanin during the war while he was commanding one of the few Russian submarines left afloat. He spoke good English then, and still does. We had a couple of real wild nights up in Murmansk, what with vodka being a major Russian pastime and all, and became good friends. He even gave my crew a couple of live reindeer to eat on the trip home that ended up in the New Jersey zoo. I wrote to him after the war and he wrote to me for a couple of years until . . . until things got bad between us and the Soviets."

"Is this the same Admiral Shumanin, who used to command the Commies' nuclear submarine fleet?" cut in Church.

"Old Aleksandr was always ambitious. I'm not surprised he made it to flag rank," continued Amery with a hint of jealousy.

"And this was the first time you had heard from him in over ten years?" Birkett asked.

"Yes sir," said Amery. "Not until he called me, five hours ago, on my home phone."

"What?" exclaimed Sharpe of the FBI. "A senior Commie naval officer has your home phone number?"

"The KGB would have *all* our home phone numbers, Mr. Sharpe," said Birkett. "It's a matter of fact."

"Jesus H. Christ!"

"Please continue, Commodore," said Birkett. "Sorry for the interruption."

"Well, Aleksandr told me he was now working on 'special projects' in Leningrad. He said they'd had an accident with some kind of programme they were using to send messages by telepathy to their nuclear submarines at sea, just like we were trying ourselves a few years back. The problem was that the sub's radio went down and the mind messages got confused. So now there's a Russian sub-driver sailing down from the Arctic who's convinced that his base has been destroyed, his family are dead and that he has orders to start using live ammunition on our blockade line."

"What is he armed with?" Admiral Cursey asked.

"Aleksandr said it was a nuclear torpedo, sir."

A collective intake of breath sounded around the table.

"Therein lies our greatest danger." cut in Birkett, "The Soviets delegate responsibility for the release of nuclear weapons to commanders in the field, which is the reason we were so concerned about the Cuban missiles in the first place."

"This is a Commie trick," Admiral Church said. "It has to be."

"Then why would Shumanin warn us?" said Sharpe. "Surely he'd know the KGB would be on to him?"

"There is no doubt in my mind that the KGB knew about this call from the start," Birkett said. "Shumanin told Commodore Amery that he was speaking from the KGB Moscow headquarters in Lubyanka Square, which makes it all the more notable. This wasn't one old war veteran calling up a long-lost buddy, or a highly placed Soviet officer looking for a chance to defect. This call to Commodore Amery represents the Soviet government looking for a credible back-channel to defuse a potentially lethal situation outside the diplomatic arena currently dominated by the Cuban Missile Crisis."

"Ah . . . excuse me, Mr. Birkett," said Carpenter. "But can all this be verified? And if it can, could it simply be a trick by the Russians to divert our attention away from the situation in the Caribbean?"

"It *was* Aleksandr Shumanin on the phone," Commodore Amery insisted. "I'd know his voice anywhere, even after all this time. He said that approval for him to contact me came right from the highest level of the Soviet Defence Council."

"Which means from Khrushchev himself," added Birkett. "We've checked out other information Shumanin sent, and it backs up his story."

"But even if the messenger is genuine," Carpenter said, "couldn't the message be false? What evidence do you have that there really is a rogue submarine heading for Cuba?"

"Yesterday morning, at around 1200 hours Greenwich Mean Time," Admiral Church said, "three US Navy Phantoms were running a search and rescue exercise in the Greenland Basin, just below the ice cap. They followed a radar contact they'd acquired and found a November Class Commie submarine on the surface with a radio balloon deployed. The water was rough and they spotted the sub on radar only because of the balloon."

"Which could confirm Shumanin's story about their main radio being out," suggested Amery.

"There's more to it than that," Church continued. "The sub dived as soon as the jets flew over it. They lost the balloon, and they lost one of their officers overboard. By some miracle the jets managed to keep a fix on him in the rough water and by a second miracle the other aircraft in their training exercise were a pair of long range Sea King helicopters."

"Did you manage to pick him up?" asked Carpenter.

"That's the third miracle," Church said. "Survival time in Arctic waters is only a few minutes. Luckily the man had an immersion suit and a lifejacket. He almost died, but only almost. He's currently under guard at the US Air Force base in Thule."

"Is he in a position to talk?" asked Sharpe.

"Only his name, rank and serial number," Church said. "He is Captain, Third Rank, Valentin Rykov, who we know to be first officer on the submarine K-6, commanded by Captain Sergei Petrachkov of the Red Banner Northern Fleet. The story checks out, gentlemen. There's a Commie nuclear submarine on the loose with an atomic torpedo. It could be rogue and it could be arriving in Cuba in less than seventy-two hours."

Silence fell as the meeting considered this new evidence.

"Has the President's Executive Committee been informed?" asked Carpenter.

"The President has, but the Ex Comm hasn't," Birkett said. "I briefed the President personally as soon as I was sure this wasn't a hoax. He feels, as I do, that to release this news would be counter-productive. There are hawkish elements on his committee who see and American invasion of Cuba as the only way forward. Given the knife-edge that both our countries are balanced on, news like this could destabilise the political process. It could precipitate an uncontrollable military situation that would spiral into nuclear holocaust. No. The President wants this situation quarantined and so, I believe, do the Soviets. That is why there are so few of you here, and why the security measures are so extreme. The only people around this table are those who *need* to know, people who can defuse this potentially deadly situation quietly."

"And how can the National Security Agency help, sir?"

"The NSA can't, Mr. Carpenter," said Birkett. "But *you* can. I want you to tell me, in as few words as possible, about your 'Project Element'."

Once more, Carpenter was nervous. Project Element had been one of his major failures, an abortive experiment he'd been ordered to abandon by sceptics in the NSA when the body count got too high.

"It's kind of embarrassing, sir."

"Tell me about it anyway."

"Ah . . . OK. We already employed trained personnel to examine aerial photographs, taken by aircraft and more recently by high altitude U2 spy planes, to see if they could pick out features on the ground that might be of military significance: guns, tanks, troop concentrations and so forth. In some cases, it seemed that a few of these photo-analysts could actually go way beyond what was asked of them. They started to see features on the photographs and on maps of the areas covered by the photos that weren't visible on paper but, when we checked out the actual terrain, *did* exist in reality. In effect, they were seeing things at remote locations without actually being there. Hence the name we chose for the technique – 'remote viewing'."

Carpenter glanced around the table. Admiral Church was getting restless. Sharpe, Cursey and Commodore Amery looked puzzled. Only Birkett and Hiscock seemed to be taking it all in.

"So I got funding from the NSA and started to take it further," Carpenter continued. "I called in psychic experts to train the people I had already found who could do this thing, trawled the photo-reconnaissance units of the Air Force for more remote viewers and set up a small unit on a base in Nevada where I could assess this technique as a practical reconnaissance gathering tool for the—"

"Now just hold on there, son," interrupted Church. "Are you telling me the NSA seriously considered risking men's lives in military action on the word of people who saw things that weren't there?"

"We knew the Russians were working with these techniques, Admiral. We knew they'd had some success, and pretty soon so did we. Within a few days we could actually verify what the remote viewers saw from their closed rooms in Nevada with over-flights by aircraft."

"And how in the hell did they see these things?"

"The technical term for it is 'astral projection'."

"I'm not a gypsy fortune-teller or a monk from Tibet, son. You'll have to explain it to me in words of one syllable."

"Astral projection is exactly what it means—the projection of a person's awareness, their very soul if you like, out of their physical body and into another place. You've heard of people having what they call 'out-of-body' experiences, looking down on themselves when they've been near death on operating tables or in traffic accidents? Well, this is similar, except that it is achieved voluntarily through the conscious will of the subject."

"You mentioned that the Soviets had been working on this," Birkett said.

"They took it a lot more seriously than we did," said Carpenter with a sideways glance towards Church, "and they got a whole lot farther. They poured in money and personnel, and their approach was far more scientific. We just wanted a practical system to gather intelligence. They wanted to pull the technique apart, see how it worked and refine it as a weapon."

Birkett put his hand on the folder in front of him. "Are you familiar with a certain Professor Boris Kharkov?"

"He worked at the University of Leningrad, initially under a guy called Vasilev, then later on his own. It was mostly on telepathy, the sending of thought waves over long distances. Ideal for communicating with orbiting spacecraft . . . or submarines. He was working with a pair of twins whom we codenamed 'Snow' and 'Ice'. I take it that he's the one behind this program that's put that sub off course?"

"He is."

"Then why can't he just get back in contact with the sub by telepathy again, correct the message and call the whole thing off?"

"Because the young woman he was using to transmit the message, this 'Ice' you speak of, has absconded with a small group of dissidents. Her twin brother was the receiver on the submarine and they have no one else who can reach him. Everything was working perfectly until she sent a counterfeit message and then vanished. That is why I need you to tell me about the people *you* got to do this work. So that we can try and make contact with the submarine ourselves."

"There are only three now, each code-named after one of the four natural elements. 'Earth' was a radio mechanic with the Air Force and now makes a living as a gambler in Las Vegas. 'Air' was a communications officer with the Navy; he had a nervous breakdown and ended up in a mental asylum in Phoenix, Arizona. 'Water' and 'Fire' were both female photo-analysts. 'Water' committed suicide. 'Fire' developed a cross-addiction to tranquillisers and alcohol, dropped out of the program and now works in the tourist trade up at the Grand Canyon. That's one of the dangers with work like this. Women have a greater sensitivity around psychic ability than men, which makes them better at it, but far less able to handle the side-effects."

"And which of the remaining three would you say was the most gifted?"

"'Air' was good, but obviously unstable. 'Fire' and 'Earth' were probably the best. I have their details on file at the NSA. I could have them sent over."

"No need," said Birkett. "I had my own sources," and he opened the slim file in front of him. From where he sat across the table, Carpenter saw a familiar list of names and addresses, along with three black and white photographs.

Carpenter felt manipulated. "Then why do you need me, sir?"

"I need you, Mr. Carpenter, to bring in these last two operatives, 'Fire' and 'Earth', from Las Vegas and Arizona, and have them make contact with the submarine. The Phoenix office of the FBI will visit the asylum where 'Air' is currently an inmate and see if he can still be of use."

"Hold on a second there," said Admiral Church, picking up the file and running his finger down the list of names. "You've got a pill-pushing drunk, a psycho and a Las Vegas gambler on this list. Are you seriously going to trust a sensitive military operation to them? Why not just find that sub and sink it?"

"Because, as you have heard, that particular submarine is not the only one the Soviets have in the Atlantic," said Birkett, snatching back the file. "The Navy knows of at least four more operating in support of the Russian merchantmen around the blockade line. Do you want us to try and sink them all?"

"Safer than trusting these three wackos," Church insisted. "Or trusting the Commies to find their missing mind-reader in a city as big as Leningrad. Who have they got running that little job, by the way?"

"A KGB officer named Vladimir Cherlenko," said Birkett. "According to Admiral Shumanin, and our own sources in Moscow, he was called to the Kremlin earlier this evening, promoted by Khrushchev himself to the rank of General, and given full authority in Leningrad to do whatever it takes to find 'Ice'. We know his reputation. He'll tear that city apart, brick by brick if he has to."

10

"What we are facing, Comrades, is a man-hunt," said Cherlenko. "A man-hunt of colossal proportions, but a man-hunt nonetheless."

He stood over the large-scale map of the city covering the table of the main briefing room at KGB headquarters on Foundry Prospeckt in Leningrad. It was a much-feared building, the scene of countless tortures and executions over many years, and known simply as the Bolshoy Dom—'The Big House'.

A score of uniformed officers stood round the table, along with four female KGB secretaries and Professor Boris Kharkov, the only non-military person in the room. Captain Slavin stood to one side, taking notes for her next report to the Defence Council.

"There are only two objectives to this hunt," Cherlenko continued. "Firstly, we *must* capture the female subject Tatyana Rospin, alive and in good health. There are photographs from her *zapista* in your files and we are in the process of posting them all over the city, along with those of the navy deserter Baybarin and the six other dissidents, who may be captured alive or dead."

"And the second objective, Comrade General?" asked Captain Slavin, without looking up from her notes.

"The second objective is that Tatyana Rospin be captured in no more than two and a half days," said Cherlenko, turning back to the group. "If that is not done, then a black mark to end all black marks will be entered into all our *zapistas*. Likewise, if we succeed, then rewards and promotions will flow. Is that clear?"

No one spoke. Nobody dared to suggest the impossibility of such a task to a newly promoted KGB General, particularly one with Cherlenko's reputation.

"In our favour, we have the combined forces of all KGB, GRU and military personnel in the city, as well as our civilian informers and police officers. Working against us is the enormous area we have to cover, some sixty-four square miles comprising forty separate islands and the main city itself. You all have your orders. Are there any questions?"

"Only one, Comrade General," asked Slavin again. "What is to have prevented these dissidents from leaving the city already?"

Cherlenko answered the question with good grace, mindful of what might appear in her report to Comrade Khrushchev. Later, when this crisis was over, he would find ways of making sure that Slavin's career was as short and as painful as possible.

"Firstly, Leningrad is a 'closed city'. Even in normal times, citizens can enter and leave only on production of an internal passport issued by the KGB. Secondly, in the knowledge that such passports can be forged, I have made it my business to commandeer aircraft and several units of the parachute regiment to fly out on all major roads and rail routes as far as anyone might have travelled by car or train since the couple went missing. Roadblocks have been set up and trains turned back. Then the troops will work inwards, tightening their search pattern into the city. Tatyana Rospin is a native of Leningrad. She grew up here during the siege of the 'nine hundred days' and has never travelled outside. She knows the streets of Leningrad as a mother knows her child, along with every bolthole, drain and sewer. If I were her, I would rather choose to hide in a place I knew than risk my life escaping over open ground. Do you not agree?"

A GRU officer raised his hand to speak. "But why the sixty-hour deadline, Comrade General?"

The smile vanished from Cherlenko's face. They were wasting time.

"All you need to know is that you must find her *before* then! Do that and you will live the rest of your life in comfort. Fail, and your best hope will be to spend it in a labour camp. Now go, all of you. The next briefing is here in twelve hours."

As the room emptied, he turned to Kharkov.

"Very well, Comrade Professor. If you were Tatyana Rospin, where would you hide?"

Kharkov stared at the map. Then he ran his fingers over the outlines of the larger islands, Dekabristov, Petrogradskiy, Velagin, Kresovskiy, Aptkarkiy, Vasilyevskiy, Gutuyevskiy and finally, the city itself.

"There," he said at last. "She grew up in this part of the city. She studied at university and has friends in the area. That is where I would start."

Cherlenko followed Kharkov's finger. It pointed to Vasilyevskiy Island.

"Interesting choice, Comrade Professor. I never had time for academic study while I was younger. Perhaps it is time I went to university myself?"

THURSDAY, 25 OCTOBER
LANGLEY, VIRGINIA
12.30 A.M. LOCAL TIME
0530 GMT

Admiral Joseph Church strode out of the main entrance of the CIA headquarters to where his staff car was drawn up. Once in the back seat, he told his driver to take him home and pulled out the small notebook he always kept on his person to record ideas during the day. Admiral Church was a highly disciplined man. One of the many things he had trained himself to do was to memorise names and addresses. So it was no problem for Admiral Church to recall the names and locations of Carpenter's remote viewers he had read from Birkett's list during the meeting.

Birkett was a weak-kneed pinko Democrat, not a man fit to be Deputy Director of the greatest intelligence organization in history. Birkett held that position over the heads of more ably qualified men like Joseph Church only because of his connection to the Kennedys.

The Kennedys! Even thinking that name brought the blood racing in Admiral Church's veins. As the staff car passed under the white metal security barrier at the entrance to the CIA complex and turned onto the tree-lined road heading back to Washington, Joseph Church comforted himself in his hatred of the Kennedys and everything they had taken from him.

Church had grown up in south-east Missouri, in the white Protestant bible belt of America, during the Depression, in a family that scrimped and sacrificed to send him to school. During vacations, he had slaved his guts out digging ditches for farmers and flipping burgers for richer kids whose parents seemed to have all the money in the world. As a result, Church had grown up with a chip on his shoulder the size of a tree trunk about those wealthier than himself, a chip that even a battlefield commission from Master Chief to Lieutenant during the war in the Pacific, and from there up the officer ladder to Admiral, had not budged. Church believed in motherhood, apple pie and the all-American way. He was devoutly anti-Communist, fanatically right wing and a silent enemy of that Catholic rich-kid John Fitzgerald Kennedy.

Church had also been obsessive that his kids would not have to graft for their place in life the way he had and did everything in his power to ease their paths. The pride of his life, his son Joe Junior, had followed him into the military with straight 'A's in Navy ROTC at college and a plum position with Naval Intelligence in Florida, thanks to his father's reputation and his own skill.

Both father and son believed that when John F. Kennedy came to power, the new President would follow through on the CIA's carefully thought out plan to invade Cuba and remove the festering sore of a Communist regime so close to home. After all, hadn't they worked on the project together, with Admiral Church in command of the strategy and Joe Junior, on the ground in Florida? Hadn't Eisenhower, the greatest warrior-President that ever lived, endorsed it during the last days of his term in office? It *had* to work. It was un-American to think otherwise.

And yet, at the last minute, Kennedy had chickened out. He pulled back the vital air support needed to protect the troops already committed to the shore landing at the Bay of Pigs. More than a hundred exiles had died, along with four Americans, including their naval intelligence advisor, Lieutenant Joseph Church Junior.

Admiral Church's world collapsed. The Kennedys had betrayed him. A blaze of hatred, built on the kindling wood of his youthful experiences of the rich and powerful, ignited by the death of his son and fanned by his own prejudices, roared up inside him. One day he would even the score with the Kennedys and all they stood for.

Now that day had come.

If attempts to stop the rogue Commie sub failed and its nuclear torpedo was launched at the blockade, then public opinion in America would swing so far in favour of aggressive action that an invasion of Cuba would be certain. As an expert strategist with access to the latest U2 spy plane photographs of Russian missile capability, Admiral Church did not believe that Khrushchev would go so far as to initiate an all-out nuclear war over Cuba. In spite of all his bluster, Khrushchev had only fifteen operational missiles on Soviet soil, compared to America's four hundred. In Church's eyes, the Cuban missiles were simply Khrushchev's way of trying to gain a little respect, a strategic advantage and a *quid pro quo* for the obsolete Atlas missiles Kennedy already had in Turkey pointing at the USSR. As things stood, Kennedy would eventually have to make a deal with the Soviets and remove his Turkish missiles. They would reciprocate by removing theirs from Cuba.

But if the balance was to change, if the Soviets launched a nuclear torpedo attack on the blockade, then Kennedy would not only have the moral right but also worldwide public opinion on his side for a full invasion of Cuba and a restoration of the American way of life to the island. With the blood of an unprovoked first strike on his hands, Khrushchev would be forced to sit back and let it happen.

Church reached into his pocket and pulled out the notebook with the list of names. All of them — the gambler, the lunatic in the asylum and the doped up Indian woman — were all within easy striking distance of Las Vegas. The lunatic and the gambler had specific addresses. The woman's location at the Grand Canyon was less certain, but then again Birkett's committee had the combined forces of the CIA, the FBI and the NSA to track her down. There couldn't be many places she could work out there to make a living.

The car stopped at Church's home in one of the more secluded suburbs of Washington. Church dismissed his driver, went inside and headed straight for his den. The house was quiet. It had been that way since John Junior had died and his wife had sunk into a valium-fuelled depression. Church looked at the photographs of his son lining the walls. He remembered the smell of his hair as a baby; the happy shout that greeted him when he came home each day, the feel of that small hand in his.

The Kennedys had betrayed him. They had killed his only son as surely as if they had put a gun to his head and then left his body to rot on some stinking Cuban beach. Now he was going to put that right, for Joe Junior, for revenge against the Kennedys, and for the all-American way.

Admiral Church still had one priceless contact from his days of planning the Cuban invasion, a key player in an organization as powerful, far-reaching and essentially American as his own, an organization he had worked with in the past and whose interests in bringing the American way back to that island mirrored those of the CIA. All it needed to start the ball rolling again was one call.

He picked up the secure phone he had been given as a high-ranking intelligence officer and dialled.

THURSDAY 25 OCTOBER
LAS VEGAS, NEVADA
12.10 A.M. LOCAL TIME
0610 GMT

A very high-class affair was underway in the main ballroom of the Tropicana Hotel in Las Vegas. Politicians, film stars, singers, movers and shakers rubbed shoulders and tried to forget the crisis outside. Beautiful girls in dazzling outfits mingled with the crowd or served glasses of champagne from silver trays. A top show band played. People danced. Sinatra was due to make an appearance.

One man was at the centre of it all. He glided from celebrity to politician to local billionaire, stopping for a quick conversation here and there, charming and at ease with everyone. He had the same dashing features, the same thin moustache and the same dark hair as a mature Errol Flynn. In public, his eyes sparkled with good humour. In private, they could be shrewd and merciless. The Venetian glass champagne flute in his left hand contained nothing but soda water.

A uniformed hotel employee caught up with him and coughed respectfully. "Mister Rosselli, sir? There's a phone call for you. A friend from Washington."

The man excused himself to the group of businessmen he was talking to and smiled.

"Which friend? I have so many of them in the Capitol."

"He didn't say, Mister Rosselli," said the man, leaning closer so that he could whisper discreetly. "But he did say you'd remember him from your business interests in Miami."

Johnny Rosselli turned and smiled at the group. "Probably the President," he said. "You've no idea how much he relies on me. Tell the switchboard I'll take the call upstairs."

Then he weaved his way out of the ballroom, and was escorted upstairs to the penthouse suite by a pair of armed bodyguards. He entered, locked the door behind him and made his way across the thickly carpeted floor to the window and the antique desk overlooking the sea of lights dancing on the Strip.

The phone rang.

"This is Rosselli. You wanted to talk to me about Miami?"

"Are you alone?"

"I am. Who am I speaking to please?"

"This is Admiral John Church, Mister Rosselli. We met at The Fontainebleau a couple of times."

"Ah yes. Of course I remember. What can I do for you, Admiral?"

"I think I can get back Cuba for you. Are you interested?"

Johnny Rosselli was extremely interested in anything to do with Cuba. His organization had lost investments worth hundreds of millions of dollars in casinos, hotels and other Cuban properties to the Communist revolution. Castro had also shut down a very lucrative operation that had allowed over a hundred million dollars' worth of illegal drugs to pass through Havana into the USA. Johnny Rosselli, and the other leaders of his organization, known by those in the business as "The Outfit", or more popularly as the Mafia, was extremely anxious to get those investments back.

To further their own interests, the Outfit had already co-operated with the CIA on a number of covert operations, under the codename "Operation Mongoose", to assassinate Castro and topple his regime.

Like the CIA, they also felt betrayed by Kennedy, as well as a certain kinship with their colleagues in the Agency as victims of his wrath. While Kennedy had publicly taken the blame for the Bay of Pigs fiasco, he had privately laid responsibility for the operation on the Agency, fired its Director and vowed to "splinter the CIA into a thousand pieces". Likewise, the President's brother Bobby, as Attorney General, was waging an unprecedented war on organised crime. Having engineered Kennedy's success in the Presidential elections, the Outfit had expected favours to be returned, in the form of relaxed laws, not a witch-hunt that threatened to put them out of business.

The Outfit and the Agency now shared a common enemy: the President of the United States.

"Of course I'm interested, Admiral. What would you like me to do?"

"Kill three people, Mister Rosselli. As soon as possible."

"Just give me their names."

Pawns

TIME TO EVENT

01:14:40

DAYS : HRS : MINS

11

The rising sun glittered on the waters of the Neva and shone warmly down the broad, straight avenues of Leningrad.

Kharkov was exhausted. His head throbbed from the beatings he had suffered on his arrest the previous day. The hollow socket of his missing tooth ached, but the pain was useful, just as it had been in the Gulag. It kept him awake. It reminded him he was still alive, while others were not.

The KGB staff car roared across the river on the Dvortsovy Bridge onto Vasilyevskiy Island. It was a centre of great learning and culture, home to Leningrad's museums, Saint Andrew's Cathedral and the university, a place of peace that was soon to be shattered by a horde of mechanised barbarians.

Cherlenko had long since sealed off every bridge in the city, with guard posts of militia and KGB officers making sure that nobody crossed without KGB authorization. Leningrad was on curfew at the highest military and civil state of alert. The streets were deserted. Armed guards stood watch on each corner, ready to arrest anyone they saw. Nobody moved, or dared to move, until the curfew was lifted.

The staff car slid to a stop outside the Naval Museum in Birziveja Place, overlooking the great semicircular lawn where wedding couples had their photographs taken in happier times. Cherlenko got out, took a deep breath of morning air and spread his arms, facing the sea.

"I love this city, Professor. It truly is the Venice of the North; such culture, such knowledge, such bracing air. It has tradition and substance. There is gentleness in the breeze here, not like the harsh winds of Moscow or Stalingrad. I was in Stalingrad, you know, Professor, during the Great Patriotic War. I killed my first fascist when I was ten."

"Those were savage times, Comrade General. It is terrible what man inflicts on his brother."

Cherlenko turned back from his meditation.

"It is not over, Professor. Come, we have work to do."

Captain Slavin appeared with a map and spread it on the bonnet of the staff car. Vasilyevskiy Island stretched before them like a leg of ham, criss-crossed with the regular pattern of streets and intersections, cut in two by the Smolenka Canal to the north.

"As logical men, Professor, we should take a logical approach. I intend to deploy my troops around the perimeter of the island and work inland, searching every building, every house, office and store without exception until we reach this park here. That way, nobody will escape the search."

"As you say, it's a logical move," said Kharkov, nodding. "It makes perfect sense."

"I take it from your tone of voice that you disapprove?"

"Of course not. I just wonder if there might be some quicker way."

Cherlenko pointed back in the direction they had come. The Dvortsovy Bridge was solid with soldiers, stretching back into the city.

"I may not have your gift for intellectual insight, Professor, but I am methodical. I have all the men I need and the island is sealed."

He turned to the semi-circle of officers who had gathered beside the car. "You have all seen the photograph of the woman we are hunting. But looks in a woman can be deceptive, can they not? Therefore *every* woman between the ages of eighteen and thirty-five is to be detained, regardless of her appearance and transported under guard to this park, here by the Smolenka Canal."

Cherlenko's finger stabbed at a patch of green.

"With due respect, Comrade General," said Kharkov. "That is not a park. It is the Smolensk Cemetery."

"No matter. It is an open space, and I don't think the present inhabitants are in any position to complain."

Cherlenko was in his element, thought Kharkov. He might have been enjoying a picnic or a sports event. Kharkov watched him planning his moves and ordering his troops around with great precision. While he did not like to admit it, he was impressed by Cherlenko's drive and efficiency, even though it was misguided. Until now, he had judged all those in high offices within the KGB to be mindless thugs or sycophantic hangers-on. But Cherlenko was different. Cherlenko had a mind, a good mind, a mind he brought to bear on the problem of finding one frightened woman in a city of eight million people.

Yet Kharkov knew he could still win.

"Well now, Professor," said Cherlenko, having dispatched his officers to their work. "It will be eight o'clock in just under thirty minutes; time for Tatyana to transmit her latest message to the submarine. Will she be able to communicate it telepathically if she is being hunted from house to house like an animal?"

"It would be difficult. She requires calm and concentration for the best results. But it would not be impossible. All she needs is the space to relax and someone to make sure she is not disturbed for as long as it takes to send the message and receive a response."

He hesitated. "That is, if she is still on this island."

Cherlenko frowned.

"If she is here on the island, then I *will* find her. My men will search every hiding place and bring every woman in for identification."

"How will we examine them all, Comrade General?" asked Kharkov.

"Simple. Our troops will check the identification papers of each woman individually. They will start by dividing them into those who most closely match the description of Tatyana Rospin and those who do not. Those who do will be brought before you for identification."

"And if I chose not to co-operate?"

"But we had an agreement, Professor."

"And if I choose to break it?"

"Then I would have every woman who obviously fails to match the description of Tatyana Rospin, in terms of age or appearance, put up against the nearest wall and shot. Hundreds of lives will be lost, perhaps thousands. And none of them would in any way reduce my chances of capturing Tatyana Rospin alive. You know my reputation. You know what I did at Novocherkassk. Is that enough incentive for you?"

"More than enough."

"I thought so. You are an idealist, Professor, not a pragmatist. That is why I will win."

He looked back to the bridge and the thousands of troops swarming onto the island.

"They will be bringing the first women to the park soon," he said. "In a few hours we should have cleared the island and have them all. Then you and I will check each of those most closely matching Tatyana Rospin's description and move on to the rest. After that, it will be time for our next briefing with the GRU and the other security forces. If nobody has found her by then, I will have to take other measures."

Kharkov ran his hand over his jaw. The pain from his missing tooth was getting worse.

"You are very methodical, Comrade General. But if I am going to be any use to you, I need to get some rest. It has been a long night and I have had no sleep."

"By all means, Professor. Rest in the car if you want to. Comrade Slavin will make sure you are not disturbed."

Cherlenko barked an order and moved off to supervise the operation. Kharkov saw the spring in his step as he marched off, the energy of the true enthusiast.

There was still time, thought Kharkov.

He opened the door of the staff car, climbed into the back seat and closed his eyes against the nightmare outside. As he relaxed, the tramp of marching troops and the roar of lorries fell away.

The sun rose in the sky. A bell at the far end of the Bolsoi Prospekt rang eight times.

THURSDAY 25 OCTOBER
SUBMARINE K-6
8.05 A.M. MOSCOW TIME
0505 GMT

"The situation has worsened," said Max. "It is imperative that we proceed as fast as possible to relieve our comrades and break the blockade."

Petrachkov compared the authentication codes Max had dictated to Doctor Chiker with the corresponding codes in the sealed packages from the ship's safe. They were identical.

What would happen now? Would the conflict spill over into other parts of the globe; Germany, Turkey, Afghanistan . . . or even China? Was he witnessing the end of the world?

He thought of his lost family. Natalya had become an expert in hoarding and trading, a necessary skill for survival in the harsh climate of the submarine base at Severmorsk. There were always food shortages. People had to queue for hours for things that never materialized.

"They have live chickens for sale at the market," she would say. "I'll be back in a couple of hours."

"Why do you have to rush out and buy food we do not need? The boys have plenty of fish in the refrigerator!"

"My dear, you have to buy things when you see them. I can trade the chicken for marinated herring with Marina next door. She has a big supply her Sasha brought back from Murmansk. Plus, on the other side of the town they have lamb for sale near the station. Sasha called and told me this morning. I can trade chicken for lamb."

He would never see her earnest, loving face again. He would never take his sons fishing or see the look in their eyes as they presented their catch to their mother.

"And what are our orders?" he whispered softly to Doctor Chiker, who put the question to Max.

"To maintain course and all available speed. To be ready again in twelve hours for a further transmission."

"Is that all?"

Max opened his eyes and spoke to him directly. "I am sorry about your wife and sons, Captain. Hold that memory of how you took them fishing."

Petrachkov stared at him across the wardroom table. He was about to speak when Chiker raised his hand.

"I think that is enough for now, Max," he said. "Rest yourself. You will be needed again."

"That was uncanny," said Petrachkov after the young man had gone to his bunk. "How did he know what I was thinking?"

"Because he has gifts, Captain. Because of the way he has been trained."

"Incredible."

"What is even more incredible is that he would not even need to be in this room to tell what you were thinking. He could reach out with his mind from any part of the world once the psychic link had been established, just as he reaches his sister."

"Then there can be no more secrets," said Petrachkov. "Every code, every message, every thought can be intercepted and read by someone trained this way. What will the world be like?"

"Different from the one we live in now, Comrade Captain."

Petrachkov thought of Natalya and his boys. "That would not be a bad thing."

He stepped out of the officers' mess and walked aft to the CCP. The submarine was on a high state of alert as they passed through the shallow waters of the Denmark Straight between Iceland and Greenland, heading for the Atlantic. The sonar room had already detected several ships in the area, although none of them had the high-speed propellers of warships. During the Great Patriotic War, the British had tried to ambush the fascist battleship *Bismarck* here and paid the price by losing the pride of their fleet, the battle cruiser *Hood*.

In a couple of hours Petrachkov would reach the depths of the Irminger Basin and the Labrador Sea and have all the water he needed to hide in. But right now he felt confined and vulnerable. He reached up, spoke into the microphone connecting him with compartment five and called for Mostock.

"I must make this ship as silent as possible," he said, when his friend emerged from the reactor room. "What can I do to reduce the reactor noise?"

There was silence as Mostock considered the problem. Both of them knew that nuclear reactors, with their constantly driving water pumps, were the noisiest things on the ship. Each reactor contained fuel rods of highly radioactive enriched uranium oxide pellets inside metal tubes. When brought together in bundles, the radiation from each fuel rod combined with the others to produce tremendous heat. To control this reaction, heavy metal plates, called "baffles", were lowered between the fuel rods to keep them apart. To dissipate this heat when the baffles were out of the way, and to produce steam to drive the turbines that generated electricity to run the ship, water had to be pumped constantly through the reactor. Those pumps made noise, and noise was a submariner's greatest enemy, but to shut off the pumps risked a nuclear meltdown.

"We could lower the baffles on one of the reactors and shut it down for a while," said Mostock. "That would at least halve your pump noise, and we would have enough power from the other one, along with the residual energy in the batteries, to reach open water."

"What are the risks?"

"Not many. You might strain the pumps on the reactor you leave running, but I'll maintain a good watch on it for you."

"Very good. Go ahead and keep me informed of progress. I'll let you know when we can come back to full power again."

"Thanks," said Mostock. "By the way, I liked that joke about me not glowing after sex. It helped raise the men's spirits in the reactor room."

"Let's hope it's still true when we get home," Petrachkov said.

THURSDAY, 25 OCTOBER
PHOENIX, ARIZONA, USA
7.00 A.M. MOUNTAIN STANDARD TIME
1400 GMT

Nurse Maureen O'Sullivan always paid attention to details. You had to when you were dealing with dangerous men. So she was careful to make sure that Robert Mann was in restraint and under sedation, well away from the TV room before she let anyone listen to President Kennedy's broadcast on this ghastly Cuban business.

While she felt it might do no harm for the other inmates at the Phoenix Memorial Sanatorium to know what was going on in the world, even if they couldn't understand it, she knew Robert Mann was different. Bobby was a paranoid schizophrenic with a very detailed delusional fantasy about being part of a top-secret government experiment to project his mind out of his body and spy on the Russians.

"More like a body out of his mind, if you ask me," Doctor James had said on his last visit, which seemed callous to Nurse O'Sullivan, who still liked to see her patients as people, no matter how oddly they behaved. But the doctor was right. For the last few hours, Robert Mann had been screaming that someone was "coming to get him" and making such a fuss that he had to be restrained. For Robert Mann to see any kind of television broadcast by the government in the state he was in would be like trying to put out a forest fire with buckets of gasoline.

Nurse O'Sullivan looked in on him through the observation window of his padded cell. He sat curled up in a straitjacket in the far corner. Even with the heavy dose of sedatives he'd been given, his eyes were clear and bright, still fixing her with that stare of his, the one that made her think he could see right inside her brain.

"They're coming for me, Sully," he pleaded. "Call the FBI, call the CIA. They're coming for me. You have to help me, pleeeease!"

"You just calm down there now, Bobby," she said through the speaker on the door. "It'll be OK. You've had these turns before and nothing's ever happened. What are the CIA and the FBI going to ever want with the likes of you and me?"

"At least let me out of this jacket! I have to defend myself when they come."

"No, Bobby. We don't want you trying to bite through your wrists again."

"Pleeeease!"

She walked down the corridor into the lounge where a score of chairs had been set in a semi-circle around the television set. Some of the inmates had their eyes glued to the screen. Others, like old Mrs. Schwimmer, were just staring into space.

Who knows what they're seeing? thought Nurse O'Sullivan. We do the best we can, make them comfortable and give them the benefit of the doubt.

The door of the lounge opened. It was Jimbo, the security guard from the main entrance to the sanatorium.

"Sully," he said, "there's a couple of gentlemen here asking for Robert Mann."

"What couple of gentlemen?"

"I don't know, but they look official."

Nurse O'Sullivan frowned at the TV and walked across the room to see who had come calling. Two men in dark suits, white shirts and ties stood at the other end of the corridor. Each had a briefcase. One of them had something wrong with his nose. It looked as if it had been broken a long time ago and never straightened.

"They say they're from Robert Mann's former employer," said Jimbo. "Something to do with the government."

"What do they want, so early in the morning?"

"They didn't say, Ma'am. They just wanted to know which room he was in. They said it was urgent."

Nurse O'Sullivan looked down the corridor. One of the men glanced at his watch. The man with the broken nose smiled at her.

"We really need to see him in a hurry, Nurse," he said pleasantly. "This is official business."

"I can't authorise visitors without a doctor being present." She felt annoyed at being dragged away from the President's broadcast. This was a piece of history and she was missing it!

"But Mister Mann is here? He's registered at this institution?"

The two men *seemed* genuine enough. They were in their late twenties, with hard expressions. Maybe they were ex-military. The shorter one with the broken nose certainly looked in good shape.

"He was, the last time I checked," she said. "Down at the end of the corridor in observation room one. But you can't see him until I get a doctor to verify that he's fit for visitors. He's been acting very strange lately."

As if on cue, Robert Mann's voice echoed down the hallway. "Don't let them get me, Sully! They're coming for me!"

"You see what I mean," said Nurse O'Sullivan.

"Perfectly," said the man with the broken nose, "but I have something here that might help." And he reached into his briefcase.

"I don't think anything can—"

He was holding a heavy automatic pistol with a thick black silencer.

"Oh my God!"

Mann's voice rose to a scream. "Sully, run!"

Nurse O'Sullivan stood paralysed. Jimbo already had his hands on his head.

"On the floor, both of you," said the man with the gun. "If you move, you die. Understand?"

Nurse O'Sullivan glanced around her for the nearest alarm button, then saw the look in the man's eyes and thought better of it. She knelt on the cold linoleum and lay down facing towards the observation room where Robert Mann was still screaming her name.

"Sully, Sully! They're coming to get me!"

The two men walked down the corridor and opened the door of the observation room.

"Sully! They're going to—"

The man with the gun aimed through the open door. Nurse O'Sullivan saw the gun jump in his hand, heard the muffled "thump" of the shots and the tinkle of spent shell cases hitting the floor.

The killer walked into the observation room. Nurse O'Sullivan heard the pistol thump again. The man who had been watching her and Jimbo bent down and picked up the cartridge cases. Then the man with the gun came out and both of them walked quickly towards the exit.

As soon as the men were out of sight, Nurse O'Sullivan jumped to her feet.

"Call the cops, Jimbo. They're gone now. Call the cops!"

She ran to the door of the observation room and looked it. The stench of cordite and fresh blood hung in the air.

"My God, Bobby!" she breathed as she looked down at the shattered body. "You were right all along."

12

The weather in Leningrad had turned to drizzle. It made the desolate scene in the Smolensk Cemetery all the more miserable. In front of Kharkov stood row after row of women separated by rope lines between the graves into one endless queue that stretched as far as he could see. Cherlenko's troops patrolled the perimeter, took away those who had already been questioned and brought fresh detainees every few minutes in lorries.

The troops seemed more miserable than the women. They stood singly with their guns at the ready, or huddled in groups for a quick smoke when they thought their officers' attentions were elsewhere. The women took it all in their stride. Groups of them gossiped and laughed. Some shared food or tried to flirt with the guards. Why shouldn't they be used to this? thought Kharkov. The average Russian woman spends most of her life queuing for food, for clothes, for life's little luxuries. Why should this be any different?

He looked up at the next woman brought before him and shook his head for at least the thousandth time. The KGB officer next to him stamped the woman's identity card and she walked off to join her friends at the next outgoing lorry. "Next!"

The process went on with face after face after face. None of them was Tatyana Rospin. It had already taken them six hours and they were barely halfway through the group of women who were *supposed* to look like her on just *one* of the islands in a city of millions.

Kharkov heard the guards snap to attention. The bureaucrat next to him stiffened in his seat.

"Any progress?" barked Cherlenko.

Kharkov put up his hand, indicating that the next woman in line should wait and got to his feet.

"None, but if I was a young and single man, this would be a marvellous way to meet women."

Cherlenko was not amused.

"This is taking too long. There has to be an easier way."

"It is your logical approach, Comrade General. It will work, inevitably, but it *will* take time. There is no doubt about that. Are there any leads from other parts of the city?"

"Not yet. It's the sheer size of the problem."

"You would not be the first military genius to make that observation, Comrade General. Napoleon and Hitler both came to that conclusion in the end."

"I cannot afford to be defeated as they were, Professor. If I fail, then you fail also. Remember that and keep on checking!"

Cherlenko stormed off with Slavin at his heels, leaving Kharkov to look into the faces of woman after woman as they came before him to be checked and dismissed. The mention of Napoleon and Hitler, the crowds of confined civilians, the masses of troops on the street and Cherlenko's curfew took Kharkov back a score of years, to the Great Patriotic War.

He had been working with Andrei Zhdanov on the defence of the city at the Smolny compound, a mile or two upriver. Zhdanov had been a tireless leader, in spite of his asthma and his endless consumption of cigarettes. The building had buzzed with activity, doors opening and closing, messengers and clerks coming in carrying papers, officers going in and out, telephones ringing, all to keep the city alive and out of the hands of the Fascists. A hundred and fifty workers' battalions, each of six hundred men, women and teenagers defended the city, armed with rifles, shotguns, Molotov cocktails, daggers and pikes. Machine gun nests and barricades had been set up in the streets and parks to protect the city from parachutists. Curfews were imposed. The shelling started and starvation set in. The siege dragged on and on and on . . . for nine hundred days.

Kharkov's wife had been a doctor. He had worshipped her for her love and her devotion to her calling. She worked herself to a skeleton to save those around her, but the medicines had run out along with the food.

That was when the children had died, Kharkov thought. Zhdanov had done all he could, so had Kharkov and his wife. What was it they used to say? "Leningrad is not afraid of death — death is afraid of Leningrad." But more people had died in that one siege than have ever died in any modern city. Over a million souls perished, mostly from starvation. Ten times as many as the atom bomb killed at Hiroshima. Kharkov and his wife had been decorated as heroes of the Soviet Union afterwards. It was terrible what Stalin had done to them next.

He looked up into the face of the next woman and, for a split second, saw the calm grey eyes of his wife Irena looking back.

"Next!" he said.

How far has the human race advanced since then? Kharkov wondered. What good were our sacrifices that it should all come to this?

"Next!"

He could still win, just as he had beaten Stalin in the end. It was only a matter of time.

"Next!"

THURSDAY, 25 OCTOBER
LAS VEGAS
9.08 A.M. LOCAL TIME
1508 GMT

Ray Mancuso was winning big, bigger than he had ever won in his life. Poker was a tough game in Vegas; far tougher and more serious than games played around the Panhandle and deeper into Texas, where there was a lot of easy money. Ray went down there every once in a while to stock up his bankroll, the reserve of cash he had been building up over the years for the one big game in Vegas which would give him the million dollars he reckoned he needed to live in luxury for the rest of his life. But in Vegas he played it safe, winning enough to make a living, but not so much as to get him noticed as a man who won too often.

But now, with this whole Cuban thing and the Commies ready to drop the bomb at any minute, the time for playing it safe was past. Ray's bankroll stood at almost seven hundred thousand. One big win and he was out of the country forever! Then the Commies could drop all the bombs they liked.

Ray understood Las Vegas. It was like the coral reef display he'd seen down at the San Diego aquarium. There were bright colours and beautiful things to catch the eye, bright lights, gorgeous women, limitless food, and free booze at the tables-twenty four hours a day. But lurking in wait behind these distractions was the natural law of 'eat or be eaten'.

In Vegas, as far as money was concerned, you were predator or prey, winner or loser. It paid to keep your mind focused. And in a mind game against other people, Ray Mancuso simply could not lose.

He looked up at the three other players around the poker table at the Flamingo Hotel Casino. Sitting to his right in the dealer's seat was a thin man in a cowboy hat and a very expensive suit worn over cowboy boots. Ray knew he owned close to fifty laundromats and a couple of restaurants back in Texas. He was good, but right now he was playing with his cock instead of his brains and his eyes were on winning not the money, but the woman sitting next to him.

She was a very attractive brunette in her early thirties with an East coast accent, old money and bright intelligent eyes. Her neckline was just north of decency and she kept exchanging glances with the Cowboy. Was she a card sharp or a high-class hooker? Ray had been around Vegas a while and hadn't seen her before. But that meant nothing. She might have been from out of town and on the prowl for an easy mark.

The fourth player, on Mancuso's left, was a professional card player like himself, an almost perfect pyramid of muscle and fat, wearing a short-sleeved tennis shirt and delicate wire-framed reading glasses. Was he a plant for the casino? That was always possible. Even now, there would be security men looking down at them from behind the one-way mirrored ceiling above their heads, watching for any signs of cheating.

The game was no limit Texas Hold'em Poker. The idea was to use the five best cards of seven; the two hidden cards you were dealt face down, along with the five face up communal cards everyone could see. The best hand won, minus the percentage to the casino. The key to winning was in the betting, the bluffing, and above all in knowing what a person was thinking, which was why Ray loved it so much.

After the minimum and maximum betting levels had been set, the Cowboy dealt two cards face down to each player and nodded at him, indicating the start of betting in earnest. Mancuso looked at the two cards he'd been dealt: ace of diamonds and king of clubs. Not bad. He raised the bet to five thousand dollars, pushing in his chips. The Pro followed suit with a further five. The Brunette looked unsure, but still pushed in five thousand. The Cowboy, with a self-satisfied smirk on his face, pushed in seven thousand.

Then the Pro discarded the top card from the pack and dealt the first three 'flop cards', face up on the table: the four of hearts, the ten of diamonds and the six of spades. Mancuso could do nothing with these, but he sensed that the Pro was feeling good and had another ten in his hand, which meant he had a pair. He also sensed mild excitement from the Brunette. She had a four, which meant another pair, but low. Nothing from the Cowboy.

The second round of betting started with the Pro. The Cowboy had his eyes on Mancuso. This was turning into a grudge match, with the Brunette as the prize, which meant the Cowboy's ego was at stake and he was going to demonstrate his manhood by bluffing. He threw in ten thousand dollars and smirked. This was just the way Mancuso wanted it.

The Pro discarded another 'burn card' from the top of the pack and dealt the second flop card: the king of diamonds. This made a pair for Mancuso, nice and high. He threw in five thousand more with a flourish, bringing his bet to fifteen. The Pro hesitated, but followed suit with another five.

Mancuso felt the Brunette's excitement rising. She had a black king in her hand, which had to be the king of spades, giving her a high pair to match his. She threw in twenty thousand.

This left the Cowboy and his ego. He smirked again at Mancuso and raised the bet to thirty thousand.

The fifth flop card was the queen of clubs.

The Pro folded.

One down. Two to go.

There was blood in the water now and, like the prowling sharks around a coral reef, punters from other parts of the casino started to gather around the table to watch the kill.

The Brunette was now less sure of herself. She still had two pairs — kings and fours—but could not tell if it was enough to beat either Mancuso or the Cowboy. Even so, she followed the Cowboy's bet up to thirty thousand.

"Well done, Ma'am," said Mancuso, touching her arm just to get under the Cowboy's skin. The Brunette smiled back at him and blushed.

Instead of showing anger, the Cowboy was over the moon. Mancuso closed his eyes for a second and focused. A picture popped into his mind. The man had a straight—ace of hearts, king of diamonds, queen of clubs, jack and ten of diamonds. Shit!

The Cowboy smiled at Mancuso, winked at the Brunette, and raised to fifty thousand dollars. Ray heard a whisper of excitement from the circle of onlookers around the table.

Mancuso saw his million getting closer. He pushed a hundred thousand dollars into the pot. The Brunette bit her lip and folded. The Cowboy gave Mancuso a look that would have peeled paint off doors and made a big fuss of trying to comfort the Brunette. Then he bet again, raising the stakes to a hundred and fifty thousand dollars.

Mancuso raised again, pushing up the bet to two hundred thousand. This was getting big now. He tried to stay focused. If this worked, then he would be out of here and away.

The Cowboy was torn between the cards and the Brunette. He threw another fifty thousand onto the table, trying to outbet Mancuso and force him to fold. But Mancuso's bankroll was good for one big game.

"Half a million!" he said, pushing his chips forward. There was a gasp from the onlookers around the table.

The Cowboy sat paralysed. He looked at Mancuso, the chips, the Brunette and finally at his own bankroll.

Then he folded.

"Goddamit to hell!"

Mancuso raked in the chips. The Cowboy slapped his cards down, face up on the table. They were exactly what Mancuso had seen in his mind.

"Show me your god-damned hand!"

Mancuso looked up from his winnings. "You know the rules of the game, buddy. If you want to see, you pay!"

The Cowboy needed to salvage his chances with the Brunette. He reached down and pushed another fifty thousand dollars onto the table.

"Show me!"

Mancuso calmly turned over his ace of diamonds and king of spades. He had been bluffing all along.

"I hope she was worth it, hot shot!" he whispered across the table. Then, to a round of applause from the onlookers, he ordered a bottle of champagne for the Brunette and the Pro, just to show there were no hard feelings.

This was it! He had his 'escape money', every last cent of it. Now it was time to get out!

He called over the cashier to arrange a transfer to his bank in the Cayman Islands. There was no sense in walking around Vegas with that kind of money just waiting to be hijacked, and he knew the casino could be trusted. They had to be. One whiff of any problem in paying a winner would have the whole place empty in less than an hour, and there was plenty of competition from other casinos up and down the Strip to make sure it would stay that way forever.

All he had to do now was to play it cool, to make like this was no big deal and put his escape plan into effect. Then, with the money in the bank, he could lay back and relax for the rest of his life.

Sweet! And all he'd done was to play it scientifically. Just like that guy Carpenter and those other eggheads in that shack out in the desert had taught him. He shrugged off the attentions of a couple of women who had been watching him win and made his way to the cashier's office. Then, with the casino bank transfer slip in his pocket, he walked out across the tiled foyer of the side entrance into the morning sunshine and waved for a cab.

The Caymans would be great. Ray had been there to sort out his bank details. The weather was warm; the women were pretty and really knew how to make a rich man happy. Not like Vegas, where the girls swarmed like leeches, looking for a high roller to suck dry before they moved on to the next victim. In the Caymans it was different. Everyone was rich, so nobody cared. Milk and honey all the way.

A couple of guys stood watching him across the Strip. They looked like government types, with dark suits and ties. Ever since he had left the program, Mancuso knew he was being watched. Every once in a while there was that odd hollowness to the phone line, or the strange car that parked across from his apartment and didn't move.

So this was nothing new, nothing to get hung up about.

One of them was looking at a photograph. Jesus! If they didn't know him by now!

A cab slowed in front of him and stopped. The window rolled down.

"Hey, buddy, you doing astronomy or what?"

The young guy behind the wheel looked familiar. He had dark eyes, a thin face and a nose that looked as if it had been broken. Girlie magazines lay open on the seat next to him.

"Take me to Elwood," Mancuso said.

"High roller, eh? No problem! Hop in!"

Mancuso pulled open the rear door and got in. The two men on the other side of the strip saw this and ran to a car. I knew it, thought Ray. Amateurs!

"I got a job for you," he said. "Two guys are getting into a dark Chevy over there."

"Yeah, I see them."

"There's five hundred in it if you can lose them."

The driver smiled.

"You got it . . . ." And before the words had left his mouth, Ray was thrown violently to one side as the cab made a ninety degree turn to the right, shot down the alley next to the Flamingo, across an intersection and left onto the Strip going east. Another turn to the left, then right and left again, and they were five blocks over and travelling back west towards Ray's place at Elwood, with no sight or smell of the other car.

"Nice work!" said Ray as the cab pulled to a stop in an alleyway next to his apartment. He passed a five hundred dollar bill through the grill. "Don't I know you?"

"I'm new in town," said the man. "Maybe it's because I look like Sinatra. I get that a lot."

"I *do* know you," said Ray, sensing something about the man. "You work in the Tropicana. I've seen you there! You work for Johnny Rosselli . . . ."

Then Ray Mancuso knew exactly what the man was going to do, just as he'd known who the men across the street were, or which cards the Cowboy had to play.

"Please," he said. "I've got money! More money than you could ever dream of. I'll split it with you. Please!"

"Sorry, buddy," said the man behind the wheel, "but business is business."

Then he pulled a silenced automatic from under a copy of *Playboy* and shot Ray twice in the heart.

13

Tony Fischetti shot Ray once more through the forehead, just to be sure. Then he unscrewed the silencer from the big .45 automatic and sniffed the smoke, as if he were savouring a Cuban cigar.

Cuba!

When they got Cuba back, he was going to live like a king, with all the women and all the money a guy could ever need. He looked back at the corpse in passenger seat. What had the guy been babbling about before he'd whacked him? More money than he could ever dream of? Forget about it! Fischetti could dream pretty big and, besides, it wasn't just about the money. It was about getting the stinking Commies out of Cuba, about doing something for his country like Frank Sinatra did in *The Manchurian Candidate*. Fischetti had taken that flick in twice already.

Fischetti loved Las Vegas and he loved the casinos. They had everything a poor boy from Detroit could ever want: style, money, booze, women and power, especially power. Fischetti had been powerless as a kid, with a drunk for a father and a mother who had walked out when he was five.

Then one day, his father had beaten up on him so bad that he broke Fischetti's nose. Fischetti decided to take his power back. He had waited that evening in the darkness and, when his father had come back drunk, Fischetti had pushed him out of their apartment window. The police suspected murder but could never prove it.

So they sent Fischetti to a juvenile correction centre, where he soon discovered that the only way to survive in a fight against the bigger kids was to go for their eyes and testicles.

People started giving Fischetti respect then. He worked out in the gym. He began to get sense. Fischetti came to the attention of people who had connections and, when he was released at the age of eighteen, he went to work for the Outfit and Johnny Rosselli.

Fischetti was good at his job. By twenty-five he was a trusted strong-arm man for the owners of the Tropicana. Their power made Fischetti feel OK about his height and his broken nose. It made women afraid of him and yet available at the same time. But when he had them, he knew it was either because he'd paid for them or because they'd slept with him out of fear. Whichever way it was, he never saw real desire in their eyes.

Then Fischetti witnessed Frank Sinatra play at the Copa Room of the Sands Hotel and came face to face with his vision of the perfect role model, a man like himself with connections to the Outfit, a man who could melt a woman's heart like butter or punch a sucker's lights out whenever he wanted, a man that all the big shots at the hotels and casinos called "sir", a man with power, the self-appointed "Chairman of the Board"! From that moment on, Tony Fischetti's mission in life was to be like Frank Sinatra.

He looked up and down the alleyway to make sure nobody was watching. Then got out of the cab, slipped the thin leather gloves he'd been wearing to hide his prints into his pocket and walked out of the alleyway into the morning sunshine, heading back to the Strip and the Tropicana. Mister Rosselli had said there was another job that had to be done quickly and Mister Rosselli was the Outfit's 'Strategist', their main man in Las Vegas.

Tony made it back in fifteen minutes, entered by the back service door where he had a key and made his way to the penthouse without anyone seeing him. The big man guarding Mister Rosselli's suite took the Colt .45, frisked him respectfully and opened the door.

"Thanks, Louis."

"You're welcome, Tony. Take it easy."

Fischetti stepped into the suite of the most powerful man in Las Vegas.

"How's it going, Tony?"

"Okay, Mister Rosselli. It worked out okay."

"So Mancuso's dead?"

"I'm sure. Three bullets. Two in the heart, one in the head."

"You're sure you got the right guy?"

"Sure, Mister Rosselli. I know him from the casino. He's been playing the card tables for years, winning some, losing some. You had me tail him, months ago, when the pit bosses told you he had a system, remember? Turned out the guy was just lucky."

"But now his luck's run out?"

"Completely."

"Any sign of the Feds?"

"The guy was running from a couple of schmucks in suits when I got to him. I picked him up just in time."

"Good. Then there's only one left, working in that tourist village by the Grand Canyon. It's a woman this time, Tony, a half-breed Indian. I want a nice clean job."

"This is important work, Mister Rosselli, big time stuff. I'll make it clean. There's a guy who owes us money working out there, north of Flagstaff. He'll know where she is, but so will the Feds. How can I get to her before they do?"

"There's a plane waiting for you at MacClarren. But even if the Feds are already ahead of you, I still want you to whack her, Tony. These people have to be eliminated. If we get them, we have a crack at Cuba. If this woman lives, then we lose it forever."

"Commie spies huh?"

"Whatever. Take as much muscle and artillery as you want, but make sure that woman is dead meat before the Feds lock her away somewhere we can't reach her."

"You got it, Mister Rosselli."

"And no messing with her, Tony. This isn't the girlfriend of some schmuck who can't pay his gambling dues. I want this quick and easy. Not like the last time."

Fischetti was getting tired of this.

"Has this broad got a name, Mister Rosselli?"

Johnny Rosselli slid a single sheet of paper across his desk.

"Make it clean, Tony, or it's your neck."

Fischetti read the name and address and folded the paper into his pocket as he left. What was it with Mister Rosselli? Always going on about that mess with that senator's daughter. If broads like that were going to show up in Vegas, with guys who lost big money and couldn't pay, they should wear signs around their necks telling honest employees like him not to hurt them when it came to getting their men to pay up.

He remembered the stuck up bitch screaming at him when he'd pushed her back on the bed and curved his finger inside the top of her dress, remembered her boyfriend yelling that he'd find the money somewhere . . . only don't . . . don't . . . .

But the madness had been on him and he'd ridden it like a wave, ripping her dress from the neck to the hemline, sliding her thin panties down around her ankles.

Shit, it had been worth it just to see the look on her face.

Fischetti walked to the elevator and pressed the button for the ground floor.

A woman . . . and a redskin at that! He'd never had one of those.

He felt himself getting hard even as the elevator started to drop.

The US Government Gulfstream turboprop droned westwards at ten thousand feet. Carpenter hated planes. The seats were always too close together for his long legs and his head hit the luggage rack when he got up to walk about. But mostly his body remembered.

It remembered being inside an Air Force EC-130 intelligence-gathering aircraft that had just been shot full of holes over Soviet Armenia. It remembered the panic, the sickening feeling of falling and the bone-shattering impact with the ground. It remembered the pain of crawling from the wreckage and the fear of hiding out in enemy territory. It remembered trying to live off the land while its wounds healed, the trek to the border and the long months of rehabilitation in a hospital. You could put something like that out of your mind with practice, but your body still remembered. Which was why Carpenter hated planes.

Hiscock was standing by the open cockpit door with a radio headset and a microphone, speaking to his wife.

"Look, Janice. If the alarm sounds, you know what to do. Get everyone down into the basement or, if you're outside, get down into a ditch right away. OK? You have that booklet I gave you from the *Washington Star*, don't you? Just do what it says and you'll be fine."

"Mister Hiscock, sir," said the co-pilot. "You have to finish on the radio now. We need it to keep in touch with Langley."

Hiscock grudgingly handed the headset back and returned to his seat, opened a booklet entitled *You Can Survive An Atomic Attack* and started to read. Carpenter wondered which would be worse: to be fried in an atomic firestorm or to be trapped in a fallout shelter for months with Hiscock and his family eating nothing but Nabisco survival biscuits. He closed the NSA file he had been reading on Ray Mancuso, looked at his watch and opened the second folder on his lap. "PROJECT ELEMENT – REMOTE VIEWER CODENAME 'FIRE'. Actual name; Ruth Abigail Weylon. Havasupai Indian name 'Little Eagle.'"

She had been working as a photo interpreter at Fort Bragg, Texas when she had been brought to Carpenter's attention. Her father, Carl Weylon, had been killed in December 1944 at the Battle of the Bulge. She had signed up with the US Air Force in the hope of learning to fly like the eagle of her Native American name, but found herself caged in a photo-reconnaissance unit staring at photographs of buildings, ports and cities. She had never been told where these places were, just *what* they were, and asked to evaluate them.

But when she closed her eyes and relaxed in that dark, quiet room they'd given her, she knew exactly where those photographs had been taken. She could go there in her mind, look from side to side and see the ground stretching out around her. She could swoop down, slip inside the buildings and see what were inside filing cabinets and drawers. In short, she could *be there*! She was the perfect spy: silent, invisible and able to see through solid walls to the secrets beyond, anywhere in the world.

Carpenter searched the file for an address, but there was none. The only clues to where she might be were the location of her Havasupai tribe, a trailer park up near the Grand Canyon, and the fact that she worked in the tourist village out on the rim, just as her mother had before she died.

"It doesn't seem right, does it?" said Hiscock. "Even when I was in Korea, I always knew Janice was safe back here at home. Wars were things that happened in other places. They didn't happen to your wife and kids. America was safe and would always be that way. Now the kids are doing 'duck and cover' drills in schools and there's surface to air missiles on the beach outside Janice's parents' house in Florida. What kind of a mess have we got ourselves into?"

The co-pilot stepped out of the cockpit.

"How long before we get to Vegas?" Carpenter asked.

"There's been a change of plan, sir. We've been ordered to divert directly to the airport at the south rim of the Grand Canyon."

"What the hell for?"

"Someone got to Mann and Mancuso. They're both dead. Langley says it looks like two professional hits."

"How the hell did they know where to find them?"

Carpenter got up from his seat and woke Hiscock.

"Uh . . . what's the matter now?"

"Mann and Mancuso—both murdered."

"Shit! That means we have a leak."

"That's academic right now," said Carpenter, glancing at his watch. "We've got to get to Ruth Weylon before whoever killed the others finds her. How long before we reach the canyon?"

"Just over an hour, sir. We should touch down at eleven o'clock, local time."

"Look," said Carpenter. "This is more important than you can possibly imagine. Get on the radio and call the local sheriff's office down there, the Park Rangers, or whoever has some authority, and have her taken into protective custody."

"Do you have an address, Mister Carpenter?"

"Ah . . . I think she lives in a trailer park north of Flagstaff. She may work at one of those hotels or gift stores on the rim."

"Do you know which one?"

Carpenter didn't. He'd never thought they would need to find her again in such a hurry. Before the news of Mancuso and Mann, he thought he had at least a day to find Ruth Weylon before things got critical. But now he had no time at all.

"Couldn't we just call her up on the phone?"

"She doesn't have one. She dropped out of life when she left the program. Look, just get onto the local sheriff's office, tell them who we are and have them search all the gift stores, hotels and trailer parks near the rim. If they need authority, refer them to Birkett back at the CIA. Just do it, will you. Her life is at stake now."

The man rushed back to the cockpit.

"You said she dropped out when she left the program," said Hiscock. "Even if we find her alive, will she co-operate?"

"She'll resist at first. She had some bad experiences and saw things she shouldn't have seen—horrible things. But when she knows what's at stake, when she knows the magnitude of all this, I'm sure she'll come around."

"Can you *make* her do it?"

"That's the last thing I could do. This kind of work has to be done willingly. Any resistance by the subject makes it impossible to relax enough for the astral projection to take place. She has to want to do it."

"Then all we can do is pray that we get there in time," said Hiscock. "Commodore Amery is still in touch with Admiral Shumanin in Leningrad. If anything breaks there, he'll let us know."

THURSDAY, 25 OCTOBER
LENINGRAD
7.55 P.M. LOCAL TIME
1655 GMT

"Your reports?" said Cherlenko from the head of the table. Night had fallen and, behind him across the Neva, lights twinkled all over the city like moonlight on ice.

"We have carried out a through search of Petrogradskiy," said a young officer from the GRU. "According to your excellent example, Comrade General. We sealed the bridges and performed a thorough sweep from door to door."

"And inside those doors?" asked Cherlenko pointedly. "You did search *inside*, didn't you?"

"Of course, Comrade General. Every cupboard in every house was ransacked, along with every attic, outhouse and cellar. I would stake my career on it."

"You might need to. Next!"

"The three islands of Kresovskiy, Velagin and Gutuyevskiy were searched in the same way," said an old army colonel with a chestful or medal ribbons. "Like you, we have all the women who even remotely match the description detained in hospitals and prisons awaiting your instructions. We have checked all their identifications. But—"

"But, you found nothing I suppose," Cherlenko said. "Next!"

The other officers around the table each bowed their heads and reported failure.

"And the parachute regiment. Did they find anything of use on the trains?"

"No, Comrade General."

"The buses? The Metro?"

"Nothing, Comrade General."

Cherlenko's patience was wearing thin. The chasm of defeat yawned open beneath him. Slavin would be drafting her report of his failure to Moscow even now.

"She must be *somewhere*!" he snapped, pointing to the map. "What do those black flags signify?"

"Places we could not access, Comrade General."

"*Could not access!* I told you to search *everywhere*! Those were my specific instructions, were they not?"

"But there are places even we could not go, Comrade General; places any human being could not hide in if they wanted to remain alive: cancer hospitals, prisons for the criminally insane, freezer warehouses, chemical stores and the like."

"How many of them are there?" snapped Cherlenko.

The young officer who had spoken first ran his eyes down a list.

"Thirty-two in all, Comrade General. There are also a few vaults beneath the major churches that have not been reopened since the great siege."

"Then, Major, I want you to take as many men as you need and search each and every one of these locations. If it is an infectious disease hospital, then give the men biological warfare suits or simply leave them behind to rot after they have reported to you. If they are chemical stores, give them gas-masks. But search *everywhere*! I want to know beyond a shadow of a doubt that we can eliminate those areas by the next briefing, or you will all find yourselves in front of a firing squad. Do I make myself clear?"

"Yes, Comrade General!" Each officer snapped a salute.

"Then get to it!"

The men shuffled out of the room, leaving Cherlenko to gaze down at the black flags on the map and Kharkov collapsed in a chair behind him.

"Are you unwell, Comrade Professor?"

"Exhausted. I never really recovered from my time in the Gulag. You have never been there?"

"There are worse things. At least nobody was shooting at you there, unless you tried to escape. At Stalingrad they shot at me all the time."

Kharkov nodded. His hand went to the small of his back and rubbed it, as if to ease some pain.

"I understand," he said. "And if your men return tonight and tell you that Tatyana Rospin is still free? Then what?"

Cherlenko looked up from the map.

"Then we will have to try a different strategy. Tell me, Professor, besides Baybarin, this man she has run off with, whom does Tatyana Rospin love most in this world?"

14

THURSDAY, 25 OCTOBER
THE GRAND CANYON
SOUTH RIM AIRPORT, ARIZONA
11.06 A.M. MOUNTAIN STANDARD TIME
1806 GMT

Carpenter braced himself, with both hands gripping the armrests of his seat and his eyes tightly closed, as the plane skimmed in low over the scrub, railway tracks and tall Pinyon trees around the airport. He gritted his teeth as the wheels bit the tarmac, and then they were down, taxiing towards the men and police cars waiting for them on the apron.

"Are you okay?" Hiscock asked.

"Fine," said Carpenter, feeling the tension in his body dissolve. "Just a previous bad experience, that's all."

The aircraft stopped. The co-pilot popped open the door and they stepped down onto the tarmac.

"So you're the guys who have us all running around like crazy down here!" said a big man in a brown police uniform and a wide-brimmed 'Smokey the Bear' hat.

"I'm sorry, Sheriff, but this is a national emergency."

"And can I confirm who has jurisdiction here, sir?"

"We do," said Hiscock, flashing his identification. "Like the man said. This is international security. In such circumstances, all civilian ground forces *will* come under the authority of the relevant federal agency, which is the CIA. Now, if we can get on with this please."

"Do any of your men know the woman we're looking for," Carpenter asked as they walked to the cars, shouting above the noise of the tourist helicopters lined up near the trees.

"Ruth Weylon? She lives in a trailer park just down the road towards Flastaff. With her grandmother," said one of the sheriff's men.

"Have you been there?"

"We *were* there, sir," said the sheriff, climbing into the first car, "but there was nobody home." Carpenter and Hiscock got into the backseats. The vehicle stank of cheap air freshener and stale vomit.

"Did you look inside?"

"I didn't have a warrant, sir. And, as a sheriff of this county, I'm supposed to be kind of sticky about the law."

"Jesus!" breathed Hiscock.

"And where does she work?" Carpenter asked.

"Could be in a hotel, in a restaurant, or one of the gift stores up on the rim."

"Are you searching them?"

"See here sir," said the sheriff, twisting round in his seat as the car pulled away. "This is one of the biggest tourist attractions in the country. You've got a National Park and enough hotels, restaurants and stores up around here to make a small city. I've only been on this case for the last hour, so cut me some slack, huh?"

"We appreciate what you're doing," Carpenter said. "Let's go back to Miss Weylon's trailer and start there. Okay? This *is* an international emergency, like my friend said. He'll take responsibility if we have to break in."

"Okay with me," said the sheriff. "Archie, turn right here. It's about a mile down on the right."

The convoy of cars pulled out onto the tree-lined highway leading up to the National Park and headed down towards Flagstaff.

The trailer park lay hidden in the trees just south of Tucsayon. Each trailer had a little wooden fence around it, a clothesline and a number. An old Indian in blue overalls and a baseball cap covering a

mane of silvery hair stepped out of the little shack by the gate as they
drew up and raised his hand for them to stop.

"What are you guys back for? I already told you she wasn't here
and I don't know where she is."

"We need to look inside her place, sir," Carpenter said. "And we
need to do it now."

"It's up along here," said the sheriff and turned to the old Indian.
"Don't you give us any more trouble, Billy. This is government
business."

The trailer stood by itself on the outside of the park, closest to the
trees. It looked lonely right on the edge.

"Okay, let's get inside," shouted Carpenter. The sheriff took a steel
crowbar from one of his men and applied it to the door.

"Hey, you can't do that without a warrant!" said the Indian.

"We've been through all that with the sheriff, sir," said Hiscock
and flashed his identification.

"CIA, huh?" said the old Indian, nodding his head. "Yup. I always
thought there was something special about her."

The caravan stank like the inside of a dirty oven. The fan was
off and flies buzzed around the tiny kitchen. Carpenter went to the
sleeping area at the back. One bed was neatly made. The other was a
mess. Photographs in cheap frames covered the walls: scenes of the
canyon, pictures of the Ruth he remembered from their time on the
program in Nevada, another of Ruth and two men by a helicopter.
His foot hit an empty whisky bottle. He saw a stack of bills and pay
slips on the bedside locker and grabbed them, shuffling through the
pages.

"Got it!"

He was looking at a pay slip from the Fred Harvey Company dated
a month previously. Written in ballpoint on the top right corner were
the words "Mather Point Gift Store".

"Do you know where that is?" he asked the sheriff.

"Yeah, it's up on the rim. The farthest place east inside the
complex."

"Okay. Let's go. Radio ahead and see if she's there now."

The sheriff's foot hit another bottle and sent is spinning under the bed. Carpenter heard the clink of glass on glass.

"Must have been one helluva party," the sheriff said.

With a hiss of airbrakes, the bus pulled into its last stop. The door folded back with a slap.

"Mather Point, honey. This is where you get off."

Ruth saw the mixture of concern and contempt in the bus driver's eyes. It didn't matter. She was in that comfortable warm glow of having drunk just enough. Too much, and she wouldn't have been able to work. Too little and she'd be edgy, wanting more. The two slugs of Jack Daniel's she'd had before leaving the trailer had been just right. She could face anything when she was like this . . . even being late for work.

She eased herself out of her seat, picked her way down the bus and stepped onto the sidewalk. It was mid-morning and the tourists would be out in force down at the main complex, shuffling along the trails between the gift stores, the hotels and the restaurants, gripping their mugs of coffee and their cameras as they peered over the canyon rim. Up this end of the complex, out beyond the Ranger station, the main hotels and the information centre it was much quieter; the preserve of serious hikers doing the Kaibab Trail down to Bright Angel and the Phantom Ranch at the bottom of the Canyon.

The bus pulled away, leaving her alone. Normally she would have just stayed in bed and slept it off. But that little shit Bob had said he'd fire her if she dodged work one more time. Which meant she'd have to sneak in around the back through the storeroom, grab a few mints to cover her breath and keep out of his way. Even if he did fire her, what did it matter? They were on the edge of a nuclear war. Who'd worry that she was late for work then?

She took a deep breath and walked up the rise to the store. Like the rest of the South Rim complex, it was neatly laid out, with wide paths, benches to sit on and signs prohibiting anyone from feeding the wildlife. There were bins for the trash and information points to tell you what you were looking at. The whole place was one vast tourist trap run by the Fred Harvey Company. It probably made more money than Vegas!

She came to the long wooden building that was the Mather Point Gift Store and Observatory, perched on the spur of rock reaching out along the western bowl of the Kaibab Trail down into the canyon. The door to the storeroom was round the back, close to the rim. She ducked under a chain, edged her way along the rough wooden walls of the building and there it was, all laid out in front of her—the limitless panorama of the Grand Canyon.

As late as she was, Ruth still stopped to stare. It was as if the world had been split in two and she was looking down into the very crucible of creation. The sky above shone pure crystal blue and the harsh light of the sun picked out every detail of the chasms, mountains and trails leading down to the Colorado River a mile below her, as it wound its way through the shadows like a band of gold in the sunlight. No wonder so much money changed hands here. Fred Harvey had taken the greatest spectacle in all creation and sold it like a peep show.

Ruth walked along the narrow trail to the storeroom door, opened it and stepped inside. Then she edged her way between the boxes of souvenirs, candy and film, gently opened the door to the store and peered in.

The place was an Aladdin's cave of canyon souvenirs. The ceiling was lined with low wooden beams in a faux-Cowboy style above a solid stone floor, and the store itself was packed to bursting point with an endless assortment of Indian pottery, little glass bottles full of different-coloured sand, dream-catchers, carvings and a pyramid of yellow Kodak film boxes. It sold postcards, colour pictures, key rings and sunglasses, home-made jams and jellies, cactus candy, blankets, linens, cups, placeholders, Indian dolls, silver spoons, hats, mugs, cutlery, beads, bags of rock, leather belts, books, baseball caps, socks and a rainbow display of loose beads in a big glass case.

She looked around for the small, mean figure of Bob Herschel, but she couldn't see him. He'd probably snuck out for a coffee down at the information centre, where he was trying his luck with one of the tour guides. Dirty little shit! Ruth thought. He'd made a pass at her too!

She opened the door and darted over to her post at the Indian goods counter by the window. "No sir," she said loudly to the nearest customer she could see. "I'm afraid we don't have that in the back room. But one of our other stores farther down the rim might. I could call them if you like and see."

Her voice sounded normal to her, but the man still stared at her.

"Are you OK, Miss?"

"Sure, sir. Just trying to be helpful is all."

The young woman on the other till came over to her. She was a Havasupai, like Ruth, with an open face and large caring eyes.

"Ruth, where have you been? Bob's been going crazy looking for you."

"What's the panic this time?"

"Oh Ruth, you've been drinking again, haven't you? This is the third day in a row."

"I ran out of pills, Joan. That's all. I just needed a drink just to take the edge off. Why all the big fuss?"

A couple of hikers stared at them. Joan smiled back and they looked away.

"The sheriff's office was on the phone. They were looking for you."

"What?"

"They were on to Bob. That's why he's going crazy. What have you done this time, Ruth?"

"Nothing. I've done nothing. I went home last night, had a few drinks and got up for work. That's it."

"Ruth, this is your friend Joan you're talking to, the one who bailed you out the last time, remember? Now what did you — ? "

"Ruth Weylon!"

A small man with a tight, rat-like face, slick backed hair and a thin moustache over slightly bucked teeth stood on the other side of the counter. The gold name badge over the lapel of his Fred Harvey jacket said, "My name is Bob. How can I help you?"

"Morning, Bob," said Ruth. "I was in the storeroom."

"Don't give me that crap! Just get into my office before you scare any more customers away."

He grabbed her arm and pulled her across the store to the glass door in the far corner. Once inside, he pushed her into a chair and slammed the door shut behind them.

"This is it, Ruth," he hissed. "I had the cops on the phone looking for you. Then you turn up here again two hours late, stinking of booze and give me some cockamamie story about being in the storeroom. Hand in your uniform. You're fired."

"But Bob, I didn't do anything. There's been some mistake. I can straighten it out, honest."

"Not this time. We're overrun with visitors who've come up here to get away from the cities during this Cuban thing and I'm under pressure from the company to keep everything running with the staff I've got. I need someone who turns up on time and does a good job, not a wino bitch who staggers in late every day and breathes booze all over the customers?"

"But Bob, you can't do this! There's just my grandmother and me and I'm the only one earning money. Please, Bob. I'll make it up to you. You've got to give me another chance!"

Bob Herschel looked down on her as if she was something he'd found on the bottom of his shoe.

"There are plenty of other people I could hire a lot cheaper," he spat. "What makes you so fucking special?"

Then, as if in answer to his question, came the screech of tyres and the flashing red lights of an entire fleet of police cars pulling to a stop outside the office window.

Carpenter followed the sheriff towards the store. There were police everywhere, throwing a cordon around the building, clearing away customers. Tourists stood staring at them. A class of schoolchildren stopped open-mouthed. A group of Japanese was taking pictures.

I should have come up here with a just couple of men in an unmarked car, Carpenter thought; this is drawing too much attention.

He ducked his head and walked into the store. The police had already rounded up the staff; a man in a red jacket and three women. Two of the women were Native Americans.

One of them was Ruth.

Her eyes widened when she saw him. She screamed and tried to run. The sheriff grabbed her with both arms and held her.

The man in the red jacket sneered.

"I knew this had to happen to her sooner or later, officer. Can you just get her out of here so I can go about my business?"

Ruth was still screeching. The sheriff was having trouble holding her. "Is there somewhere these gentlemen can talk to Miss Weylon in private, sir?" he asked. "Somewhere quiet?"

"You can use my office," said the man in the red jacket.

"We should get her into the car and away from here now," Carpenter said.

Tony Fischetti loved flying.

He had been crooning *Come Fly With Me!* all the way from Vegas under the clear blue sky. Sinatra travelled like this. It had style.

The little Beechcraft touched down on the airstrip and taxied over towards a red minivan parked by the line of helicopters at the edge of the field. Fischetti opened the cabin door and the four of them climbed out into the sunshine. The air was cold, colder than Vegas. Fischetti felt alive, ready for action. This was going to be fun. The other three men went to the rear of the plane, opened the luggage locker and pulled out three golf bags, with bright plastic hoods over the heads of the clubs and bulging side pockets. The bags were heavy. The men were very careful not to let them drop.

Fischetti peered back along the runway. Beyond the choppers and the other light aircraft stood a larger military plane with a police car next to it and an armed guard. That did not look good.

The door of the red van slid open and a heavy-set man with thinning black hair walked over to him. He wore a red nylon jacket with an embroidered logo that matched the one on the van — "Eagle Helicopter Tours". He seemed worried.

"This is Ed Marino," said Fischetti. "Ed, meet Gus Russo, Moe Spilato and Jimmy Snyder."

"Hi, Tony," he said as they shook hands. Fischetti knew Marino from the casinos.

"We got problems," Ed said. "I tried to call you, but you'd already left. The Feds are here. They landed half an hour ago and went off with the county sheriff and a whole army of cops."

"We need transport," said Fischetti, taking Ed by the arm and leading him back towards the van. "And we need it in a hurry. Something without the name of your fucking company plastered all over it, something we can dump after the hit."

"Hey Tony, I don't want any violence, okay? I got a business to protect."

Fischetti remembered Johnny Rosselli's instructions and the tone of voice he'd used. There was no going back now.

"Just get in the van, Ed, and take me to where I can find a nice discreet set of wheels. We can talk about protecting your business on the way."

They got into the van and shut the doors. Gus, Moe and Jimmy had their golf bags with them.

"I tell you, there's an army of cops up there," Marino said. "They'll be packing a whole heap of guns."

Fischetti reached over and pulled the bright covers off the clubs in one of the bags.

"So are we," he said. "Now get in the van and drive."

Ruth heard Carpenter's voice but not the words. All she heard were his instructions from her nightmare; "Then this is the place. You're on target. What can you see?"

He had come to drag her back and suffer it all again, just as she had known he would. She had planned for this. She had made preparations, mapped escape routes. But now, the one time the pills had run out and she'd had dropped her guard, he had caught her.

Damn! Damn! Damn!

She tried to sip the coffee Joan brought her from the machine. It was too hot. She spilt some on her shirt and tried to wipe it off. The Air Force dog tags fell out through the open neck and hung there on their chain. Joan brought her water and she gulped it down too fast. She felt sick.

Carpenter's words started to make sense.

" . . . only you can help us, Ruth. We need you for a mission. Nobody else can do it but you."

She took a deep breath. If she pinched her leg with her fingernails, the pain gave her something to focus on.

"What about the others . . . Earth, Air and Water?"

"They're all dead, Ruth. Water committed suicide and the other two were murdered. That's why you must come with us now. We can keep you safe. If you stay here, then whoever killed Earth and Air will find you."

It had to be a lie to get her back where he wanted her. The man with Carpenter stared at her with angry eyes.

"Forget it," she said. "I'm not going."

Then the man with Carpenter snapped. He leant forward so that his face was right next to hers and grabbed her uniform shirt, popping the buttons as he hauled her towards him. "You selfish bitch," he spat in her face. "My wife and kids are about to fry down in Florida and all you can say is you're not going!"

Carpenter pulled him back. "Cool it, Sam!" he said. "That's not going to help."

"Selfish bitch!" repeated the man through clenched teeth. But he backed off and stood against the wall opposite the window, still glaring at her while Carpenter continued.

"It's what you signed up for, Ruth. Millions of people will die if you don't help us. It's your duty."

His eyes fell to the dog tags, hanging loose around her neck after Hiscock had ripped her shirt open.

"Don't talk about duty to me," she shouted, pulling the ripped cloth together. "I just wear these to remind me of the pain you put me through the last time and to never *ever* listen to you again. Do you hear me? You'll have to kill me first."

She tore at the dog tags, broke open the chain and threw them at Carpenter. They bounced off his chest and fell to the floor. Joan bent down, picked them up and then, seeing the look in Ruth's eyes, slipped them into her own pocket.

Carpenter turned to the sheriff.

"Could you leave us alone with Miss Weylon for a moment?" he said. "There's some classified information we need to show her."

Fischetti held his favourite automatic under the jacket he had folded on his lap as Marino drove their stolen Ford pick-up to the roadblock near the Kaibab Trail. A pair of State Troopers walked over to them. One raised his hand. Fischetti smiled to him and waved, beckoning him round to his window, which he had rolled down.

"What's all the excitement, officer?"

"I'm afraid you can't go up there, sir."

"That's fine. We're just looking for a place to eat is all. What's the matter? It looks like something out of *Dragnet*."

The officer stood so close to the window that Fischetti could smell his aftershave. He was looking at the golf clubs in the back and at Gus, Moe and Jimmy, sitting up there alongside them.

"Nothing for you to be concerned about, sir. If you just turn the truck around, you'll find a coffee shop back there on your right, down at the main information centre."

"Thanks, officer," said Fischetti, "but we already had a bellyful. Now it's your turn."

The .45 calibre bullet from the silenced automatic, fired upwards through the open window of the pick-up, caught the policeman under the chin and blew off the back of his head. Even before the other cop could register what had happened, Fischetti had brought the Colt up over the dashboard and fired straight thought the windshield, catching him in the chest and spinning him around.

Behind them, Fischetti heard the clatter of weapons being cocked as the boys emptied their golf bags, followed by the single crack of Moe's high-powered rifle. On the other side of the roadblock, tourists scattered, dodging behind bushes and trees, grabbing their loved ones, diving to the ground.

In a few seconds all four men were out of the truck and running towards the gift store, each with a Browning sub-machine gun and a satchel of army surplus grenades.

"Kill them all!" shouted Fischetti. "I don't want any witnesses. Just leave the Indian woman to me!"

There were just the two of them with her in Bob's office; Carpenter and the angry man from the CIA. They had spread out a chart on Bob's desk, along with some papers. Carpenter went through them with her while the other man remained by the wall facing the window, keeping watch.

"And this submarine whose commander thinks we're at war," she said, trying to focus on the chart. "You're telling me there's no way to communicate with it, except by telepathy?"

"That's what we understand," said Carpenter. "In Washington, they've set up some sort of hotline with a Russian Admiral called Shumanin. If nothing can be done to reach the sub and it attacks the blockade, then the Russians wanted us to know that it was an accident and not a premeditated act of war."

"And the scientist in charge of the experiment?"

"His name's Kharkov. Professor — "

"Boris Kharkov of the University of Leningrad," said Ruth. The water was clearing her head now. She was sobering up fast.

"Are you fit to travel?" Hiscock said.

"You mean when can I be moved without throwing up all over your car?"

"You can throw up over whatever or whomever you like, Ruth," said Carpenter, packing the charts and files back into his folder. "But we have to get you back to the facility in Nevada right now. That sub will soon be within torpedo range of the blockade. This is a matter of national security."

"Is that why you brought all those guns?"

She saw Carpenter and Hiscock exchange glances.

"Someone got to Bobby Mann at the asylum early this morning," said Carpenter. "And later on today Ray Mancuso was found dead in the back of a taxi in Vegas. Both were professional hits. That's why we brought all the guns, Ruth. They're to protect you . . . ."

She heard a sharp crack, as if someone had thrown a stone through the window, a kid with a catapult maybe, or a pebble from a car tyre outside. She glanced over at Hiscock. He still sat looking out at the car park with a vacant expression on his face. Behind him on the wall was a splatter of red and grey. Between his eyes was a neat round hole, oozing blood.

Carpenter dived across the desk, grabbed Ruth and pulled her to the floor, covering her body with his.

"They've found us!" he shouted.

"Who?"

"How the hell should I know? All that matters is that we get you out of here alive."

A deafening roar erupted from the front of the building, like a giant chainsaw ripping into wood. Glass shattered. People screamed.

"Jesus, they've got machine guns!"

"Joan," cried Ruth. "I have to save Joan."

"No time. I have to get you out of here."

"I'm not leaving without her!"

"Can you use a gun?"

"What?"

"You had small arms training in the Air Force. Can you shoot a gun?" He reached towards Hiscock's body, unbuttoned the jacket and pulled out a neat German automatic. "I'll look after your friend. Take this, stay low and don't move. I'll come back for you."

She watched as he scuttled towards the door of the office. The machine guns opened up again, tearing through the office door and sending shards of glass skidding off the desk. Then came the 'whump' of an explosion, close by, and the whiz of flying shrapnel.

Ruth's head spun. Who was doing this? Why did they want to kill her so badly? She had to see if Joan was okay.

Ruth's heart pounded as she crawled across the broken glass to the office door and peered into the store. Bob Herschel lay in a pool of blood, staring at the ceiling. Carpenter crouched just beyond him, shielding someone. He moved. Joan was against the film counter, as if she had just sat down for a rest. A wide scarlet smear rose from behind her shattered chest and up the side of the display. Her dead eyes stared across the room at Ruth. Her mouth was open, as if to speak.

"Joan!"

Another explosion rocked the building, bringing down a wall of Indian pottery, jars of sand and glass beads, filling the air with dust. Ruth rolled herself into a ball behind the office wall. As the air cleared, she saw Carpenter's file of papers on the floor by the desk.

"This way!" she screamed back into the store. "There's a back way out!"

As another volley of shots from the machine guns ripped into the building, Ruth grabbed the papers and scuttled next door into the storeroom. Carpenter followed her, his head low. Hidden under the boxes of Indian trinkets and guidebooks lay an old rucksack, packed with spare clothes and supplies, ready to go. Ruth pulled it out and stuffed the gun and the papers inside. Then she reached up for the back door and her escape route.

"Yee – hah!"

Fischetti felt the adrenaline rush he always got from a heavy gunfight and the knowledge that, once again, he was on the winning side. The Browning sub-machine gun in his hands kicked and stuttered like a power hose, sending a spray of bullets into the gift store, punching in windows, splintering doors and tearing whomever was inside to shreds.

A State Trooper ducked out from a doorway and raised a shotgun. Fischetti had him nailed before he could pull the trigger. He heard Moe open up behind him and another man fell. Jimmy threw a grenade and one of the huts where a cop had been hiding dissolved into matchwood.

"I want the woman," screamed Fischetti above the din. "Leave her to me. You can tear this place apart all you want after I've got the woman."

He ran across the narrow lawn and kicked in what was left of the store's front door, heard the ridiculous tinkle of a wind chime and swung the Browning to cover the room.

"I want the woman!"

Then he saw her sitting on the floor with her back against a counter. She looked pretty. Fischetti reached down and stroked her cheek with his fingers. She had a bullet hole in her chest and her uniform was soaked in blood.

Pity, he thought. We could have had a bit of fun, you and me, before I had to whack you. At least Mister Rosselli will be glad I kept it clean.

"I got her!" he shouted. "Let's get out of here!"

The last shots echoed around the gift store. Fischetti stood up, still looking down at the dead woman, wondering . . ..

Next to the hole in her chest was a plastic name badge, covered in blood. Fischetti ripped it from her blouse and rubbed the blood off on her hair. It read, "My name is Joan. How can I help you?"

Oh shit! Fischetti thought. It's not her!

The sound of someone scuffling across a wooden floor reached him from the room beyond the office.

"Hey!" he screamed, "we still got a live one here!"

He reached into his satchel with his left hand, grabbed a grenade and pulled out the pin.

Ruth heard something hard hit the floor and bounce across the wooden planks. She turned and saw a metal ball rolling towards them, hissing smoke as it came. Without stopping to think, she dived through the door of the storeroom onto the narrow path behind the building, Carpenter right behind her. A voice shouted to her left. She heard the crack of a shot and a bullet hissing close by.

Before she had time to get clear, the building behind them exploded in a shower of splinters and broken glass, lifting Ruth, Carpenter and the rucksack off the path and out over the shoulder of the Canyon.

15

Carpenter hardly had time to register his terror at the vast chasm in front of him before the blast of the grenade sent him flying out over the sloping shoulder of the canyon towards the lip. He was airborne! All he registered were whirling trees; a flash of sky, rocks . . . . Then the breath was crushed out of him as he slammed onto the slope, tumbling towards the edge. Scraggy bushes flashed past. He snatched at them and missed, caught one and it was torn from his hand. Ruth screamed at him to hold on. Carpenter rolled faster and faster towards the precipice.

He could not stop.

She grabbed his right hand. For a moment they were sliding together, staring down at the abyss rushing towards them. He *knew* they were going to die. Then his left hand snagged a bush. Her foot bit into the ground. And they stopped.

As the breath whooped in his lungs, Carpenter gently lifted his head. He lay shaking in terror, his legs hanging out into space and his body perched on a solid outcrop of rock. Below him, far distant and faint, he heard the patter of small rocks on the cliff below. In front of him, the empty air of the Grand Canyon stretched limitlessly in all directions.

He closed his eyes to block out the view, gritted his teeth against the fear and tested the bush with his left hand. It held. He felt Ruth move beside him.

"Pull yourself back slowly," she whispered. "We haven't got much time."

Carpenter looked straight up at the sky and pulled with his left arm, grabbed another bush with his right and slid back until his legs reached the rock. Then he shuffled far enough onto the shoulder until he felt safe and sat up.

"Thanks," he said.

Ruth turned onto her knees, looking up at the blazing building and the column of smoke rising. "No time. They'll be after us in a moment. This way."

At the top of the shoulder, silhouetted against the clear blue sky, he saw the round head of a man. Voices reached him.

"She's down there. She's got a guy with her!"

"Get after them!"

Carpenter rolled to his left and shuffled upwards away from the edge, following Ruth into the bushes and heading east along the rim.

"Hold it, lady, or I'll shoot!" yelled the man above them.

Ruth was not stopping, and neither was Carpenter.

"You asked for it, lady!"

The man followed them down the shoulder for a better shot, raised his gun to fire and lost his footing. He stumbled, hit the slope and started to roll.

"Jesus Christ! Help me!"

More men with guns appeared on the skyline. Carpenter saw Ruth scamper towards the shelter of the trees. Behind him the cries of the rolling man grew more and more desperate until they rose to a scream as he reached the edge and fell.

A volley of machine gun fire rattled above them. Bullets whined off the rocks and hissed out over the canyon. Carpenter pumped his legs as hard as he could go. The trees bounced nearer and nearer. A puff of dust spurted beside him. Then he was in the trees and out of sight, running into the deep shade. He kept running, just in case the bullets could reach him through the branches. Then he slowed . . . and stopped.

Where the hell was Ruth?

Ruth ran along the narrow path she had scouted long ago, into the ragged forest that stretched around the bowl of the rocky inlet leading to the Kaibab Trail, reached the trees and fell headlong into the shadows, gasping for breath. She pulled herself to her knees and glanced back to where Carpenter was still struggling through the scrub. She had to lose him if she was ever going to escape. So why had she saved him from going over the edge? Maybe the men with guns would kill him for her?

She took a deep breath to clear her head before the next part of her escape route: the traverse across the sheer rock face at the end of the forest. If she could not focus on the hand and footholds, she would fall and die. She ran on, deeper into the trees. The foliage was denser, the forest darker. It offered her more protection. She stopped, unshipped the rucksack and let it fall to the ground in front of her, undid the ties and pulled open the cover. There were the charts and papers Carpenter had showed her, the two bottles of water she replaced every week, the emergency rations, the waterproof matches and the long-bladed knife. She reached down through all this to the bottom of the rucksack.

There, safe inside its nest of tightly packed clothes, lay a hip flask of Jack Daniel's. Her fingers closed around it, pulled it out and unscrewed the top. The heady scent of liquor bathed her nostrils. She raised the flask to her lips . . . and then threw it spinning into the trees. No! She had to stay sober to survive this. She couldn't let them win again and send her back into hell. She bent down and tore at the rucksack, pulled out a flannel shirt, moccasins and a pair of cotton trousers, and ripped off her Fred Harvey uniform. Her legs had been badly scraped during the tumble outside the gift store.

She was just repacking the rucksack when her fingers hit the hard metal of the gun Carpenter had taken from the dead CIA man. She took it out and turned it in her hand. During her photo-reconnaissance days in the Air Force, everyone had been taught basic small arms drill. Ruth had been a natural. This gun was a German Walther PPK automatic. She let the magazine slide out of the butt onto her palm, checked the number of bullets and pushed it home. Then she pulled the slide back to make sure there was one bullet chambered and ready to go, clicked on the safety catch and pushed the gun into her trouser pocket. She was just taking a long swig of water from one of the bottles to clear her head when she heard the snap of a branch behind her.

"Jesus! . . . That was . . . close!" panted Carpenter as he reached her.

"You stay here until the cops come for you," she said. "I don't want you following me!"

Carpenter was still getting his breath back.

"No way! I have to take you back. This is too important, Ruth. You know what's at stake."

She reached down, pulled out the pistol and aimed it at his thigh.

"If you follow me, I'll shoot you in the leg."

Something heavy thumped to the ground behind Carpenter. The faintest wisp of smoke rose from the scrub between the trees.

"Down!"

The grenade exploded with a sharp crack, throwing a geyser of damp earth into the air, sending a hail of shrapnel screaming through the trees above their heads.

Another crack, closer this time, and the thud of metal tearing white gashes in the tree bark around them.

She couldn't stay. All the men above had to do was to drop a grenade close enough and she'd be torn apart.

Ruth pushed the gun back into her pocket, crouched as low as she dared, and ran.

Fischetti peered down into the trees on the curve of the bowl below the gift store but saw nothing. Unless he went down there, he would never know if he'd killed the woman, injured her, or missed her all together. He couldn't lob down grenades all day; the cops would have reinforcements soon and he'd need to be long gone before they showed up.

He peered down into the trees again.

"Moe, give me that rifle with the scope!"

Moe Spilato handed over the rifle grudgingly. It could have been because he liked his gun, or because he didn't like Fischetti. Fischetti knew that Moe was just itching to elbow him aside and take his job at the Tropicana. You had to watch your back twenty-four hours a day.

Fischetti raised the rifle and squinted into the telescopic sight. There, in the cross hairs between the trees, he saw movement.

"Quick," he said passing the gun back. "She's in the forest. Pick her off quick before the cops get here!"

Moe Spilato raised the rifle in one fluid motion and aimed. Fischetti had to hand it to him. He was good with guns. The rifle cracked and kicked in Moe's hands.

"Did you get her?"

"I don't think so. She's running in the trees. It's hard to get a bead on her."

"Shit!" swore Fischetti, turning back to the truck. "Now that broad's on the loose in the canyon. The Fed's will find her and Mister Rosselli will have my balls for breakfast."

"You got a problem, Tony."

"*We* got a problem, Moe! If I go down, then I'm sure as hell not going down on my own. I need ideas. You got any?"

"You have to get down into the canyon. Ed's got a chopper company. He and his partner ferry tourists around the canyon all the time. You could lean on him a little. Get him to fly us down there while it's still light."

The distant wail of sirens reached them over the crackling of the burning store.

"And how are we going to do that with the whole place swarming with Feds? They'll be out there looking for her too."

"Only if they think she's alive. Back there in the gift store there's another Indian broad that got stiffed as we came in. I could mess her up a little, make it look like—"

"That's okay," Fischetti said. "I'll do that myself."

Ruth arrived at the edge of the trees, where her escape trail finished and the rock face began, reached out with her fingers for the first hand-hold and started to climb. Below her, the cliff plummeted five hundred feet into the bowl of the Kaibab Trail. One slip and she'd end up like the man who'd tried to chase her back at the gift store, crushed and broken on the rocks below.

Her toes found the foothold.

"Where the hell are you going?" Carpenter shouted, staring down at the chasm and the rocks far, far below.

"Away from you. Away from all of them. You want to follow me? Then start climbing!"

"Ruth. You can't."

Her left hand found the hold and gripped it. She moved her weight from the right foot to the left, shifted across to the new position and moved again. If only she hadn't had that booze! This was an easy climb when her head was clear!

She took a deep breath through her nose, held it and let it all out through her mouth in a rush. For a moment her head cleared and she moved again, inching across the cliff face to the east, under the overhang and out of sight of the rim.

They'd never catch her now.

She was home and . . . .

Her foot slipped! She gasped as all her weight came onto her fingers and arms. The muscles in her shoulders screamed. Her legs swung in empty space. Beneath her, she heard a stone fall, bouncing and rattling on the rocks, far below.

She scrabbled desperately with her left foot, praying that the thin skin of the moccasins would help her find the holds on the rock face.

It did! There was the left one . . . and the right. She took her weight very slowly on her legs, rested for a moment to let herself calm down. When her breathing was back to normal and she felt strong enough, she reached out again for the next hand-hold, crabbing her way closer to the Kaibab Trail.

Carpenter watched Ruth edge her way around the rock face and disappear. Once she hit that trail and got a good start on him, he might never find her. She was in her element down in the canyon, while he was a plodding beginner.

He followed the line of her climb around the rock face and looked down into the bowl of the cliff. His head spun. His body remembered the pain of the air crash and he began to shake. If he started to climb and fell, he would die. If he started to climb and froze out of fear, he would die. If he stayed where he was and did nothing, so that the submarine got through and World War III broke out, then he would die, and so would millions of other people. Carpenter did the math. He was a brilliant mathematician. He had to start climbing.

He tried to relax and put things into perspective. After all, he told himself, if that was only a five-inch drop with a wooden floor under your feet, you'd do it, wouldn't you? So make yourself believe it's only five inches and the floor *is* there, and not five hundred feet down onto rock! Mind over matter!

He took a deep breath to steady his nerve, put out his left hand and found the hold. Then he put out his left foot, moved his weight and swung himself out into space.

THURSDAY, 25 OCTOBER
LANGLEY, VIRGINIA
3.04 PM LOCAL TIME
2004 GMT

The phone on the CIA Deputy Director's desk rang.

"Is that Mister Birkett?"

"Speaking. Who's this?"

"My name's Ramster, sir. I'm sorry to call you like this but Doctor Hiscock told me before he left the airfield that if anything was to happen, I should contact you."

"And who are you exactly, Mister Ramster?"

"I'm the CIA pilot who took Doctor Hiscock and that NSA fellow out to the canyon, sir. I have the Arizona State Police here at the airport and they tell me there's been a major incident over at the rim. It seems there was a big shoot-out at one of the gift stores an hour or so back. Doctor Hiscock and almost a dozen police were killed and that NSA fellow is missing, presumed dead. The place was burned to the ground. I can see the smoke from here. It was a massacre, sir. I'm sorry."

"And the woman Doctor Hiscock was looking for? Ruth Weylon? What about her?"

"The fire service got the blaze under control a while ago and found a couple of bodies in the store. One of them was a woman, a Native American. But she'd been badly shot up and burned, so they couldn't tell who she was at first. They found a pair of dog tags on her though. Tell me, Mister Birkett. Had Ruth Weylon ever been in the military?"

"Air Force, yes."

"Then I'm sorry, sir. But it looks like she's dead."

Don Birkett pressed the receiver to his forehead and closed his eyes.

"Mister Birkett, are you still there?"

"I am. Do they know who did this?"

"The FBI's on it now. They've sealed off the crime scene and are looking at tyre-marks and shell casings. There's also a body they haven't managed to reach yet, down in the canyon."

"Man or woman?"

"It looks like a man. But it's not a cop or anyone who worked at the store, so it could be your NSA guy. The Park Service says it's too close to the cliff to lift out with a chopper, so they'll have to run a line to it or hike down on foot. That'll take a while."

"Call my office when you have any more news. I'll be out there to you as soon as I can."

"Yes sir. I'm sorry it had to end this way."

"So am I," said Birkett, and hung up. Then he dialled again.

"Admiral Cursey? Don Birkett here. I'm afraid the soft option of using our own telepath to communicate with the Soviet submarine has fallen through. I need an immediate meeting with you to discuss a strategic naval approach, using force. Yes. Anywhere you say. Thank you. I'll be right over."

He put down the phone and stared at the sweeping second hand of the clock on the far wall. God help us! he thought. It's all up to the Russians now.

16

"In any good game of chess," said Cherlenko, "even one as vast and complicated as we are playing now, it is wise to remind ourselves of the basic rules. What are the choices of move? What are the relative values of the pieces on the board? It is also valuable to consider the motivation of our opponent. If we know what drives them, if we study their past behaviour in times of crisis, then we are more likely to predict their moves in the future. Is this not so?"

"I do not see how the rules of chess apply here," said Kharkov. "You said it yourself when we started this morning: 'Comrades. What we have here is a simple manhunt. Nothing more and nothing less.' Those were your exact words. Please correct me if I'm wrong."

They were in the second floor briefing room of the KGB headquarters in the Bolshoy Dom. Cherlenko stood by the window, gazing out over the Neva and the darkened city. Kharkov sat slumped in a chair at the table. Captain Slavin was examining the maps of the search. The other officers of the KGB and GRU were out in the city, still looking for Tatyana Rospin.

Cherlenko turned and smiled at Kharkov across the table. If the stakes had not been so high and the deadline so tight, this might have been an amusing battle of wits with a worthy opponent. But there was no time to be sentimental, not when his career and the fate of the World depended on the outcome.

He reached down to his briefcase, pulled out ten *zapistas* and laid them on the table, picked out four and put the other six back in his case. Then he laid out the four files side by side. One was considerably thicker than the other three.

"You know Tatyana Rospin better than any person alive," he said, leafing through her file. "Tell me what motivates her. Why did she do what she did?"

"I already told you, Comrade General. She is a beautiful, gifted and highly strung young woman with her own mind, a woman who espouses great causes and great passions. The State trained her to project her consciousness beyond her body and travel instantly to any point on the globe. As an unfortunate by-product of this training, from the State's point of view, she also has the ability to roam at will *within* this great Soviet Union of ours, to pass through any fence or barrier, and to see things those in power do not wish ordinary citizens to see."

"What sort of things?" challenged Captain Slavin, looking up from her maps.

Kharkov snorted. "Imagine a young and impressionable mind looking down into the innermost workings of our labour camps in Siberia, where innocent people are sent to rot for years on the slightest pretext. Think of her roaming the wards of our cancer hospitals or our mental asylums where people are incarcerated until they contract an incurable disease or go insane for merely questioning the State. Picture her watching the germ warfare and poison gas experiments where innocent men and women are used as live subjects to study the effects of deadly toxins on human flesh. Consider a sensitive and gifted young mind being flooded with this vast amount of evil. Imagine all that, Comrade Slavin, and I am sure you will find it easy to see her motivation."

Cherlenko closed Tatyana Rospin's *zapista*.

"Did you know this might happen, Professor?"

"I suspected she was emotionally disturbed by what she saw, but, then again, we were exploring uncharted territory. When I voiced my concern about Tatyana to my masters in the Navy and the KGB, they would not allow me to relax the programme and reduce the stress placed on her. They told me we were engaged in a 'Mind Race' with the West every bit as important as the Arms Race or the Space Race. They insisted that I win this new race for the Soviet Union, so that was what I did."

Cherlenko opened the other three folders.

"You've told me what she hates, Professor. Now tell me: whom does she love?"

"She loves her brother. They have been inseparable since birth and it was difficult for her to see him sent away on that submarine. She feels what he feels, knows what he knows and hates what he hates. I know she loves him, Comrade General, but then . . . ."

"But what?"

Kharkov smiled.

"But then you cannot use him as a hostage against her, now can you? He is thousands of miles away beneath the sea. If you had this lover of hers, this Baybarin, you might be able to force her to give herself up to you. But he is hidden from you also."

Cherlenko nodded and closed the Max Rospin's *zapista*. Then he looked down at the two remaining files and the photographs on the inside cover of each one, those of Baybarin and Kharkov himself.

"I do not think she would give herself up for Baybarin, or for any of her other friends whose files I have with me," he said, closing that *zapista*. "Her cause is too great and the stakes are too high. I think the clever Miss Rospin just used Baybarin as a key to unlock the authentication codes for Petrachkov's Apex orders. Now that she has what she wants from his mind, she may have no further use for him."

He closed that *zapista* too.

"No, Comrade Professor, I think the person Tatyana Rospin loves most in this world is sitting right here with me in the room. I think the best hostage I have against Miss Rospin is you."

Kharkov shrugged. "I am just her mentor, Comrade General. Even as a child, she loved my wife, her stepmother, more than me. Do not forget that my wife and I were both arrested and taken from her to the Gulag for the most formative years of her life. I was the only one who returned, and I am sure Tatyana resents me for it. No, she does not love me, any more than you would love the men who trained you at the KGB."

"You do yourself a disservice, Comrade Professor. In my own experience, great teachers of great ideas pass on far more than knowledge to their students. They pass respect, moral values and even affection. Your moral values are strong. You were jailed for them once. I detect a similar set of values in your stepdaughter."

"I had gone astray. I allowed the loftiness of my academic position and the grand theories discussed around me go to my head. Luckily, this illness was detected by my superiors, who assigned me for appropriate treatment. Now I am cured and able to perform my duties to the State unhindered by my previous wrong thinking. All that is in the past."

Cherlenko ran his fingers down the outside of Kharkov's *zapista* until he came to a bookmark; then he opened it at that page.

"You and your wife were relocated to Siberia, Comrade, for promoting subversive ideas amongst your students and patients here in Leningrad after the Great Patriotic War. She was sent to work in an experimental facility, where she died of a mysterious illness. You were sent to a State Mental Hospital, from which you were released after the death of Comrade Stalin. That is correct, is it not?"

"It is. Does your file state which 'mysterious illness' my wife died from, and how?"

"It does, Comrade Professor," said Cherlenko, closing the file. "Tell me, what became of your stepchildren, the Rospin twins, during this time?"

"The State provided for them, Comrade General," said Kharkov, twisting the wedding band on his left hand. "They were placed in an orphanage until I returned."

"Indeed. Comrade Slavin asked you to imagine Tatyana's motivation at the beginning of our discussion, Professor. I can also imagine *your* motivation upon your return from Siberia, having been robbed not only of your wife but also the love of your stepchildren for all that time."

"I do not see what you mean, Comrade General. I told you that I went astray and was cured. What other feelings could I possibly have but gratitude to the State, particularly for meeting the expense of both my treatment and the upkeep of my children? My wife died from an unfortunate illness. That was fate. I have no ill feelings towards the State for that? How could I? It was almost ten years ago and out of their hands."

Cherlenko stared at Kharkov, remembering what he had read in the man's *zapista*.

"I am still not convinced, Professor. Furthermore, I find myself faced with two possible scenarios regarding your influence on Tatyana Rospin."

"Which are?"

"Either she did what she did out of some misguided love for you, or you *directly* instructed her to carry out the crimes she has committed. In any case, your only use to me now is as a hostage against her safe return. You will be executed, or better yet, returned to your mental hospital in Siberia immediately after she is found."

"You cannot use me against her. I'd kill myself first!"

It was Cherlenko's turn to smile. "So, Professor, for the first time I see you as an emotional man. That is refreshing. As to your suggestion of suicide, I would remind you that I still have thousands of women awaiting questioning out there in hospitals, jails and army barracks. If you do not co-operate willingly, I will execute those who do not match Tatyana's description as potential enemies of the State—a hundred at a time, every hour, on the hour."

"Even you would not be allowed to slaughter so many innocent citizens, just to reach one person."

"You forget what Comrade Khrushchev himself told us. I have unlimited power here in Leningrad. No expense, resources or even civilian safety are to be spared. I would not simply be allowed to do it, I would be *ordered* to do it if there was even the slightest chance it would achieve my aim."

Cherlenko stared down at Kharkov. For the second time in their brief but interesting battle of wits, he was certain that he had won.

"You are right," said Kharkov, shaking his head. "What do you want me to do?"

THURSDAY, 25 OCTOBER
WASHINGTON.
4.00 P.M. LOCAL TIME
2100 GMT

A chart of the north-west Atlantic filled an entire wall of the naval operations centre at the Pentagon. The room had been emptied of staff for this special briefing and the only other person present with Don Birkett was Admiral Cursey of the US Atlantic Fleet.

On the chart, a blue line stretched from the edge of the ice field in the Greenland Basin, through the Denmark Strait and past the Grand Banks of Newfoundland to the Bermuda Rise and on into the Caribbean.

"That course represents the fastest route from the sighting of Petrachkov's K-6 by our aircraft off Greenland to Cuban waters," explained Cursey. "Of course it's not the only route, but it's the one that will get him there in the shortest time."

"And these red dots?" asked Birkett, pointing to the clusters of symbols off Greenland, in the Mid-Atlantic and around the approaches to the American coast.

"Those are top-secret. They represent the SOSUS or 'SOund SUrveillance System', chains of sensitive microphones, hundreds of miles long and placed on the seabed to pick up the noise of enemy subs, or indeed any ship, to warn us of their approach. Like I said, SOSUS is top-secret. The Russians don't know we have it, nor should they. If they did, they would modify their subs to make them quieter and more difficult to detect."

"So we should be able to listen in on Petrachkov's submarine as it passes those SOSUS arrays?"

"We should, and we will," said Cursey. "The problem is, we may not know what we're listening to. SOSUS is new. The first array was installed off Newfoundland only three years ago and we don't yet have a full library of sounds in our computers to identify each source of noise. We might detect a sound and not be able to tell if it's a surface ship or a sub. Or, we may know it's a sub but, unless we have its sound signature in the computer, we won't know whose sub it is."

"It's not very encouraging. I'd hoped we had better capabilities than this."

"Sorry to depress you, Mister Birkett. The Atlantic's a big ocean, with a lot of water to hide in, but don't let it get you down. Knowing where Petrachkov started from and where he's going to helps us a lot, and we did get a noise signature from a nuclear sub in the Denmark Strait a while ago. We have that recorded sound on file and should be able to follow it if he comes near any of our SOSUS arrays. Don't forget we also have a whole arsenal of conventional anti-submarine detection gear at our disposal. We can drop floating hydrophones into the water from aircraft and we can use both passive sonar, which just listens for noise, and active sonar, which sends out that distinctive 'ping' you hear in war movies, both of which we have mounted on all the warships making up the blockade around Cuba. So that's a whole lot of listening power."

"And if they find Petrachkov's sub? What then?"

"Our warships have instructions to order him to stop and surface."

"I beg your pardon," said Birkett. "Are you seriously suggesting that they politely ask a Soviet captain who thinks he's on a war footing, commanding a fully armed nuclear sub, to pull over as if they were traffic cops?"

Cursey laughed. "Yeah, but not quite. Each of the ships in the blockade, and those patrolling here around the Grand Banks and Bermuda, has been supplied with a message from Admiral Shumanin in Leningrad. The message is to Captain Petrachkov himself and can be broadcast through the water as simple sound waves that Petrachkov's passive sonar can pick up. It contains personal information only he would recognise, along with other information that would be known only to his crew. It does not ask him to surrender his ship. It simply asks him to surface and, if he can, to make radio contact."

"And if he doesn't?"

"I understand that you've already brought this matter to the personal attention of the President, Mister Birkett. If Captain Petrachkov does not, as you put it, 'pull over', then orders will be issued to engage and sink his submarine, as discreetly as possible."

THURSDAY, 25 OCTOBER
GRAND CANYON SOUTH RIM AIRPORT
1.55 P.M. MOUNTAIN STANDARD TIME
2055 GMT

Matt Hooper pulled the fuel line out of the new Bell 204 'Huey' helicopter and looked along the canyon rim to where a plume of smoke rose into the afternoon sky. It looked as if it might be coming from one of the hotels or viewing points down along the rim, or even as far east as the Kaibab Trail. If he didn't get any customers in the next half hour or so, he might take a drive down there and have a look, just to put his mind at rest. At least it would make a welcome change from waiting around the office beside the hanger, fighting his endless battles with the IRS, the bank and his ex-wife's lawyers.

Ex-wives were a problem for Hooper. He'd never been able to adjust to normal living since he had come back from the war in Korea. They'd trained the human feelings out of him. How can you stroke your wife's cheek and caress the most intimate parts of her body with the same hands you used to ram a bayonet into another man's guts? It hardened you inside. It cut you off. It made you wake in the middle of the night yelling in terror, or lash out at people who tried to touch you when you didn't expect it.

You just weren't the same any more.

Ruth had understood. She'd known. But the problem with her was that she'd known too much. She had a way of seeing right into his soul, and this he found deeply uncomfortable. After all, a man has to have his places to hide, his little escapes from reality. But she'd wanted to see the truth, the whole truth and nothing but the truth, all the time.

Which was perhaps, why he'd given *her* greatest secret away: to show her how it felt. She wouldn't give him any peace after that. He had broken her deepest trust and she never opened herself to him again.

So finally, in frustration at not being able to reach her as he once had, he'd decided the easiest thing was to walk away. She'd taken it calmly. The papers had gone through. The divorce was clean and painless. For a while, that worked for Hooper. His second wife Beth accepted his silences. She was happy to be apart sometimes, if that was what he wanted. And when he came back to her, she was always glad to see him. They had three kids together, and they were always happy to see him too.

But for Hooper something was still missing, and that missing something was Ruth. She had been his first love and part of his soul was still with her. Beth picked up on it. They had spats, fights, stuff that Hooper could do without. This time it was Beth who left. She took the kids, hooked up with a teacher in Phoenix and stung Hooper for the alimony.

At least he was free to be as private as he chose. Free to do whatever he wanted. But what was that?

Something about the canyon still held Hooper. He didn't know why. He didn't know if it was the place, which was breathtakingly beautiful in itself, or the memories of his first wife and the love they'd shared before it had all gone wrong.

I should get away, he told himself. I should sell my share in the business and go down to one of those flying schools in Florida where they teach pilots to fly choppers in three weeks. It'd be good down there, lots of sun and girls in bikinis. I could escape down there. But from what?

His eyes went back to the rising column of smoke.

What if that *was* her? I could just drop in, say I was passing and—

Looking up, he saw his business partner Ed Marino draw up in the company van with three other men.

"Matt!" Ed shouted. "Are you booked up? There's an emergency out on the rim and these guys from the FBI need a chopper to do a missing persons search. They'll make it worth our while if you can take them up right away."

Hooper locked off the fuel line and walked across the pad towards the van.

"Sure, Ed," he said, eyeing the guys in the van. "I can take all four of you."

The thickset guy with the broken nose in the front beside Ed seemed to be the agent in charge.

"That's great," he said. "On behalf of the Bureau, can I just say how much we appreciate it. What's your usual fee?"

"A hundred dollars for the first hour and eighty after that."

The man was already pulling notes off a thick billfold.

"Here's a thousand," he said. "There may be an element of risk."

Matt had been getting bored with milk runs for tourists anyway. "No problem," he said "Mister . . ?"

"The name's Tony," said the man. "I work out of Vegas."

Pawns Attack Queen

TIME TO EVENT

01:01:55

DAYS : HRS : MINS

17

Ruth jogged around the steep S-bends of the Kaibab Trail, heading down. The path was difficult, deeply grooved from the feet of hikers and the hooves of mules, stepped with high wooden boards to stop it washing away in the flash floods. She could not afford a fall. The drop over the edge was at least fifty feet to the next curve in the path below, with no handrails to stop her.

She was getting into her stride. Three steps forward and a drop over the board, step, step, step, drop! Step, step, step, drop! Down the zigzag trail, into the canyon and safety.

Carpenter was nowhere in sight, slowed or stopped altogether by his fear of the rock traverse. He had no water or supplies. The heat of the canyon was dangerous, even this late in the year. Experienced hikers still died of thirst if they had no water, and Carpenter did not look like an experienced hiker. If she kept ahead all the way to the river, there would be no way he or anyone else could catch her.

The sun blazed down, but she welcomed it. Heat would help her sweat the last of the alcohol out of her system. She reached back to her pack, slid out a water bottle and took a swig. The only problem with being sober was that the nightmares would come back. But what choice did she have? Staying drunk would have meant getting caught, and that was the biggest threat. You were right to throw the whiskey flask away Ruth, she told herself. Stay sober and survive.

She stopped at a turn and looked back at the rim. The smoke was thinning above the smouldering ruin of the gift store. She thought of Joan, who had always been like a sister to her, who had laughed at Granny Moon's jokes and known how to deal with Bob when he made advances to them in the store. Joan, her friend, gone.

Should she go back now? Should she have waited until the cops came and took her into protective custody? Carpenter had shown her the mission. It was 'a matter of national security' he'd said.

Yeah, right! She'd heard that one before . . . .

The Kaibab Trail levelled off on the red rock of "Ooh Aah Point", the first stopping-off place for hikers descending into the canyon. Properly known as Cedar Ridge, it was a high plateau with a rest room, a hitching rail for mules, and spectacular views of the green shoulders of the inner canyon. The yellow and white earths of the upper trail gave way to brick red dust. A cool wind blew across the plateau, bringing peace. Ruth took another long drink of water and ate a packet of peanuts from her rucksack to keep her salt levels up and stop her muscles cramping. Then she jogged out along the ridge to Skeleton Point and down the steep trail towards Natural Arch and the gorge of the Colorado. The heat rose. The sheer red cliffs fell away into shadow as she descended into the darkness below.

She had seen darkness on that last mission too . . . .

They told her the target was a laboratory in Siberia, a secret installation in the middle of a remote forest, surrounded by minefields and electric fences. They told her it was a matter of national security to know what was going on there. They showed her photographs from a U2 spy plane to get her started. They said it would be easy . . . .

But she came back covered in sweat, shaking and sobbing in wave after wave of tears that would not stop. The people in the laboratory had been experimenting on live human beings, without the use of anaesthetic! She had come back to the room where Carpenter had been sitting calmly, writing everything she had said in a neat little notebook on his knee. She had come back scarred, her life in pieces, and nightmares that could only be deadened by pills or alcohol.

That was why Fiona, the sensitive girl they had codenamed 'Water' had hanged herself, why Bobby Mann had gone insane, why

Ray had taken to gambling and she herself had tried to lose herself in the bottle. "Earth", "Air", "Fire" and "Water"; the four subjects of Carpenter's "Project Element", four human beings destroyed or twisted out of shape for the sake of "national security".

A mule train passed her, heading up from the Phantom Ranch with its load of laughing tourists and a sunburned cowboy in the lead. She moved into the rock face to let it pass as she was supposed to. Once they reached the rim, in an hour or two, the police would question them, along with all the other hikers she'd passed on the way down. They would recall seeing her but it wouldn't matter. Not once she'd reached the river.

The trail curved westwards below Skeleton Point. The ground flattened out onto a scrubby shoulder where the Tonto Trail joined the Kaibab. She saw prickly pear cacti, tumbleweed, scrub and a black wooden hut around a simple pit toilet. Beyond it, the trail curved past a piece of flat ground and over the final shoulder of the canyon, heading down to the Colorado. Ruth stopped, took another drink and looked up at the sky. It must have been two hours at least since she had started her descent.

The sun dropped lower and lower along the rim. In an hour or so the bottom of the canyon would be in shadow, bringing an early darkness to the river. It would take them hours to mobilise a search party and come after her, and all the time her head got clearer as she drank more water and sweated the alcohol out of her blood. She slipped the water bottle back into her pack and tightened the straps on her shoulders. Soon she'd be safe.

She had just started to run again when the first sounds of the helicopter reached her.

18

Hooper sat in the pilot's seat with Fischetti on his left. Ed Marino and the other two FBI agents, Moe and Jimmy, were in the back where the sightseers normally sat. They all wore padded headsets against the din of the turbines and the rotors, with little microphones attached so that Hooper could do his 'tour guide' routine when ferrying sightseers around the canyon.

He had been tempted to ask if they wanted the 'Standard' or the 'Deluxe' tour package, but somehow he didn't think Fischetti had a sense of humour. He looked a very hard man, especially with that broken nose and those broad shoulders. He was also packing a gun, as were the other two agents in the back.

"Just take us east up the canyon rim. Then follow the Kaibab Trail down to the river," shouted Ed. "Matt and I go back all the way to Korea, Mister Fischetti. He flew choppers there, didn't you, Matt?"

"War veteran, huh?" said Fischetti.

"That's right," Matt said. "Were you ever in the Army, Tony?"

"I volunteered, but I had a bad lung. So I joined the FBI instead."

"Oh? I thought their medical tests were even tougher?"

"That was later, but I still saw a lot of action." Fischetti smiled. It was the sort of cruel smirk that told Hooper he and Ed were really going to have to earn their thousand dollars.

As they gained altitude, Hooper saw the north rim cliffs and the desert way beyond, shimmering in the distance. Then the canyon unfolded beneath them in precipices, valleys and mountains of rust-red rock. The rotor blades chopped the air as Matt banked east and the helicopter shot out over the south rim and the spectacular fall off to the canyon floor, five thousand feet to the Colorado River.

"Wow!" shouted Jimmy and Moe behind him. "Ain't that somethin'?" They were right. Even though Hooper had made that manoeuvre a thousand times, he still felt the tingle of excitement as he took the Huey out over the edge. Behind them, the sun sank farther towards the horizon, casting deep shadows in the canyon, which rose slowly over the cliffs and buttresses like the rising of a dark tide. Hooper wondered if they would be able to find whomever Fischetti was looking for before the light went. Beneath them, the scrub and sandstone of the upper shoulder, the souvenir stores, hotels and restaurants slipped by to the right. Ahead of them, a fading column of smoke rose from the head of the Kaibab Trail. At its base the blue and red lights of a dozen patrol cars, ambulances and fire department vehicles winked and glittered.

"Jesus H. Christ, it looks like a bomb hit it!"

"You got that right," said Fischetti. "There was a whole gang of them, punks with guns looking for an easy mark. They shot up the staff, cleaned out the cash register and torched the place. The sooner we catch them, the better."

"I know someone who works there!" said Matt. "Can I radio to see if she's okay?"

"She'll be fine," said Fischetti. "Right now we've got to get the punks that did this."

"You mean they went down into the canyon?"

"Just follow the trail and do exactly what we say. It'll be a lot safer that way."

Hooper saw Fischetti unbutton his jacket and reach inside with his right hand. He was checking his gun, a big .45 calibre government model. At least that fitted. All FBI and military men carried guns like that. He'd had one himself in Korea.

But he was still worried sick about Ruth.

He banked the Huey over to port and followed the zigzag of the Kaibab Trail down along the red rock of Cedar Ridge to 'Ooh Ah Point'. Hikers looked up and waved. In the back of the chopper, Hooper saw Moe scanning them with binoculars. He swung the helicopter over the shoulder of the ridge, correcting for the wind sheer, and dropped down over the deep red cliffs on the other side down towards Cremation Creek. On the trail below, a mule train crawled its way up from Phantom Ranch.

"Pity we can't stop and ask them if they've seen anything," shouted Hooper.

"Yeah," said Fischetti. "Real pity."

"What's that?"

Farther on down the Kaibab, just before it levelled out onto the flat ground at the Tonto Trail, a man was waving at them, crossing his arms above his head. He was tall and blond and looked in a bad way. His shirt was dark with sweat.

"Shall we get closer?" asked Hooper.

"Don't worry about it," Fischetti said. "He's one of our guys. I told him to wave to us if he saw anything."

"Don't you want to pick him up? If he's got no water, that's a dangerous place to be."

"Just follow the trail on down. We can pick him up on the way back."

Ruth heard the faint thud, thud, thud of the helicopter and looked up to see which direction it was coming from. Echoes were deceptive in the canyon. Down at the river the cliffs blocked the sound of choppers so well that you'd never know one was coming until, with a whine of turbines and the thud of rotors, it suddenly appeared around a bend.

She looked for a place to hide. If this thing with the submarine was as important as they said, then Carpenter would spare no expense to get her back, and choppers were freely available for hire up on the rim. She started to run towards the shelter of the pit toilet, tightening the straps on her rucksack as she ran down the trail and off to the left over the low scrub.

The sound of the helicopter changed. She heard the whine of its turbine above the rotor chop. That meant it was coming down the Kaibab Trail on the far side of The Tipoff and that it was close. She had only twenty yards to go now. The chopper could sweep around the bluff any second. She glanced back to see . . . .

Her foot twisted underneath her, the scrub leapt at her face and she sprawled in the dirt, winded and helpless, as the helicopter burst around the bluff.

"There!" shouted Fischetti. "Over by that shack!" He pulled out the big Colt automatic and pointed to the pit toilet on the Tonto Trail.

Hooper peered through his sunglasses at the figure sprawled in the dirt, a woman with a rucksack, a woman with long black hair, an Indian woman. There was something familiar about her. But they were still too far off to tell.

Ruth pulled herself to her knees, in full view of the chopper. She heard its engine noise change as it swooped round behind her and slowed to a hover. They'd seen her all right. Now all they had to do was land and bring her in. They'd have guns and there was nowhere to run.

She looked up and saw the red fuselage of the machine, the words 'Eagle Helicopter Tours' and Matt Hooper staring out at her.

Matt, of course! He would have heard she was in trouble and come to get her before the cops could raise a search party. He'd have known she'd run down here, known where to find her.

She got up, raised her hands in mock surrender and started to walk to the hovering helicopter. The downdraft of the rotors whipped at the scrub, raising a cloud of dust, making it difficult to see. She lowered one hand across her face to shield her eyes. Something felt wrong.

Looking up again, she saw that Matt wasn't the only person in the chopper. The rear door slid back. She glimpsed Ed Marino and a thin man with black hair. The man raised his arm to point at her.

Something wasn't right.

She blinked again.

She was staring down the barrel of a gun.

"Wait until we're down . . ." screamed Matt into his headset. A storm of wind and noise filled the cabin as the rear door slid back, bursting on Matt like a wave. He twisted in his seat just in time to see Jimmy Snyder take aim.

"Noooo!"

Ruth threw herself to the ground, as a bullet whizzed above her head. The chopper whirled out of control, spinning on its axis like a child's toy.

She pulled herself to her feet, darted behind the pit toilet and ripped open her rucksack, scrabbling for the gun.

"What the fuck are you doing?" Fischetti screamed. "We could have nailed her right there!"

"Nobody said anything about killing anyone!" shouted Hooper. He was out of his mind with anger at Ed for talking him into bringing these guys along. They were no more FBI than he was! He should have known that by Fischetti's remark about his bad lung. These guys were organised crime. They had it written all over them.

"What do you think I paid you a thousand bucks for, Mister fuckin' War Hero?" screamed Fischetti above the din of the rotors. "To take us on a fuckin' picnic in the woods?" He pushed the gun barrel up under Hooper's ear. Hooper steadied the Huey, coming to a hover at around a hundred feet and pointing away from the pit toilet.

"You can't kill her!" he shouted. "You can't!"

"And why the hell not?"

"Because she's my ex-wife. That's Ruth Weylon down there!"

"I don't give a fuck if she's your mother. You circle around that shack and hold steady until my boys have picked her off or you'll find your brains plastered all over this cockpit!"

"Do that and your guts will join them," shouted Hooper. "You got wings, Tony? Huh? Can you fly? Just pull that trigger and let's find out?"

Fischetti lowered the gun and rammed it into Hooper's ribs. The madness in his eyes faded.

"Okay," he said. "Just set us down on that clear patch of ground over there and we'll work something out. Jimmy and Moe, you go and bring in the woman, nice and gentle like, with no rough stuff. Mister War Hero, you stay in the chopper with Ed and me."

From the shelter of the pit toilet, Ruth saw the helicopter settle beyond the Kaibab Trail and two men get out. The engine was still running. They'd want to keep it that way for a fast takeoff if things went wrong, or if an armed Park Ranger showed up. The two men separated and started to walk around the pit toilet from different directions. Did they know she was armed? Matt couldn't tell them. She'd never owned a gun before.

Matt Hooper! Why had he done this to her? Why had he sold her out? She pushed back the safety catch on the Walther and waited. The two men were coming for her with their guns still holstered, nice and confident. They knew they had a helicopter right behind them with its engine running. They thought they had a frightened woman with nowhere to run. There were two of them and one of her. They weren't even being smart.

Jimmy Snyder was on a high. Today had been full of firsts for him: his first big shoot-out with the cops and his first ride in a helicopter. It didn't get any better than this! He was still excited from the whirling, crazy-making riot of moving bodies, crashing guns and falling cops up at the gift store. This was major league action, not slitting some schmuck's throat in a dark alley off the Strip because he wouldn't hand over his wallet, or beating some old fart to a pulp because he woke up at the wrong moment when Jimmy was robbing his house.

This was big time, with big people, people who could get him places. Maybe he'd be up there with Tony one day, or even Mister Rosselli himself. Now, that *would* be something!

He walked away from the chopper and around the shack to the left, keeping a careful eye out in case the broad tried to make a run for it. Jimmy worked out at the gym at the Tropicana, so if she did run, she'd get caught. No doubt about it. He looked to his right, where Moe was walking round from the other side. They had her. It was just a matter of grabbing her as quickly and cleanly as possible, so the schmuck in the chopper would fly them back. They could always bump her off when they got back on the ground, and him along with her.

"Come on, lady!" he shouted towards the shack. "That shot was just a mistake. You come with us now and you won't get hurt. Okay? Nice and easy now. That's it!"

She peered around the corner of the shack, about ten yards away. He looked to his right and saw Moe start to hurry now that her full attention was on Jimmy. Good thinking. He'd keep her talking and Moe would grab her. It would only take a moment.

The broad had long black hair and the darkest eyes Jimmy had ever seen, like a cartoon princess out of a Disney movie.

"That's it, lady, you can—"

He heard the crack of a shot at exactly the same time as something thumped him in the chest, real hard. Then he was lying on his back looking up at the sky. It was getting dark, a lot darker than it had been a second ago. He was having trouble breathing. He tasted blood in his mouth, a lot of it! He reached up to his chest to see where he'd been hit and his hand came up red.

The darkness closed in.

Moe Spilato heard the shot on the other side of the shack and thought Jimmy had loosed one off at the broad. How would they ever get back out of here if that chopper pilot's wife got whacked? he wondered. They'd have to fucking walk, that's how!

He drew his weapon, ran forward the last few yards to the corner of the shack and peered round.

Moe saw her, looking around the opposite edge of the shack towards Jimmy. She had a gun! The fucking broad had a gun! Where was Jimmy? Was he dead? She was going to get it right now if he was, helicopter or no helicopter!

He levelled his Smith and Wesson at the back of her head and said, "Okay, lady, freeze. That's it. Now, nice and slow, throw the gun to your right and turn around. That's it. Nice and . . ."

Something smashed into the side of his head, like a hand grenade going off between his ears! The world exploded in a hissing, whirling sea of pain as he collapsed to his knees with blood pouring down into his eyes.

"Jesus!"

The guy who had thrown the rock was running at him down the rise from the trail above. He was a long skinny man with blond hair . . . and no gun.

Moe raised his pistol with both hands, took aim at the man's chest. A hammer hit him, just below the left armpit. He turned to defend himself when another blow smashed into his chest, high on the left-hand side. Moe crumpled to his knees. The gun in his hands was heavy. He tried to pull it up and aim, but the Indian broad had the drop on him. Slowly and carefully, she took aim between his eyes and fired.

"Holy shit! Who is that guy?"

Fischetti heard the first shot, saw Jimmy Snyder go down and saw the tall blond man, the one they'd passed on the trail coming down, step out from behind a rock, throw something and run to the shack. Then three more shots, close together, and then nothing.

"What the hell's going on?"

"Could be a *real* Fed," said Hooper, and if he hadn't been the only one who could fly them out of there, Fischetti would have shot him dead on the spot. "Ed?" he said, twisting in his seat, "are you sure you can't fly this thing?"

"No, Tony. I'm just the mechanic."

"Shit!"

"You got another problem," said Hooper. "Your boys aren't coming out. Which means that Ruth and the guy who just ran in there have at least two guns between them, three if they run out and grab Jimmy's. I wonder how long it'll be before they start shooting?"

"We need more firepower," Fischetti shouted. "And we ain't going to find it around here."

A loud 'smack' sounded on the Plexiglas windshield as a bullet from Ruth's gun smashed through, bursting the padding on the bulkhead above Fischetti's head and showering fireproof stuffing into the cockpit. He saw Hooper twist the throttle and haul on the collective control, sending the Huey leaping into the air to the west before diving towards the river, out of pistol range. Hooper flew a mile or so west and up out of the canyon, heading to the airfield.

"Where the fuck are you going?" Fischetti yelled.

"Back to the field. The game's over, Tony, and you lost. Someone's sure to have heard the shooting, seen this chopper and put two and two together. If you're lucky, you'll just have time to make a getaway before the cops seal off the airfield. If you're not, then they'll be waiting for you when we get back."

"How much gas have you got in this thing?"

"Just over half full, but you can't — "

"How long is that in the air, Ed?" asked Fischetti looking back at Marino. "And don't try to bullshit me or it's your ass."

"About forty minutes, depending on how you fly."

"Okay then," said Fischetti. "I want you to fly down the canyon until you come to a nice quiet spot. Then I want you to get on that radio of yours and contact our plane up at the airstrip. I've got a few arrangements to make. We'll try again tomorrow at first light."

"Aw, Tony, you're out of your mind," said Ed. "The place will be crawling with choppers tomorrow."

"And your dead body will be crawling with maggots if we don't get that woman," hissed Fischetti. "Mister War Hero, get me that plane on the radio! Then you and I have to have a serious talk."

Ruth watched the helicopter climb into the sky and dive for safety behind the rise leading to Phantom Ranch, following its line of flight with her gun. She let the chopper go. It was moving too fast to guarantee another hit and she had only six rounds left, plus whatever the two dead gangsters had.

She ran over to the man lying flat on his back and looked down at him. He lay with both eyes open, an expression of surprise on his face. She searched him for anything she could use. The padded vest did not have too much blood on it and might be useful for warmth once the sun set. So she stripped it off. Then she took his bootlaces and a very sharp folding knife she'd found in his jeans pocket. The money in his wallet was useless to her now, so she left it. But she took the gun. There was already spare ammunition in the vest pocket. He had no food or water on him. He hadn't counted on being in the canyon that long. Now he was going to be here forever.

"What are you doing?"

Carpenter stood over her, looking down at the body.

"Taking what I need. I know how to survive. You don't. You haven't even got any water."

"But you have," said Carpenter.

"What makes you think I'm going to give you any of mine?"

"I saved your life. I hit that man with a rock. He'd have shot you."

"And I saved yours, *twice*. Once up on the rim and again just now. I shot him *after* you hit him with the rock. Remember? He was aiming at you before he died."

She pushed the things she had taken from Snyder's body into her rucksack and ran around the shack to where Spilato lay dead. The only thing of value was his gun. Ruth took it.

"You have to give yourself up at the Phantom Ranch," said Carpenter. "You know what's at stake."

"No. You lied to me before and you could be lying again now. This is your problem and you can get yourself out of it. I'm not putting myself through hell again. I'm getting out of here."

"And what if I stop you?"

Ruth smiled. "If you wanted to stop me, John Carpenter, you should have remembered to pick up one of those guns, shouldn't you? Are you going to stay here and die of thirst? Or are you coming with me to the river? You can get water there at the Phantom Ranch."

Carpenter shrugged. "It looks like I'm coming with you."

"Then walk in front of me and don't try anything. It'll be dark by six thirty and difficult to see our way on the trail."

The little airstrip outside St. George was deserted, which was one reason Ed Marino had suggested it. The other reasons were that it had a large, abandoned hanger and was within a few miles of the main highway into Vegas. Hooper set the Huey down gently on the tarmac outside the great yawning doors of the old building, shut down the turbines and said, "That's it! I'm finished!"

"What do you mean?" said Fischetti. "We haven't even started."

"I mean it. You get yourself another pilot. You can't force me to fly for you against my ex-wife. So shoot me or let me go!"

He pulled off his headset and threw it across the control panel. Behind him, he heard Ed open the passenger door and walk around to speak to Fischetti. Looking back, he saw Ed write a name and address on an old aviation fuel receipt and give it to the gangster, who smiled that cruel smile of his and slid it into the breast pocket of his jacket. Then Ed came around to Hooper's side of the cockpit and opened the pilot's door. Fischetti got out and stretched his legs but still had both his gun and his eye on Matt.

"Just listen to me for a few minutes, Matt. Okay?" said Ed. "I don't want Tony to take it into his head to shoot you and get another pilot up here from Vegas? So just play it cool, for old time's sake."

"You heard the man," shouted Fischetti. "For old time's sake. Like real Army buddies, huh?"

"I'm not helping him hunt down Ruth," Hooper said. "She was my wife."

"But not your *only* wife, was she, Matt?"

Ed had a sad smile on his face, the sort of smile he'd used in Korea to tell guys their buddies wouldn't be coming back from a mission, the sort of smile that meant *really* bad news.

"What do you mean?"

"There's Beth down in Phoenix, isn't there? And there are your three children. Is Beth happy now? You'd want her to stay that way, wouldn't you?"

Hooper felt sick. It was worse than having Fischetti blow his brains out. Beth wasn't part of this and neither were their kids. Now he had put their lives in danger, just as he'd fucked up Ruth's life years ago.

"You bastard!" he spat into Marino's face. "We were friends."

"Don't give me that 'friends' crap," Marino snapped. "Who had to scrape around for the money to hold this company together while you were flitting around the sky or getting your ass burned by lawyers because you couldn't hold a marriage together? Who had to sell their soul to the devil just so you could have a fancy new chopper to keep up with the competition? Me, buddy boy! That's who! And now the devil is looking for a piece of my ass in return. So act nice and do what he wants or it won't be too pretty for Beth and the kids!"

"And speaking of friendship and love and all that shit," said Fischetti. "Don't think that croaking yourself or sabotaging that chopper is going to get your family off the hook because it's not. I'll just get another pilot, take out that squaw of yours in the canyon and then pay your wife and kids a visit."

He patted his breast pocket and smiled cruelly. "I'd enjoy that, War Hero! Your buddy Ed can tell you all about my reputation up in Vegas, can't you, Ed? You know what a thrill I'd get out of it."

"I'm sorry, Matt. You've got to do what he says."

"So you two old buddies just sit there and swap war stories for a while," said Fischetti. "My reinforcements from Vegas will be here pretty soon."

19

The canyon lay in darkness as Ruth and Carpenter trudged across the black metal bridge over the Colorado. The sun had set and the moon had not yet risen above the rim. Then they were on the other side and moving along the narrow path to the Phantom Ranch.

"Keep moving," she said. "We're almost there."

He had her second bottle of water in his left hand and had already emptied it. At least he would not die of thirst.

"And then what happens?" asked Carpenter.

"I leave you and disappear. It's as simple as that."

She sensed him thinking of ways to trap her. The alcohol was gone and her old powers were coming back. It was frightening and exhilarating at the same time. She only dreaded the darkness, when the nightmares of the woman with the grey eyes in that operating room would return.

They walked down into a dip, where a small stream flowed into the Colorado. The moon rose over the canyon rim and its light played on the gently overhanging trees, the reeds and the babbling water. Farther upstream was the welcoming glow of lights.

"There it is," she said, moving to a drinking water tap and filling her water bottle. "Phantom Ranch. You'll get food and water there."

"Is there a phone?" asked Carpenter, looking up to where a set of wires was silhouetted against the sky.

"Yes, there's a . . ." Then he grabbed her, knocking the gun from her hand and scrabbling to get her arms pinned against her body.

"Help! I'm a Federal Agent. I have a prisoner here. Help!"

Ruth clawed at his face. He tried to beat her into unconsciousness with his fists. A blow struck her shoulder, spinning her round but, before he could connect again, she had her knee in his groin. Carpenter folded, wheezing in agony. Ruth picked up the gun from the path and hit him very hard behind the left ear.

She watched him for a moment, to make sure he was still breathing, and then rolled him into the brush so that people coming down to the water tap wouldn't see him. Then she ran back to the beach.

A row of rafts, kayaks and canoes lay pulled up tight against the shore, each with their oars or paddles tucked neatly inside. Ruth chose a fifteen-foot slalom kayak, with float bags in the bow and stern, and a spray cover that would seal the cockpit. Then she searched amongst the other craft, found a fibreglass helmet and a thirty-three-pound buoyancy life jacket. The helmet had scour marks on it, as if it had saved a cracked skull in the past. Ruth hoped it would do the same for her.

She lined up the kayak near the water, pulled the Walther automatic out of her rucksack and slipped on the dead gangster's padded vest against the cold. Then she ran back up the beach. Twelve feet above her, the ceramic insulators of the phone lines to Phantom Ranch stood white against the night sky. Ruth planted her feet squarely on the path, legs slightly apart, took the pistol in the two-handed grip she had been taught and aimed. The shot boomed like a cannon, the insulator shattered and the broken wire dropped free. It took two more shots to shatter the second insulator and break its wire. Lights flicked on up at the ranch. Voices raised in panic reached her from the camp ground.

Ruth ran back to the beach, pulled on the lifejacket and helmet, and pushed the boat into shallow water. She slipped in as the sound of running feet got closer, took the two-bladed paddle in both hands and pushed off.

"There are two kinds of paddlers:" her instructor had told her years before when she and Matt had learned to run the rapids "*instinctives*, who feel the river and can navigate without thinking, and *technicians*, who study each rapid and run it like the pages of a textbook."

Ruth had been an instinctive. In a few strokes of the paddle, the current of the Colorado had her in its grip and she was sliding westwards at around thirteen miles an hour, away from the Phantom Ranch, Carpenter and her slavery to the NSA. She passed under the graceful latticed arch of the Bright Angel Suspension Bridge into a timeless world, where only two things mattered: herself and the river. The river had been there for millions of years and would be there for millions more. So Ruth knew that survival lay not in trying to fight the great Colorado but in harnessing its power. Her one hope would be to understand the river and its spiteful children, the rapids.

And to safely shoot each rapid between her and Havasu Canyon, Ruth had to feel its 'run', that invisible ribbon of safe passage, sometimes only inches wide, between its eddies, rocks and snags. If she followed the run of a rapid, it would carry her with it. If she missed the run, she would be fighting for her life.

The first rapid, at Pipe Creek, was small. Ruth steered the kayak to the left along the narrow beach to avoid the strong eddy she knew lurked in waiting on the right. The water roared softly like a sleeping giant. She tried to get the feel of the run, but could not.

This worried her. Sheer cliffs towered on either side, cutting out the moonlight and throwing the river into shadow. With the passing of Pipe Creek, there was no way she could hike back to the Bright Angel Trail to escape from the canyon on foot. Had she been foolish to try and run the Colorado in darkness? Should she stop now and head for the shore?

Then it was too late and she was committed. The current carried her onwards to Horn Creek Rapids where the river dropped ten feet between two massive boulders. Ruth moved in for a run, going right of the right-hand horn and pulled back across the tongue of the rapid, picking up speed over the drop. Adrenalin surged through her body. Her mouth went dry. She took a deep breath to focus herself, lined up the kayak and was drawn in . . . .

She shot past the rocks on the left. The river took the kayak in its grip and hurled it at the left-hand cliff. Ruth fought back. Her pulse raced as the water threw her forwards, into calmer water. Had her feeling for the river returned?

She paddled on, wary of her first easy victory and the need to keep focused. To lose concentration for even a second meant disaster. The next rapid, at Salt Creek, was what kayakers call a 'read and run'. She got through easily, but knew it was just a curtain raiser for what was ahead at Granite and Hermit, two of the most dangerous rapids on the Colorado.

The river curved gently to the right as she tried to remember all she knew about Granite; a seventeen-foot drop, with rocks on the left forcing the current into the cliffs on the right. She heard the roar of white water ahead and took her run . . . .

The throat of the rapid sucked in the little kayak and flung it towards the cliffs. Ruth threw her weight backwards and dug deep with the paddle in a back sweep, forcing the stern into the current and sending the bow skywards. The kayak pulled back from the rocks, landing flat on the water. Ruth caught the edge of a wave and surfed it, looking for the run. She planted the paddles downstream and pulled. The kayak turned on the spot, gaining speed until she was skipping over each crest, falling and sliding, and all the time watching for waves curling back from the canyon wall.

At the foot of the rapid lurked a large eddy, a living hole in the river that could suck her down and crush her. Ruth aimed at the run down the right on the lateral waves. She felt the rush of rock near her face, the churning water hurling her on, and then she was through!

Ruth let out a yell of triumph. She couldn't help it. She had beaten Granite! The blood pounded in her ears. Her hands shook. Ruth felt wonderful. Better than she had in years. Why hadn't she kept this up after Hooper had left?

Ruth paddled on down the straight gully towards Hermit. She knew its waves could flip an eighteen-foot raft. So what would they do to her in a kayak? The roar of water sounded in the canyon. Ruth took her run to the right of the cauldron of standing waves looming out of the darkness, and was into the jaws of the rapid.

The water rose ahead of her in a huge standing wave. Ruth shot up over the top and down. The second wave growled around her, sucking at the kayak. The third wave caught her unawares. It slapped the front of the kayak left, so that she hit the fourth wave off-balance, and flipped over. Ruth plunged into the deafening maelstrom of the Colorado, arched herself back so that her helmet hit the rear deck of the kayak, and reached up with the paddle until it broke the surface. Then she pushed it away and flicked her hips. The kayak flipped upright just in time for Ruth to see the fifth wave towering over her for the *coup de grâce*.

The wall of water smashed down. Ruth plunged back into darkness. Her helmet smashed into a rock. She clung desperately to the paddle and fought to hold her breath as the pressure lanced into her ears. Her strength was ebbing away. She tried to roll back upright again, but all she got was a snatched breath of air and a mouthful of water. Another roll, another failure. Her lungs heaved. Fighting back the panic, Ruth put all her strength into one last flip of her hips. The kayak rolled. The thunder faded. The water calmed. Ruth drifted downstream, with her face pressed against the front deck as tears of pain streamed from her eyes. She pulled herself upright, dazed and shaking with the fear, and tried to calm her breathing. Ruth had survived Hermit, but only because of luck. She was truly scared now, scared that her feeling for the river had gone and that next time she would lose her nerve. The river carried her onwards, towards Crystal Rapid, with its seventeen-foot drop, but Ruth could not face it.

She heaved the kayak ashore above the rapid at Crystal Creek. It was now fully dark in the canyon. Ruth drank her water, ate her dry rations and lay down to sleep, clear-headed and sober for the first time in years, looking up at the stars and praying that the nightmare of the woman with the grey eyes would not return. She thought of Hooper and the joy of their early life together on the river, of how he had called her 'Princess', and of how the war had killed him inside with wounds that only she could see. She waited for the nightmare to come, but it didn't.

Her spirit soared above the river and the canyon to where Hooper lay. There were other men there with him, evil men who held him prisoner, and he was deeply troubled about what he might have to do the next day . . . to her.

Fifty miles away to the north-west, Matt Hooper lay awake on the rickety camp bed Fischetti had placed next to the Huey after they had moved the helicopter inside the hanger. His right hand was handcuffed to a steel pole running from floor to ceiling. Fischetti, Ed and three more goons from Vegas were on the other side of the chopper, playing cards. Their laughter echoed in the big steel shell of the hanger and it was unlikely that he'd get any sleep, even if his head hadn't been spinning in silent desperation.

Ever since Marino had given Fischetti Beth's name and address, ever since he had seen Ruth on the Kaibab Trail, Hooper had been wracking his brain for a way to get them all out of this mess. But there was only one way that would work, only one plan that would succeed for sure, as long as Fischetti didn't pass that piece of paper in his top pocket to anyone else. The evening wore on and the card game finished. He heard Fischetti talking softly to his men and Ed Marino snoring.

Only one plan that would work . . . .

Matt finally fell asleep and dreamt. In his dream Ruth, his 'Princess', came to him in the hanger and knelt by his bed. He was scared that the other men would see her, but they didn't. She looked as she had when they first met. The light of love was still in her eyes as she bent over and kissed him.

"Why did you try to kill me, Matt?" she asked.

"I didn't know it was you. They tricked me, Princess. I'm sorry for everything. I'm sorry I gave away your secret and for what I put you through. I'm sorry I took the love we had and destroyed it. I'm sorry for the pain."

"It's not your fault," she said. "Love goes on. One day we'll be together again and things will be as they were . . . believe me."

20

Cherlenko looked up from the planning table as the doors of the briefing room opened. A young naval officer ushered former Admiral of the Red Banner Northern Fleet, Aleksandr Shumanin, inside. Shumanin's splendid uniform and decorations were gone, replaced by a simple dark suit and an open-necked shirt. He looked as if he had not slept in days. Dark rings of fatigue hung under his eyes and his chubby face seemed pale. He regarded the uniformed KGB and GRU staff with a mixture of envy and shame.

Cherlenko motioned him to an empty seat on his right, at the top of the table next to himself and Professor Kharkov.

"Comrade Shumanin," he said. "Thank you for coming in so early to update us on progress in detecting your submarine K-6."

Shumanin seemed to regain some of his confidence now that he had been asked to speak from his own expertise.

"I have to inform you, Comrades, that naval operations to locate Petrachkov have taken a new turn," he said, beckoning to the young naval officer, who spread a large chart of the Northern Atlantic in front of them.

"With your permission, Comrade General. As of early yesterday morning we have been co-operating secretly with the Americans to contact K-6, using every means at our disposal. This has meant sharing information on unidentified sonar contacts detected by our warships, intelligence trawlers and sonar buoys dropped from the air."

He leant over the chart and, with his stubby finger, drew the meeting's attention to five red crosses.

"This first point represents the position Petrachkov was at when he was spotted by the American jets; the second contact in Denmark Strait was also reported to us by the Americans. They say it was obtained from a sonar buoy dropped by an anti-submarine aircraft from one of their Greenland bases. The sound signature does not match any of the American or NATO fleets. Neither does it match any of the four diesel submarines we have in the Atlantic. Therefore, we must conclude that it was Petrachkov's K-6, on course for Cuba.

"This contact here," he continued, drawing his finger to the south-west, "was obtained by one of our spy trawlers on the fishing grounds off the Grand Banks of Newfoundland, near the Flemish Cap. It was thought to have been one of our other submarines. But this has since been proved not to be the case, making it likely that it was Petrachkov."

"And these last two contacts farther south?" asked Cherlenko impatiently. He wanted Shumanin to give his information and go as quickly as possible. It irritated him that his own search of Leningrad for Tatyana Rospin had still nothing to show, while Shumanin, who had been searching the entire Atlantic Ocean, had all this information to lay before the meeting.

"These last two contacts were given to us by the Americans. Once more, they say they were obtained from sonar buoys deployed by aircraft. If you join these five points in sequence, you see this pattern . . . ."

He took a blue wax pencil from his pocket and, with the aid of metal ruler, drew a jagged line from the Greenland Basin to the Denmark Strait, to the Grand Banks, on down the coast towards Boston and along the continental shelf and Georges Bank to the waters off New York.

"This is almost certainly the course Petrachkov has taken," said Shumanin. "It is a classic stealth attack on the US mainland, making the best advantage of oceanographic conditions and the masking effects of noise from other vessels, fishing fleets and shipping lanes, to cover his submarine's progress."

"Then why has it not been possible to intercept him?" asked Cherlenko.

"Because it takes time to relay and process these contacts, Comrade General. We are dealing with opposing fleets and agencies poised on the brink of war. There is a great deal of suspicion on both sides. The Americans predicted Petrachkov would take the shorter, more direct course from the Grand Banks straight to Cuba by way of the Bermuda rise. Admiral Cursey of their Atlantic fleet built his career in surface ships. He sees the best course between two points as a straight line, whereas we submariners are more devious. That is why Petrachkov has beaten him so far."

He gave the faintest hint of a smile.

Professor Kharkov peered at the last contact, east of New York.

"When was this contact made?"

"Approximately two hours ago. In that time we have been in constant communication with the US Atlantic fleet regarding ways of intercepting Petrachkov. We know he is making for the US blockade line. In consultation with Admiral Cursey, two additional anti-submarine screens have been prepared, one relatively close to the shore by a squadron of six US destroyers, and the other by two of our four diesel submarines in offshore waters farther south."

"I have a question," Kharkov said. "If we have Russian submarines operating in these waters and the Americans are using anti-submarine warships, what is to stop them mistaking our other boats for Petrachkov's K-6?"

"The noise made by a nuclear submarine like Petrachkov's K-6 is quite different from that of a diesel submarine, which runs on electric batteries while submerged, Comrade Professor," explained Shumanin patiently. "A nuclear submarine has to run its pumps and turbines continuously to cool its nuclear reactors and avoid melt-down. This produces far more noise than a diesel submarine running on electrical batteries alone."

"Thank you, Comrade *Admiral*," said Kharkov. "Do you think that will make it easier for our combined forces to detect the K-6?"

"I do," said Shumanin. "Captain Petrachkov is an experienced submariner with a shrewd mind. But he is pitting his vessel against ever-increasing odds. We have twenty-four hours in which to stop him and I am now confident that we can. May I ask, Comrade General, how the search in Leningrad is progressing?"

Had Cherlenko been alone with Shumanin, he would have ignored that question and dismissed the man. As it was, there were a great many high-ranking officers of the GRU and the Army present, along with Captain Slavin, the Defence Council's private spy. He needed to maintain their confidence in the ultimate success of the search if he was to succeed.

"There has been a change of strategy," he said. "Now that we have exhausted conventional methods of finding Tatyana Rospin, her confederate, the deserted *naval* officer Baybarin and the other dissidents in their group, we will be moving to more subtle means. This will require the direct involvement of Comrade Professor Kharkov, who has intimate knowledge of their motives. It will also necessitate a number of, shall I say, 'volunteers' from your naval headquarters, *Comrade* Shumanin—brother officers who know Baybarin and can assist by providing intelligence. I have found such methods to be extremely effective in all but the most intransigent cases and I expect they will be equally effective now."

"And . . . can I ask what these methods might be?" asked Shumanin. The man looks afraid for his staff, thought Cherlenko, as well he might. It would be pleasant to let him suffer a while longer.

"I have other matters to discuss with the members of this group," he said. "Come back here at noon and I will explain my methods. Until then, you are dismissed."

FRIDAY, 26 OCTOBER
SUBMARINE K-6
8.40 A.M. MOSCOW TIME
0540 GMT

Petrachkov scanned the rows of dials and gauges around him in the CCP. Men worked silently at their stations. The ship hummed with activity and purpose. Where they had started this mission as a group of individuals, they had truly become one united crew. Each man performed his duties to the utmost of his ability and relied in turn on the others to perform theirs. There was great comfort for everyone in this, great simplicity. Only Petrachkov, as Captain, had to bear the burden of the world outside the simple community of this hundred-metre steel cylinder.

He thought back to the last 'séance' he had witnessed with Max Rospin and Doctor Chiker. Petrachkov attended all these sessions now. The fate of his submarine hung on this one remaining link with the Admiralty in Leningrad.

The latest intelligence Max had relayed to them was that two hunter-killer groups, one composed of surface warships and the other of two diesel-electric submarines, lay in wait farther south. They had received the warning just in time to make preparations and to study the charts for escape routes.

K-6 was proceeding at full speed along the shoulder of the American continental shelf, south-east of New York. To the north, the shelf sloped upwards into shallower water, to the south it plunged to the Hatteras Abyssal Plain, over five thousand metres deep. Above the thermocline, that sharp divide separating the cold waters of the deep from the warmer waters nearer the surface, the Gulf Stream flowed north-east at a steady five knots. The K-6 was safe, protected from active sonar sweeps by the shoulder of the slope to the north and the reflective thermocline above.

Petrachkov leant forward and examined the detailed chart on the plotting table. Their own course and the reported positions of the two hunter-killer groups were clearly marked. The first group could not be far away.

A buzzer sounded. Petrachkov reached up and took a microphone.

"Sonar, have you heard something?"

"Very faint, Comrade Captain. High speed screws bearing two two five degrees."

"I'll be right there."

Petrachkov got up from his commander's chair, handed over control of the ship to the officer of the watch and walked forward to a tiny cubicle, just off the narrow corridor leading forward to the torpedo room. The cubicle was tightly packed with not only the standard passive and active sonar systems for military operations, but also with the special *Arktica* sonar unit Petrachkov had taken on board to avoid deep icebergs during his scientific mission under the ice.

"What is it?" he asked.

The rating in the compartment removed his padded earphones and pointed to a flickering oscilloscope display. Looking carefully, Petrachkov could just make out faint stirrings along the thin fluorescent line at its base.

"Nothing definite, Comrade Captain, but I have started to pick up faint noises. It sounds like more than one ship."

"Let me listen."

Petrachkov put on the headset and closed his eyes. He heard the faint but regular chop of high speed propellers above the hiss of background static. The sonar man was right. And there was more than one source.

"Very good," he said, laying a hand on the young man's shoulder. "If even so much as a fish breaks wind, I want to know about it. Is that clear?"

The sonar man nodded and replaced his headset. Petrachkov went back aft to the CCP. "Comrades," he said. "As ever, our superior Soviet science has come to our aid and predicted what has just been confirmed on passive sonar. We have a reception committee waiting for us to the south-west, immediately in our path. Show me the high definition underwater maps for this area."

The navigating officer spread a new chart on the plotting table. Ever since the success of fascist U-boats against the Allies in the Great Patriotic War, the Soviet Union had poured limitless resources into oceanographic research. In particular, it had supported a number of extensive projects to map the seabed with extreme accuracy all over the world. As a result, the Soviet Navy had a very clear picture of the underwater terrain in which its vessels operated, essential knowledge for any submarine commander wishing to hide from his enemies.

Petrachkov ran his finger along the bunched depth contours of the American continental shelf. The chart looked like a large-scale map of a mountain range. It showed the Hudson Canyon, a vast submarine trench stretching almost from the shoreline off New York for seventy kilometres into the deep, deep water of the Hatteras Abyssal Plain.

"How far until we reach this?" asked Petrachkov.

The navigating officer looked at the instruments on his panel, did some calculations and bent over the chart.

"We are here now, Comrade Captain," he said, drawing a precise pencil cross close to the 200-metre contour line south of Block Island. "The entrance to the Hudson Canyon is only thirty kilometres away, on course one nine zero."

Petrachkov reached up and spoke into a microphone.

"Sonar, do you have a course, speed and range to those warships yet?"

"Range around sixty kilometres, Comrade Captain. Speed thirty knots. Six vessels with high speed screws in a standard sweep formation, probably destroyers."

"And their course?"

"Zero four five degrees, Comrade Captain. They are heading this way!"

"Keep me updated every five minutes!"

He turned to the chart, took the navigator's pencil and drew a line to the canyon entrance. Then he drew another, extrapolating the estimated course of the American warships. The two lines met.

"We have a race on our hands, Comrades," he said. "Come left to one nine zero. Make revolutions for full maximum speed. Depth two hundred metres."

He reached up and took another microphone.

"Comrade Mostock, could you join us in the officers' wardroom right away?"

Petrachkov and the commanders of each compartment crowded around the officers' wardroom table with the high definition chart of the American coast in front of them.

"If we are to be successful in attacking the blockade, as instructed, we need to slip undetected past the squadron of six destroyers currently bearing down on us from the south-west. We are making maximum speed in their direction, which should put us within their active sonar range in just over forty minutes."

"But why sail towards them, Comrade Captain?" asked Dudko. "Do you intend to attack them with the torpedo?"

"No, Petr Anatoly. I intend to save your bright new toy for much bigger game. I am heading towards those warships because between them and us is a large submarine canyon, an ideal escape route into deeper water and the open sea. Once at the entrance, I intend to use this chart and our *Arktica* sonar to navigate as deeply into it as we can. Its rock walls will not only shield us from their active sonar, but also muffle our reactor noise.

"However there are risks," continued Petrachkov. "We may be detected on passive sonar before we reach the canyon, if those ships choose to slow down and listen carefully. It will also be difficult to navigate safely in the confined space of the canyon without hitting the walls, although the *Arktica* sonar will help us there. So I want your best men at all the key positions as we perform these manoeuvres, understood?"

He looked at the faces around the table.

"How can compartment five best help you?" Mostock said.

"By giving us enough speed to get to the canyon ahead of those ships and by being as silent as possible once we reach it. You remember that drill we performed in the Denmark Strait to reduce reactor noise? Can we do it again?"

"It's risky. But yes we can."

"Right then. Get to your stations, all of you. This is going to be a tight run race."

"Sonar, what do you have to report?" asked Petrachkov.

"The warships are maintaining course and speed. No alterations. No active sonar."

Good, thought Petrachkov. They don't know we're here. Not yet!

"Range to those ships?"

"Twenty kilometres."

"Time to the canyon?"

"At this speed, just over sixteen minutes."

He walked forward to the sonar room and listened again on the headphones. The warships' screws seemed deafening. As the sonar man changed the direction of the receiver mounted on the bow, he could make out the six ships distinctly. They were destroyers, no doubt about it, and he was heading towards them at a combined closing speed of over a hundred kilometres an hour!

"Switch on the *Arktica*."

A screen jumped to life, showing the image of an electronic landscape made up of green moving lines, like a moving picture taken from an aircraft.

"Can that display be piped back to the CCP?"

"Yes. Comrade Captain. We had it rigged through to the console above the main helm when we were under the ice."

"Do it quickly please."

He walked back to the command post. Tension in the cramped compartment was as thick as the cigarette smoke. Nobody spoke. Everyone listened for the first sound of enemy propellers, the first active sonar ping, the splash of a homing torpedo entering the water!

"Time to canyon?"

"Four minutes, Comrade Captain."

The screen above the man steering the ship flashed into life, showing the moving underwater landscape beneath them. Petrachkov hoped the charts were accurate.

"Sonar?"

"Still no active sonar transmissions, Comrade Captain. Warships maintaining course and speed. Range now two kilometres and closing fast."

"Two minutes to canyon!"

Then he heard it clearly, the thud, thud, thud of propellers from outside the submarine.

If I can hear them, then surely they can hear me. Or are they still going too fast to notice?

"One minute to canyon."

He stared at the moving green display. At the very top of the right-hand corner, a denser patch of darkness crept down the screen.

There it was, the entrance of the Hudson Canyon. They had to turn into it and dive.

"Stop port engine. Full left rudder. Back dead slow on port engine. Forward dive planes ten degrees down."

To reverse the port engine at this speed was a risk. It could create 'cavitation', tiny bubbles that formed in the water behind a churning propeller and then collapsed, making a tell-tale noise a warship could hear.

"Rig for silent running!"

The submarine tilted as it banked in a tight left-hand turn, heading downwards into the safety of the underwater canyon below.

The thud of the warships propellers grew louder and louder, as if they would smash through the hull at any moment.

Then, from behind them on the port side, came a low vibration. The portside screw was cavitating as it went into reverse.

"Dead slow!" hissed Petrachkov.

The noise faded. The enemy screws thumped above their heads. The submarine slid forward towards safety.

A deafening 'ping' slammed into the hull, bringing a cry of pain from the sonar man in his cubicle as his eardrums were almost shattered by the screaming blast of amplified sound through his headset.

Petrachkov swore under his breath. "They've found us!"

21

"Depth?" demanded Petrachkov, staring at the green display of the *Arktica* sonar above the helmsman's position. On either side of the screen, green digital walls rose around them.

"Two hundred and twenty metres and increasing."

"Distance to canyon wall, port and starboard?"

"A hundred metres on each side, Comrade Captain. We have good clearance."

"Angle on bow?"

"Ten degrees down."

The noise of warship screws above them changed. It's as if they're circling, thought Petrachkov. Did they get us on that first 'ping'? Will they try again or will they just listen with their passive sonar until they sniff us out?

Petrachkov ordered the electric motors on the K-6 switched off. Their big brass propellers feathered gently in the slipstream of the submarine as it glided silently downwards. The only noises in the CCP were the whir and click of the depth metres and displays, the hiss of the passive sonar and the nervous breathing of the men. A creaking groan sounded from the hull.

"Depth?"

"Two hundred and fifty metres and increasing."

He knew their ship was good for around three hundred metres. To go deeper was risky. The weight of seawater above them, crushing in on the hull at a force measured in tons per square inch could find the weakest point of the pressure hull and punch it in. Then the sea would flood through, crushing bulkhead after bulkhead until the submarine lost so much buoyancy, it would never rise again.

"Speed?"

"Fifteen knots, Comrade Captain."

They were gliding downwards on the residual momentum of their turn into the canyon and the weight of the submarine, five thousand tons submerged displacement of metal and men.

Another 'ping' sounded behind them at the top of the canyon, fainter and farther away this time.

"Sonar, have those ships moved? Are they following us?"

"No. Comrade Captain. They are still circling."

"What is their range?"

"Two kilometres and increasing."

"Very good," said Petrachkov and smiled. They had managed to show the hunter-killer group a clean pair of heels and would now be protected by the canyon wall from detection by any ship except one directly above them. All they had to do was to slide along silently, following the contour of the canyon until their safe depth of three hundred metres, then level out and go on their way.

"Captain, Sonar here. I have a contact. Submerged high-speed screws dead ahead. Range two kilometres. It sounds like another submarine."

"What kind?"

"Conventional. I don't hear any reactor noise."

A submarine dead ahead could listen directly into the canyon with its passive sonar, pick up their reactor noise and send an active sonar 'ping' right into the canyon.

Petrachkov reached for a microphone.

"Comrade Mostock, I need complete silence. Shut down the baffles on both reactors and run on batteries for a while."

"That could be risky, Comrade Captain. What if I cannot restart them?"

"That's an order, Mostock," said Petrachkov. "Shut them down now."

"Yes, Comrade Captain."

Petrachkov replaced the microphone and stared at the gently rolling landscape of the canyon on the *Arktica* monitor. Right now, Mostock would be in his reactor control room forward of the CCP in compartment two, controlling the electric motors and pullies that lowered the thick lattice of metal baffles separating the uranium fuel rods in each of the two reactors. Once this was done, the rods would cease to achieve their critical mass of radiation and the nuclear process in each reactor would stop. It was like putting a wet blanket over a fire. But would that fire rekindle itself once the blanket was lifted? It had not always worked in the past.

"It that submarine still there?"

"Yes, Comrade Captain. It is motionless at two hundred metres depth. Range now one point six kilometres."

In a few moments, they would pass right underneath it, if they were lucky.

The lights in the CCP dimmed, switched automatically to red emergency power, and then brightened as the main batteries cut in.

"The baffles are down in both reactors," said Mostock over the intercom. "We have about two hours of battery life, but only six knots of speed. I hope you are not planning to call for full speed!"

"Depth two hundred and fifty metres and increasing."

"Sonar here. The other submarine is heading away on course zero eight zero. Range two kilometres and increasing."

Petrachkov and the men around him in the CCP relaxed.

"Well Comrades. It looks as if we've won. Wait another five minutes and then tell Comrade Mostock to go and blow some life back into his precious reactors."

"We need a course correction, Comrade Captain! Rocky outcrop coming up on the port side about five hundred metres away!"

"Come starboard ten degrees. Slow ahead, port engine."

Machinery whirred into life behind Petrachkov, running on the power of the main batteries. He looked up at the green display of the *Arktica*. A bright clump of digital lines protruded into their path.

"Starboard fifteen. Port engine, half ahead. Starboard engine, back slow."

The noise of the engines increased. Would the other submarine hear it? Would they clear the rock on the—?

The periscope housing leapt at Petrachkov as the submarine keeled over to starboard. A screaming roar thundered past him from the bow of the ship, through the CCP, and on down to the stern. Glasses of tea, charts, pencils and ashtrays crashed onto the grating. Hanging microphones swung wildly from the ceiling.

He fixed his eye on the rolling display. The submarine had careered off the left side of the canyon and was heading for the right-hand wall.

"Starboard engine, ahead full! Port engine, back! All compartments report damage."

An alarm sounded in the depths of compartment five. Mostock came through from his control panel in compartment two, heading aft to the reactors. He glanced at Petrachkov.

"We have a problem!"

"I heard. Sort it out as fast as you can. Damage control, what's happened?"

"We have minor leaks in the torpedo room, Captain. Comrade Dudko has them under control."

"And the special torpedo?"

"It is undamaged, as are the firing tubes. No damage in compartments two or three."

"Engineering?"

"We have a problem with the batteries, Comrade Captain. Some of the main cells have shorted out. Comrade Mostock is inspecting them now."

Petrachkov looked back at the green display of the *Arktica*.

"Where are we?"

"Back in the centre of the canyon, Comrade Captain. We're moving forward at around ten knots. Depth three hundred metres and increasing."

"Forward planes ten degrees up. Aft planes five degrees down. Let's try and raise her by the nose. We can't afford to go much deeper. Sonar, any news of that other submarine?"

"It has changed course and is circling above us. They must have heard something."

Mostock appeared in the aft doorway of the CCP. "Can I speak with you, Comrade Captain?"

Petrachkov followed him aft, past the generators, compressors and evaporators in compartment four, into one of the narrow corridors running alongside the huge chambers containing the nuclear reactors.

"We have a very serious problem," Mostock said. "That collision bent the rails on which the reactor baffles slide. They will not come back up on their own. In the meantime, the batteries are shorting and electricity is leaking away. If we don't get those reactors back on line in less than half an hour, we'll lose all power. If that happens— "

"I know," said Petrachkov. All the systems on the ship—the engines, the sonar, radar, weapons systems—ran on electricity. If their submarine lost power, the only thing they could do would be to blow the ballast tanks manually and surface, right into the waiting arms of the Americans.

"Then the only way is for someone to go in there and crank up the baffles by hand," Petrachkov said.

"That's right."

To enter the outer chamber of a nuclear reactor was to risk a painful death from radiation poisoning. To raise the baffles manually meant clambering in through the sealed hatch on top of the outer chamber and climbing down inside, next to the two reactors themselves. A metal crank would be needed to raise the baffles. That would restart the reactors by exposing each fuel rod to the full nuclear radiation of all its neighbours to create a critical mass. But it would also expose the body of whoever was carrying out the task to dangerous levels, depending on how long he spent close to the nuclear cores.

"Get one of your younger men to do it," said Petrachkov. "I need you in one piece for the rest of the mission."

"But they're *my* reactors, Comrade Captain. I am in command of compartment five," Mostock said seriously. Then he smiled, "Besides, what do young farm hands and coal miners from Siberia know of nuclear physics?"

"Get someone else, Viktor. That's an order. But be as quick as you can."

Petrachkov hurried back to the CCP.

"Where is that other submarine?" he asked as he reached the command chair.

"Circling away to port. Range two kilometres."

"And the flooding in the forward torpedo room?"

"Under control. All weapons have been secured. Comrade Dudko is checking over the special torpedo again."

"How much electricity do we have in the batteries?"

"Enough for less than an hour's running at low speed on the engines. Comrade Mostock is entering the reactor chamber now."

"What!"

"Comrade Mostock is—"

But Petrachkov was already on his feet and running aft to the reactor room, along the catwalk and down the narrow ladder to the observation window at the base of the nuclear chamber. Viktor Mostock was crouched inside the cramped space of the reactor core, with the long black crank handle of the baffle control. He had it connected. As soon as he turned the crank and raised the baffles, the atoms would start to flow. The longer he took, the greater his risk of radiation poisoning as the reactors came back to full power.

"What are his chances?" Petrachkov asked Mostock's assistant, who was standing next to the window beside him. The man had a small microphone in his hand and his ear to the speaker on the wall of the reactor chamber, so that he could talk to Mostock directly.

"Not good, Comrade Captain, unless he can get out of there in less than a minute after the reactor starts."

Petrachkov watched as Mostock struggled with the lever. At first it would not turn. Then, painfully slowly, it started to shift. Beneath the visor of his radiation suit, Mostock's face was pouring with sweat. Petrachkov saw his teeth clench as he heaved the control crank round and round. He took the microphone from Mostock's assistant.

"Just the one reactor, Viktor. Then get out of there as soon as the reaction starts!"

Mostock's assistant glanced over at a panel on the reactor wall. "Fission is taking place, Captain. The reactor has started. Radiation levels in the inner chamber are rising."

Behind them, in the turbine and motor compartments, machinery hummed back into life.

"Viktor, that's an order! We can make do on one reactor."

Mostock's voice sounded, strained and grunting, over the loudspeaker. "Come now, Sergei Nikolai . . . would you rather make do with one testicle . . . when you could have two?"

Mostock unclamped the crank handle from the first reactor and moved to the second.

"No, Viktor, you are to come out now!"

"I'm sorry, Comrade Captain. Your voice is breaking up. Badly made electronics, I'm sure. I can't hear you."

"I know you can hear me, Viktor. Come out of there now!"

But Mostock just waved and went on cranking.

"I cannot watch this any more," said Petrachkov to the assistant. "Tell me when he is finished. I'll be back in the CCP."

He climbed the narrow ladder to the corridor and walked back to the control room.

"Power from the generators is rising, Comrade Captain," reported the officer of the watch. "We'll have sufficient for full manoeuvring in a few minutes."

"And the other submarine?"

"Moving away. Range almost three kilometres and increasing."

He reached up to a microphone connecting him to the reactor chamber.

"Any word on Comrade Mostock?"

"He is out of the chamber, Comrade Captain," said Mostock's assistant.

"I'll be down there directly. How is he?"

The voice on the other end of the line hesitated.

"Comrade Mostock has been taken to the sick bay, Comrade Captain. The surgeon says nobody is to come near him." But Petrachkov had already hung up the microphone.

He hurried back through the machinery compartments four, five, six and seven to the second last compartment in the ship which the crew's quarters and galley. Crew members stood quickly by to let him through.

Viktor Mostock was lying on a fold-down bunk in the tiny compartment that was the ship's hospital.

"Good afternoon, Sergei Nikolai," he said. "Now I am truly glowing, but without the pleasure of having all that sex beforehand."

Mostock was sweating profusely. His blotchy red body looked as if it had been cooked from the inside out. A sheet and a lead blanket covered him. The ship's surgeon wore a lead apron, gloves and a facemask. He looked up.

"You cannot come in here, Comrade Captain. Mostock has suffered a severe dose of radiation. It could be dangerous. He is radioactive."

"You know that vodka sweats it out of the blood," said Mostock. "I'll take mine now, if you please, with a slice of lemon."

Petrachkov motioned the surgeon outside.

"What are his chances?"

"No better than fifty percent, Comrade Captain. The radiation has penetrated his body, causing extensive cell damage. If we were not at war, I would insist you surface and airlift him off to a hospital where they can take care of him properly."

"Where's my vodka?" Mostock shouted from the sick bay.

"Just do what you can," said Petrachkov. "And report any change to me immediately."

FRIDAY, 26 OCTOBER
LENINGRAD
10.00 A.M. LOCAL TIME
0700 GMT

"I have been reading through Comrade Baybarin's *zapista*," said Cherlenko. "And I've passed the names and addresses of all his family and friends to my colleagues in the KBG and GRU. As we speak, those close to Baybarin are being arrested. It seems he is a very popular young man, Comrade Shumanin. Quite a number of your former staff are on this list."

"It is not a crime to be a good comrade and companion, *Comrade General*," Shumanin replied.

The gathering around the table in 'The Big House' was far more select than that of the twelve-hourly briefings. Only Cherlenko himself, Captain Slavin, Kharkov and the head of the local GRU were present. Cherlenko was tired of large committees. All they did was waste time.

"I know, Comrade Shumanin, but it *is* a crime to desert your post to collaborate with a dissident in a major act of sabotage. Has there been any word from either the American surface fleet or from our own submarines standing between Petrachkov and his target?"

"Nothing definite. The American task force thought it had detected noises at the head of a submarine canyon off New York and even 'pinged' what they thought was a submerged contact, but it vanished from their screens and was interpreted as a ghost echo of our own submarines farther out to sea. Other noises in the canyon were investigated, but these were analysed as having been the result of an underwater rockslide, since no reactor or propeller noise was detected and no other contacts made."

"Captain Petrachkov?" Cherlenko asked. "Is he good at his job?"

"You have his *zapista*, General. The facts speak for themselves."

"Indeed I do. But what is *your* opinion of him?"

The former admiral looked uneasy. It was obvious to Cherlenko that Shumanin despised him, but Cherlenko was now a General of the KGB and Shumanin a civilian in disgrace. I have taught you the stupidity of playing politics with me, thought Cherlenko. Even your powerful friend, Admiral Gorshkov, cannot help you now.

"Sergei Petrachkov is one of our best captains," said Shumanin. "He is a brilliant strategist and a person with great cunning when he needs it."

"So if anyone is likely to slip through those barriers, it would be him?"

"I'm afraid so. If I had been commanding that American task force or our submarines over the canyon, I would have dropped warning depth charges and attempted to contact Petrachkov as soon as I heard those noises. It would not be beyond him to use a geological feature like that to his advantage."

Cherlenko tapped his teeth in thought.

"So perhaps the commanders of your other submarines should be reprimanded?"

"No, Comrade General. But the Americans should be warned of how capable Petrachkov is."

Cherlenko's smile broadened.

"That's a very good answer, Shumanin. I see there is a bright future for you in the diplomatic corps now that the military has no further use for you."

He turned to address the rest of the group.

"So, to business. We shall shortly have all Comrade Baybarin's friends and family in custody. We are already putting out announcements on the local radio, through the newspapers, posters and our network of informers here in the city that unless Baybarin surrenders himself and the Rospin woman immediately, his loved ones will face a firing squad in Nevsky Prospeckt, starting in two hours' time with his father and mother. That should have some effect, no?"

"And the woman?" asked the head of the GRU. "What leverage can you bring to bear on her?"

Cherlenko turned to Kharkov. "My colleague Professor Kharkov is the key to that lock," he said. "If Tatyana Rospin does not reveal herself, along with Baybarin, in two hours, he will join Baybarin's parents in Nevsky Prospeckt and be shot to death."

22

FRIDAY, 26 OCTOBER
ST. GEORGE, NEVADA
5.30 A.M. MOUNTAIN STANDARD TIME
1230 GMT

Hooper was dreaming that he was back in North Korea at the Chosin Reservoir, flying old bubble-nosed Bell 47s for the Army. The air was bitterly cold—so cold that it hurt to breathe, so cold that the gasoline sometimes froze in the tanks of the choppers.

He dreamt he was in the air, over the combat zone. Rifle fire from the ground smacked into the helicopter, shattering the big Perspex bubble over the front of the cockpit, tugging at his flight gear. Beneath him, a forest of hands reached up, pleading for him to save them.

People were dying down below, people he knew, people he loved. They grabbed the skids of the chopper, hoping to be pulled free of the ground. But there were too many of them, far too many. They pulled him down into the yawning barrels of the rifles. He wrenched the throttle control around until the engine screamed, but there was no lift. The rotor blades clawed the air . . . . Whup! Whup! Whup!

"Matt, time to get going!" Someone shook his arm. "Come on, Tony's waiting."

Hooper opened his eyes as Ed Marino unlocked the handcuffs. Beyond the helicopter, Fischetti and the goons from Vegas were checking their guns, joking and laughing. Fischetti holstered his big automatic and ducked under the tail of the chopper.

"Okay, War Hero! Let's get this bird out of the hanger and up in the air. I want to have this over and done before the Feds figure out that the Indian broad I mangled back there at the gift store isn't your old lady."

That had to be Joan, Ruth's friend.

"You piece of shit," Matt said. "I bet that gave you a thrill too, didn't it?"

The heavy Colt came out of Fischetti's holster so fast that Hooper had no time to dodge it. The back of the slide smacked into the left-hand side of his face, knocking him sideways. Blood spurted as the gun's foresight ripped into his cheek.

"You watch your fucking mouth, War Hero!" Fischetti spat. "That's if you want to still be alive after all this."

Matt knew Fischetti would never allow him to live. He knew too much. Fischetti would shoot Ed as well, only Ed was too stupid to realise it. Hooper didn't care about himself, or about Ed. They were both as good as dead, but Beth and the kids had to be okay. They *had* to be.

He wiped the blood from his face with the back of his hand.

"Still got the name and address of my wife and kids in Phoenix, Tony?"

Fischetti smiled and patted the breast pocket of his jacket.

"You bet I do! Carry it with me wherever I go. So get over here and help us push this bird out onto the tarmac!"

Hooper smiled. His plan was going to work. Ruth, Beth and the kids would be OK after all.

John Carpenter opened his eyes. It was still night-time, although the sky had turned from pitch black to gunmetal grey, which meant that dawn wasn't far off. His lips were parched; he was dying of thirst. Carpenter moved his head. It hurt like hell. He reached up with his left hand and found a lump the size of a hen's egg behind his left ear. He hauled himself onto his feet, staggered out of the scrub to the drinking tap and turned it on, pushing his head under the spout so that cool water filled his mouth and ran over the back of his head, easing the pain of whatever Ruth had hit him with the night before. He wondered how long he had been lying there and looked at his watch. It read 5.45 a.m., which meant she had at least ten hours' start.

Carpenter looked around to see if she had left anything behind, but she hadn't. For a pill-popping alcoholic, she was damn well organised. He looked up the creek to where the yellow lights of the Phantom Ranch shone between the trees. On the other side of the stream he heard the rattle of pots and pans as the hikers made breakfast.

He had to get to a phone. He had to tell someone Ruth Weylon was still alive and down in the canyon somewhere. He started towards the ranch, trying to ease out the pain of his strained leg muscles, and mounted the wooden steps to the glass-panelled door. The room was laid out like a diner, with row after row of tables full of hikers tucking into breakfast.

"Sorry, sir, but you'll have to wait for the next sitting," said a man in a cowboy hat and an apron, piling plates onto a tray. Then he looked up. "Hey, fella, what the hell happened to you?"

"I don't want breakfast. I'm a federal agent. I need a phone. This is an emergency."

The man with the apron put down his tray and looked at Carpenter's ear. "Who did that to you?"

"A prisoner. She's out there with a gun. Now show me a phone!"

"Good shot, is she?"

Carpenter thought of the way Ruth had taken out the two men at the pit toilet.

"Yeah, you could say that. Why?"

"Because some sharp-shooting son-of-a-bitch shot down our phone line," said the man. "Then we had the National Park Service helicopter down here just before dark and the Rangers asking about a couple of guys they found shot full of holes up near the Tonto Trail. You wouldn't know anything about that now, would you?"

"I was there when it happened," said Carpenter, pulling out his NSA identification. "And I need to contact the police. Did anyone here see an Indian woman around the river last night? She's twenty-nine, five ten, slim build, long black hair, good-looking."

"If you find her, can I marry her?" shouted a voice from the back of the mess hall. There was a ripple of laughter.

"I saw someone like that leave here last night in a kayak, right after all that shooting," said a woman at the first table. "Rucksack, padded vest, flannel shirt and moccasins. She looked like she knew what she was doing."

"That's her," said Carpenter.

The man with the apron raised his eyes. "She'd want to be real good with a paddle or damn stupid to try and run them rapids in the dark. Chances are she's dead by now."

Carpenter looked back out of the ranch house door and up at the rim of the canyon. Arc lights shone brightly around the ruin of the gift store.

"Has anyone here got a really powerful flashlight?"

Ruth had been on the river for four hours. Her arms screamed with the pain of paddling and her legs kept cramping. She was freezing cold. But there was no other way to make it to Havasu Canyon before the helicopters came at dawn. She knew they would come as soon as it was light enough to fly, either from the police or the men who had tried to kill her the day before. Whichever got to her first would be bad news. So the sooner she was down to Havasu Canyon, the better. She knew she could hide in there, and the narrowness of the gullies would make it impossible for a helicopter to land.

The journey so far had been a nightmare of cold, fear and mounting pain. The confidence she'd felt when she'd first pushed out onto the river had evaporated and now, with only a fitful night's sleep and five major rapids behind her, she was wrung out.

The last big rapid, the Deubendorf, with its great cockscomb of rock splitting the river in two, had been a close call. She had taken the left-hand run, fought her way through the holes of pounding water and then tried for a cross-river move to pass left of the huge rock at the end of the rapid. But the river had turned on her. It had enlisted the whirling eddies against her to slam the little kayak against this last rock, cracking the bow high up on the right-hand side.

The boat was taking in water. Ruth felt it sloshing around her backside as the kayak moved. If the river had turned against her, then it was playing with her as a cat tortures a mouse, savouring her pain before it moved in for the kill.

And between her and the Havasu Canyon was Upset Rapid, with its enormous eddy hole that could swallow her alive.

Don Birkett peered out of the helicopter at the great black sea of the darkened canyon and marvelled at the sheer scale of it. It was a country in itself. A person could lose themselves down there and never be found. No wonder this Indian woman had chosen to live close to it, to have a limitless place to hide in. The canyon looked vast and unconquerable from the air. Birkett wondered what it must be like amongst the gullies, valleys and crevices that stretched for mile after mile.

"We're almost there, Mister Birkett. Right ahead, sir!"

His eyes followed the hand of his National Parks Service pilot up along the canyon rim. On the crest of a rise, about a mile ahead, an entire fleet of police cars and fire trucks stood around a tangled mass of smouldering beams and blackened panels that sent a weak column of smoke into the dawn. On the canyon's shoulder, below the ruin of the gift store, a makeshift crane of thin metal rods stood illuminated by powerful arc lights shining down over the cliff, as if a rescue operation was in progress.

The helicopter turned above the wreckage, pirouetted beyond the mass of parked vehicles, and set down on a patch of open ground. Birkett waited until the rotors had stopped turning, unclipped the passenger door and got out. The stench of burning wood caught in his throat.

Two men ran over to meet him, one in the uniform of a county sheriff, the other in a dark suit, shirt and tie, with an FBI identification badge stuck in his breast pocket.

"You must be Mister Birkett from Langley," the sheriff said. "I'm Bill Poxton and this is Art McGraw from the Phoenix office of the Bureau. I'm told you lost a couple of men here, sir. Along with all the rest."

"Two," said Birkett as they walked toward the gift store and the rim. "A senior member of my own staff called Samual Hiscock and a colleague from the National Security Agency, name of John Carpenter."

"We found Hiscock in the wreckage of the store. We haven't located the NSA guy yet. His body could still be down in the canyon somewhere." The sheriff shook his head. "We had a real battle on our hands yesterday, Mister Birkett, a full-scale war. What's it all about, sir? I've got all these bodies up here, one over the rim and now two more down on the Kaibab Trail. I got the CIA, NSA and FBI involved. What the hell's going on?"

"Tell me about the bodies down below."

"Two guys with criminal records and both out of Vegas," said the FBI agent, thumbing through the pages of a notebook. "Moe Spilato and Jimmy Snyder. Both worked at the Tropicana, which has ties to the mob. The guy we're pulling up on the hoist is Gus Russo, again with mob connections. Tell me, Mister Birkett, why would an organised crime syndicate that makes millions want to knock over a souvenir store?"

"That's classified, I'm afraid," said Birkett, "but I need to confirm the death of a Native American woman who worked here named Ruth Weylon."

"We found the body of an Indian woman in the gift store. She'd been killed by a shot to the chest and badly disfigured when the burning building collapsed on her."

"Can you confirm it was Ruth Weylon?"

"We found a pair of old Air Force dog tags on her that check out. Is this what all this was about, Mister Birkett—one woman?"

"Like I said, that's classified information. Can I see the body?"

"It's in that ambulance over there, sir, waiting to go to the coroner's office in Flagstaff."

"Thanks."

Birkett walked to a group of people clustered around the ambulances. One old woman in an Indian blanket seemed particularly upset, wailing over and over in a long keening song as if calling on God, or the spirits. Birkett found it eerie and chilling, like a death dirge.

"I need to see the body of the Indian woman," he said, showing the ambulance man his identification and then reaching into his pocket for the file photograph of Ruth Weylon. "Can you get these people to step back?"

The sheriff stepped in and moved the crowd. The ambulance man opened the door of his vehicle to reveal three body bags on fold down beds.

"Are you sure you want so see her, sir? She's beaten up pretty bad."

"Yes, I'm sure."

"Okay then. The head's up this end." He unzipped the body bag. Birkett's nostrils were assaulted by the stench of burnt flesh.

"Oh my God!" The photograph of Ruth Weylon fell from his fingers.

"I told you she wasn't a pretty sight, sir."

The obscene mask staring up at him was not a face any more. Something, or someone, had made sure of that. The features had been smashed into a bloody pulp and what flesh remained was charred and black. The hair had burned off, leaving the red scalp bare and singed.

"You can zip her up again," he said. "I'll just get some air."

He stepped back slowly and propped himself up against the ambulance.

The old Indian woman stood in front of him. She held up the photo of Ruth Weylon he had dropped.

"Are you looking for my granddaughter?" she asked.

"I'm so sorry," Birkett said. "You've had a terrible loss."

The old woman nodded. "Yes," she said. "Joan was a very dear friend. But now it is time to find my granddaughter before the evil men do. She is in great danger."

"But she's dead, ma'am. She was shot and killed."

The old woman looked at him, speaking slowly as if she was explaining something to a child. "No. The body in that ambulance is Joan. Ruth is down there in the canyon. Soon men will come to kill her, just as they tried to kill her yesterday. We must take your helicopter and go down to save her. I have tried to tell these other policemen that, but they think I'm crazy. Will you listen? We need to save her *now*."

"How can you be so sure she's alive?"

"Because she spoke to me in the night," said the old woman, fixing him with her bright brown eyes. "She spoke to me in a dream. She's down there in the canyon."

"Mister Birkett, Mister Birkett, come and look at this!"

"What is it?" The sheriff was calling him from the edge of the canyon rim and pointing down towards the distant lights of the Phantom Ranch. One of them was brighter than the rest, and it was winking.

Birkett remembered his signals training in Army Intelligence.

"That's Morse Code!"

23

The roar of Upset Rapid reached Ruth as the Colorado pulled left below Matkatamiba Canyon. Cold water from the crack in the bow of the little kayak slopped around her legs. It made the boat sluggish and hard to handle. Should she stop and bail it out? There wasn't time. The men in Matt's helicopter would be coming for her soon. Already the sun had risen and its hard light shone down on the inner canyon. Far above her head the upper reaches of rock turned from dull grey to brilliant reds, browns and yellows as the sun caught them. She could see clearly now and, if she could see, so could they.

The river turned farther to the left, the roar of water reached a crescendo and the current sucked her in, pulling her towards Upset Rapid, where the main flow of the Colorado joined the stream from 150 Mile Canyon. She knew the main danger was the large eddy hole at the bottom of the rapid, where the pounding waters from the two rivers collided so violently they could suck down anything trapped inside. She had to avoid that hole. She had to glide round it either to the left or the right. Rock walls flashed past her as she gained speed. She slid right and then left, tried to pull the kayak back right to avoid the hole, but the little craft was too slow and too full of water. The tail dragged and the kayak fell back. Ruth twisted around. The hole opened and the river rose up and swallowed her.

There was no light, no sense of up or down. The current tore at her, wrenching at her arms and shoulders, twisting her neck to breaking point. Pain lanced through her ears as she was sucked deeper. The dark water around her became quiet. Ruth felt the air bags pull the kayak towards the surface. It broached, rolled and Ruth was sitting upright in the air with the paddle still in her hand and the thunder of the river all around.

But the river was playing with her.

Looking round, she saw the hole sucking her back again. She flailed with the paddles. The kayak reached the downstream edge and tipped into the darkness. Darkness and light flashed before Ruth's eyes. Her helmet slammed against rock, again, and again. Her lungs screamed.

Ruth tore at the shoulder straps of the spray deck, ripped them from her body and pushed with her arms and legs. The water sucked her free of the kayak. Pain lanced up her leg. The current whipped her left and right, up and down, over and over. Her chest began to burst. The darkness turned red . . . and she was on the surface again, trying to cough and breathe at the same time as the eddy spat her out into the river. A rock leapt at her from the right as she tore downstream. She fended it off with her legs. Another lunged at her from the left. Then, just when she thought she was going under for the last time, the roaring water ceased and she drifted gently in the current towards a long narrow beach. Her feet touched bottom, she hauled herself into the shallows and up on to dry land. She pulled off her helmet and collapsed onto the muddy sand.

"Where do you want to start?" yelled Hooper. He had to shout now, even with the microphones and headsets. Ed Marino had taken the doors off the helicopter, just like they'd done in Korea, to give Fischetti and his boys nice clear shots. Fischetti sat next to Hooper in the co-pilot's seat, his gun cradled in his lap. Ed was behind him in the seat facing aft and the two other goons from Vegas sat right at the back, looking forward. Both had high calibre hunting rifles with scopes. There was no way they were going to miss this time.

"Take us back down to the river below that shack where we lost her yesterday," Fischetti shouted. "Then we'll move downstream with the flow. Ed tells me you and that Indian bitch of yours were great kayakers in your day. Is that right, War Hero? He reckons that's how she'll move, using the river."

"Sorry, Matt," said Ed over the headphones. "War is war!"

"I hope this business was worth it, Ed," Hooper shouted. Up ahead on the rim stood the ruin of the gift store, with its circle of police cars and an NPS helicopter set down just beyond it. He banked left into the bowl of the first valley and dived down over the Kaibab Trail towards Cedar Ridge and Skeleton Point. The canyon's green shoulders stretched out on either side as they dived around Natural Arch, and there was the Tipoff, with the little black shack of the pit toilet. Hooper saw two squares of yellow crime scene tape fluttering in the breeze as they roared overhead: Moe and Jimmy. Fischetti shuffled in his seat. Hooper thought of Beth and their kids, safe in Phoenix. Would she ever know what he was about to do for her? Part of him hoped she never would. He had caused her too much pain already.

They reached the final gorge at the base of the canyon, where the coffee-coloured water of the Colorado flowed relentlessly westwards. Hooper lifted them over the black metal bridge above Bright Angel Creek and slowed towards the beach at Phantom Ranch. He saw canoes, kayaks and rafts. People stared up at them from the campgrounds as they slid by.

"Do you want to land?" he shouted.

"Probably been too many cops around here asking questions already," Fischetti said. "Head on down the river. The sooner we nail that bitch, the better."

"You're the boss," Hooper shouted and pushed the joystick forward, bringing up the engine speed and sending the Huey sliding down the gorge over the silvery lattice of the Bright Angel Suspension Bridge. Just as they moved off, he saw a man run to the beach by the boats and shake his fist at them. It was they same guy he'd seen the day before at the pit toilet, when Moe and Jimmy had been killed.

Carpenter went crazy as the red Huey flew off down the river and disappeared around the bend. There was nothing he could do! Those goons in that chopper would catch up to Ruth and hunt her down like an animal.

He picked up a rock and smashed it down into the water in frustration, sending up a shower of spray. But the river flowed on as it had for millions of years, the ripples from his rock vanished and it was as if nothing had ever happened.

Helicopter engines and the whirling chop of rotor blades burst in on him again from the left over the Kaibab Bridge. For a moment he thought the guys in the Huey had circled back to get him. Then he glimpsed the blue and yellow stripe and the letters NPS on the National Park Service helicopter.

"Yes! Yes! Yes!"

He leapt up and down on the beach, waving his arms above his head and screaming out across the water as the machine slowed, hovered and turned towards the windsock at the ranch's makeshift helipad.

"She's alive!" screamed Carpenter, running to the chopper as it set down. "She's alive. We have to get after her!"

The door slid open and Don Birkett peered out. A little old Indian woman in a woven shawl sat next to him, along with two NPS Rangers armed with hunting rifles. Carpenter climbed up over the skid and squeezed in beside the old woman.

"The guys who attacked her yesterday just came past in a big red Huey," he shouted above the din of the rotors. "They have guns and they've gone downstream. We have to get after them."

Birkett had a headset and a microphone. "Call the sheriff and that FBI agent, McGraw, up on the rim," he shouted to the pilot. "We must have more helicopters in here, fast!"

"We need to get a full remote viewing unit set up and ready as soon as we bring Ruth in," Carpenter yelled. "Can you patch me through to the NSA so that I can round up the old support team from Project Element?"

The old woman tugged at his sleeve. "She won't go with you, Mister Carpenter," she shouted. "You've hurt her too much already."

"How did you know my name?"

"You are the one Ruth speaks of—the man who made her crazy. She won't work with you again."

"But she *has* to! Millions of lives are at stake."

"I know. That's why I asked Mister Birkett to bring me with him. Ruth trusts me. You cannot force her to reach out with her mind if she does not trust you. You know that. Let me guide her!"

Carpenter stared at the old woman. She seemed so tiny and frail beside the Rangers and their guns, yet her eyes regarded him with the same uncomfortable directness that Ruth's always had. They held the same power and confidence, the same ability to see right through him.

"All right," he shouted. "If we can still reach her alive, then you can guide her."

The NPS helicopter lifted off from the Phantom Ranch and headed down river.

The warmth of the rising sun fell on Ruth's face. She opened her eyes and looked round. The narrow campground followed the river along the base of the gorge's towering cliffs. Ruth pulled herself to her feet. A sharp pain shot up her left leg. She looked down. The leg of her pants was sliced open and blood was oozing from a deep gash on her calf. She ripped off a strip of material and tried to bind it, but the blood kept seeping through. Maybe it would heal later. Her helmet lay in the mud. She picked it up. The left-hand side had been stove in by the force of the blows taken in the "washing machine". If that had been the side of her own head, she would be dead now, she thought.

She looked around for the kayak. About a hundred yards away, on the other side of the river, she saw a flash of yellow. That was it, or what was left of it, trapped against a rock. The only way to reach it would be to swim across. She had her life jacket. If she started far enough up and eased herself out with the current rather than fighting it, she could slide over to the far bank in time to reach the kayak. The water felt cold. She was still shivering. But her rucksack, the guns and her supplies were all in the boat. She would need the guns when the men in Matt's helicopter came back.

She tried to calm herself, to slow the shivering, focus her mind and reach out to Matt. But all she heard was the chuckle of the water.

She tried again. The voices in her head were confused. But someone was coming; someone with a sense of purpose, and all she felt was death. The roar of the helicopter's turbine swept around the bend of the river upstream. The thud of its rotors biting the air on the turn reached her. She searched desperately along that narrow shelf of beach for somewhere to hide, but there was nowhere. She was trapped!

"Well, what do you know?" Fischetti whooped. "There she is!"

Hooper had already spotted Ruth on the narrow beach to the right of the canyon as the helicopter rounded the bend in the river. In some way he knew she would be there. He had felt her presence, in much the same way as he had known she was home when he came back at the end of a day. He pointed the nose of the chopper straight at her, blocking the line of fire from Fischetti and his goons in the back, and slowed to a hover above the river.

"Let's get the bitch now!" screamed Fischetti. "She's running. We need to bring her down before she gets away. Flip this thing around so that I can get a clear shot!"

Fischetti was excited, like a kid landing his first big trout. Hooper smelt the raw animal lust in him, the joy of killing, the same feeling they had taught him to welcome to his heart in Korea.

Ruth turned and ran, pumping her legs on the flat shale above the mud. There had to be a place to hide! Her eyes searched the face of the gorge frantically for a crevice, a cave or even a pile of rocks, anywhere she could shelter until the helicopter had passed. But the cliff was smooth and uncompromising. Her feet slipped on the wet shale. Her body slammed down onto the beach. The red helicopter slid towards her. She saw the sun sparkle on its windshield and the downdraft of its rotors raise a halo of spray that caught the light in rainbow colours as it hovered over the river. The noise of its turbines filled the canyon as the machine hung there, waiting.

She saw Matt looking down at her and the men behind him with guns. The one next to him in the cockpit was arguing with him to turn the chopper side on so that they could get a clean shot.

Matt looked straight ahead at her. He had a sad smile on his face.

She was helpless against them, naked. She was going to die.

She got to her feet facing the helicopter, closed her eyes and focussed on Matt Hooper.

"Turn this fucking chopper so we can get a shot!" Fischetti screamed, hopping up and down in his seat, but Hooper held the Huey with its nose facing his wife. He looked down at her, standing proud and defiant next to the river, their river, in the place she loved. She closed her eyes and he could hear her voice.

"Turn this helicopter, you bastard!" Fischetti shrieked. "Let me kill the bitch!"

Ruth opened her eyes.

Even from where he was hovering, so far away, Hooper could reach out and touch her.

"Goodbye, Princess," he said out loud. "I'm sorry."

Then he rammed the joystick forward, sending the Huey screaming down into the river.

"Maaaatttt!"

Ruth's heart leapt in her chest as the helicopter tilted at a crazy angle, staggered and fell. It smashed into the water in a fountain of spray, its rotors crumpled and its fuselage snapped, sending the whirling tail rotor spinning into the air. The gas tank exploded, throwing a mushroom of boiling orange flame upwards in a plume of thick black smoke. Pieces of wreckage flew skywards, cart wheeled in the sunshine and tumbled back into the river. Ruth ran to water's edge, screaming Matt's name, desperate for a glimpse of him in the relentless flow of the current.

"Matt! Matt!"

But there was none. Finally, she fell to her knees on the shale, sobbing with grief and shock, as the great river pounded the wreckage until all that remained was a ghostlike wreath of black smoke, fading as the wind took it, like an ascending soul.

24

Ruth felt her heart ripped from her body and smashed along with the helicopter. She knelt staring out across the water, sobbing with grief and trying to make sense of it all. Hooper had done what he told her he would do in her dream. He had taken his own life, and with it the lives of the men who had threatened them both.

She remembered the happy times they had enjoyed together before he had gone to war: of running the rapids, of lying on its banks between their kayaks in the sun, of making love. What war does not destroy it corrupts. Nothing can ever be the same. War had killed Hooper deep inside and twisted her own mind into tortuous shapes. It had driven her to pills and booze as a means of escape; cutting her off even more from those she loved.

She hardened her heart and looked across the water. Every trace of the helicopter had vanished, carried away by the irresistible force of the river that had carved this massive canyon. She saw the bright yellow hull of the kayak downstream on the far side, wedged between the rocks, waiting for her. She reached down, tightened the makeshift bandage around her calf, waded slowly out into the cold water of the Colorado and pushed off with her feet, angling across the gorge to the other side. Would she make it, or was the water flowing too fast? She pushed with her legs and struck out with her arms. The rocks on the other side rushed past at an alarming rate. She kicked harder. The kayak slid towards her, fifty yards away, forty, thirty . . . . She heaved with her arms and pumped with her legs. Her foot touched bottom and she pulled herself upright, just ten yards upstream of the little boat.

It was in bad shape. The crack in the bow had widened to a hole about six inches wide. The paddle was gone, but the rucksack was still there, wedged into the bow where she had left it. She heaved the kayak out of the river far enough to let it drain, pulled her old uniform out of the rucksack and jammed it into the hole in the bow. Then she pushed the rucksack back in place, climbed into the kayak and, using her hands as paddles, edged her way out into the flow of the river. The Sinyella Rapid, the only one between her and the entrance to Havasu Canyon seven miles farther on, was a simple 'read and run'. With luck and the river on her side, she should make it in just over half an hour.

"Ruth is in pain!" cried Granny Moon.

"What the hell's that?" shouted the pilot.

Looking forward, above the rim of the inner river gorge where they were flying, Carpenter saw a ball of smoke rising into the clear blue sky.

"It looks like a chopper went down!" he shouted.

"How far away?"

"A couple of miles. Hard to tell from here."

The NPS helicopter shot past Matkatamiba Canyon and banked right, following the gorge of the Colorado below them. Carpenter saw the broiling brown water of Upset Rapid as they started into the next left-hand turn.

"That looks like a paddle down there!" he shouted, pointing to the base of the gorge.

"Could be," said the pilot. "Look up ahead. I'd say this is where the crash happened."

"I don't see anything."

"Look there in the middle of the river! That standing wave!"

Carpenter peered forwards. What he had thought to be a rock showing just above the water was in fact painted bright red. There were white letters painted on it ' . . . copter Tours'.

"That's it! It was an 'Eagle Helicopter Tours' chopper they were using. I wonder what brought it down?"

"She did," said Granny Moon. "She and her husband. He gave himself for her."

Carpenter stared at her. "How do you know that?"

"She is my granddaughter."

"Is she still alive?"

"Let us land and find out," said Granny Moon, looking at him again with those penetrating eyes. "There's a place over there on that beach. It looks wide enough to land on."

"Are you sure this is really necessary?" Birkett asked. "Shouldn't we just get on down the river?"

"We need to know where my granddaughter is. To do that we must land."

Carpenter shrugged. "We should do as the lady says," he said. "She's been right all the way so far."

Birkett looked uncomfortable, but ordered the pilot to set down anyway. In a few moments, Carpenter and the little old woman were kneeling by the shore of the narrow beach some fifty yards from the NPS helicopter. Birkett was still on the radio, checking on the progress of his reinforcements. The two NPS Rangers stood guard. Granny Moon reached out and touched the muddy sand. Carpenter saw two footprints, with deep imprints in front of them, as if someone had knelt down hard.

"What can you tell?" he asked.

"Nothing except what you see for yourself," said Granny Moon, smiling impishly at him. "Ruth collapsed here when her husband crashed his helicopter and sacrificed himself. See, the line of the knee marks and her feet point to the river and the wreckage of his aircraft."

"So why did you insist that we stop here?"

"So that I could speak with you in private away from the others. Ruth will never come with you. She is too scared. If you bring in your Army, with their guns and soldiers, she will retreat into herself and be of no use to you. Let me guide her alone, here in the canyon at a place we both know, and she may do what you ask."

"How can I make that happen?"

"Ask the men in the helicopter to drop us off where I tell you, near Havasu Canyon. Say that I'm certain she has gone downstream towards Lake Mead and that you need them to search the river farther on as thoroughly as possible. Tell them we have to pick up something she needs at Havasu to contact the submarine and that they should go on ahead while we get it. Say what you like. But they must not take her from the canyon or be present when she tries to reach the Russians. Otherwise, she will not succeed and millions will die. Can you do this?"

"I can," said Carpenter. "Thank you."

Ruth paddled the kayak over to the left bank of the river, just above Havasu Creek. Normally a lot of folks tied up at this spot so they could trek up and see the Havasu Falls. Today there were just two boats moored there, probably belonging to hardened canyon runners taking one last trip in spite of the crisis. She heaved the rucksack out of the bow and pushed the little boat back into the stream, almost sad to watch it go. The kayak drifted into the current of the Havasu Falls, rolled slowly and sank from view. Ruth reached into the rucksack, pulled out the Walther PPK and pushed it into her pants pocket. Then she dressed her wound as best she could and started to scrabble along the rough trail leading up Havasu Creek. The going was difficult, with a lot of rock-climbing and scrambling.

She thought of Matt and the sacrifice he had made for her to live. Then, as the tears returned to her eyes, she hardened her heart once more and climbed on.

25

FRIDAY, 26 OCTOBER
LENINGRAD
5.55 PM LOCAL TIME
14.55 GMT

Kharkov watched the flood lamps glare down into Nevsky Prospeckt with their cold, hard light, catching the first flakes of early falling snow and the gleaming steel bayonets of the troops lining the street. A crowd of nervous citizens dragged from their beds to act as witnesses, wore hurriedly grasped coats and blankets over their pyjamas and nightgowns. The small group of frightened prisoners, men and women in their everyday clothes and uniforms, crowded together between the columns on either side of the gateway to the Strogonov Palace. North of the assembled crowd, towards the Admiralty Garden and south towards the Kazan Cathedral, the great street was deserted.

Ever since his time in Siberia, Kharkov had never been able to stand the cold. It bored into him like a worm and lodged under his skin. It never left him, even in summer. He shivered beneath his Naval overcoat.

"Do you think they'll come, Professor?" Cherlenko asked.

"Baybarin might, Comrade General," said Kharkov. "Tatyana will not."

"You sound very sure."

"My wife and I raised her. I know her mind. Even with me as a hostage, you will not force her out. She will expect me to see the higher good in all this and be ready to sacrifice myself for the cause."

"And are you?"

Kharkov looked up at him.

"I was ready to die when they sent me to Siberia, but I was not ready for my wife to die as she did."

"Millions more will be killed if we do not turn back that submarine, Professor."

"I know."

"And that doesn't bother you?"

"Of course it bothers me. Why do you think I'm helping you? If I'd wanted Tatyana to succeed, I'd have run away myself, or even put a bullet in my brain, so you could not use me against her. I do not want to see innocent people killed any more that you do."

Then Kharkov remembered whom he was talking to. This was 'The Butcher of Novocherkassk', the man who would cheerfully have shot all the women at the Park on Vasilyevskiy Island that morning if he'd thought it would have brought him one single centimetre towards his goal. The man who had rounded up Baybarin's family and friends to stand in front of a firing squad.

Cherlenko pushed back the sleeve of his tailored overcoat to glance at his watch.

"It is almost time," he said, raising a loudhailer to his lips.

"Gregor Baybarin! I am General Vladimir Cherlenko, officer commanding all KGB personnel here in Leningrad. By the emergency powers invested in my by the People's Defence Council, I am authorised to execute all the suspected dissidents here before me, including your mother and father, your two sisters, your brother and their families, as well as your former colleagues from the Admiralty, who no doubt aided and abetted you in your treasonous crimes against the State."

He paused. The word "State" echoed between the great buildings like artillery fire.

"In just two minutes, on the last peel of six o'clock. I will start by executing your mother and father, unless you make yourself known. Do you hear me? Captain Slavin, bring them forward."

Cherlenko stood in silence as the last echoes of his words died away and the snow fluttered down. The men and women in front of the Strogonov Palace huddled a little closer together.

Cherlenko switched off the loudhailer and turned to Kharkov. "You see? Baybarin leaves me no choice. And to think that this street was once called 'The Street of Tolerance'! I will take command of the firing squad, Captain Slavin."

"Yes, Comrade General."

Ludmylla Slavin stepped aside. Cherlenko raised his hand to the sky.

"Firing squad, ready!"

With a single 'clack' a dozen rifles lifted to a dozen shoulders and their bolts drew back. The old man and woman who had been brought forward put their arms around each other.

From the depths of the city the first chime of six o'clock rang out. It had a deep and mournful sound, more like a heartbeat than a bell. Kharkov tried to think how many times he had heard it over the years. The second chime sounded. During the years of the 'Siege of the Nine Hundred Days', that bell had been the pulse of Leningrad, a signal that the city was still alive. Now it was a death knell. Cherlenko and his kind had perverted even that.

The third chime rang.

"Take aim!"

Kharkov looked into the eyes of Baybarin's parents. There is no death, he thought. Not for those who understand.

The fourth chime came, echoing up through the buildings, from the House of Books and Yeliseev's famous delicatessen to the Aeroflot Building and the Great Curved Façade of the Kazan Cathedral.

Cherlenko is enjoying this, thought Kharkov. He wants me to share his twisted belief that this act of slaughter is his sad duty, but really he relishes it. He is an animal who disguises murder behind a uniform and a smile. I hate him and everyone like him.

The fifth chime sounded. The old couple closed their eyes.

A single gunshot cracked in the cold air.

"Wait!" screamed a voice beyond the southern barricade.

"Stand easy!" snapped Cherlenko. The dozen rifle bolts snapped back. Every head in the crowd turned.

A tall young man in a naval uniform stood in the middle of Nevsky Prospeckt. He had blond hair, an open face and mild blue eyes that looked resolutely towards Cherlenko and the assembled soldiers. He held a pistol in his right hand, pointing at the sky.

"I take it you are the traitor Gregor Baybarin?" Cherlenko's voice boomed from the loudhailer.

"I am."

Soldiers raised their rifles and machine guns.

"Kill me now," shouted the young man. "And you will never know where Tatyana Rospin is hiding."

Kharkov saw Cherlenko smile. "In chess, my young friend, it is unwise to leave your Queen unguarded. Tell me where she is at once, or I will order this firing squad to complete their work."

"I play chess too, Comrade General," Baybarin shouted. "You keep people afraid, because you promise death. But there is no death!" Then before anyone could stop him, he opened his mouth and pushed the barrel of the pistol between his teeth.

Kharkov held his breath. He heard a muffled crack, saw a mist of blood blossom like a halo in the flood lamps. The young man collapsed to the ground. All that remained of him was his broken body and the dying echo of his last shot, rising into the darkened sky.

Cherlenko cursed violently. Kharkov ran to the young man and knelt beside him. Baybarin's face had collapsed from within. A growing pool of blood trickled between the cobblestones, staining the newly fallen snow. Kharkov reached out his hand and touched the young man's neck. There had never really been any doubt about it. Baybarin was dead.

He heard a rush of footsteps. Soldiers surrounded him, their black boots like the trunks of trees in a forest. He looked up. Cherlenko pushed his way through, with Slavin right behind him.

"Is this Baybarin?"

"Yes," said Kharkov. "You saw his face before . . . before he shot himself. You have the photographs on his *zapista*."

"Strip the body!" Cherlenko shrieked like a petulant child. "I want every stitch of clothing he's wearing examined for clues, right down to the skin. Do you hear me?"

Kharkov saw Slavin snap a stiff salute. A stretcher passed through the crowd to the front. Two soldiers lifted Baybarin onto it and covered his body with a blanket.

Cherlenko punched his fist into his other hand. "Now we are back where we started! Why did that idiot show himself and then put a pistol in his mouth? What was he hoping to achieve?"

"He gained the lives of his family and friends," said Kharkov, still staring at the pool of blood on the cobbles. "Without him, you have no hold over Tatyana. He gave his life for them all."

Kharkov watched Cherlenko try to think of a clever response, but none came.

"I still have you, Comrade Professor. Don't forget that. You are hostage enough for Tatyana Rospin."

"And Baybarin's family and friends?"

Cherlenko glanced at the huddle of men, women and children hemmed in by the soldiers against the Palace gates.

"They are associates of a proven terrorist," he said. "As such, they are enemies of the State. A long stay in prison would be the best thing for them!"

Then he ordered two soldiers to take Kharkov back to the Bolshoy Dom and turned to talk to Captain Slavin.

Kharkov bowed his head and walked meekly to the KGB staff car, settled into the back seat and allowed himself to be driven away. His left hand held his coat closed tight against the cold. His right hand was tucked deeply into his coat pocket, around the pistol he had taken from the ground beside Baybarin's body.

Cherlenko was furious at the way Baybarin had robbed him of his key to Tatyana Rospin, at the incompetence of his staff, his own inability to predict what had just happened, and at Kharkov's constant reminders of his failure in front of Captain Slavin. But he was also deeply afraid. Afraid because he knew that what Comrade Khrushchev could give one moment, he could take away the next —witness Admiral Shumanin's fall from grace, in spite of his powerful ally Admiral Gorshkov, a venerated hero of the Soviet Union whose portrait adorned the Ministry of Defence. If he, Cherlenko was to fail in this mission, then he would surely be stripped of all rank and possibly even shot for treason. That was if he escaped the nuclear fallout from the American reprisals after Petrachkov had unleashed his torpedo.

He glared at the assembled faces around the briefing room at KGB headquarters, seeing only incompetents and informers. His gaze was constantly drawn to the big electric clock above the table, as it counted down the hours until Petrachkov reached the American blockade. Several times during the introductory reports from the local KGB and GRU commanders, Captain Slavin had called him away to take calls from high officials in Moscow requesting progress updates, and after each one he had come back to the table more angry and afraid than before.

"So in summary," he asked pointedly, "you have at last searched every building in the city, including the chemical warehouses, hospitals and deep freeze facilities you overlooked the first time and *still* found nothing?"

Heads nodded with fear and embarrassment. Each officer knew that his career, if not his own life, now hung in the balance, just as Cherlenko's did.

"Then enlighten me," continued Cherlenko, "as to how the traitor Gregor Baybarin could appear on Nevsky Prospeckt, having passed like a ghost through all those roadblocks of yours, in front of all your troops, and still be allowed to draw a gun?"

Cherlenko noted the long silence that followed, broken only by the soft click of the electric clock.

The senior officer of the GRU was the first who dared speak. "He must have been hiding close by, Comrade General. Perhaps he came up through the sewers or the drains. Perhaps he found some service passageways for the Metro that we missed."

Cherlenko was amazed that the man should have the audacity to flaunt his own incompetence. "Perhaps! Perhaps! Perhaps!" he taunted. "We are drowning in uncertainty. The only *certainty* is that my head will roll in less than eight hours if you do not find Tatyana Rospin! And if my head rolls, then it will not be the only one. Do I make myself clear?"

Nobody answered.

Cherlenko glared at Shumanin. "And what of the naval situation? Have you had any more luck in detecting the submarine, or is it just the same litany of excuses?"

Shumanin looked him straight in the eye.

"We have no further news, Comrade General. If that was Petrachkov's submarine our combined forces heard off New York, then he is on schedule to reach the blockade around Cuba in approximately eight hours. In our favour, however is the fact that the Americans have a special anti-submarine task force out looking for him, including a squadron of destroyers and the aircraft carrier *Essex*. Even a man of Petrachkov's cunning will not get through, and there is one additional ray of hope."

"And what is that?" Cherlenko asked hungrily.

"Gregor Baybarin is dead. If he was feeding the authentication codes via Tatyana Rospin to Petrachkov, then that conduit is now closed. Petrachkov will expect to hear from the girl in a few minutes' time at the regular hour and find that her message cannot be confirmed. At that point he will realise that something is amiss and call off his attack."

"But couldn't Baybarin have passed several days' worth of codes on to Tatyana Rospin, enough to authenticate as many messages as he needed?"

"No, Comrade General. At that level of security any officer below flag rank knows the codes for only twenty-four hours in advance. By deserting when he did, Baybarin was able to take code words for that day and the day after. But now that period has elapsed; new codes have been issued to senior personnel here in Leningrad that correspond with those in Petrachkov's safe."

"Who knows these codes?"

"Only myself," said Shumanin. "In view of the critical situation, and until my replacement is appointed, I had all Apex code books at the Admiralty withdrawn and locked in my personal safe. I have memorised the codes for the next twenty-four hours and no more, just in case they are needed to call off the attack."

Professor Kharkov raised his hand. "Could I lie down for a few moments, Comrade General? I got a chill out there in the snow and I haven't slept for days."

"Very well, Professor. I may need you again this evening as a hostage, so please do not sleep too soundly. Guards, take him next door."

"Do we have any useful evidence from Baybarin's body?" Cherlenko asked once Kharkov had left.

One of the police officers carefully emptied the contents of a large brown envelope in front of Cherlenko.

"Very little, Comrade General. There was a set of identity papers in his pocket, in his own name, a few roubles and a watch. He also had his military identity tags."

"And what of the gun he shot himself with?"

"It must be with the rest of his uniform, Comrade General. I thought his personal effects would tell us more."

"Never mind," snapped Cherlenko, seizing upon the other items and turning them in the light.

Between the two flat metal tags hung a tiny silver cross.

"Tell me, Comrade," he said, turning to Shumanin. "Was Baybarin a religious man?"

"Religion is frowned on by the State, Comrade General."

"I know that, but I ask you again *Comrade* Shumanin, as a commander who knows his men, was Baybarin religious? Was he a Christian perhaps?" He held up the little silver cross for all to see.

"I cannot say, Comrade General."

"Are *you* a religious man, Comrade?"

"No," said Shumanin, sensing a trap. "I put my faith in the State."

"Another good diplomatic answer," said Cherlenko, turning back to the other officers in the room and the map of the city. "Tell me, have you searched all the churches around the Nevsky Prospeckt?"

"All churches in the city have been boarded up and closed for years, Comrade General," said the senior officer of the GRU. "They have been searched, yes, but . . . ."

"But what?" barked Cherlenko, glaring at him.

"But not exhaustively. As I said, they've all been boarded up."

"And this building here?" Cherlenko was pointing to a large building on Nevsky Prospeckt, within a hundred yards of the Strogonov Palace.

"It is the Kazan Cathedral, Comrade General."

"A church!"

"Yes, Comrade General. A church."

Cherlenko took a deep breath.

"Indeed, Comrade. A church. Comrade Captain Slavin, I want an airtight blockade around it within ten minutes, with every door, window and shutter covered and any tunnels sealed. Then I want full architectural blueprints on this table and a squad of troops lined up outside this building. I will be on the phone to Moscow. I think we may be closer to finding Tatyana Rospin than we thought."

FRIDAY, 26 OCTOBER
THE GRAND CANYON
10.06 A.M. MOUNTAIN STANDARD TIME
1706 GMT

Ruth climbed on up the Havasu Canyon, across rocky outcrops and boulders slick with spray from the turquoise blue water of Havasu River. The going was difficult, but she was sure-footed enough, in spite of the wound on her leg. Her clothes, washed of the mud from the Colorado by the clear Havasu water, had dried on her back.

She climbed on, higher and higher, towards the secret place where Granny Moon had brought her all those years before, a place where she felt safe.

She pulled a water bottle from the rucksack, drank a few mouthfuls and chewed on some emergency rations for a while. Then she looked down. The cut in her leg was still bleeding into her moccasin. She took another bandage from her pack and strapped it tight. Would the blood have left a trail?

She repacked the rucksack, pushed the wrappings from the dressing under a rock out of sight and walked on, still thinking of Hooper and what Granny Moon had told her about peace so many years before.

Black Queen

TIME TO EVENT

00:05:21

DAYS : HRS : MINS

26

"With all due respects, Comrade General, Professor Kharkov insisted he not be disturbed," said the guard. "He is sleeping."

"And the next bed you sleep in will be a heap of stinking straw in a cattle truck on the way to the Gulag," hissed Cherlenko. "Let me pass!"

"Of course, Comrade General. At once."

Another guard sat by Kharkov's bed. He snapped to attention when Cherlenko burst in.

"Kharkov," shouted Cherlenko, "we're going hunting. Get up!"

Kharkov seemed in a deep trance. At first he did not respond but then suddenly he woke like a man hit by an electric shock.

"Uh . . . Oh, Comrade General. I'm afraid you took me by surprise. I was dreaming."

"Get up! I think I know where your precious stepdaughter is to be found."

"Oh . . . where?"

"Nearer than expected," said Cherlenko, bundling Kharkov to his feet and leading him out of the door. "She may be in a church not far from here."

FRIDAY, 26 OCTOBER
SUBMARINE K-6
8.30 P.M. MOSCOW TIME
1730 GMT

On the submarine, morale had swung from a wild euphoria to a sense of impending doom. The achievement of having managed to slip undetected beneath the noses of the American ships and submarines into the safety of deeper water had raised everyone's spirits. Petrachkov had sanctioned a double ration of vodka for everybody not actively on watch and even Dudko and Muhkin, the KGB and Party representatives on board, had joined in the celebration.

But now, as Viktor Mostock's condition began to deteriorate and the rendezvous with their target crept nearer, they remembered their terrible losses at Severmorsk. What had begun as a patriotic quest to avenge their families was moving towards the stark reality of an act of mass destruction with a live atomic torpedo.

In the officers' wardroom, the evening's session with Max Rospin and Doctor Chiker was underway.

"The authentication codes are correct, Comrade Captain," whispered Kapitulsky after the first communication had been established with Tatyana Rospin.

"Very well," said Petrachkov. "Doctor Chiker, can you please ask Max what the strategic situation is regarding our conflict with America and if our instructions have been modified in any way?"

Chiker relayed this message to Max, who sat in his trance-like state at the head of the table.

"Admiral Shumanin sends his regards to Comrade Captain Petrachkov," he said. "He would like to congratulate you and your crew on evading the American anti-submarine group, but fears that even greater challenges lie ahead. You are to proceed according to your first instructions and attack the flagship of the American blockade, the aircraft carrier *Essex*, east of Bermuda."

Petrachkov whispered to Chiker. "Is any other information available?"

"Admiral Shumanin repeats his warning against the American use of deception," said Max. "You are to be particularly wary of any voice messages transmitted through the water than may pertain to come from his headquarters on another . . . ."

His voice trailed off.

"Another what?" asked Petrachkov out loud, forgetting himself for an instant.

"I . . . I do not know. Tatyana has cut herself off. Perhaps she was interrupted or disturbed. This sometimes happens if she is upset."

"I am sorry, Comrade Captain," said Chiker. "This is, after all, an experimental technique. I only wish we could have perfected it before we had to use it under these circumstances."

"Never mind," Petrachkov said. "We have the main elements of the message confirmed and I'm sure Max must be tired. Please tell him to rest."

When the two scientists had gone, Petrachkov called his watch officers to the wardroom, pulled out a detailed chart of the Caribbean and spread it on the table. On it he drew a straight line representing their course from the Hudson Canyon off New York to the estimated position of the *Essex* battle group. Across that he marked a second line in red. Then, taking a pair of compasses and a ruler, he worked for a minute or two at estimating distances and then drew a third line around Cuba, which he hatched in green.

"According to Max, the outer escorts of the *Essex* battle group are here," he said, pointing to the red line. "The green area around Cuba represents the sea currently within the American 'quarantine zone' behind the blockade commanded from the *USS Essex*. Her aircraft also patrol the area to make sure none of our blockade-runners gets through and to guard the destroyers from attack by submarines such as ourselves. Our first objective is therefore to run the gauntlet of this outer destroyer screen and its protecting aircraft from the *Essex*. Does anyone have any suggestions?"

"The underwater landscape does not look conducive to the sort of manoeuvre we executed off New York," said the navigating officer. "But the warmer surface water will form a distinct separation layer over the colder ocean below and we could hide under this. Any sonar waves will bounce back to the surface without us being seen."

"We could try," agreed Petrachkov. "But it's an old trick that's been used a great many times before."

"There are numerous commercial shipping lanes, Captain," Kapitulsky suggested. "Some of them even pass through the *Essex*'s protective screen. If we were to spot another surface ship going at any respectable speed, a large American oil tanker perhaps that would not have submarine detection equipment, we could ride along in its shadow. That way, the sonar echo reflected back to the warships would be perceived as the tanker's hull and any propeller or reactor noise we might make would be lost in the cacophony of sound and vibration from the larger ship."

"A good plan," said Petrachkov. "And one which I myself have used to great effect before. In my time we called that manoeuvre 'buggering the whale'. Go to your stations now and prepare your compartments. When Kapitulsky's whale does emerge, we shall have to act quickly if we are to bugger it successfully. That is all."

The officers filed out of the wardroom into the corridor heading back to their stations. Petrachkov stopped Kapitulsky.

"You show a great deal of initiative, Comrade. I would like you to accompany me on a visit to Mostock, if you will."

The two men threaded their way back through the CCP, to Mostock's old empire of the reactor room, turbines and engines, and the tiny sick bay off the main galley. Viktor Mostock's face now showed severe signs of radiation poisoning. Blisters covered his skin. Sweat soaked his pillow and the blanket around his neck.

Petrachkov felt helpless to do anything for his oldest friend, but he still needed Mostock's knowledge and experience if they were to survive this ordeal. Perhaps Mostock would appreciate the chance to serve. It would prove Petrachkov had not yet written him off.

"I hope you brought vodka, Sergei Nikolai," said Mostock. "You know that is the best cure for radiation sickness."

"Perhaps later, Viktor. Right now I need your mind to be sharp."

Mostock smiled. "Ah, you are not yet ready to put me in a torpedo tube and blast me out into the ocean then?"

"Not yet. Comrade Kapitulsky and I have a problem we need to solve."

"Concerning communications obviously," said Mostock eyeing the younger officer.

"Indeed," Petrachkov said. "I am still anxious that we should establish some conventional link with Leningrad to confirm our orders. You, Comrade Kapitulsky, saw how Max stopped suddenly in mid-flow. While I accept that telepathy is new and experimental, and while I don't doubt Max or Doctor Chiker's abilities or their dedication, I would feel a lot more comfortable if I could talk to Admiral Shumanin myself by radio."

"The main challenge, Sergei Nikolai, is to be able to deploy an aerial without surfacing," said Mostock. "There are no hatches or air locks one could use to pass a wire outside the submarine without flooding it."

"However," said Kapitulsky, "it occurs to me that there will certainly be Soviet commercial vessels, and indeed other submarines of our own, in the vicinity of the American blockade. While our long-range VHF and low frequency systems are useless, it might be possible to rig up one of the short-range low-power units we hold in reserve. Then, if it was possible to surface, even for short periods of time, with only the conning tower above the water, we could try and contact one of our Russian comrades for news and ask them to relay orders from Leningrad using their own long-range radios."

Mostock nodded. "The kid's good," he said. "But even the conning tower might show up on radar. What is the range of these sets anyway?"

"Only about fifty miles, Comrade," Kapitulsky said.

"It's better than nothing," said Petrachkov. "Kapitulsky, you put that work in progress. Viktor, see if you can think of a way of sending a message without surfacing. In the meantime, please keep your brain clear of vodka. We are about to go to war."

FRIDAY, 26 OCTOBER
LENINGRAD
9.06 P.M. LOCAL TIME
1806 GMT

Cherlenko's Zil limousine, a motor cycle escort and two troop transports, swept down Malaya Konyushennaya Ulitsa, across Nevsky Prospeckt and up the semicircular drive to the great entrance of the Cathedral of Our Lady of Kazan. From the back seat beside Cherlenko, Kharkov saw the flood lamps shining up at the imposing dome, the spire and the grand columns of the great colonnade that stretched round on each side of the entrance like the embracing arms of God. Throughout the years of the 'Siege of the Nine Hundred Days', he had always wondered why the Germans had never succeeded in obliterating such a proud landmark. Perhaps God looks after his own after all?

"Impressive, isn't it?" he said.

"As an extravagant edifice to an outmoded luxury, possibly," said Cherlenko. "As the scene of my final victory over the elusive Tatyana Rospin, definitely."

Captain Slavin greeted Cherlenko with a smart salute as they stepped out of the staff car into the snow.

"Comrade General," she said. "The cathedral is surrounded and sealed. Nobody can get in or out without being intercepted."

"And the tunnels and passageways?"

"We have the architect's drawings you sent us. We are searching now."

They walked smartly up the Cathedral steps. Cherlenko and Slavin took them two at a time. Kharkov found it difficult to keep up.

"Very good," said Cherlenko. "How long do you think it will take to comb this place thoroughly?"

"We have started a systematic search, beginning with the outlying rooms and working inwards to the main body of the church," reported Slavin. "To thoroughly examine each room, as well as the passageways and tunnels, could take at least an hour."

"You have men on the roof?"

Slavin stopped, turned and pointed. "I have snipers and searchlights on the House of Books across the street, as well as on other buildings, covering the cathedral from different angles and of course, there are men on the roof of the cathedral itself."

"That is good. Professor, come with us please."

They entered the main body of the cathedral, with its gleaming marble pillars, murals and high curved ceiling decorated with hexagonal panels. A huge silver sun hung above the altar, looking down on them all, just as it had when he and his wife had worked there throughout the Siege. During those years the cathedral had been used as a casualty station for the wounded and a refuge for the homeless. It had been hard to keep the children alive, to protect them from the bombs and to make sure they did not starve. Kharkov had relied on his wife so much, as he went scuttling to and fro from the front line ferrying munitions into Leningrad across frozen Lake Lagoda to the east. Irina had tended the dying, nursed the wounded and protected the children. She had found food for them all. She had kept them alive.

He felt the old anger rise as he thought of what men like Cherlenko had done to Irina in Siberia. It had been an obscene death for a woman who had cared so much for the sick.

But the children had survived.

"Comrade Professor, you are familiar with this place?"

Cherlenko stood at the high altar with Captain Slavin by his side.

He had swept the candles from the holy marble slab and laid out the architectural plans of the building in their place.

Look at those two, thought Kharkov, the High Priest and Priestess of the new religion of power. See their vestments in their uniforms, their religious texts in the dictates of the Praesidium, and their bloody vengeance in the labour camps, the insane asylums and cancer wards from here to Siberia. See their faithful worshippers in the faces of the Party members, the bureaucrats, informers and uniformed thugs of the KGB and GRU who hang on their every word.

"Yes," he said, standing below the altar and looking up. "I know this place well. My wife tended the sick here during the Great Patriotic War."

"And if you were to hide here, Comrade Professor, where would you choose?"

Kharkov's eyes travelled around the body of the church, from the rows and rows of abandoned pews, the confessionals, the choir stalls and alcoves, back to the altar itself.

"I would not hide here in the main church, Comrade General. It is too obvious a place and too easy to search. I would hide in the maze of corridors and passageways *beneath* the Cathedral. It is the oldest, safest part of the building. We used to shelter the sick there during the fascist artillery bombardments."

"Very well," said Cherlenko, studying the plans carefully. "I will go and direct the militia on where to focus their efforts. Comrade Slavin, you stay here and drink in the wonderful atmosphere of this holy place with my learned friend, Professor Kharkov."

Slavin tried to protest. It was amusing, thought Kharkov, to watch their mutual mistrust at work. Slavin had been assigned to transmit Cherlenko's mistakes back to Moscow. For all his power, Cherlenko was still a prisoner of the State.

"It will be my pleasure to demonstrate the beauty of this historic church to Comrade Slavin," said Kharkov. The young woman scowled at him. Cherlenko rolled up the plans and marched off towards the back of the cathedral, his boots clattering on the stone floor.

Kharkov was alone with Slavin. He pointed up at the great domed ceiling, described it to her in detail and began strolling towards the confessionals, with Slavin at his side. But she was more interested in immediate issues.

"So, Comrade Professor, you are nearing the end of your chess game with Comrade Cherlenko. Will he succeed in capturing Tatyana Rospin alive?"

"That all depends on if she wants to be caught, Comrade Captain. She is a very strong-willed young woman."

"Like her mother, I imagine. Comrade Cherlenko said your wife was a doctor, a hero of the Soviet Union, and that she died after the Great Patriotic War?"

Kharkov turned to face her.

"I fear you are confused, Comrade Captain," he said. "Tatyana Rospin and her brother Max were not our natural children. They were both left in our care during the great siege after their own parents were killed. Our own children had died of starvation the year before. My wife said it was only right that we take care of the Rospin twins as if they were our own."

"But you and your wife were sent to Siberia. You could not have taken care of them then."

"That is correct, Comrade Captain. The children were put into care, for the good of the State."

Captain Slavin turned to look at him. Kharkov noticed the keen mind working behind her dark brown eyes. "I sense a note of cynicism in your voice, Comrade Professor," she said. "Do you blame the State for the death of your wife?"

"It is hard for me not to, Comrade Captain. She was tortured to death in a State research facility, where she had been sent without trial to assist in experiments that she would have found an obscene corruption of her oath as a doctor."

"Individuals must sometimes suffer for the greater good of the many," Slavin said.

"Nobody would ever have benefited from the results of this

research," replied Kharkov. "They would just have died a more painful death."

"Be careful, Comrade Professor, I could send you back to a mental asylum for expressing criticism of the State."

"Have no fear. Comrade Cherlenko already has me consigned there, just as soon as Tatyana is captured and he no longer needs my assistance."

"You do not seem too concerned. Do you not fear death?"

"Not any more."

"Then you have faith in a life after death?"

"Religion is frowned on by the State, Comrade Captain. You heard that already from Admiral Shumanin."

He could tell she was growing weary of his company and only wanted to find Cherlenko, so that she could document his actions for her next report to Moscow. They were nearing the ornate confessional boxes lining the wall of the cathedral. Kharkov looked around the vast space. They were still alone. Inside his coat pocket, his fingers tightened on the pistol he had taken from Baybarin's body.

"I believe in the survival of the human spirit, Comrade Slavin. It cannot be destroyed, no matter how many mental hospitals or labour camps the State builds . . . ."

The crack of a distant shot echoed around the empty church. Kharkov heard shouts and a scream. A volley of concentrated fire crackled and died.

"He's found them!" Slavin gasped. "I must go . . . ." She turned towards the sound, reaching for her pistol. Then she looked back at Kharkov, torn between her orders to ensure that he did not escape and to spy on Cherlenko for the Defence Council.

"Go," Kharkov said. "You have the cathedral surrounded by guards. I will not try to escape. Go!"

Another volley of shots sounded. Slavin nodded, drew her pistol and ran off between the pews heading for the altar.

Kharkov waited until she was well out of sight, made sure no other guards were lurking in the cloisters or the body of the great church and stepped over to the nearest confessional box. He pulled back the curtain. Looking up at him was a young woman with blonde hair and soft grey eyes.

"Hello, Tatyana," Kharkov said. "We may not have long. Cherlenko is very good at what he does. Your friends will not be able to hold out against him for much longer."

"I know. Is everything going as planned?"

"It is. They do not suspect. You have done well, Tatyana. You led them a merry chase around the city."

She smiled. "I would have held out longer, but Gregor wanted to save his family. He could not bear the thought that they might suffer because of him."

"He was very brave. He played his part well. We will succeed now, because of the time he bought us."

"And how much time is left?"

"Only a few hours before the submarine attacks the blockade."

"If they catch me alive, they will use me to contact Max and stop the attack."

"Yes. And they may not let me stay to assist you."

Her eyes looked into his.

"I wanted to see you one last time," she said softly.

"I know."

"Did Gregor give it to you?"

"I took it from him afterwards," said Kharkov, showing her the gun.

"Then do what you have to do," she said, looking into his eyes with calm certainty. "I am ready."

"You are so like your mother," he said, raising the pistol. "There is no death, Tatyana. You know that, don't you?"

"I do, Father. Thank you for my life."

"I love you."

He pressed the muzzle of the gun to her forehead, where he was sure he would require no second shot and, as her grey eyes closed, he pulled the trigger.

27

Cherlenko heard the single shot and wheeled round, leaving the officer in charge of the militia to deal with the remainder of the terrorists. Kharkov had been right. There had been only a handful of them, five or six at most, and they were no match for his trained soldiers with their automatic weapons. But they had fought valiantly, drawing the soldiers onwards and falling back from the main chamber of the cathedral one room at a time.

Had it been nothing more than a diversionary tactic?

To divert him from what?

Then came the single shot from behind him, the crack of a small calibre pistol. He ran back into the main chamber and called out. Kharkov's voice sounded from over by the confessionals.

"Over here! She's dead!"

Cherlenko rushed towards the voice. Kharkov sat slumped in a pew near an open confessional. Cherlenko saw a pistol on the floor near his feet.

"Who is dead? Who?"

"There," said Kharkov, pointing to the confessional.

Cherlenko looked inside. A young woman sat slumped in the seat. She had blonde hair, a ragged hole in her forehead and a halo of blood and brains behind her on the wooden panelling.

Cherlenko's heart leapt.

"Is that Tatyana Rospin?"

Kharkov looked up at him.

"Yes, it is."

Cherlenko felt the gates of hell opening beneath him. He had failed in his mission of capturing Tatyana Rospin alive. He had failed in the presence of the assembled military of Leningrad and General Secretary Khrushchev's own personal emissary. There could be no doubt. His life now hung in the balance.

"What happened?" he shouted, reaching down and grabbing the older man by his coat. "Why couldn't you stop her?"

"Tatyana had a gun. I thought she was going to kill me, but she turned it on herself just as Baybarin did. I could not cry out for fear of her pulling the trigger."

"Did you not try and reason with her?"

Cherlenko was shaking the old man now, anxious for answers, desperate to avoid the black hole that would swallow him, once news of Tatyana's death reached Moscow.

"I had only a few seconds before she died, Comrade General. She knew that once you caught her, you would use her to contact Max and stop the submarine. This was her only way of escape, to make her mind unavailable to you."

It made sense of course. It all made perfect, logical sense, but was there some other motive lurking behind Kharkov's eyes?

"She meant a great deal to you. You raised her as a child. Why are you not weeping for her?"

Kharkov glared at him. "Of course she meant the world to me! Of course I tried to stop her! But the choice to take one's own life is the last remaining freedom the State *cannot* take away, Comrade General. I have seen too many friends and loved ones tortured by the State to cry when one of them truly liberates themselves."

Cherlenko held his gaze, waiting for the little man to break. But Kharkov did not. Cherlenko threw him down onto the marble slabs.

A clatter of footsteps echoed around the cathedral. Captain Slavin entered from behind the altar and ran down to them.

"Where were you?" Cherlenko hissed. "I ordered you to guard this man. I ordered you to remain with him. Look what your disobedience had achieved!"

Slavin peered into the confessional. Her face was white when she turned back.

"Is . . . is that Tatyana Rospin?"

"It is, or it *was*! She took her own life while you left this man unguarded. What do you have to say for yourself?"

"I . . . I heard firing, Comrade General. I thought you might need me. I had guards posted all around the cathedral. Kharkov could not escape. There was no reason for me to stay . . . ."

"Except that I ordered you to!" Cherlenko screamed. "I should have you both shot!"

"Then why don't you?" shouted Kharkov, pulling himself to his knees. "You and your kind have taken everything I held dear. Shoot me now and release me for ever. As soon as that submarine attacks the blockade, we're all going to die anyway."

Cherlenko reached for his leather holster, hauled out his pistol and aimed right between Kharkov's eyes. Those eyes stared back at him with the same defiant light, the certainty of having won . . .

Cherlenko's finger caressed the trigger. Then the madness passed.

"No," he said, pulling himself together. "I will not give you such an easy release. A better death for a man who values his sanity over his life would be to imprison it in his body as he rots inside a mental institution."

He slid the pistol back into its holster and turned to face Slavin.

"I want nothing but praise for my actions in your reports to the Defence Council from now on. Is that understood? Support me and you shall live. The death of Tatyana Rospin was as much your negligence as it was mine."

Cherlenko saw his words hitting home. Slavin had lost her arrogance. She was now as much at his mercy as he had been at hers.

"Yes. Comrade General. There will be nothing in my reports but praise for your unceasing efforts."

"Very well. Throw this prisoner into a cell at the asylum until I need him again."

As Slavin summoned the guard and led her prisoner away, Cherlenko thought of that last look of victory on Kharkov's face. He felt outmanoeuvred in their game of chess, a game he had been so desperate to win, but took some small sliver of comfort from the fact that he had restrained himself from executing Kharkov on the spot. If Kharkov were dead, Cherlenko would never know what secrets lay behind those eyes. With a better understanding of how Kharkov thought, and how his experiments worked, there might still be time to snatch the victory he needed to save himself from the jaws of defeat.

Cherlenko spent the drive back to the Bolshoy Dom wracking his brains for a solution, looking for the key to the puzzle; Kharkov and his experiments, the Rospin twins, Kharkov and his wife being sent to Siberia after the Great Patriotic War. What had been their crime? What had happened to the Rospin twins while they were away? Who were the real parents of those children? What abilities did *they* have? Could those abilities be duplicated before it was too late?

Back at his desk, he picked up the telephone and called the university where Kharkov had worked, speaking to anyone who had access to Kharkov's research, his notebooks and files, demanding that they bring all written material to him personally and at once, no matter how late the hour. In less than forty-five minutes, he had a pile of notebooks, transcripts, textbooks and experimental records laid out on the table of the briefing room.

"You!" he barked, pointing to a thin, bearded man who had been one of Kharkov's postgraduate students. "If I wanted to know exactly what your professor was doing and needed to duplicate it immediately, where would I start?"

The young man was frightened out of his wits at being dragged in front of a high-ranking officer in the KGB so late at night. He stammered so badly that he was almost incoherent.

"You . . .you would start with these personal notebooks, Comrade General. The ones you told us to break out of his desk."

"Bring them here now! What do they mean?"

"They are like a journal, Comrade General," said the young man, placing the books before him. "They record Comrade Kharkov's progress on a daily basis. Do you see? This is a record of his work with the Rospin twins. Here are the details of the experiments and their success rate. Here are the shapes and symbols used for transmission and the number of times they were communicated successfully, Comrade General. I could interpret his notes, if you wish?"

"I am not a moron," snapped Cherlenko. "Wait in the outer office. I will analyse this material myself and, if I need your assistance, I will call."

He flicked through Kharkov's journals, turning page after page of carefully recorded notes, searching desperately for answers amongst the tables of results. There had to be an answer here somewhere. There had to be a way of communicating with the submarine . . . .

FRIDAY, 26 OCTOBER
SUBMARINE K-6
9.45 P.M. MOSCOW TIME
1845 GMT

"It looks as if we have found your whale, Comrade Kapitulsky," said Petrachkov, leaning back from the periscope. Sitting squarely in the cross hairs was a large tanker, flying an American flag. Petrachkov noted the wide red waterline showing all around the hull, which meant that the ship was riding high in the water, empty. Her propeller would be thrashing the surface at the upper edge of its arc, making plenty of noise. So much the better.

"Range, course and speed of target?" he asked.

"Range to the tanker is three kilometres, Comrade Captain. Speed fifteen knots, course zero eight five degrees."

"Probably out of Miami, heading for the Mediterranean, the Panama Canal and the Gulf," said Petrachkov. "Those Americans need lots of oil for their big, expensive cars. How would that whale suit as a candidate for buggering to get us past the destroyer?"

"It would suit us very well, Comrade Captain. There are high speed screws in the water about ten kilometres beyond her. They must be the destroyer escort around the *Essex*."

"I want the best helmsman we have up here in the CCP now and the best sonar man on watch. Set course to intercept that tanker and make revolutions for twenty-five knots."

Petrachkov had twice been in submarines that had pulled off this deception, once in the narrow entrance to the Mediterranean and once in the Denmark Strait, but this was the first time he had been in command. He tried to picture the manoeuvre in his mind, as if he was looking at it from outside the ship. The trick was to slide in under the tanker from the side, so as to avoid her propeller, and then stick as close to her hull as a sucker fish sticks to a shark.

"Steady as she goes," he called to the officer of the watch.

Above the hum and click of the CCP, a new symphony of sound started to make itself felt. Petrachkov heard the roaring thrash of the tanker's giant propeller astern and to port of them, drawing closer and closer, louder and louder.

"Call out your depth!" he said.

"Thirty metres and steady."

"Make that thirty-five!"

"Thirty-five it is."

Just to keep a constant depth beneath a giant ship ploughing through the water at twelve knots was a complicated balancing act of trim, speed and dive plane settings. Too deep and the submarine would be a sitting duck for any listening sonar array. Too shallow and the submarine risked a collision. Petrachkov knew of just such an accident in the Baltic, which had caused a diplomatic incident and forced the submarine commander to serve the rest of his time on shore. Petrachkov had pitied the man. Now he would gladly have traded places with him.

The noise of the tanker was deafening, and it was getting louder.

"Increase speed to eighteen knots!"

"Eighteen knots."

The thrashing of the propellers softened slightly.

"Back to fifteen!"

"Fifteen it is."

"Hold steady at that!"

"I would like to report one whale, successfully buggered, Comrade Captain," said the officer of the watch, grinning from ear to ear.

"Thank you, now all you have to do is keep us there. What is the range to the destroyer screen around the *Essex*?"

"High speed screws reported port and starboard of our track at eight kilometres range, Comrade Captain. We should draw level with them in around thirty minutes and be in attack position on the *Essex* in less than an hour. We'll pass right through the escorts and they will never know."

"Let us hope so," said Petrachkov. "Put a relief of your best men on the controls every fifteen minutes to prevent fatigue. I don't want anyone making a mistake and chewing off the conning tower. I'm going to see how Comrade Mostock is and ask him if he has had any ideas regarding our communications problem."

28

**FRIDAY, 26 OCTOBER
THE GRAND CANYON
12.00 NOON MOUNTAIN STANDARD TIME
1900 GMT**

Ruth left Havasu Creek and climbed into the cool shade of a tiny gully almost hidden by a rocky outcrop and dense cottonwood trees. She stopped to drink from her water bottle and listened. From the far end of the gully came the familiar hiss of a waterfall and the rustle of leaves on the wind. This was the place, the very special place where Granny Moon had brought her the first time she had known about her gift, the place where it had seemed so natural for her to possess it. It was also the place where, as a child, she had watched Granny Moon and a small group of people from her tribe light the funeral pyre under her mother's body and release her spirit to the Other World.

Granny Moon was older than anyone could remember. She had been alive at the time of the Great Indian Wars, when stories of Custer and Sitting Bull were told around the camp fires. Legend had it that she had been a great medicine woman who could heal wounds with herbs and a broken heart with a spell. People would consult her to forecast the weather, to tell if an unborn baby was to be a boy or a girl, or to advise on how the ceremony of the Ghost Dance should be performed. If anyone could understand what it felt like to fly into a photograph, it would be Granny Moon.

So the old woman had listened and when Ruth had finished, she told her they were going on a long walk and might not be back until nightfall, maybe not even then. She packed water and food in a haversack, brought out her favourite walking stick and took Ruth deep down into the Havasu Canyon on one of her special trails, that not even the Havasupai guides knew. That night they camped below Beaver Falls, in a beautiful secluded clearing, near a waterfall that fed a bright blue stream to Havasu Creek.

"You have a gift, Little Eagle," said Granny Moon, calling Ruth by her Havasupai name as they sat looking up at the stars. "It is the same gift your mother had before you, the gift of second sight. Nobody must know, beyond you and me."

"But why, Grandmother?" To Ruth, it seemed such an easy and natural thing to be able to soar with your thoughts. Surely many other people could do it but had never bothered to say.

"Because other people will enslave you," said Granny Moon. "They will prod you and poke you and make you do things you do not want to do. That is all they ever do, those people in power in Washington. They take things of natural beauty and make weapons out of them. And if they can't do that, they spoil them, destroy them, or sell them to the highest bidder."

Granny Moon raised her hand, taking in the waterfall, the rocks and the sky. "Look around you. What do you see?"

Ruth looked up, to where the stream of crystal water leapt into space, fell in droplets of moonlight and crashed into the stream in a living cloud of rainbow colours.

"I see a place of great beauty, Grandmother."

"You are a child of nature, Little Eagle. Those in power see nothing but fish to be caught and sold, water to be dammed to make electricity, and rock to be mined. They see burger bars, parking lots, hotels and money—lots and lots of money. That is why I keep this place secret."

Ruth knew this to be true. Her mother had worked in such a place up on the canyon rim after her father had been killed in the war. By day she had sold trinkets to the tourists and by night had performed traditional dances in the hotels with her friends, until the emptiness of selling her soul night after night had grown too much to bear.

"But what has that to do with my gift?"

"Yours is a gift from nature. You must keep it secret. Do your job with the photographs as well as you can, for it is important work. But tell nobody what you can *really* do."

"I'll tell nobody."

Which was how it had remained, until Ruth had fallen in love with a handsome young helicopter pilot at Fort Bragg.

Ruth put away the water bottle and walked on through the gulley. A family of mule deer looked round at her and trotted away. The hiss of the waterfall and the rush of water in the brook grew louder and the gulley opened up.

It was the same as it had always been. The curving arc of water leapt from the rock into the deep blue travertine pool. Cottonwood trees bowed towards the water and shady grass banks rose on either side of the little stream as it ran off to join the Colorado far below. She ran down the last few steps from the mouth of the gulley and stood on a rock by the waterfall, her arms open wide, feeling the spray on her face.

"Hello, Little Eagle! I was wondering how long it would take you to get here."

"Granny!!"

The old woman sat cross-legged on a ledge by the waterfall, out of sight of anyone except a person standing on the rock where Ruth now was. She was smiling sadly.

"Granny Moon, what are you doing here? What's wrong?"

"Ruth, you remember when I first brought you here and we talked about your gift? You remember how I told you to keep it secret?"

"I do." Ruth was worried. It was not like Granny Moon to address her by anything other than her Havasupai name, or to talk so seriously in a place of such peace and joy.

"And you remember all the bad things that happened to you afterwards and all the pain the men from Washington caused you?"

"Of course I do. Why? What is wrong?"

"You are to work with them again."

"I can't and I won't. Please don't ask me such a dreadful thing in this happy place. They bent my mind, those men in Washington. They made me see things I should never have seen—horrible, unspeakable things."

"Ruth, there is no other way. Millions of people will die if you are not strong. You always trusted me, didn't you? And I trusted you by bringing you to this place. Trust me now. You have to do what he asks!"

"What *who* asks?" said Ruth, suddenly on the alert.

"Him," said Granny Moon, turning to look behind her. "You can come out now, Mister Carpenter. I have spoken with her."

John Carpenter stepped out of the shadows beside the waterfall.

"No." Ruth shouted. "I won't. And you can't force me to. It won't work!"

"Listen to him, Ruth," said Granny Moon gently. "This task is vital. Your husband gave his life so that you could succeed with it. Joan was killed for it and all those policemen died for it at the gift store. You are the only one who can stop this thing, the only one in the world. I need you to be strong, Little Eagle. A terrible evil has been set in motion and you are the only one who can stop it."

"I will never work with that man again. Never. Just hearing his voice causes me pain."

"I will guide you," said Granny Moon. "Like I did when we explored the canyon together in our minds long ago. Mister Carpenter is only here to tell me where to send you. It will just be you and me."

"No. You don't realise what it's like, either of you. You don't know what it feels like to stand in the presence of pure evil, or to be attacked by a thing that has no shape and no name, a thing so powerful that it could snuff out your existence just by a thought. You have never been hanging by a thread in a world made of nightmares and known that thread could snap at any second. You don't know what you are asking me to do."

Granny Moon looked at her across the clear blue pond. "Little Eagle, I am old enough to remember all the wrongs done to our people over the years. I witnessed how the land was taken from us, how we were banished from the rim and the Indian Gardens to the base of the canyon. I remember how our farms were taken, our hunting grounds confiscated and sold, and how we were forced to live on reservations, selling souvenirs and singing songs for the tourists. It will be many years before we are recognised and accepted for who we are. But that day will *never* come, and disgrace will be poured on us for all eternity, if one of our people held the key to saving the world and would not turn it. Imagine, Little Eagle, the shame that would bring."

Ruth looked into Granny Moon's eyes and saw the sorrow of a dozen generations. She was right. The Havasupai and all Indian nations would be reviled until the end of time.

"Then what must I do, Granny?"

Carpenter explained to Ruth the charts and papers he had shown her at the gift store. Ruth had to reach into the mind of Max Rospin on the Soviet submarine K-6 somewhere east of Bermuda. She had to convince him that the messages from his sister in Leningrad were false. He in turn had to make the Russian commander bring his vessel to the surface and stand by for authentic messages from his base in Severmorsk.

"I do not speak Russian," said Ruth. "How can I tell him anything?"

"You will be speaking directly into his mind," said Carpenter. "There is no need for language at that level, remember? Just think of what you have to make him understand. Here is a diagram of the submarine. The captain's name is Petrachkov. He could already be preparing to attack."

Carpenter laid the chart of the North Atlantic, the list of names and the diagram of the submarine on the grassy bank where Ruth was sitting. Granny Moon laid Havasupai charms and totems around the chart and the diagram. Then she looked up at Carpenter.

"You leave now," she said. "Ruth knows all she needs to know."

"But I'm the one most familiar with the mission."

"And you have told us what we need to know," said Granny Moon. "Go now. I made a promise to Little Eagle and I must keep it. You have hurt my granddaughter enough, Mister Carpenter. Go now!"

Carpenter knew she was right. If the mission was to succeed, if Ruth was to be relaxed enough to try, then he had to back off. So he left the information behind him on the grass, surrounded by Indian totems, and walked up the trail to the gully leading to Havasu Creek. The last thing he saw, looking back, was Granny Moon laying a blanket on the grassy bank next to the waterfall.

"Close your eyes," whispered the old woman gently. "Close your eyes and listen to the waterfall. You are part of this place. It is part of you. Its energy is your energy. Your life force is the life force of the waterfall. You are safe here. You are at peace here. Feel it, Little Eagle. Feel it being part of you."

Behind her eyelids, Ruth imagined the scene around her. She saw the waterfall in her mind's eye, the stream and the soaring rock above her head. She saw the hills above the gully, Havasu Creek and the faraway line of the canyon rim. Above her, in the dazzling blue sky, an eagle soared on the rising air.

She looked down. On a grassy bank an old woman knelt with her hands gently holding the head of a younger woman.

She was out of her body!

She had the sense of a chord joining her to the young woman on the ground. Ruth floated, like a balloon on a string, weightless and shapeless. She felt part of the sky, the hills and the river—part of everything.

"There, Little Eagle," said a voice, which she knew was Granny Moon's. "You are there, aren't you? What do you see?"

"I see us on the ground below me. I see my lips moving and you nodding. Can you hear me?"

"I can, Little Eagle. Now I want you to fly to the place you were shown on this chart, a place very far away to the east. I want you to go there and reach beneath the sea to where Max is waiting. Go now, Little Eagle. Go!"

"I'll try," said Ruth, and even the very thought of doing so sent her sailing off across the canyon, the desert and the mountains, eastwards towards the Atlantic ocean.

FRIDAY, 26 OCTOBER
SUBMARINE K-6
10.28 P.M. MOSCOW TIME
1928 GMT

"I have an idea," said Mostock. "It will work, if the shipbuilders in Leningrad have not let us down again."

"What is it," Petrachkov asked.

Viktor Mostock was dying. His eyes were so swollen, they were almost closed. He had difficulty speaking and could drink water only through a straw. He was holding on to life by a sheer act of will.

"It is so simple and yet so brilliant you will promote me to Admiral the moment you hear it. You know we have two emergency radio buoys, in case we ever sink and cannot surface?"

Petrachkov knew of these devices, floating waterproof transmitters connected to the inside of the submarine by a radio wire, which could be released in an emergency and used to communicate with the outside world.

"Very good, Comrade Admiral," he said. "I congratulate you on your promotion to flag rank."

"See how simple and brilliant it is," whispered Mostock, smiling painfully. "I bet that young genius Kapitulsky could transmit a coded signal through one of those buoys to any of the Russian merchantmen who are, at this very moment, sunning themselves while they hang around the American blockade line. They could relay the message to Leningrad, get you your answer on the emergency channel and confirm your orders."

"Get some rest, Viktor," said Petrachkov, turning to go. "I'll have the surgeon prescribe you an extra ration of vodka."

"Sergei Nikolai," gasped Mostock, "whatever happens, to me or to this ship remember what I told you. The men need you as their captain. It has been a pleasure serving with you, Comrade." He raised his blistered hand in a weak salute.

"Likewise, Comrade, and thank you," replied Petrachkov, returning the salute and walking back through the engineering spaces to the tension and cigarette smoke of the CCP. He went over to Kapitulsky's station, told him Mostock's plan and ordered that preparations be put it into effect. Then he returned to his commander's chair and scanned the dials and gauges. Outside the submarine, the thud of the tanker's propellers and the roar of its machinery overhead still drowned out the other sounds in the CCP. On the master plotting table, the blue disc indicating their current position had moved closer to the coloured counters of the warships in the American fleet.

"By my reckoning, Comrades," he said loudly, "we should be coming up on the destroyer screen any moment now."

The 'ping' of an active sonar sweep lashed their hull. Every eye in the CCP looked up, as if they could see through the steel hull of the submarine into the water beyond.

"No need to worry," said Petrachkov calmly. "Just because we've been swept, doesn't mean we've been detected. Is there anything to report on passive sonar? Any sudden changes of course by those warships?"

"No, Comrade Captain," came a voice from the sonar station. "Their engines are all at normal speed and there is no cavitation from their screws. Nobody is going anywhere in a hurry."

"So nobody is chasing us. That is good. Maintain our position under Comrade Kapitulsky's whale for a while longer."

The intercom buzzed. Petrachkov reached for the microphone.

"Comrade Captain, this is the ship's surgeon."

"What is it?" asked Petrachkov flatly. But he already knew.

"Comrade Mostock died just after you left the sick bay. There was nothing more I could do."

Petrachkov looked at the faces of the men in the command post. All their eyes were on him. Mostock had been their friend too.

"I understand," he said, choking back this latest blow. "Thank you." He released the microphone. He thought of Mostock in the early days of the old diesel-electric boats, of fishing with him in the cold waters of Severmorsk, of all the years they had shared together. Petrachkov had never had a brother, not until he and Mostock had served together. He remembered Mostock's last advice to him before he died.

"It is time for Comrade Muhkin and I to arm the torpedo," he said. "Ask him to join me at the safe."

"Yes, Comrade Captain."

He left the CCP and walked forward to the officers' wardroom. Muhkin was already there, standing to attention by the safe where the nuclear key was kept.

"I have dialled my combination, Comrade Captain," he said solemnly.

"Very well," said Petrachkov and bent down, dialling his own set of numbers and opening the small metal door. He took out a sealed brown paper envelope and showed it to the political officer.

"By the power delegated to me by the people of the Soviet Union and the Defence Council, I am taking charge of the nuclear trigger key," he said solemnly. "Do you witness this?"

"I do, Comrade Captain."

"Very well then, follow me."

They made their way forward through narrow corridors and tiny watertight doors to the very bow of the ship. There, in the cavernous space of Compartment One, row upon row of torpedoes lay stacked against each side of the hull, like felled steel treetrunks.

Security officer Dudko stood solemnly by the top torpedo on the starboard side. Its purple nose, housing the atomic weapon, stood out from all the others. Just where the bright paint of the warhead finished and the black paint of the torpedo body began, a steel panel had been removed, showing a single slot.

Petrachkov reached up and slid the key into place.

"I am arming the weapon. Do you, as security officer, concur?"

"I do, Comrade Captain," Dudko said.

Petrachkov turned the key.

A red light glowed on the panel above the slot. To Petrachkov, it was as if the atomic monster inside this terrible weapon had suddenly come alive and was watching them with its evil eye.

"Replace the panel," he said. "Then load the torpedo into the tube and tell me when it is ready to fire."

"Yes, Comrade Captain," said Dudko.

Ruth soared above the clouds to the east, drawn irresistibly to her destination. Below her the rolling landscape turned to a coastline.

"Where are you?" asked Granny Moon. "Talk to me, Little Eagle."

"I am over the coast. I see waves breaking."

"Good. You know where to go?"

"To where Max is."

She soared out over the ocean. Ships scratched white lines on its deep blue surface. She passed over islands and more ships, grey and sleek this time, moving with purpose, searching. A much larger vessel, riding high in the water, moved slowly between them, its hull scoring a long straight line on the sea.

"I'm being pulled down."

"Let your mind guide you," Granny Moon whispered. "It will take you where you have to go."

She felt drawn to the big ship. Was Max there? Wasn't he supposed to be on a submarine? Then she passed through the ship, through decks, bulkheads and into the darkness of the sea.

"He's here, beneath the ship!"

"Is he in the water? Is he dead?"

"No," Ruth said. "He is here, with his friends."

She glimpsed a huge black fish that stretched on forever. She was in a brightly lit space. She felt men, tension, and long narrow corridors. She saw small rooms on either side. Men came and went around her, moving with great purpose.

"I'm in the submarine," she said. "It's hiding here from the warships. The men are tense. They know they will be hunted and destroyed if they are not careful."

"Good, Ruth, very good. Now go and find Max."

Ruth slipped through the corridors and the tiny rooms, trying to get a feel for Max amongst all the other men. She came to a room towards the front of the submarine, a much larger room than all the rest, a room where men were watching dials and gauges, a room full of controls. A short, squat man with wide shoulders and a kind face sat in a big chair. The other men liked him. They followed him. But the tension in this room was greater than all the rest.

Ruth passed on down the submarine. Men were sleeping in small rooms, in bunks one on top of the other. She passed a room where a small man with thick glasses and a beard sat bent over a book. Ruth sensed he was close to Max and waiting for something to happen, so she reached out to touch his mind and find out what it was. She had the briefest sense of the number 'eight' before the man looked up from his book and seemed to stare at her. But he was not Max. After a moment he shrugged and went back to his book. In the next room a young man, hardly more than a boy, lay asleep. He had blond hair. Ruth sensed that he too was waiting for something to do with the number 'eight' and that he was deeply troubled.

"I've found Max," said Ruth.

"Speak to him," said Granny Moon. "Think the things you have to say. He will understand."

Ruth touched the boy's head. She felt her hand pass into his mind and reach him. Max stirred in his sleep.

Max, she thought. *You must make them stop. You must make them turn around and go home. The orders are wrong. You have to make them listen.*

Stop . . . thought Max. *Turn around . . . Listen!*

Max, you must tell Captain Petrachkov to stop the submarine and turn around.

Father?

She heard his voice so clearly inside her mind that it took her by surprise.

Father, thought Max again. *Is that you?*

No, Max. I am not your father. But I wish you well. Stop the submarine, Max. Tell them to turn the ship around. Go home!

No! thought Max. *We cannot go back. We cannot fail. Evil will triumph if we fail. My father said . . . .*

Max! Listen to me. People will die unless you turn back. Millions of people! Please listen to me. Your orders are wrong!

Max writhed in his bunk, like someone in the grip of a nightmare.

No. I cannot. My father told me we must not fail!

Then, beside them in the room, Ruth felt another presence—vast, and terrible, and familiar . . . .

"Granny Moon. There is someone else here with us!"

"Of course there is. The ship is full of men."

"No. This is not a man from the ship. This is the presence from my nightmare. Someone that has come here in their mind . . . someone like me!"

Black King

TIME TO EVENT

00:00:52

DAYS : HRS : MINS

29

The dark presence poured into the room, just as it had on that last mission to Siberia and in her nightmares ever since. Ruth sensed enormous energy, strength and a deep, deep feeling of loss.

Who are you? she thought, fighting back the panic.

Go! said the presence. *You are not wanted here. Leave the boy and go!*

I cannot!

You must. He has work to do. The triumph of good over evil is at stake. You must leave.

Max squirmed in his bunk. Ruth felt his pain. Sweat broke out on his face. He called out words. The little man with the beard was coming.

Then Max screamed. His fear filled the space.

GO! screamed the presence, *or I will destroy you! I see your darkest fears and your innermost weaknesses. I read your secret thoughts. I will take those you love and crush their minds. I wil cut the chord that binds you to your body and leave you in limbo forever. GO NOW!*

The most profound sense of dread crashed over Ruth like a wave. She was a child again, in the grip of her most terrible nightmare which drove cold fingers into her soul. This dark presence, powerful beyond her wildest imaginings, had her in its grip.

She leapt back in panic, up through the hull of the submarine, through the water into open space. She fled blindly, across the sky an down through the clouds. Running home to . . .

"Ruth!"

She woke with a jolt. Granny Moon held her head in her hands. Her body lay drenched in sweat. She shook with fear.

"Hold me!" she cried like a frightened child. "Hold me!"

"What is it, Ruth? What have you seen?"

"Someone was in the submarine with Max. The same presence I felt in Siberia all those years ago when the nightmares started. He could have crushed me like an eggshell. He could have cut me off from my body forever. He could even have reached out and killed you too. He was powerfull, Granny Moon, more powerful than you could ever imagine."

She felt Granny Moon's arms around her, cradling her like a child. The old woman whispered to her softly, trying to comfort her. But all Ruth could do was cry.

"This presence," whispered Granny Moon. "What did you feel from him?"

"I felt pain. There was anger there too, but also a deep, deep loss. He was like an old wounded lion striking out at the world. It was terrible, Granny Moon. I've never felt anyone as strong . . . ."

**FRIDAY, 26 OCTOBER
LENINGRAD
10.40 P.M. LOCAL TIME
1940 GMT**

Cherlenko had shut himself away and told Captain Slavin to hold all calls so that he could think. Kharkov's journals and experimental notes were fascinating. Those in power were right to have sponsored his work with the Rospin twins. The potential was there to send messages in complete secrecy, to spy on anyone, anywhere and even to kill a man remotely with a single thought. With the power to project one's consciousness outside the body, there would be no secrets an enemy could hide, no files that would remain closed, no obstacles to advancement to the very top. What if he himself could train his mind the way Kharkov had trained the Rospin twins? The possibilities for advancement were endless . . . .

Cherlenko rubbed his eyes, lit another cigarette and glanced up at the clock. It had just gone midnight and nuclear war could break out at any minute unless he solved this problem. He sat back from the briefing table and tried to visualize the elements of the puzzle as separate pieces on a chessboard. What were they?

There was Kharkov himself, obviously as the Black King, with Tatyana Rospin as the Black Queen and her brother Max as a Black Knight. There were the experiments on the submarine with Doctor Chiker (a Black Rook perhaps?) Shumanin (a fat White Bishop), Petrachkov (a White Knight) and the traitor Baybarin (a Black Pawn).

How had the moves of the game played out? It had started when the submarine's radio systems had conveniently broken down. The long wave system had malfunctioned, or could that have been sabotage? Then the VHF aerial had cracked off on the ice. That had been reported as an accident, but could it have been deliberate? Who had been present when Leningrad knew that the only way to reach the submarine was through the Kharkov experiment? The radio operator at the Admiralty building would have known, followed by Kharkov, Tatyana Rospin, Baybarin and Shumanin. Tatyana was dead now, as was Baybarin, both by their own hands. Had they died to protect someone? Shumanin was in disgrace. He had been on the periphery of it all anyway. Petrachkov was under the Atlantic. Who was left?

Kharkov!

He pulled the Professor's thick *zapista* from the pile of documents and leafed though it yet again, taking a large sheet of paper and a pencil to make a single list of dates, events and places so that he could see the whole of Kharkov's life at a glance.

Born 1905, in Leningrad.

Married 29 March 1938 . . . childhood sweetheart, Irina Asanov, medical student at the university and subsequently a qualified doctor, also born in Leningrad.

First child born 1939 . . . and the second child? Perhaps the record was missing? Unusual.

Both husband and wife had played a significant part in defending the city during the great siege. Kharkov himself had worked with Andrei Zhdanov and the City Council of Defence to co-ordinate the effort against the invading Fascists. Irina had coordinated medical services and tended the sick in the Kazan Cathedral. No wonder Kharkov knew that place so well.

Both children had died of disease and complications brought on by malnutrition . . . 1943 . . . hmm!

Family friends Igor and Galina Rospin killed during a Fascist artillery bombardment, also in 1943. The Kharkovs adopted their children, Max and Tatyana, as their own that same year . . . all paperwork present, witnessed and genuine, or so it appeared.

Kharkov received the decoration Hero of the Soviet Union, along with his wife in 1945, decorated personally by Stalin.

Then in 1950, rounded up with his wife, as part of 'The Leningrad Affair'—Stalin's purge on those he suspected of being isolated from his influence for so long during the great siege that they were trying to set up a separate Russian Communist Party. The Kharkovs probably escaped being shot only because of their decorations for bravery.

Exiled to a State mental hospital in Siberia. Wife sent to experimental facility, also in Siberia . . . see separate secret annex. Cherlenko flipped through the pages to find it. The facility in question had been experimenting with new forms of chemical warfare. Because of her medical expertise, Irina Kharkov had been ordered to perform tests in which live subjects such as convicted 'dissidents' were exposed to chemical weapons under controlled conditions. She had refused and was beaten. When she still refused, she was placed in the chamber herself, exposed to toxic gas and then dissected alive without an anaesthetic to gauge the effectiveness of the poison.

Even Cherlenko felt his skin crawl as he read the details of the examination. He noted the date of her death on his list . . . 28 February 1953.

Meanwhile Kharkov had been a model patient at the asylum. Notes from the supervising 'doctors' indicated long periods of isolation and meditation without incident. Then suddenly, on the day of his wife's death, he had become so uncharacteristically violent that he had been locked in an isolation chamber and left in darkness for six days until he had calmed down. This had happened between the 28th of February and the 5th March 1953. Cherlenko noted those dates also. They looked familiar, like dates he should have remembered from a history class? On the 6th March Kharkov had then been let out of the isolation cell, never to cause any more trouble. He had finally been released from captivity in 1956 following the commissions of inquiry set up by Khrushchev to examine the cases of prisoners in the camps and had returned to Leningrad from Siberia in 1958.

What had happened in those two years? What was it that would hold a man in the frozen wastelands of Siberia if he were free to return home? A note had been written in the margin of the file: "Reported living with Shamanistic peoples in the area to further his meditation studies."

Strange?

Following his return to the University of Leningrad, Kharkov took up a junior position at the Department of Psychology, studying telepathy. Within two years he had demonstrated such brilliant results that he had been elevated to the position of Professor and given the resources to run his own programme of telepathic experiments with Chiker and the Rospin twins, financed by the navy, and under the supervision of the KGB, naturally enough.

The Rospin twins again . . . Max and Tatyana . . . .

Cherlenko looked at the list of dates he had written, lit another cigarette and opened one of Kharkov's personal notebooks. He scanned the columns of results from the naval experimental programme and then started flicking through the pages, faster and faster . . . .

He was right! That was it!

The significance of 5 March 1953 burst upon him like a blinding white light, along with the realization of what had been going on from the very first moment this crisis had broken. Ever since he had entered into his mental chess game with Kharkov, there had only ever been two kinds of pieces on the board.

One Black King had dominated the whole game, while Cherlenko and all the other pieces had been nothing but pawns!

And now Kharkov was lying in solitary confinement, in a dark and isolated cell, exactly as he had been on that momentous day back in 1953, when life in the Soviet Union had changed forever.

Cherlenko grabbed the notebook and *zapista*, ran to the briefing room door and into the outer office. The young postgraduate student leapt to his feet. Captain Slavin snapped to attention.

"Yes, Comrade General, what is it?"

"Get my car around to the front of the building at once!" Cherlenko shouted. "And call the asylum. I must get to Kharkov right away!"

FRIDAY, 26 OCTOBER
SUBMARINE K-6
10.48 P.M. MOSCOW TIME
1948 GMT

Petrachkov heard the commotion in the corridor forward of the CCP just as news that the *Essex* had been located came through. Someone shouted and then screamed. He heard running feet.

"What's going on?"

Max Rospin burst into the command post, dressed only in his underwear, eyes wide with fear and his body drenched in sweat.

"Stop. You have to stop. The orders were wrong!"

"Someone call Doctor Chiker," Petrachkov yelled above the din. "Chiker, get him out of the control room now. He's gone mad."

Kapitulsky ran in from the communications cabin behind Max and tried to grab him but Max lashed out with his fist, sending the young officer reeling across the attack table onto the grating.

"Security to the CCP!" ordered Petrachkov. "Somebody hold him down!"

But Max seemed to have strength beyond his own body. He punched, kicked and clawed his way through the crowded room until he stood facing Petrachkov. "You must stop!" he screamed. "You must turn the ship around! Your orders are wrong!"

Petrachkov raised his open palms and faced the boy.

"Calm down, Max," he said. "Calm down. Everybody else stay at your posts. We have to keep this ship in position under that tanker if we want to stay hidden."

Two armed sailors entered the CCP from compartment two, with Doctor Chiker right behind them. Chiker had a cut above his left eye. One of the lenses in his glasses was cracked.

"Max," said Petrachkov gently, "I want you to go back to your bunk. Do that for me, son. It's just a nightmare. We're all under a lot of pressure, you especially. Get to your bunk, Max. Go back to sleep."

Chiker reached out and touched Max's shoulder. The boy turned, saw him and suddenly realised where he was.

"They were fighting . . ." he whispered again softly. "Fighting!"

Then he burst into tears. Chiker threw a blanket around Max's shoulders and led him away.

"Everyone concentrate on their duties," ordered Petrachkov. "Do we still have that contact for the *Essex*?"

"Yes, Comrade Captain. Range five kilometres, bearing zero nine two degrees."

"Comrade Kapitulsky, are you all right?"

"I'm fine, Captain," said the communications officer, wiping the blood from his lip. "It's just a scratch."

Then the implications of what had just happened hit Petrachkov like a blow to the chest. Every action he had taken since radio contact with Severmorsk had been lost had been based on orders received through Max. And now here was Max screaming that those orders were wrong. If Max was unreliable, could it be that the situation in the outside world was not as Max had said it was? Could it be that Natalya and his sons were still alive? Were they really at war with the Americans or was he, Sergei Nikolai Petrachkov, about to bring that war about by mistake? He *had* to be sure.

"That radio transmitter in the emergency beacon?" he asked Kapitulsky. "When can we try contacting Severmorsk?"

"It's ready to go, Comrade Captain. The coded messages can be transmitted as soon as the buoy hits the surface . . . ."

Kapitulsky suddenly looked up at the ceiling. What was it? thought Petrachkov. What was the man hearing?

Then he knew.

The roar of the tanker's engines and the thud of its great propeller were fading. During the commotion caused by Max forcing his way into the CCP, the tanker had suddenly changed course and moved away from them.

They were alone and naked in the open sea.

"Sonar," shouted Petrachkov, "where is that tanker now?"

"Pulling off to port, Captain. I . . . I'm sorry!"

"Helm! Port twenty degrees! Get us back underneath it!"

But even as he called out the order, the deafening 'ping' of an active sonar pulse lashed the hull.

30

Carpenter heard the scream and rushed back down the gully to the waterfall. Ruth lay there in the old woman's arms, shivering like a frightened child.

"It was terrible, Granny Moon. I've never felt anyone as strong."

Carpenter knelt beside them, next to the charts and Indian totems.

"What happened?"

"It was like being a frightened child in the presence of an adult," Ruth stammered. "He could anticipate every move I made, overcome any trick I might try. I felt powerless before him. I felt his energy, his anger and his own indescribable pain."

"You say 'he'," said Carpenter. "You think this other presence is a 'he'?"

"I do."

"Because the only telepaths the Soviets are admitting to are Max and Tatyana Rospin. If you were with Max at the time this presence appeared, that means another telepath has penetrated the submarine, someone we know nothing about."

"I got the sense of age," Ruth said. "It was an older man."

"The only two men who might be involved are Doctor Chiker on the submarine, or Professor Kharkov, who pioneered their program. Neither of them has been reported as being telepathic."

"It's not Chiker. I saw him reading and reached into his mind. He's not the one."

Ruth drew her knees up to her chin and sat rocking gently.

"It must be Kharkov," she said at last. "That's where the anger, the pain and the awful sense of loss I felt must come from. Max called him 'Father'. It has to be him."

"Then Kharkov's hold over Max will be absolute," Carpenter said. "I don't know how you're going to break it when you go back, Ruth. I really don't."

She glared at him. "Who says I'm going back?"

"You have to. Nobody else can reach that sub but you . . . ."

"Kharkov's out there in the ether! He's waiting for me like a big black shark in a cold dark sea. He'll stand guard over Max and crush me if I come anywhere close. I can't do it. I don't have the strength."

"But we're so near, Ruth. We cannot fail! You know we can't!"

"I won't go!"

"You *have* to!"

"I'll try," said Granny Moon. "I have gifts of my own. I will go in Ruth's place. I don't fear this man as she does. I'll go. You guide me, Mister Carpenter. You show me the chart."

"No," said Ruth, "you can't!"

"It's my choice," replied the old woman. "It has to be done. And if you are not strong enough, then I must do it."

Carpenter watched Ruth, torn between her fear of going back to face Kharkov and the certain knowledge of what he could do to Granny Moon if she went in her place. The old woman may have possessed gifts he could only imagine, but she had not been to the submarine or reached into Max's mind as Ruth had. Maybe the only way to defeat Kharkov was to get Ruth in and out of the submarine before he knew she was there. Granny Moon would need to orientate herself inside the maze of rooms and corridors to reach Max. She would take too long. Kharkov would destroy her. Ruth would understand that too.

"I'll try again," Ruth said, "just once more. You can stay this time John, if you want to. I may need you."

He watched her lie back on the blanket, close her eyes and try to calm herself. Granny Moon spoke to her softly.

Then Ruth said, "I'm floating. I'm floating above you. I see you below me and the canyon all around. I'm drifting eastwards, very fast now. I'm over the ocean. I see ships, lots of warships. They are steaming with great purpose towards a target."

"Ruth?" asked Granny Moon, "can you see the big ship under which Max's submarine is hiding?"

"It has changed direction, but the submarine is still there. I'm going down to find Max."

Ruth lay silent for a few moments. Carpenter watched her eyes moving beneath their lids, just as he had done years before on Project Element.

"I feel his presence," she said. "He is deep under the ocean where the other ships move in great circles. He is in the middle of it all, frightened and alone. The water is closing over me. I feel the cold darkness."

"Keep talking to us, Little Eagle."

"I am in a long narrow corridor bathed in soft red light. Men stand all around me, or sit on bunks waiting. Anyone who moves does so as carefully as possible. I sense their tension; they're waiting for something terrible to fall on top of them."

"What is it?" asked Granny Moon.

"They're being hunted!"

FRIDAY, 26 OCTOBER
SUBMARINE K-6
10.53 P.M. MOSCOW TIME
1953 GMT

"What are the Americans doing?" Petrachkov asked.

"Just circling above us, Comrade Captain," reported the sonar man. "They are transmitting propaganda into the water. I can hear it quite clearly on the passive sonar."

"What does it say?"

"That our orders from Leningrad were in error and that we should surface and contact Severmorsk for new instructions. Admiral Shumanin orders us to call off the attack. He gives what he says are today's Apex security codes."

"We were warned that they would use deception," Petrachkov muttered. He was at the worst point of his career, faced with the impossible decision to continue the mission and launch the nuclear torpedo, or to surface and contact Severmorsk, if it still existed. Launching the weapon was only the press of a button away. Trying to contact Severmorsk meant laying his ship open to attack by an overwhelmingly superior force. Max had said the Americans would use deception. Yet Max had become unhinged. Could he, Petrachkov, take responsibility for firing an atomic weapon without a definite confirmation of orders? The temptation to know his family's fate was overpowering. If they really were at war, why had the Americans not released their own weapons by now? They must have an accurate sonar lock. What was he to do?

"Comrade Kapitulsky, is that emergency buoy ready to launch?"

"It is, Captain."

"Come to periscope depth. Dead slow ahead!" He reached up for a microphone to speak to compartment one, the torpedo room. "Comrade Dudko, is the weapon ready?"

"Tube number one is flooded, the outer door is open and the

torpedo is ready to fire, Comrade Captain."

"Very well. If the Americans fire their weapons, then we shall fire ours."

He looked around the CCP. Everyone stood at their stations, waiting for his orders.

"Depth?"

"Periscope depth, Comrade Captain."

He *had* to know about Natalya and his boys.

"Up periscope," he said. "Release the emergency radio buoy!"

Ruth slipped through the submarine, between the men in the control room and into the long corridor to where Max was lying. Doctor Chiker sat on the bunk near him. He did not glance up this time, but kept on watching Max, as a concerned parent stands a vigil over a sick child.

"What are you seeing?" Granny Moon asked.

"I'm with Max in his cabin. He looks very ill."

Max Rospin lay in the grips of a fever, curled up in the narrow bunk, his arms over his head. A half-empty glass of water and some pills stood on the little metal ledge by the bunk.

They've sedated him, she thought. They've tried to keep him quiet after the last outburst. How will I reach him now?

She stayed by the bunk, looking down at the gently rocking figure. Was this how she'd been a few minutes earlier in the arms of Granny Moon, a terrified child too frightened to go on? Maybe we were never meant to have these powers. Maybe we aren't ready, any of us. Look what we've become!

She reached out and touched his mind.

Max, Max, listen to me! You have to stop the ship!

His lips moved. She saw him mouthing her words in what must have been Russian . . . *stop the ship!*

Doctor Chiker leant forward and put his hand on Max's forehead. She saw his lips move too, but couldn't hear a word he was saying. Was he comforting the boy? Was he asking him what he had meant?

In this world of theirs, outside the body, there was nothing but silence.

Max, she thought again. You *have to stop the ship!*

Max sat up suddenly in the bunk. His mouth moved. He was shouting! Chiker grabbed his shoulders and tried to quieten him, but he still shouted.

She reached again into Max's mind to try and understand what he was saying.

Mmmmmm . . . Iiiiii . . . Faaaaaa . . . . Thuuuuuh!

My father?

Then the terrible presence she had known before poured back through the walls and engulfed her like the sea.

"Kharkov's here now!"

"Talk to him, Ruth," said Carpenter. "Tell him you know his name."

The presence filled the tiny cabin, a black cloud of anger and hate, pressing in on her.

I know you, she thought, fighting against her own panic. *You're Kharkov. They hurt you, just like they hurt me. Talk to me. We both want the same thing! Please, speak to me.*

Get away from my son, screamed a voice inside her mind. *He's mine. Go now, or I will destroy you!*

I cannot leave. Not without stopping this ship!

The presence gripped her and spun her like a leaf on the wind.

You will leave now!

No!

I am master of this world beyond the body, boomed the voice. *I have studied under men who know more than you could learn in a thousand lifetimes. Go, or I will cut you off from the earth and you will roam like a ghost for the rest of eternity. Go now, or be destroyed!*

No, I cannot!

Then you leave me no choice!

As that thought reached her mind, Ruth was pierced by a fear so great that she screamed out in terror. Her whole existence, everything that she had ever been, or done, or loved was being snatched away from her and crushed.

Nooooo!

She tried to pull back, to leap home to that special place where Granny Moon was waiting for her. But Kharkov had smothered her in the folds of his black presence and she was lost in the darkness.

She tried to sense the silver cord connecting her with her body, but it was gone. She drifted in the blackness of an eternal, silent limbo, with no way home.

31

"Ruth! Ruth!"

Carpenter saw Ruth Weylon's head loll to one side on Granny Moon's lap. Her mouth opened, as if to speak, but no words came out. A drool of saliva rolled out over her lips and slid down her cheek.

"She's gone!" cried Granny Moon. "Kharkov was too strong for her. Now she is lost in the Other World!"

"What do you mean, lost?"

"When you were working with those other people on your program, did you ever have subjects go mad? Did they go off on one of your so-called 'missions' and come back changed?"

"Just once," said Carpenter. "Our first guy, in the early days before Ruth and the other three. He looked as if he'd had a stroke."

"He was lost in the Other World. He left his body, severed the cord that bound his spirit to it and could not find his way back. From then on, his body would have been nothing more than an empty shell. My Ruth is lost, Mister Carpenter. And I am going to get her back. Quiet now!"

Then she put the palms of her hands on Ruth's forehead and began to chant . . . a deep, keening wail that lifted from her throat and soared into the sky, rising, falling and building, like the song of a lost soul.

Ruth tried to move in the blackness, but there was nowhere to move to, no up, no down, no anywhere. All she felt was her own presence, a single conscious dot in a limitless sea of nothingness.

She tried to recall the energy of the waterfall and that special place, the love of Granny Moon and the music of the brook. But she felt nothing.

Then the faintest memory came to her: the memory of a song from long ago when she had been a child in her mother's arms. Her grandfather had sung it one evening as the sparks from the campfire had flown into the night. "Yo-Heya-Hee, Ya-Na-Hana-Hee." Over and over again.

She felt herself floating up through water. The darkness softened into grey. The greyness lightened into deep purple and then light blue. She was on the surface of the ocean and then above it, floating into space.

"Yo-Heya-Hee, Ya-Na-Hana-Hee."

Could she stop herself? Or would she just float out into space, to the edge of the universe? Every time she had been in the Other World before with Granny Moon, or on a "mission" with Carpenter and his remote viewers, she had always had a sense of where "home" was.

Now that was gone.

She floated in space, lost. Was this what happened when you died? If you were good, did you float up to heaven? If you were bad, did you sink down to hell?

Far away, in a distant place, she heard the song again, "Yo-Heya-Hee, Ya-Na-Hana-Hee," and found herself drifting towards it, into the light.

"Ruth? Ruth?"

"I'm here! Is that you, Granny Moon?"

"It is. You lost your way. But now I hear you again. Tell me what you see."

Ruth hovered above the water. Near the horizon, she saw a huge ship with a great flat deck. Around her, much closer, the leaner, faster shapes of destroyers circled. Below her, the great black fish of the submarine moved slowly beneath the water, with Max inside.

She described all this to Granny Moon.

"Can you see your way home again?"

The silver cord was back, stretching home to the waterfall and their special place.

"I can."

"Do you feel strong, Little Eagle?"

"I don't know, Granny. I don't know."

"You must go back and make sure that weapon is not fired. It still depends on you."

"I can't go back a third time. I can't. I'm too weak and he's too strong. He'll destroy me this time for certain."

"Then do not fight him directly," said Granny Moon. "Is there some small thing you can do that would influence the outcome of events? Is there any way to distract Kharkov without confronting him?"

"I don't know."

"I'll be with you. I'll guide your hand. My power will be yours this time. If he confronts you, come straight back. Do not stand and fight him. Nobody can ask you to take on someone as powerful as Kharkov in a contest you cannot possibly win."

SATURDAY, 27 OCTOBER
SUBMARINE K-6
11.08 P.M. MOSCOW TIME
FRIDAY 26 OCTOBER
2008 GMT

"Where is the escort screen?" Petrachkov asked.

"Holding position around us, Comrade Captain," said Kapitulsky. "The nearest ships are only two kilometres away, on either side."

"And the emergency buoy?"

"It is transmitting, Captain. But no response to our message yet."

"How long will we have to wait?"

"It depends on who receives the signal and how long it takes them to relay it to Severmorsk, Captain."

Petrachkov's nerves were at breaking point. His ship lay naked in the ocean, hovering at periscope depth with a bright yellow radio buoy floating above it in full view of the American destroyers. In his favour was the fact that they had not yet opened fire. In his forward torpedo tube he had a fully armed nuclear weapon, ready for launch.

"Just like those cowboy movies the Americans love so much, eh Comrades?" he joked. "What do they call this kind of gunfight, 'A Spanish Stand-Off'?"

"I think the term is 'Mexican Stand-Off', Comrade Captain."

Max Rospin stood in the door leading forward to compartment two, fully dressed in a blue boilersuit and sandals. He looked nervous. His right hand played with the fingers of his left, as if he was twisting an invisible wedding ring.

Petrachkov saw the security guards stiffen and move towards the young man. He waved the men back.

"How are you, Max?" Petrachkov asked, watching the youth for the first sign of trouble.

"Much better, thank you, Captain," said Max in a calm, even voice. "I was delirious for a while. It must have been the strain of this operation. But I am fine now. I'll be ready to give you the next message from Leningrad when the time comes. Doctor Chiker asked me to tell you he will be sleeping until then. I think the strain has affected him too."

"That won't be necessary Max. Comrade Kapitulsky has rigged our emergency radio beacon to broadcast a message we hope will be relayed to Severmorsk. We are expecting a reply within minutes."

Max's face darkened.

"You don't trust me then? I already told you Severmorsk was destroyed."

"Of course we trust you, Max. But this is a nuclear weapon we are about to release. I am sure you understand that I must do all in my power to confirm the orders you relayed to us from Leningrad."

"Of course, Captain. May I stay here by the door and watch?"

Petrachkov noted the guards between Max and the sensitive controls on the torpedo firing panels.

"Yes, Max, you may, but do not come inside. We are at a very tense phase of the mission and I wouldn't want you to get in the way."

"Thank you, Captain. I've enjoyed being part of your crew."

Petrachkov was touched. Maybe it would all work out for the best after all.

A buzz sounded over his head.

"Radio room, Comrade Captain. We have two responses to our signal."

He grabbed a microphone and pressed the toggle.

"Who from?"

"One is from the Soviet ship *Gagarin*, sixty kilometres away and relayed back from . . . from Severmorsk! The other is directly from the *USS Essex* herself."

So it was true! Severmorsk still existed! Were Natalya and the boys alive?

"I'll be right there," replied Petrachkov and darted across the command post, past Max and into the radio shack.

Ruth sank through the blue water into darkness, following the line of cable from the little yellow buoy. The great black shape of the submarine loomed out of the murk and she slipped inside, forward of the conning tower, into the corridor to the control room.

Max's bunk lay in the tiny room right in front of her. She slipped through the closed door. Max was not there. But Doctor Chiker was. He lay slumped across the bunk with his arm drooping towards the floor at an awkward angle. His mouth hung open and a livid bruise was forming in the bald patch at the back of his head. Ruth reached into his mind, but he was out cold. At Chiker's feet lay the pieces of a heavy glass ashtray.

Someone had hit Doctor Chiker and then left him unconscious, closing the door behind them. Could it have been Max? She slipped through the door and down the corridor. The Captain stood hunched over a radio set in one of the small cubicles off to the left. She saw Max standing in the doorway to the control room. Only it was not Max! The boy's body was wrapped in a living black cloud.

It was Kharkov.

He had found a puppet to do his bidding, here on the submarine.

32

"It's all here in Kharkov's *zapista* and his experimental journals," said Cherlenko, "but nobody ever compared the two sets of documents before!"

He felt elated at having made this breakthrough and needed to share his excitement with someone. Captain Slavin, sitting stiffly next to him in the back seat of the limousine, seemed a natural candidate. After all, they already shared the common bond of conspiracy regarding blame over Tatyana Rospin's suicide.

The car swept away from the Bolshoy Dom and turned left on to the bank of the Neva, heading west. The great city lay in darkness. A light flurry of snow glittered in the headlights. Cherlenko knew that tonight he finally had the answer to the puzzle that would set his career back on track towards the very top.

"And what do these documents show, Comrade General?"

"Look here," said Cherlenko, snapping on the internal light and opening Kharkov's *zapista*. "Kharkov's natural children were Yuri and Maria who died, or so he claims, during the 'Siege of the Nine Hundred Days'. Then the Kharkov's old friends Mikhail and Olga Rospin were killed during an artillery bombardment, leaving a pair of orphaned twins, Tatyana and Max."

"But that is already known, Comrade General."

"Yes indeed, but tell me how it could be that their birth certificates show a pair of twins born twelve months apart?"

"Perhaps the record is incorrect?"

"Or perhaps it was doctored in too much haste to conceal the fact that Tatyana and Max Rospin are in reality Yuri and Maria, Comrade Kharkov's own children!"

"But why would Kharkov conceal the truth?" asked Slavin. "It does not make sense."

"It would make perfect sense if you were a Russianist dissident trying to protect your family. Kharkov and his wife knew the children of dissidents were often sent to the labour camps with their parents. By distancing them as the adopted children of others, the Kharkovs ensured their survival in a State orphanage. But the clever Comrade Professor had a far more important reason to hide the fact that he was the children's real father, a reason that relates directly to the telepathic powers they possess."

"I don't follow you, Comrade General."

The car swerved onto Troitskiy Most Bridge, and hurtled across the Neva towards the Petrograd side of the river. To their left, Cherlenko saw the long, low walls of the Peter and Paul fortress looming out of the night like a giant warship.

"Look at Kharkov's journal," he said, "and the comparison experiments he performed on Max and Tatyana to compare their telepathic abilities. See here, in these three columns, the figures for success rate in transmitting information over various distances? The first and second columns represent Max and Tatyana's progress through their training. Their scores increase over time, as you would expect. More and more, as the months progress, they come to resemble the extremely high score achieved in this third column here."

Slavin stared at the journal, almost as if she was afraid of it.

"What does that third column represent?" she asked. "Is it a benchmark of some kind, a control?"

"It is the only realistic benchmark there *could* be," said Cherlenko, closing the notebook. "It shows Kharkov's own perfect score."

Captain Slavin looked forward past their driver to the approaching gates of the Peter and Paul fortress.

"So Kharkov is also a telepath?" she said slowly.

"Not just a telepath, but a grandmaster in a wide range of paranormal abilities. The basic building blocks of such gifts are hereditary; passed from a parent to his children. That is why Kharkov falsified those birth certificates, to protect *himself*. By persuading the State to let him act as mentor to Max and Tatyana, he gave himself the opportunity to expand his own considerable gifts to the point where he could exact a terrible revenge on the State."

The car entered the fortress, weaving its way through the complex of buildings to the prison compound at the far end of the island. A towering spire topped by a weather vane scratched the night sky. The car reached a long façade of grey stone, punctuated by curved windows barred with steel and a cavernous entrance flanked by unforgiving stone pillars.

"But how do you know Kharkov had these powers before he returned to Leningrad from the Gulag?" Slavin asked.

"Kharkov's notes contained records of people who claimed to be able to kill a person with pure thought? Tell me, whose death occurred on the fifth of March, 1953?"

The car stopped. The driver came round to open Cherlenko's door.

"Why," said Slavin. "Comrade Stalin of course."

"Yes. He died of a stroke that had happened at around 6.30 in the evening six days before, on the twenty-eighth of February, the day Kharkov's wife was killed. That stroke was caused by the haemorrhaging of blood vessels in his brain, an effect that Kharkov may well have been responsible for."

Cherlenko gathered up the papers and marched across the snow-swept courtyard, through the yawning entrance and into the prison, with Slavin beside him.

"I was a fool," he admitted. "I kept Kharkov close to me during this investigation so that I could learn about these protégés of his.

He was at every meeting held to organise the hunt for Tatyana Rospin. By being there, he was able to see into the minds of fools like Shumanin and extract the authentication codes he needed to validate his messages to his son Max on the submarine."

They entered the reception area of the prison, originally built to hold enemies of the Tsars in secret isolation and currently in use as an interim holding facility for criminals, dissidents and those 'insane' enough to question the State.

"What do you intend to do once we reach Kharkov?" Slavin asked.

"Force him to contact his son and stop the attack."

"And if he will not?"

"Then I will execute him. He is already a danger to the State beyond anything you or I can imagine. He is too dangerous to live, whether he helps us now, or not."

A worried man in a white coat came running across the tiled floor.

"Comrade General, we have a serious problem."

"Where is Kharkov? I must see him *now*!"

"When your office telephoned to say that you were coming to interrogate the prisoner, I had my guards go down to prepare him for you. But he has somehow locked himself in his cell. I have men down there now, trying to force their way in, but he has jammed the locking mechanism of the door from the inside. It will not open."

"Then get a cutting torch!" screamed Cherlenko. "Blast it open if you have to! But get that man out of there alive immediately or I will take you and your staff out into that courtyard and have you all shot!"

SATURDAY, 27 OCTOBER
SUBMARINE K-6
11.38 P.M. MOSCOW TIME
FRIDAY, 26 OCTOBER
2038 GMT

"The messages from the emergency buoy," said Petrachkov, leaning into the tiny radio cubicle. "I must see them."

The radio operator passed Petrachkov two sheets from his message pad. "The first one is from the *Gagarin*, Comrade Captain. It was relayed back from Severmorsk."

Petrachkov scanned the message. It looked genuine enough. It came from Northern Fleet headquarters and congratulated him on re-establishing radio contact. The messages he had been getting from the Kharkov experiment in Leningrad were part of a Russianist dissident plot. A number of conspirators, including Tatyana Rospin, had been killed, and Kharkov himself was now in custody. No hostilities existed between Soviet forces and the Americans. He was to disarm and lock down all weapons at once.

"You should reply in person to this second message, Comrade Captain," said the radio operator. "It is from the *Essex*."

"Why should I talk to an American warship?"

"Read it, Comrade Captain, and you'll see."

He then turned to the message from the *Essex*. This was in perfect Russian and addressed to him as commander of the submarine K-6. The sender gave his personal greetings to Petrachkov and his crew, along with a short but sufficiently detailed account of his credentials and apologised for his absence without leave. He begged Petrachkov to call off the attack and verified Shumanin's instructions.

Petrachkov read the message again in disbelief.

"Can you raise the *Essex*?" he asked.

"At once, Comrade Captain!" said the radio operator and bent over his control panel. He handed Petrachkov a microphone.

"Pipe this through the intercom all over the ship," said Petrachkov. "I want the men to hear it."

Contact was established. "This is the commander of the Soviet submarine K-6," said Petrachkov. "To whom am I speaking? Over."

"You are speaking to Captain Third Rank Valentin Rykov, first officer of the Soviet submarine K-6 and temporarily on board the United States ship *Essex*," said the voice. "Please do not sink us, Comrade Captain. I do not wish to go into the sea twice in one week. Over."

A muffled cheer reached Petrachkov from the CCP and grew into a wave of applause along the length of the ship.

"The crew is pleased to hear you, Comrade Rykov. Can you confirm our new instructions? Over."

"The People's Defence Council, the Admiralty and the Northern Red Banner Fleet have instructed you to ignore instructions sent to you as part of the Kharkov experiments and return to Severmorsk immediately. I, of course, would be grateful if you would delay long enough to surface and take me on board before you leave. American food is good, but the pickled herrings they serve here simply do not have the same bite. Over."

"I will confirm that with headquarters, comrade," replied Petrachkov. "In the meantime, please prepare to come back aboard. Out."

He flicked off the radio switch and reached for a hanging intercom microphone.

"Comrade Dudko, send a security detail to the CCP. I want Doctor Chiker and Max Rospin put under arrest until further notice!"

Ruth watched the seething cloud of Kharkov's presence around Max Rospin change and harden as all the crewmen in the control room erupted in a spontaneous round of applause. She saw them silently shouting and laughing, shaking hands and clasping each other in bear hugs. Had peace broken out? Had the attack been called off?

The energy in the ship had changed. The tension had been defused. The men were like prisoners released from a death sentence.

Only Kharkov's energy intensified in its purpose.

Petrachkov walked back to the command post, happier than he had ever felt in his life. They were going home! He would take his sons fishing and see Natalya's smiling face welcoming him back when they reached the dock! As soon as he could, he would go back to his cabin and take their photograph out of the drawer and replace it on his wall. It was like waking from a bad dream into the sunshine.

He put out his hand to comfort Max. "It's all right, comrade," he said, "but we'll have to confine you to quarters until . . . ."

Suddenly he was flat on his back in the corridor outside the CCP, wondering how on earth Max Rospin could have thrown him, a former weightlifting champion, without so much as turning his head.

The young man moved into the CCP and the crowd of rejoicing men, heading for the torpedo control board with its red illuminated button on the panel for tube number one. All Max had to do was to raise the safety cover and push!

"Kapitulsky!" screamed Petrachkov. "Lock down all weapons, NOW!"

33

Ruth slid into the control room. Max was already halfway across the room, heading for one of the illuminated control panels. Men around him moved forward purposefully, reaching out to stop him. The black swirling presence of Kharkov reached out to each of their minds and they jerked back, just as the Captain had done.

Ruth could do nothing but watch. Kharkov had found his puppet in Max and could pull his strings to do his will. To stop him, Ruth needed a puppet of her own.

A young officer rose from a panel near the Captain's chair. She reached into his mind and thought *Stop Max!* as hard as she could. The officer reached forward, grabbed the swirling black form with both arms and dragged Max to his knees. Ruth was dazzled by an explosion of blinding light as Kharkov resisted them both, but Max was down. The other men in the control room piled on top of him, pinning him to the grating. The black form of Kharkov whirled above them. The red light on the panel Max had been reaching for winked out and changed to green as the weapons system shut down.

A deafening howl burst in Ruth's mind, the howl of a tortured soul robbed of revenge. The black cloud hardened into the form of a man's face, a man with a beard and bright piercing eyes. His voice screamed in her brain.

You will pay for that! You and all those you love!

Then the cloud expanded and engulfed her, reaching into her soul with tendrils of black fear.

SATURDAY, 27 OCTOBER
LENINGRAD
11.51 P.M. LOCAL TIME
FRIDAY, 26 OCTOBER
2051 GMT

Cherlenko watched impatiently as the arc of the oxyacetylene torch crawled around the lock of the prison door. Dense smoke poured from the blistering paint and smouldering wood. Cherlenko lifted the padded handkerchief he had placed over his mouth.

"How long is this going to take?"

"Only a few more seconds, Comrade General."

Cherlenko's driver ran down the narrow passageway. "Comrade General, Comrade General, a message from the Admiralty! They have made contact with the submarine. Captain Petrachkov has called off the attack!"

Cherlenko grinned and turned to Slavin.

"There," he told her. "You can put your recommendation for my elevation to the Praesidium in your next report to Moscow, eh?"

He unbuttoned the holster of his pistol and pulled out the weapon, flicked off the safety catch and cocked it. Captain Slavin watched him.

"You do the same," he told her. "There is no further reason to keep the traitor Kharkov alive. The longer he lives, the longer he is a danger to the State."

The arc of the cutting torch reached the upper doorframe and the hissing gas stopped. Without waiting for the metal to cool, Cherlenko raised his right foot and smashed the heel flat on the cell door, just below the lock. The door swung open with a crash and a hiss of burning metal.

Cherlenko rushed into the smoke-filled cell, Captain Slavin behind him. Kharkov lay motionless on a tiny cot with raised metal sides. His breathing was fast and shallow, like a man in a nightmare.

His closed eyelids bulged as the eyeballs flickered to and fro beneath them.

Cherlenko raised his pistol and aimed directly at the older man's chest. Behind him, he heard the cell door bang shut.

"Boris Kharkov," he said, "on behalf of the People's Defence Council and the People of the Soviet Union, I sentence you to death!".

Cherlenko squeezed the trigger. The gun kicked in his hand. The deafening roar of the shot exploded in that confined space. Kharkov's body shuddered as the bullet tore through his chest.

Ruth screamed as the terror took her, pulling her out of the submarine and deep into the depths of the ocean. She felt the silver cord connecting her to her body strain as Kharkov twisted her within his grip. She felt his pain, his frustration and the incredible power of his mind in complete domination over her.

We were wrong to think we could ever match him, she thought. *There is nothing that he cannot do. He is the devil. He is God. He is . . ..*

Kharkov's energy changed. Ruth had the briefest sensation of panic from the great force surrounding her. She felt Kharkov pause, reach back into a far distant place for an instant . . . and then he was gone, leaving her alone to struggle upwards from the dark water into the sunlit realm of the sky, helpless, drained and lost.

Faintly, like a distant puff of wind, came the chanting voice of Granny Moon: "Yo-Heya-Hee, Ya-Na-Hana-Hee."

Ruth relaxed and let herself be drawn towards it.

Cherlenko moved forward to the metal cot. Kharkov was still alive. His breath came in short, desperate gasps. Blood welled up from the wound in his chest and spread across his thin hospital gown. Cherlenko raised the pistol again and aimed at the man's forehead for the *coup de grâce*. His finger tightened on the trigger.

Kharkov's eyes snapped open.

"The secret . . ." he gasped. "You want to know how it is done, don't you? Come closer. I do not have much time."

Cherlenko remembered Kharkov's notebooks and the promise of unlimited power they offered to anyone who could understand them. He turned to Slavin.

"Wait outside. I'll deal with this."

She looked at him suspiciously.

"Go! Immediately!"

Slavin retreated reluctantly into the corridor and swung the ruined door shut.

"Quickly!" hissed Kharkov. "Come closer."

Cherlenko was alone with the dying man. He had a loaded pistol. He felt safe.

"What is it?" he said. "Tell me."

Kharkov's blood spread onto the sheets in a widening circle. He would be dead in seconds.

"Closer," the old man whispered.

Cherlenko leant forward.

"There is no death," breathed Kharkov. "Not even for you!"

Then, with a last tremendous act of will, he grabbed Cherlenko's head in his hands and slammed it down onto the metal rail around the bed; again, and again, and again . . . .

Cherlenko was too surprised to pull back. The first blow stunned him and the gun fell from his hand. He saw flash after flash of red light. His knees buckled as he lost consciousness and slid to the floor. His world was a whirling kaleidoscope of sensation; the ringing pain in his head, the stink of blood and cordite, the cool metal of the bed, smooth linoleum and the sound of running feet fading further and further into the distance . . . then darkness as he slipped into unconsciousness.

And then . . . the strangest thing.

He was floating above his own body, looking down on himself as he lay crumpled on the floor beside Kharkov's cot. Cherlenko's cap was off, his gun lay near his feet and a trickle of blood seeped from his forehead. But he was still breathing. His chest rose and fell. Saliva drooled from his mouth.

Slavin came into the room, followed by the doctor. He watched her reach down to him, move his head and check his pulse. He saw her mouth open to speak and the doctor respond, but there was no sound. It was then that he noticed a strange silvery cord that seemed to connect him to his body.

This was the secret Kharkov had promised to share with him, the ability to move outside the body. What a wonderful thing! He, Cherlenko now possessed the power to move invisibly anywhere in the world, to see everything, to spy on anyone. All he had to do was to render himself unconscious, slip into this netherworld and travel wherever he wanted.

What was it the old man had said before he died?

"There is no death. Not even for you."

He looked at Kharkov, still lying prone on the bed. The old man's life was ebbing away fast now. Cherlenko sensed it pouring out of him, like a dark storm cloud seething around his dying body . . . What will happen when *his* spirit is set free?

Then, in a terrifying rush, Cherlenko realised the enormous danger of facing Kharkov in a world where the old man was master. He tried to reach back down the silvery cord into his own mind, to return to the safety of his physical form, before it was too late.

But a great black presence burst from Kharkov's lifeless corpse, filling the tiny prison cell and snapping the silver cord connecting Cherlenko's spirit to his body as if it were made of cobwebs, crushing his puny spirit in its grip. Cherlenko screamed silently in pure animal terror. His whole existence, everything he had ever been, or done, or loved—his very soul—was being snatched away from him and crushed.

Nooooo!

But Kharkov had smothered him in the folds of his terrible black presence and Vladimir Cherlenko was lost in the limitless darkness . . . forever.

Carpenter looked down at the lifeless face of Ruth Weylon, cradled in Granny Moon's lap. She was dead. She had to be. Either that or she was lost for all time outside her body. He reached forward gently for her wrist and took felt her pulse.

"Yo-Heya-Hee, Ya-Na-Hana-Hee," chanted Granny Moon. "Yo-Heya-Hee, Ya-Na-Hana-Hee."

She stopped.

Carpenter stared at the old woman.

"Is she lost?"

The old woman smiled, opened her eyes and looked down at her granddaughter.

Ruth Weylon lay there looking up at him.

"I'm back," she said. "The submarine has been stopped."

"That's . . . that's great news . . . wonderful!"

He put his arms around her. For a moment she responded, and then drew back.

"It is over," she said. "You must call your people and tell them where to pick you up again."

"What about you? You must come with me, both of you. The government will be grateful for what you did."

"Maybe," said Ruth, glancing up at Granny Moon. "Call your people first. Radio reception is better on top of those rocks over there, above the gulley."

Carpenter went to where he'd left Birkett's radio and walked back up to the top of the ridge. Then he pulled out the aerial and switched the set to 'Transmit'.

"Hello? Is that you, Don? Yeah, she did it! She contacted the sub and made it stop! What's that? It's on the surface near the *Essex*? That's great. Yes. I'll pass your congratulations on to her and Granny Moon. But you can tell them yourself when you come to pick us up. No. I don't think she'd come back to work for us. Not right now anyways. But I'll work on her. She'll come around. Yeah, that's right! Same spot. Okay. See you in ten!"

He slid the radio aerial back into its housing and shut off the set. Reviving Project Element and the remote viewer program wasn't such a bad idea. They could recruit a whole new team and really perfect the technique. Don Birkett and the CIA would be a hundred percent behind it and that would cut a lot of ice over at the NSA. It would be like the old days, only better. He could . . . .

"Ruth?" he called out, looking back towards the waterfall.

But she and Granny Moon had gone.

The End

BIBLIOGRAPHY

Below is a list of books and journals and articles that I found particularly helpful in creating this novel. For details on how close the Russians *actually* came to deploying nuclear–tipped torpedoes during the Cuban Missile Crisis please read Peter Huchthausen's excellent book *October Fury*. For eye–witness accounts of what it was like to be part of the US remote viewing programme please see the accounts by David Morehouse, Tim Rifat and Jim Schabel.

Andrew, Christopher and Gordievsky, Oleg. *KGB: The Inside Story*.
     London: Harper, 1991.
Beloff, John. *Parapsychology: A Concise History*.
     London: Athlone Press, 1993.
Blackmore, Susan J. *Beyond the Body: An Investigation of
     Out-of-the-Body Experiences*. London: Paladin Books, 1983.
Brown, Dee. *Bury My Heart At Wounded Knee: An Indian History
     of the American West. London*: Vintage Press, 1991.
Daniloff, Nicholas. *Two Lives, One Russia*.
     London: Futura Publications, 1990.
Doxey, William. *ESPionage*. New York: Leisure Books, 1979.
George, Alice L. *Awaiting Armageddon: how Americans faced the
     Cuban Missile Crisis*. Chapel Hill and London: University
     of North Carolina Press, 2003.
Gregg Iliff, Flora. *People of the Blue Water: A Record of Life Among the
     Walapai and Havasupai Indians*. Tucson: The University of
     Arizona Press, 1954.
Huchthausen, Peter A. *K-19, The Widowmaker: The Secret History
     of the Soviet Nuclear Submarine*. Washington: National
     Geographic, 2002.
Huchthausen, Peter A. *October Fury*.
     New York: John Wiley & Son, 2002.
Huchthausen, Peter A., Kurdin, Igor and White, R. Alan.
     Hostile Waters. New York: Saint Martin's Press, 1997.

Korotov, Dr. Konstantin. *Aura and Consciousness: New Age of Scientific Understanding*. Saint Petersburg: Federal Technical University "SPIFMO", 1998.

Kress, Kenneth A. *Parapsychology in Intelligence: A Personal Review and Conclusions*. Published in the winter 1977 issue of *Studies in Intelligence*, the CIA's classified internal publication and released to the public in 1996
(see: www.parascope.com/ds/articles/parapsychologyDoc.htm)

Lyons, Eugene. *Workers' Paradise Lost. Fifty Years of Soviet Communism: A Balance Sheet*. New York: Paperback Library Inc., 1967.

Morehouse, David. *Psychic Warrior: Inside the CIA's Stargate Program: The True Story of a Soldier's Espionage and Awakening*. New York: Saint Martin's Press, 1996.

Ostrader, Sheila and Schroeder, Lynn. *Psychic Discoveries Behind the Iron Curtain*. New York: Marlow & Company, 1971.

Owen, Joseph R. *Colder Than Hell: A Marine Rifle Company at Chosin Reservoir*. New York: Ivy Books, 1996.

Purvis, Vaughan. *The* Nautilus *Affair*. Extracted from *The CIA and the Battle for Reality*. 1997
(see: http://www.raven1.net/mcf/hambone/nauti.html)

Rawicz, Slavomir. *The Long Walk: The True Story of a Trek to Freedom*. London: Robinson, 2000.

Rifat, Tim. *Remote Viewing: The History and Science of Psychic Warfare and Spying*. London: Century, 1999.

Schnabel, Jim. *Remote Viewers: The Secret History of America's Psychic Spies*. New York: Dell Books, 1997.

Salisbury, Harrison E. *The 900 Days: The Siege of Leningrad*. London:Pan Books, 2000.

Sewell, Kenneth and Richmond, Clint. *Red Star Rogue: The Untold Story of a Soviet Submarine's Nuclear Strike Attempt on the U.S.* New York: Simon & Schuster, 2005.

Shipler, David K. Russia: *Broken Idols, Solemn Dreams*. New York: Times Books, 1983.

Suvorov, Viktor. *Inside the Soviet Army*. London: Book Club Associates, 1982.

Targ, Russell and Harary, Keith. *The Mind Race: Understanding and Using Psychic Powers*. London: New English Library, 1985.

Targ, Russell and Puthoff, Harold. *Mind-Reach*. London: Paladin, 1978.

Taubman, William. *Krushchev: The Man – His Era*. London: Simon & Schuster, 2003.

Tomlin, Simon. *The UnXplained: Psychic Powers*. Bath: Parragon, 2000.

Weir, Gary E. and Boyne, Walter J. *Rising Tide: The Untold Story of the Russian Submarines that Fought the Cold War*. New York: Basic Books, 2003.

Wilson, Colin. *The Occult*. London: Hodder & Stoughton Ltd. 1971.

Now read the first exciting chapter of John Joyce's next novel . . .

MASTERPIECE

▬▬▬▬▬

THEN

PARIS

Sabaut crouched in the darkness of the tiny cave it had taken him six weeks to dig. Light from the small torch strapped to his head glistened on the bare clay walls, on the two steel cases and the waterproof canvas bag he had hauled in on his hands and knees. Now only a flat metal plate, held in place by turn clips separated him from the storeroom.

Planning the crime had taken a year of Sabaut's life. There had been the special equipment to prepare, surveys to carry out, endless research into computer security systems and, of course, the tunnel to dig. During all that time, he had marvelled at the ultimate simplicity of the crime. It had the same perfect form a masterpiece of art presents to the untrained observer, the same fusion of inspiration, sweat and pain into a seemingly effortless beauty.

He held his hands up to the light and watched them shake from the exertion of climbing those last few metres from the sewers below. The sickly sweet stench of those endless caverns still filled his nostrils. The walls of his tiny cave pressed in. The strain of the past year seemed to rise up and crash down on him like a wave. Sabaut was not a young man. His arms and legs ached from his weeks of work on the tunnel. His vision swam. Points of red light danced in front of him. A cold sweat broke out on his face. He closed his eyes and tried to steady himself. The red lights faded and his breathing returned to normal.

Nicole! I am doing this for you.

Sabaut opened his eyes again. His hands no longer shook.

He leant forward and reached for the four metal catches that held the panel in place.

"I'm at point one," he said into his throat microphone.

"Proceed," said a familiar voice in his earpiece.

Sabaut opened each of the catches in turn, switched off his head torch and lifted the panel aside. He was peering into a dark silent space, filled with shapeless forms. He waited for a moment and then, satisfied that nobody was in the room, he reached up and turned on his light. A face stared at him out of the blackness. Its sightless eyes did not blink in the torch beam. Nor did its expression change.

"*Bon soir,*" Sabaut said softly. "*Ca va?*"

The statue did not reply.

Sabaut played the torch around the vast low-ceilinged chamber, taking in the rows of exquisitely carved faces, curving bodies and prancing animals, all frozen in stone. The building had started life as a fortress almost a thousand years before and this room, deep below ground level, was now used as a storehouse. Sabaut knew there were no alarms here, and no cameras. They would begin at the next level.

He reached back through the panel and pulled the two cases and the bag inside. Slipping the straps of his torch over the head of the statue, Sabaut peeled off the mud-stained boilersuit he had worn in the tunnel and changed into an old shirt, worn jeans and scuffed brown shoes. Then he pulled on a light blue work coat, checked that the security badge was prominently displayed on the breast pocket and turned to the first case. With practised ease he assembled the collection of stainless steel plates, rods and rubber wheels inside. Finally, he turned to the second case, opening the clasps and lifted the lid gently to reveal the two exquisite oil paintings inside.

In another two minutes, he stood before a thick wooden door at the end of a narrow stone corridor, lit only by strips of fluorescent light. He knew he was still more than ten metres below ground level, in one of the fifteen kilometres of underground passageways and service tunnels that honeycombed the ground beneath the great buildings above. Beyond the door the security cameras would start.

"I'm at point two," he said.

"Shutting cameras down now!" came the reply. "You have fifteen minutes."

Sabaut opened the door and stepped into a brightly lit passageway with white walls and a smooth concrete floor. The Cyclops eye of a security camera peered down at him from the ceiling.

Was it still live?

An orange light flashed on the walls around him. The hiss of tyres and the whirr of an electric motor sounded as a yellow cart pulling a trailer loaded with wooden crates and cardboard boxes rolled past. The driver raised his hand in greeting as he drove on.

Sabaut walked for over fifty metres to a service lift, stepped inside and pressed the button for 'Entresol'. The polished steel door slid shut and he saw the reflection of a tall, grey haired porter with a stainless steel trolley looking back at him. The heavy moustache he had grown especially for the job and the thick-framed spectacles, repaired with adhesive tape, gave just the right impression of a hard-working man on an honest wage. Sabaut smiled as the lift doors slid open. He turned to his left and, pushing the trolley in front of him, made his way down a darkened mall of exclusive retail outlets, information points and souvenir shops to the vast space beyond.

He hardly looked up as he passed beneath the soaring lattice of metal and glass that formed the giant pyramid above his head, or took in the escalators, ticket kiosks, coffee docks and balconies that welcomed over six million visitors a year. For six days out of seven, this atrium would be thronged with visitors from all over the world, people who had come to pay homage to one of the greatest art collections in existence. But now, early on the morning of the one day in each week when the museum was closed to the public for maintenance and repair of its collections, the only sounds to be heard in the Museé de la Louvre were the distant drone of floor polishing machines, the squeaking wheels of Sabaut's trolley and the hollow clap of his shoes on the marble floor.

He walked across the great atrium and into a corridor closed to the gaze of tourists and art lovers. A pair of grey-painted double doors stood shut across his path, protected by a security camera, a swipe card reader and an electronic key pad.

Sabaut glanced up at the camera. Then he patted his pockets, drew out a swipe card and ran it through the slot. A green light blinked on the key pad. Sabaut entered four zeroes and the door shuddered. He pulled it open and wheeled the trolley through into a long, brightly lit corridor that smelled of floor polish. He glanced at the names on the office doors as he passed.

At the far end of the corridor, marked it out from all the rest by the pair of armed security men standing guard, was the room that really interested him. Sabaut peered at their faces as he approached. They looked familiar but, with a staff of over two thousand men and women at the Louvre, it was unlikely that either of them would recognise him from his fleeting visits to the restoration area in the years Nicole had worked there.

However, it was not impossible.

"Good morning," he said, wheeling the trolley in front of him. "What are you guys doing here? Is it that time of year again?"

The guard on the left glanced at Sabaut's identification badge.

"She's down for analysis and restoration before she goes back up to that new exhibition area in the Salle des Etats tomorrow," he said, "the one the Japanese TV company sponsored."

"The one with the bullet-proof display case?"

"Bullet-proof glass, hermetically sealed, new alarm systems — the lot! I heard it cost almost five million euro."

Sabaut shrugged. "Perhaps it's worth it," he said. "After all, she is worth over eight *hundred* million? Can I leave this inside for the restorers?"

"What is it?" asked the other guard, leaning forward.

Sabaut carefully lifted the dust sheet covering the trolley.

"A Monet from the Grand Gallery, down for its annual check up. They forgot to bring it across last night and the curators want it back on display by the end of the week. I wish the management took as good care of its staff as it does with its precious paintings."

Both guards nodded in agreement. The one on Sabaut's left pulled the dust sheet back into place.

"Not one of my favourites," he said. "Hurry up then. They're paranoid about security when she's down." The door opened with a hiss.

"I'll just be a moment," Sabaut said and pushed the trolley forward. The restoration room was vast and smelt of surgical spirit. Its white walls, complex X-ray machinery and tables of tools and long-stemmed lamps gave the impression of a hospital laboratory or a workshop for luxury cars. There were no windows and no other exit. The room was sealed, airtight and hermetically-controlled, with security cameras panning down from every angle. Sabaut took a deep breath and stared down the endless rows of tables bearing covered paintings. Were those cameras still live? Or were they watching nothing more than the image of the empty room that had been frozen into their feedback circuits before he had entered?

"I'm at point three," he said softly.

"You have ten minutes and twenty seconds," said the voice.

Sabaut pushed the trolley down the main aisle between the covered paintings, to the far end of the room. There, on a table set apart from all the rest, was a single small painting covered by a Plexiglas dust shield.

He slipped a pair of fine cotton gloves from his pocket, checked the dust shield for hidden alarms and lifted it off, laying it gently down beside the table. For a moment, he allowed himself the bittersweet luxury of gazing down at the enigmatic smile of the young woman sitting on a balcony with her hands crossed on the arm of her seat.

Colours came to him . . . the blues and greens of Nicole's palette as she worked during the evenings in their apartment near the Pompidou Centre . . . the spun silver and gold of her hair . . . and finally, the dark red swirls of blood on white porcelain. . . .

Jean Jacques Sabaut pushed that memory aside and lifted the Monet onto the table. Then he leant down and began to work on the bottom shelf of the trolley.

This is for you, Nicole. This is my masterpiece. Just as the paintings you left behind will be recognised some day for the works of genius they are, so this act in your memory will also find a place in history.

The lower shelf of the trolley was made of stainless steel with a lip eight centimetres deep. Reaching underneath with his right hand, Sabaut found a hidden catch and released a lower sheet of stainless steel from below the shelf. It swung open to reveal a padded tray. He bent down, gently removed the contents and laid it on the workbench.

It was an expertly aged and treated sheet of poplar wood, seventy-seven centimetres tall by fifty-three centimetres wide, with four wooden battens running across its back to prevent it from warping. On its upturned face a portrait had been painted, identical in every respect to the original that lay beside it on the restorer's table.

How many years had Nicole worked here in the Louvre, studying the art and form of this painting's legendary creator; copying his pictures, matching his brush strokes, studying his pigments, so that she could do his genius justice in her restorations?

She had started the project as a joke—just to see if it *could* be done. But, as the reviews of her original works had grown more and more hostile and Nicole's artistic spirit had begun to buckle, it had become a serious obsession. If the critics would not accept Nicole Sabaut as an artist of the present, then she would expose their hypocritical worship of the artists of the past. Nicole had unlimited access to the restoration room. She had the talent, the expertise and the materials to create the ultimate forgery. Then all she had to do was to substitute it for the real thing, and then take her vengeance upon the jackals of the art community when she finally unmasked them as the mindless hypocrites they were?

Sabaut slipped on a pair of thin cotton gloves, lifted Da Vinci's masterpiece from the restoration table and turned it carefully in his hands, examining the front and back of the poplar wood sheet, noting the inventory number. Nicole had been right. The wood was warping ever so slightly. The museum had been justified in building the new display to protect it from further damage. Sabaut smiled. If he succeeded tonight, and Nicole's forgery was encased inside that bullet-proof display before it was hermetically sealed, then it could remain that way forever.

His fingers touched what appeared to be a blob of wax on the bottom edge of the poplar panel. Looking at it closely, it seemed as if the wax had been there for centuries, but Sabaut knew better. Taking a pocket knife and unfolding the blade, he gently prized what was actually a red plastic plug away from the wood and allowed a cylindrical electronic security tag to fall into his palm. He smiled again, remembering Nicole's precise instructions, and transferred the device and its 'wax' cover to a corresponding hole in her perfect forgery. Then he laid the two paintings side by side on the table and looked down at them. They were identical in every respect except one—the knowledge that Leonardo's masterpiece carried the very soul of its creator in the delicate brushstrokes and that it was a priceless national treasure of France, the essence of which could never be replaced. Taking this painting from the Louvre now was an awesome responsibility. What if something were to happen in the tunnel? Was it fundamentally right, in spite of his solemn vow to Nicole's spirit, to proceed?

A cold sweat broke out on Jean Jacques Sabaut's face as he gazed down at the two masterpieces in front of him—one genuine, one not. Their eyes looked back at him from the table, begging him to choose.

"You have six minutes," said the voice in his ear.

"I hear you."

To hesitate any further risked discovery and capture.

Sabaut took a deep breath, covered one of the paintings with the Plexiglas lid, gently placed the other into the secret compartment on the trolley and raised the metal flap.

To anyone looked at the trolley from above, the bottom shelf was empty.

He took the fake Monet that Nicole had made and hid it behind a stack of other paintings in the corner of the restoration room. Nicole had often told him that, for all its security arrangements and cataloguing, the Louvre had still not managed to make a complete inventory of its three hundred thousand pieces of art.

He turned, glanced back at the painting beneath the Plexiglas cover one last time, and pushed the seemingly empty trolley back to the doors of the restoration room. The two guards hardly glanced at it as he pushed it past them and down the brightly lit corridor to the atrium, the elevator and down into the bowels of the great museum to the storeroom where he had entered.

He turned on the light, shut the door behind him and started to dismantle the trolley.

"You can release the cameras now," he said into his throat microphone. "I'm back."

"Understood."

Sabaut pulled his boiler suit back on, carefully removed the painting from the stainless steel tray of the trolley and placed it lovingly in the reinforced carrying case. The stench of the sewer flared his nostrils as he reopened the panel in the wall. Then he took his headlight back from the statue, bid it farewell and, with a last deep breath of sweet air, he was gone.

Forty minutes later, he stood by a rusted metal ladder leading upwards to a steel plate set into the pavement at the south-east corner of the Place de la Concorde on the north bank of the Seine. From above came the muted roar of traffic bursting from the underpass beneath the Pont de la Concorde. Below him was the babble of gently flowing water. He had dumped the trolley and the bag containing the clothes and security tag in the tunnel. Now all he had was the precious case.

"I'm at the manhole," he said.

"I'm in place," said the voice in his headset. "Hurry."

Sabaut took the case in his left hand, gripped the wet metal rungs with his right and climbed to the top of the ladder. Once there, he braced his shoulder against the steel plate and pushed, sliding it sideways onto the pavement. The sound of distant sirens, the roar of traffic and the muffled hum of a city at night time washed over him. Cold, clean air rushed through the manhole and into his lungs as he slid the case out and climbed onto the pavement.

After the silence and the stinking blackness below him, he paused for a moment to take in the lights, the sounds and the wide open space of the Place de la Concorde as the great sweeping searchlight from the Eiffel Tower swung across the stars. Then he pushed the manhole cover back into place and looked across the Quai de Tuileries to the Seine.

The black van was there, on the other side of the road.

Sabaut got to his feet, took the case and ran towards the vehicle, glancing to his right at the underpass as he went. He had reached the middle of the road when a silver BMW, travelling at speed, burst out of the tunnel. Sabaut darted forward and twisted his body to one side, just in time for the offside wing of the speeding car to slice past him harmlessly.

There. The devil looks after his own—

With a roar and the briefest flash of blue light, the police motorcycle that had been chasing the BMW, exploded out of the underpass, swerved out of control in an effort to avoid him and smashed into his legs.

Sabaut felt no pain. He felt nothing but the unimaginable impact of the machine, as it caught him below the knees, spun him upwards into the whirling lights of the city and slammed him down onto the unforgiving surface of the roadway. His head slammed against the edge of the pavement. A deafening hiss roared in his ears. He closed his eyes against the pain. As it cleared, he heard the sound of running feet and the wail of sirens. Cars skidded to a halt close by. He heard men shouting and the sound of twisted metal being scraped against stone. Voices crackled over radios.

Footsteps sounded close by. He heard a man's voice ask him if he could hear them.

He tried to move his legs, but his body was numb.

Far away in the distance he heard a familiar engine pull away and fade into the distance. The van had gone!

All that planning . . . all that risk . . . his revenge against the art world for Nicole's death . . . and twenty million dollars . . . all gone in a second!

The painting! What about the painting?

"I . . . I have a case," he said. "Where . . . where is it?"

The voice told him to lie still. Then, somewhere off to his right, he heard the unmistakeable sound of the case scraping on the roadway. Someone was lifting it.

"Don't . . . don't open . . ." Sabaut said. But then came the snap of the catches being flicked back. For a moment, it seemed to Sabaut that the world had fallen silent. Then he heard a man's voice, raised in excitement, calling to his colleagues to come and look. There was a clatter of footsteps.

Sabaut turned his head. He blinked his eyes to see. But there was nothing . . . nothing but the dark.

DUE FOR PUBLICATION - OCTOBER 2013 FROM

SPINDRIFT PRESS

www.spindriftpress.com